FIELD OF THUNDER

OF

ROSE FLEM-ATH

A THRILLER

Stoddart

Published in 1997 by
Stoddart Publishing Co. Limited
34 Lesmill Road
Toronto, Canada
M3B 2T6
Tel. (416) 445-3333
Fax (416) 445-5967

01   00   99   98   97   1   2   3   4   5

Stoddart Books are available for bulk purchase for sales promotions,
premiums, fundraising, and seminars. For details, contact the
Special Sales Department at the above address.

Canadian Cataloguing in Publication Data

Flem-Ath, Rose
Field of thunder

ISBN 0-7737-3042-7

I. Title.

PS8561.L45F53 1997   C813'.54   C97-931512-3
PR9199.3.F53F53 1997

Cover design: Bill Douglas @ The Bang
Text design: Tannice Goddard
Computer graphics: Mary Bowness

Printed and bound in Canada

Although some of the characters and situations are based on real life,
this is a work of fiction and is not intended to be an historical account.

*We acknowledge the Canada Council for the Arts and the
Ontario Arts Council for their support of our publishing program.*

for Rand
as always

Incens'd with indignation Satan stood
Unterrifi'd, and like a comet burn'd . . .
In th' arctic sky, and from his horrid hair
Shakes pestilence and war.

JOHN MILTON
PARADISE LOST

PROLOGUE

MARALINGA
AUSTRALIA
October 1956

The blast slammed into Corporal Charles Emory like a clenched fist. He gasped and sucked in his breath like it was his last.

Sergeant Larry Fisher whistled. One long, clear note.

Slowly, very slowly, Charles unclenched his hands. Light crept under his lids as the initial roar of the explosion receded into a distant thunder. As he opened his eyes, a mustard yellow cloud rose from the earth and hovered over the desert. Dust swirled at his feet.

It was then that Charles saw the rabbits. Hundreds of them tumbling from the low, dry brush. Pink-laced ears flattened against their skulls in terror. "Jesus H. Christ . . . !" he whispered. The rest of his words were seared from his mouth by a second shaft of hot wind.

The men stood motionless, mesmerized by the sight of the frantic creatures stumbling across the ground. One fell against Tony Lawson's ankle and jerked away, streaking across the sand.

"Poor little bastards," Tony murmured. "Nobody told them to close their eyes until it was over . . ."

Charles Emory stared after the helpless animals. "They're blind," he muttered hoarsely. "They've bloody well been blinded . . ."

FORTY-FIVE MILES EAST

Taking a wooden peg from between her teeth, Phyllis Emory pinched her husband's best shirt to the drooping clothesline and wiped the perspiration from her forehead with the back of her hand. She squinted into the sun's punishing heat. It was just past ten in the morning as she dragged herself up the wide stairs to the welcoming shade of the verandah. She refilled a glass of lemonade from a large pitcher and lowered herself into a cushioned chair. Fingers flicking at her white blonde hair, Phyllis let the sweet drink, already too warm, run over her lips. She could just glimpse the shimmering desert above the porch railing. This godforsaken place was a heck of a long way from home. From rainy, lush Oregon. But at least Charles had found them a house graced by the shade of a few sparse gum trees.

A high wind gathered the heat before releasing it in hot gusts across the verandah, drawing her cotton dress across her thighs. The leaves of the gum trees shivered. Phyllis offered her face to the wind and licked the sugar from her lips. No, it wasn't Oregon. But something in this dust-choked air and sterile ground had done what years of the thick rain forest and turbulent rivers of her home state couldn't: made her fertile. She closed her eyes to the breeze and rolled the cool glass along her cheek.

Suddenly the trees shifted violently, lurching in the thin soil as if being strangled at the roots. Phyllis leapt to her feet. The branches that touched the roof rolled in a heavy rhythm. And then were seized by a final spasm before shuddering into a deathly calm. She turned her eyes to the horizon. A harsh light boomeranged along the earth where the sky had been, stripping the trees, the earth, of colour. One hand flew to cover her eyes. The other dropped to shield her belly.

The next day the silver leaves that brushed the house turned the colour of mold.

The day after that they dropped, rotting, to the verandah floor.

MARALINGA
One Hour Later

An oily dust covered the woman's dark skin, her wide face, her bare shoulders. And the infant at her breast. She shivered and spit dirt from her mouth. Wetting her thumb, she touched it to the child's face, wiping the sand from his eyes and nose, digging it from his ears. Gently pushing his mouth from her teat, she ran her finger across the baby's pink gums. He squirmed and howled into the blue sky, choking on the grit that filled his throat.

Two men walked beside the woman. They muttered to each other and eyed the tent, which was pitched a few hundred yards ahead, its canvas flapping in the hot wind. The younger man pressed his hand against his ear as if in pain, and moaned softly.

"Jesus! What're they doing here? Where's Corporal Taylor? He was supposed to keep the whole bloody area clear!" Larry Fisher jumped from the canvas chair where he'd been scratching out some notes for Headquarters. "This is going to mean a goddamned avalanche of paperwork if we don't get rid of them. And quick!" He marched towards the straggling band of Aborigines.

Charles Emory followed, coughing and clearing his throat, spitting a bloody mass of phlegm into the sand. "Our boy genius Maher won't be very happy," he rasped. "It might mess up all the neat little statistics he's compiling back there in his cosy bunker." He coughed again and wiped his mouth with the back of his hand. "Counting dead bugs — the bugger . . ." He laughed at his own thin joke.

But Fisher wasn't listening. He was flailing his arms at the group as if they were nuisance birds crowding a soccer field. "Stupid wogs. There's bloody warning signs everywhere. Can't they read?"

"Not English, sir." Charles blinked — his eyes hadn't stopped watering since the blast and his throat felt like one huge, raw blister.

The woman ducked her head but not before Charles saw the tears cutting through the film of dust that covered her face. Her husband stepped between the soldiers and his wife while the older man grumbled some question at the soldiers. The infant wailed relentlessly, kicking his arms and legs at the sky.

Larry Fisher examined the group as if they were loutish guests at an exclusive party. "All right. Toss them in one of those portable showers. God knows where they've been. Lawson — you got that Geiger counter thingamajig? Run it over them, why don't you."

Tony Lawson lifted the boxy instrument. The woman shrank back, covering her baby's head. Her husband's eyes widened in fear as the counter spit frantic darting beeps into the desert air.

"Look at that," Charles whispered. "It's jumping right off the scale!"

Larry scratched his crotch. "Not very pretty."

The older man looked back over the scrubland from where they'd wandered, muttering a single word over and over.

"What the hell's he saying?" Larry demanded. "You understand the local lingo, Emory — what the hell's he saying?"

Charles leaned closer, trying not to meet the fear bubbling in the old man's black eyes. "Sounds like . . . something like . . . Maralinga, Sergeant. Yes . . . Maralinga. Means a plain . . . no . . . a field. Explosion . . . maybe . . . thunder. Yes — that's it. Field of thunder."

1

BURNT PAW LAKE
ALASKA
October 1990

August felt it before he saw it. He raised his head slowly. The sky was the same thick grey as when he'd slid the canoe from the lake. Only the silence seemed different — solid and impenetrable. The kind of stillness that usually supplied the tonic he needed. But now it weighed against him.

Waves licked the sand. A few tarnished leaves hung from thin branches as if suspended in a July heatwave instead of bracing for the first freeze. But it was the silence of the birds that really disturbed him. Their nervous twitter had stopped sometime after he'd flipped the canoe over and begun to dry its smooth skin. The irritable crows had ended their screeching and the honk of the Canada geese resting in a far cove had been muted. Even the solitary loon, so temperamentally suited to this place, had slipped away.

The sky was maddeningly blank, a neutral face. Squinting, August adjusted the Oakland A's cap Sam had given him for his fortieth birthday last month. A rustle pulled his gaze behind him. Nothing. A rat maybe. Or a nervous badger. Grizzlies didn't wander here anymore. He studied the rolling hill that carpeted the land between the lake and the high cliffs to the east. The vegetation was sparse, like the discoloured mat of an old pool table, scruffed and tarnished from the punishing weather and the trails of a hundred small animals.

And then he saw her.

The gyrfalcon, its blazing white breast marking a large female, hovered high above him. She rode the air streams, weaving them into a pattern to her own advantage as she honed in on a target. She circled again, lazily.

A scraping in the mossy rock. And then a rabbit, split with panic, zigzagged across the mercilessly open rise. August squeezed the rag in his hand tight against his knuckles.

Sound sped at him. Wind rushing against mass as the falcon accelerated towards the ground, wings flattened against her body.

The rabbit froze. It was as if the raptor's gaze had paralyzed it.

August crouched, anticipating the gyr's attack. He licked his lips, leashing the part of him that wanted to urge the creature to run . . . *run!* But the moment was lost. The rabbit turned as if the memory of some warm shelter beckoned. It jumped once more, an involuntary twitch of fear. A vestige of instinct warned that to move meant death. The instinct was too late.

The falcon was there.

The rabbit staggered and then collapsed as the gyr swept over the ground once more, clearing the area of interference before claiming its prey. And then she seized the limp body, lifting it from the earth and disappearing over the cliff.

A crow cawed in malevolent congratulation and small white-caps spit against the shore. Suddenly it was very cold. August straightened up, a twinge in his ankle from an old fracture sig-nalling that he'd been crouched too low. But he continued to watch the far shore as the gyrfalcon keened from somewhere lost to him.

Reluctantly, he turned away and hoisted the canoe over his

head, breathing the familiar smell of cedar. It was a comfort he hadn't felt in years. The pressure of the canoe's narrow struts and enfolding shell was a welcome burden, preferable to the mental weights he'd been carrying lately. It had been a good idea to come back to this wild place. Even though he'd told himself that he was too soft now; too cynical to make it here. This notch in the earth demanded decisions. Not committees. Not memos in triplicate. And any compromise was usually on nature's terms.

The canoe fit snugly into a natural bracket between the grey sand and a thicket of stunted fir that crept to meet it. Lots of scrap wood for a fire. Plenty of shelter. The pup tent would fit right up against the bracken. He glanced at the sky. A few bullying clouds were shoving past the sun. There might be snow tonight. Winter was licking its lips for a good solid bite.

He'd just poured the coffee, boiled and stewed, four sugars, no milk, when he heard the plane's engine buzzing into the falling night. August jumped up, spilling the drink, the hot coffee burning through his pants. Shit! He tossed the cup aside and strode to the edge of the lake. Hell! The last thing he needed was a bunch of dilettantes on a trendy trip to the wilderness packing a wolf carcass or a pair of antlers ripped from a Bighorn into their designer trunks.

The drone of the engine grew louder, chopping at his nerves as it churned and sliced at the air. The birds had dropped into silence again. The plane dipped into the valley; it reminded him of some great insect in a Japanese horror movie. Skidding along the surface of the water, it cruised to a stop.

Sam's round face, still as smooth and flushed as an excited kid's, popped out of the pilot's window. "Hi, guy! What do ya want first? The rotten news or the miserable news?" The door squeaked on its hinges as he swung it open, and the engine sputtered impatiently a few times. The plane rocked under Sam's weight as he jumped onto one pontoon and then swung himself, surprisingly gracefully, over the few feet of water towards the gritty shore. But he missed the last step, and water rushed over the rim of his boot. "Damn!" He shuddered and lifted his leg out of the water to shake it.

"Is something wrong? Is Katy okay? What the hell are you doing here?"

Sam flung his hands up as if to fend off an attack. "Whoa! Katy's fine. Perfectly okay . . ." He limped up to August, still shaking his leg. "Jesus! Why don't you just go camping in Antarctica? It's about as comfortable." He gestured at the trees swaying in the building wind and the shoreline cluttered with bleached wood and scattered boulders. "You got no cable here, no bar, and," he swivelled his head in mock surprise, "you sure as heck got no women. *None* of the necessities for survival! Oh," he glanced at the fire, steam rising from where August had tossed his coffee, "but I do see you have room service. What is it tonight? No — don't tell me . . .," he pressed his fingers to his forehead like a cheap psychic, "it's coming to me. Yes. Wieners and could it be . . . yes, yes, it is — beans. That's it. Beans!"

"What do you want? Why aren't you with Christa and the baby where you belong? I've only been here three days, you bastard. You'd better have a damned good reason for showing up. And it better be that somebody's died. Somebody important. Since my daughter's all right and my wife gave up on me long ago — and you're obviously still breathing — then it seems to me you don't have a good reason for being here." The wind had started to nip through August's flannel shirt. He walked to the campfire and picked up a parka from where he'd tossed it over a tree stump. "And if it's World War Three," he shouted back at Sam, "I don't want to know either."

"Well hello to you too, old buddy." Sam was still smiling. He came up behind August and put a hand on his shoulder. "It might not be World War Three," he said quietly, "but it *is* war."

August stopped moving, the zipper on his jacket halfway up. Sam released his shoulder and waved towards the sputtering campfire. "I think you'd better plug the kettle back in and sit down."

The coffee was still hot but somehow not quite as satisfying. Sam dumped spoonfuls of dry milk into his cup and shook it vigorously as if he could will it into the real thing. "Rumour has it," he raised a hand as if warding off attack, "far be it from me to pass on rumour, but Wendell Laine did send me after you without so much as a please, let alone a decent explanation, so I'm entitled. Anyway, rumour has it that you might be needed for this Gulf mess. Save the world from Saddam. Keep us safe from nasty oil prices. You know the drill."

"My Arabic stinks, Laine knows that. I barely passed the refresher and that was two years ago. My tongue was in intensive care for a month afterwards!"

Sam noticed the hint of rough beard and hunched shoulders that matched the weariness gathered around his friend's mouth and eyes. "I don't think it's groundwork this time, buddy. Jamie Watts, the new kid upstairs, told me on the q.t. that the more reliable rumour is that there's some glitch in satellite reconnaissance. Everybody's screaming that we can't afford any glitches right now. Not with Mr. Hussein being so difficult. The powers-that-be are jumpy. They don't want so much as a hairline fracture in Desert Shield." He took a sip of the hot liquid and winced as it hit the back of his throat. "And let's face it, August. No one knows satellite imagery like you. Laine wants you in on this. Whatever it is."

August ran his hands over his hair. It was getting long. His fingers grazed the recently discovered balding spot. It irritated him. "Jesus, Sam — my concentration is shot to hell. It has been for months. Why do you think I'm up here at the end of the earth?! If I have to look at one more space shot or argue with one more prick of a politician, I'll go into orbit myself. I mean, Christ almighty — did Laine tell you I nearly punched him in the mouth last month? I'm lucky I just got sent on a little R&R instead of premature retirement." He watched the lemon yellow plane bobbing against the lake.

"Well there you go then! That's the good news! They can't live without you. This will be a fresh start. Go in there. Knock 'em dead. And you'll be the golden boy again."

August raised one brow. "Two things. I've used up my quota of fresh starts — as Lena will tell you, for as long as you want to listen. And number two, I haven't been a *golden boy* for fifteen years."

Sam shrugged and took a bigger gulp of coffee. "Hey, I'm just the messenger."

"Okay, Mr. Messenger. How about you just hop back in your noisy machine there and go tell Laine you couldn't find me? Some jackass hunter picked me off. Or I fell into a hole in the woods or something. I mean, it's not like it isn't possible. Many a jerk has tossed dice with the elements out here and lost big."

"Look, August, I know you don't like it. But you've gotta go back. In fact, I can't leave here without you. I come up with a bullshit story like that and they'd probably just send the marines to get you instead. There's no gettin' away from it."

The sky had slid from a dark grey to charcoal, the raw red of an interrupted sunset scratching at its insides. "Weather closing in. We better not risk flying out tonight," August said.

Sam slurped back his coffee. "No way. I'm not sharing any pup tent with you. I gave it up when we were twelve, remember?" He tossed back the dregs of his cup. Standing up, he kicked sand over the flames.

August watched the fire sputter and steam before it suffocated.

The plane left the earth behind so easily. From inside the cockpit the engine was just a dull drone. A few fat flakes of snow were squashed against the windowpane, and Sam switched on the ridiculous, carlike, windshield wipers. It was too much like being inside one of those remote-controlled toys. Any minute now the giant who held the control panel would let them crash to earth.

They swept over the rise where the rabbit had died, the plane's wings flirting dangerously with the feces-streaked cliff where the gyrfalcon had disappeared. Over the next cliff lay the clearcuts, the slash and burn of civilization. Tomorrow.

August watched the place that had been his refuge fall away. It was as if it had never been.

NATIONAL PHOTOGRAPHIC INTERPRETATION CENTER (NPIC) WASHINGTON, DC

"Counting cholesterol I see?"

Damn! There was no mistaking the sarcastic tone and no escaping Wendell Laine. Here he was, crowding August's shoulder, his smile pinching into little lines of condescension.

August took the plate of overdone sausage and slippery eggs from the bored girl behind the counter and slid them onto his tray. He added a strawberry Danish that he didn't really want. He'd spent so many years explaining himself to Wendell Laine, he didn't intend to start justifying his choice of breakfast menu now.

Wendell gestured with a brittle move of his elbow towards a small table crowded into an alcove of the cafeteria. "Let's get some privacy," he said in a stage whisper, lifting his tray, which held a plate with two pieces of gritty-looking toast and a pot of tea.

"Oh sure, the only table with a reserved sign on it in the joint. Let's make ourselves inconspicuous and private, Wendell," August said. He glanced around the room. Windowless like the rest of the six-storey cement building at the corner of M and First streets, the cafeteria reflected the staleness of a place that never admitted light. Only a few of the round tables were occupied at this hour in the morning. Several large murals dotted the walls: "Earth As Seen from the Moon"; "Relief Map #183 — the Grand Canyon"; and a few distorted close-ups of the streets and alleys of Washington. Some rebel had pinned a poster of Elvis in his prime near the cash register. At the table next to it Marilu Jarvis and another secretary from the third floor picked at something wholesome and brown. August had dated Marilu once last year. A disaster. A Bon Jovi concert he'd lost the spirit for about five minutes after his ears started ringing.

Marilu waved a small, shy wave at him. He smiled a forced, unnatural smile. The women's heads moved closer together and someone giggled.

August squeezed into his side of the table, its edge pressuring his recently expanded middle. Wendell sat daintily on the other side, seeming to hold the fabric of his expensive suit slightly away from the insult of the cheap plastic chair. The ease with which he slid into position and straightened his napkin, spoon, and plate irritated August. "If you wanted privacy you've got a leather couch in your office that the taxpayers are paying for through their gritted teeth. I'd rather slide my ass onto that."

Wendell took his time opening a minuscule capsule of marmalade. He shook his head conspiratorially. "Never know, August. You never know who's listening these days." He rolled his eyes upwards, glancing around the walls until they rested on Elvis, then he shuddered slightly and went back to picking at the lid of the capsule with one manicured finger. "Much more private here, I am sure."

August watched him spread the marmalade very carefully on the toast. Maybe it had finally happened. Old Wendell had spent so many years entombed in this godawful place, Federal Building No. 213, stuck next to the old Washington Navy Yard on the banks of the Anacostia, that he'd finally succumbed to paranoia. He jabbed a fork into his mustard yellow eggs. Wendell had always been good at his job, no one could take that away from him. It was all they really had in common. Enough to sustain years of meals like this.

"There's a leak." Wendell tore off a piece of the rigid toast and placed it delicately against his tongue. "One of the whiz kids upstairs, Jamie Watts, thinks he might know where. So the mole might not be as smart as he thinks he is. But one thing's clear. Somebody's spilling information. And . . .," Wendell studied August Riley as if doubting whether to continue. The thinning blonde hair pulled back into one of those foolish ponytail things like his own hopeless son wore. The denim jacket and jeans that looked like the same pair he must have worn in the back of beyond. "Riley, must you have your mid-life crisis during work time?" Wendell demanded with about as much passion as he ever revealed.

The fork stopped halfway to August's mouth. "If you recall, I was supposed to be on a month's leave. We don't all have the good taste to quietly drown our burn-out in a glass of Jack Daniels, Wendell."

An unaccustomed flush traced Wendell's neck. He cleared his throat.

"You were saying?" August asked quietly as he tasted the eggs.

The hint of a small triumph crossed Wendell's face. August's blunt reminder of a minor embarrassment over a minor hiccup in Wendell's career — it could hardly be called a drinking "problem" — was worth enduring if it meant nailing Riley to this assignment. As a result of his "non-problem," Wendell needed some points upstairs. He needed the best for this assignment. And Riley was the best no matter how much it choked him to admit it. "Desert Shield is escalating every day. No one wants to commit to a ground war if all the Polaroids aren't right."

The eggs were cold in August's mouth. "What's that got to do with me?"

"Don't be coy." Wendell chewed his food like a fussy cat. "You've been stationed at every major satellite reconnaissance base we've got. Xinjiang, Trabzon, Vetan . . ."

"Yeah . . . beauty spots all." August ripped a napkin from the dispenser and rubbed his mouth. "I've done my time, Wendell. Both for you and the NSA boys."

Wendell ignored him. "None of our other people have your kind of experience." He poured the pale tea from the tin pot, holding the warped lid down tight. "We're . . .," he raised his brows, glancing around the room briefly, "not sure where the leak's originating. Could be any one of the ground stations that are receiving the stuff. Or any of the personnel who handle the information. Anyway, that's what we want you to find out." A dribble of tea managed to escape the pot. Wendell placed the thin napkin over it. "And we want you to find out fast."

August watched the spilt tea slowly stain the napkin. "How much leeway do I have?"

Wendell offered a tight, condescending smile. "As much leeway as you've always had. The same kind of leeway that got you kicked out of China and put the Brits' noses out of joint at Menwith Hill."

August forced himself to swallow another mouthful of eggs, then tossed his fork onto the tray. It clanged in the early morning quiet of the cafeteria. Marilu glanced at him. "My reports were sustained in both those incidents. The Chinese were selling off the info to the Pakistanis and that old boy at Menwith had been in the Russians' pocket for ten years trying to support the decrepit family estate."

"Ah, but diplomacy. A little art of diplomacy would not go amiss in these situations."

"I told you after the last stint overseas — a desk job will suit me just fine until I collect my pension."

Wendell smiled thinly. "Well, we're calling your bluff. This is just a straightforward analysis job."

"Why do I have a feeling there's a bit more to it than that? Why do I have the feeling that if I blow this one I might as well forget about a pension?"

August saw the little quiver of temper zip around the other man's nostrils. Wendell squeezed the damp napkin between his fingers. "We've tolerated your . . . eccentricities for a long, long time, Riley. And as you've probably guessed — it's not me that you've got to thank for that. It's strictly the quality of your work. You've been right," he swallowed as if the words stuck in his throat, "more than you've been wrong. A lot more. So, your various periods of going AWOL — your Greta Garbo, I vant to be alone act — well, there are those above me who felt you were worth it. But yes," Wendell carefully squeezed the wet napkin over his saucer and then folded it into quarters, "yes, if I was you I'd be putting some thought into your future — or lack of it — around here. I understand you've got a daughter who might be needing a transfer to another special school soon? Quite an expensive special school?"

August shoved his plate aside and stood up, pushing back his chair. It bounced off the wall and punched him in the lower spine. "Shit . . .," he muttered. The secretaries' heads swivelled towards him. "Meet you upstairs," he growled. Wendell, tiny smile, placed one sugar cube in his cup. "When you've finished your tea, of course."

August marched past the yellowing photo of Elvis — Elvis in his prime in black leather cradling a microphone — and headed for the fourth floor.

Upstairs hadn't changed much since his last stint. Anonymous, colourless. The monotonous din of the eighty-foot air-conditioners droning twenty-four hours a day, summer or winter, cooling the delicate innards of the NPIC computers as they chewed up billions of pieces of data every year. The finely tuned high-technology trap enclosed August once again as he stepped farther into the main analysis room.

It hadn't always been like this. Twenty years ago the place had been divided into a dozen cubbyholes, so-called "offices," pressed hardboard dividing one analyst's few yards of space from the next guy's. The tinge of excitement as they'd plunged into a new frontier had kept an invisible chord of camaraderie pulled tight around the room. Although the bricked-in windows had bothered him from the start. But the view wasn't exactly a tourist's dream even if you did catch a glimpse of daylight. They'd shoved the NPIC building into a rancid area of the city that hadn't become any more palatable over the years. Guards dotted the perimeter. And just in case anyone still didn't get the idea, two slices of barbed wire curled along the top of the Cyclone fence that surrounded the place.

But all that had been overshadowed in those first years by the knowledge that he was taking up the challenge of Arthur Lundahl's original team. The pioneers who in 1962 had propelled the NPIC into the forefront of reconnaissance after they zeroed in on Castro's buildup of missiles. It was the stuff of legend how the interpreters had been yanked from their cubicles, along with the frames of U-2 film they were studying. An hour later they were in the White House Cabinet Room pointing out the location of nuclear warhead storage sites and missile shelter tents to the President. By the end of that session John Kennedy, on the basis of a few rather innocuous-looking shots taken from a U-2 at 70,000 feet, had decided to initiate the action that would leave a legacy of humiliation for Nikita Khrushchev and the scent of nuclear war burrowed into the consciousness of a generation. The next day the NPIC was pushed onto the White House priority list. August had jumped on for the ride as soon as he could.

He'd left Salt Lake City behind two days after his eighteenth birthday and had detoured around that particular dot on the map ever since. His parents had four other boys and two girls to keep them busy and August had been somewhere in the middle. So while his absence was a disgrace and they probably still prayed for him to this day, they'd spent only minimum form searching for him. He'd been a thorn in their side anyway since he was eight years old and screamed bloody murder both before and after his baptism. Some violent rebellion had led him to plunge his teeth into the priest's hand as he'd tried to bless August with the holy water. He thought then that the guy had a damned nerve and he still believed it now. Priest or no priest.

His mother never forgave him and his initial punishment was a ban that summer on the annual trip to Alaska to visit his Uncle Olsen. August's immediate kindred spirit of few words, Olsen had escaped to the wild country decades before. He'd been his sister's favourite and she was still trying to save him from himself.

August had met Sam Whitman during his first summer up there, envying his rugged existence with a dad who was a real life guide and trapper. Sam later enlightened him as to how unromantic life without running water or Howdy Doody really was.

August worked two jobs after he got to LA, bartending on weekends, night delivery during the week for a courier service that carried suspicious little parcels to some of the swankier areas of town. He never asked, just took the usually generous tip and got home in time to get in a few hours studying. The scholarships were in short supply and the student loans barely kept him in macaroni and cheese. He messed around with a few biology courses the first year. But the dissecting, the statistics, and the endless note taking in the field robbed his joy in the wild. So he'd been drawn back to another obsession — an obsession seeded when the Sputnik went up, the same year as his farcical baptism. He'd won the Grade Three ice-carving contest depicting the bumpy, clumsy-looking satellite. What a perfect escape from the earth that capsule had seemed to his young eyes.

NASA was too fussy for him. He didn't have the eyesight or the science marks. But the CIA was recruiting for their newly formed NPIC section and August's enthusiasm and knowledge of satellites overcame his bad math marks. They figured his Mormon background made him extra reliable. August didn't bother to point out that the religion was rooted in rebellion and even charges of treason.

He looked around his old office. Far too quiet now. Years ago Led Zeppelin and radio talk shows had blasted through the air ducts. Crusting Styrofoam cups and stale ashtrays had been buried amongst piles of top secret documents. Snapshots of wives and kids, plaques with "words of wisdom" were tucked into cluttered bookshelves. Sam had even kept a stuffed bald eagle perched on the back of the one extra chair in the office until Laine had made him get rid of it. Wonder if Sam still had that thing? Those dull glass eyes so awful in the perfectly shaped, lifelike head.

Now the place seemed too clean, too tidy, too timid. Pulsating, clever chaos bowed to the nineties pace of information gathering. Budget cuts and manpower shortages forcing double-paced work for three times the amount of stuff August had had to deal with every day. These men and women had to be twice as smart, twice the technician that August had been. But they weren't having half the fun. Comparing, contrasting, magnifying, over and over again. Was that smudge a nuclear reactor or a grain elevator? Bomb shelter or storage bunker? Civilian or military target? He glimpsed a few heads bent over the dust-free desks of smooth modern line, with matching adjustable chairs.

"Mr. Riley?" The voice was unnaturally loud and eager in this place.

August turned. A broad friendly face and wide grin punctured by a row of the most crooked teeth August had ever

seen. A thick hand seized his and pumped it up and down.
"I've been waiting for you."

August tried to hide his puzzlement.

"Jamie Watts. Mr. Laine said you'd be coming in today."

It fell into place. The whiz kid Sam had mentioned. The
new golden boy. Could he really be so young?

August gripped the hand in return. "I understand you've got
something to show me."

The kid's eyes lit up. He gestured August into a beige-
coloured square of space, its narrow area covered with
blow-ups of enhanced satellite images. He pointed to one of
them. On the surface it looked like one endless, empty plain.
But clustered into the lower left-hand corner were what
appeared to be a dozen little black boxes.

"Tanks?"

Jamie nodded. There was no sign of delight now. Just intense
concentration.

August leaned closer. "What's that next to them?" Before
Jamie could answer, he demanded, "You got a comparison shot?"

Jamie pulled another sheet from below and slid it smoothly
over the original. "This was taken two days ago."

August's brow wrinkled. He traced a finger, careful not to
actually touch the shots, in between the black boxes. "They've
pulled out those Scud launchers."

The grin was back. "That's what I say!" His face realigned
into carefully neutral tones. "Laine . . . Mr. Laine," he glanced
at August as if expecting an admonishment for the slip in
respect. When he saw only August's intense interest he continued, "Mr. Laine thinks I'm imagining it and the other guys
around here aren't sure. And well, frankly . . ."

"Nobody wants to tell the old fart that his eyes aren't what
they used to be?"

An involuntary guffaw shifted the boy's features back into
their bright enthusiasm. "Something like that."

August turned back to the photos. "Well, they're difficult to
spot all right. They've parked them in the shadows. Probably
to keep them out of the heat."

"The reason I'm pushing it, Mr. Riley . . ."

August raised a hand. "Cut the mister stuff — I'm feeling my age too much lately as it is."

Jamie nodded, his tightly curled black hair gleaming in the fluorescent light. "Well, the thing is — we expected the Iraqis to leave the Scuds in those positions. Misinformation has been spread around that our troops were going to be building to the south. They're in a perfect position. So why would they move them? Except if they knew that it was misinformation?"

August looked at the photos again for one long moment as a traitorous wave of excitement dipped across his chest. "I guess that's what we're here to find out, Jamie."

CAMP DAVID
Late December 1990

August could feel the two men behind him and see the two in front even though they were keeping what was probably considered a discreet distance. The brown and white spaniel scampered ahead, sniffing deeply into piles of frost-bitten leaves clustered along the path. August had been summoned with an hour's notice. He wasn't dressed for it. His jacket was too light and his boots felt awkward and heavy as he tried to match the easy stride of the angular man beside him. He wished they could either walk faster or slow down to a stroll but the President insisted on a measured, steady pace.

The briefing had been succinct. August had felt vaguely uncomfortable under the tight gaze of the narrowed, dark eyes. They'd stood in the large, airy kitchen sipping coffee, the President in an open-necked sports shirt, August leaning against a counter ledge, a leaky faucet dripping steadily into the stainless steel sink. A gap-toothed Santa Claus had been cut from red construction paper and stuck on the kitchen window. A guy built like a locomotive stood on the other side of the window. Every so often he swivelled his head around the maniacally grinning Santa in a way that made August draw back. He wanted out of here. Wanted to get on with the job. What he didn't want was to be any man's excuse for a macho fistfight over so-called leadership qualities to wave at the next primary. And he didn't want to be some kind of ghost-buster for the poltergeist of Vietnam. On the other hand, he had a lot of problem with dictators. And as far as Saddam was concerned, better late than never. But he figured now wasn't the time to ask about the buddy-buddy plan with Hussein during that nasty incident known as the Iran-Iraq War.

He might have liked Camp David under other circumstances. It had a certain qualified wildness to it. The cedar buildings and sheltering low eaves invited you inside. But there were too many guys with thick necks and unblinking eyes appearing without notice from around corners to suit August's taste.

The President had motioned for August to follow him outside. "So, it's not as bad as it could have been?" Bush asked as they stepped onto the trail leading from the cluster of living quarters to several wooded acres.

"No, sir. I've eliminated the National Security Council as being the source of the leak. Our mole doesn't appear to be working out of there."

"How do you know?"

"We've tossed a little misinformation into their daily data. We suggested that several countries were getting soft about the Resolution. That some might be open to a bit of dealing with Hussein. There was no reaction from Baghdad. We could be reasonably certain that if Hussein had any inkling of that piece of news he would have taken the bait. So — it looks like your men are clear."

"But?"

"Sir?"

The narrow lips pulled back on one side. "There's always a 'but,' Mr. Riley."

August couldn't help smiling. "Well, you're speaking to a natural pessimist, I suppose. I almost wish the leak had been in the NSC. Now we only have to eliminate the possibilities in the rest of the world."

"From what I've been told you're more than up to it." The President reached down and in one smooth move, one hand still in the pocket of his overcoat, grabbed a fallen branch from the ground. The spaniel turned towards him, her chocolate nose twitching in the air.

August felt the men behind them stiffen. "It might take awhile," he said.

George Bush tore a few rough strands from the branch and tested its strength between his hands, bending it up and down. The dog jumped at their feet, emitting little excited yelps. "How long is awhile?"

Bars of cold sun slanted between the bare trees. He should have tried to see Katy. But he'd been busy. The awful old seduction of late nights and obsessive pursuit once more coming between them. August tried to snap the metal tags on his jacket closed. Two of the tags were missing and the other had to stretch too far to do its job. "Six weeks. Eight. Maybe longer. Depends on how clever our mole is."

Bush stopped walking. So did the four men. The two in front fanned into the trees. "We don't have that long, Mr. Riley. We have an eight-million-dollar Lacrosse satellite about to go up on the Atlantis shuttle. That thing's gonna tell us how many grains of sand are getting up Saddam Hussein's nostrils every day. We don't wanna find out a week from now that its shots have been so compromised that we might as well send him copies for his family album. It's up to you," he raised the suddenly solid-looking stick as if about to jab August with it. "It's up to you," he repeated, "to target your best bet." He flung the stick in a high curve along the leaf-strewn road they were following, barely missing the tallest secret service guy. "And to give me answers." The dog scampered through the leaves, its stub of a tail twitching wildly.

The President turned back to August. "Where do you wanna start?" he asked, the slanted smile lifting half his face into a lop-sided grin.

August watched the dog bite into the soft wood of the stick and toss it in the air. "I think it better be our tracking station on Heard Island, sir. From there I can throw some false data into the system and see who scoops it. I can narrow down the leak. Send each station — from Incirlik in Turkey to Pine Gap in Australia — the misinformation. If the bait is swallowed, I'll have to pay a trip in person to wherever the mole is hanging out. But Heard is our best bet to start. There's not much there. And the fewer bodies snooping around, the easier my job."

"Where's this Heard Island?"

August grimaced. "The middle of nowhere, Mr. President." He watched as the sun slid behind the black trees. "The middle of nowhere."

2

ULURU (AYERS ROCK)
AUSTRALIA
January 18, 1991

Charles Emory placed a hand over Larry Fisher's camera and reached for the plastic nub at his throat which substituted for a voice box. "Don't," he rasped.

"Watch it, old boy! You'll get your damned fingerprints all over the lens!" Fisher shouted. He yanked the camera out of Charles's reach. "I didn't cart the thing halfway 'round the world for you to go mucking it up." He pulled a tissue from the pocket of his shirt and carefully wiped the lens. Anything to avoid looking at Emory. It was a bloody effort to keep his eyes from being drawn like a magnet to that damned awful . . . well . . . that hole right smack in the middle of the old boy's throat. A fellow had to be polite after all and not stare. But Jesus, it was hard with that yellow, plastic thing — didn't look quite hygienic somehow — sticking straight out at you at eye level.

He'd known about the throat cancer, of course. Matching up longevity levels was practically a hobby for the Maralinga survivors. And who didn't remember the brouhaha Emory had kicked up? A very nasty piece of business it had been. In fact, Larry himself had occasionally been at the receiving end of Emory's infamous temper. But still it was a shock to see him. He'd heard through the grapevine that the quacks had taken the voice box in the late seventies.

Not being able to speak properly must have really irritated old Emory. No one had loved to bark out orders more than Emory once he had the chance. But now the thick head of raven hair was reduced to a few strands of white against a mottled skull. His skin hung in untidy folds about his face. And his tall, once commanding frame seemed inadequate for the weight of his light clothes. But the eyes were the same. Dark, bottomless, blue. And wary.

Fisher felt he had to rush in with something to fill the silence, which was growing as long as the shadows behind them. "Don't look so poe-faced." He glanced back at the tall black man who stood silhouetted at the edge of the trail, red dust settling across his scruffed running shoes. "I was going to give the geezer a quid for the privilege of snapping his ugly mug." His high, dry laugh boomeranged from the massive rock face that crouched around them.

Emory's fingers whipped to his throat in a practised, but staccato gesture, as if he were still learning the choreography of his handicap. "Mr. Tjilkamata is hard of hearing. He's trying to tell you that he doesn't want you to take his photograph." He gulped and plugged the hole.

Larry tried not to watch the mechanics of Emory's speech, cocking his head to catch each syllable of his mutilated voice. "What's he going to do, eat me?" He laughed uproariously and capped the camera. "Light's just about gone anyway," he shrugged. "We'll see if we can talk him into it tomorrow. Maybe for a fiver." Stretching in exaggerated weariness he glanced around at the cluster of vehicles in the parking lot, metallic scabs along the edge of the magnificent rock. "Well, we'd better be finding our beds if we're going to tackle that little hill in the morning."

"No." The Aborigine's voice was thick. His flesh lay on him in smoky layers barely covering his bones. He stepped forward into the harsh light thrown by the concession stand behind them. It became clear that the shadows of evening and his straight figure had concealed his true age. Deep ravines ran beside his mouth and some great burden had gouged a chasm across his forehead. But he held his head erect and looked at the two men with a certain confidence that carried his history, despite the ill-fitting park warden's uniform that hung loosely on him. "I would advise against hiking tomorrow."

"Johnnie?" Charles Emory was alert, his own emaciated figure a pale reflection of the other man's ash-coloured body. "Johnnie?" he repeated, leaning towards the man's left ear, the undamaged ear.

But Johnnie Tjilkamata was watching Larry Fisher, his eyes probing.

Larry turned away, fussing with the camera strap. "What's he on about?" he muttered to Charles out of the side of his mouth as if Johnnie were an animal whose hearing operated on a different wavelength.

"The mountain isn't as smooth as it looks," Johnnie said. "Many believe that they can cling with their hands and feet like a koala to a eucalyptus and conquer the top. But there are few footholds for those of little experience. Danger hides in the secret places of the Uluru. Only the Kunia Snake-people can explore with impunity."

Charles spoke to Fisher but didn't take his eyes from Johnnie's face. "The Aborigines believe that the Kunia were murdered here. And their bodies transformed into the boulders around the base of Ayers. It's sacred territory which must be approached with respect."

Fisher snorted and pulled the zip on his camera case closed with a vicious snap. "Hocus-pocus." He winked at Charles. "A bunch of morbid malarkey to keep gawking tourists like me out of the way. But I'll have you know," he stepped towards Johnnie waving three fingers, "that Larry Fisher's been around the world three times." Johnnie stood resolute, a full head taller than Fisher. "And it'll be a cool day in hell before I get the wool pulled over my eyes by the likes of you and your rubbish."

Charles pushed Fisher's hand away from Johnnie's face. "You don't remember him, do you, Larry?"

"Pardon?" Larry's face wrinkled into a caricature of an old man. "Remember him?" Jesus. It was like talking into one of those one-way radios he'd heard they still used on some of the sheep stations in this backward country. The awkward uncertainty of not knowing for sure when it was your turn to speak. He wished Emory would signal over and out or something.

"Think about it," Charles was saying. "Maralinga. You and I and the rabbits weren't the only ones in the desert that day."

Larry looked from Charles to the Aborigine, who was watching him with quiet bemusement. "You're making about as much sense as this bloke's superstitious poppycock." He couldn't tell if it was a smile or a grimace that punched Emory's mouth.

"Think about it just a little bit."

Larry tipped back on his heels, hands on his hips, camera bouncing against his belly. And then slowly the memory seeped into his eyes. "Jesus! You're not telling me? Nah, couldn't be . . . that skinny little wog with the other old guy? Came wandering in after the fireworks were over?" He looked eagerly at Charles for confirmation, like a grade schooler flinging his hand in the air to answer a question.

Charles nodded. "A woman and child were with him as well." His look glanced off Johnnie before returning to Larry who now stood openmouthed. "But you probably don't remember that either."

Larry screwed up his eyes and stared at Johnnie as if trying to squeeze the vision of that day from the past. "You're absolutely right, Charles. My God, what a memory you've got! No wonder you went so far in this godforsaken place. But hey," he gestured towards Johnnie. "Don't say he's coming . . ."

Charles smiled thinly. "Oh no, don't worry. The last thing he'd be interested in is attending our little reunion. The very last thing. I just make a point of getting in touch whenever I'm out this way." He turned to the other man. "Staying long this year, Johnnie?"

"Time to go soon." Johnnie's face touched a grin. "Shirt's no good. It sticks." He pulled the clinging cotton away from his thin chest.

Charles laughed and put out his hand. "All the best."

The Aborigine's reed thin arms rested briefly like a hovering insect on Charles's shoulders. "Next season?"

"Perhaps." Charles waved one hand, almost in benediction, over his own body and tilted his head slightly as if listening for some internal signal. "But perhaps not."

Johnnie turned again to Larry. With a small gesture like a potter smoothing a glazed vase, he brushed his arm. Larry flinched. "Don't climb tomorrow." Fisher laughed and hitched up his pants. "Yeah, yeah, we know — only the snake men and all that."

Johnnie, holding his shirt away from his body with two fingers, walked into the lengthening shadows at the base of Ayers Rock.

HEARD ISLAND

If there was one thing August hated more than small planes it was helicopters. "Have we finally hit hell frozen over?" he shouted at the pilot over the sound of the rotating blades. He'd been comforting himself for the past hour with the thought that as long as he could hear that damned chop, chop, then the contraption was at least still defying gravity. The pilot, who didn't look old enough to cross the street without his mother let alone fly this thing over the roughest seas on the planet, lifted one corner of his mouth, which August concluded would have to pass for a smile. Well, he could live without a sense of humour if it meant the boy was concentrating on flying.

August had started this trip three days and several datelines ago. He'd picked up this deathtrap and its baby-faced captain at a place in the South Indian Ocean with the encouraging name of Desolation Island. He'd figured things could only get better.

He was wrong.

Hail was pelting the chopper's windscreen, great round balls of ice that seemed to take the presence of the humans in the fragile machine personally. Below, the ice cap that made up ninety percent of the island gleamed in an occasional slice of sun penetrating the cloud. It didn't exactly conjure up August's usual image of an island: Hawaii, where he and Lena had spent their honeymoon, or even the tiny mound of rock and wild flowers that flared out of the middle of Burnt Paw Lake. Many a late summer evening he'd dragged the canoe onto its rocky shore and set up camp. An island was a place of refuge. But not Heard Island. Named after yet one more poor fool sailing around looking for El Dorado, but finding instead a slab of ice never meant to be trod by shivering humans dressed in peaked hats and leggings who couldn't sprout a decent fur pelt between them as shield against the unremitting cold.

"You gonna be able to set this baby down without skis?"

The pilot ran a finger over the light fuzz on his upper lip, the start of an adolescent-looking moustache. August's optimism plunged another notch. "It'll be difficult, sir. But my orders are to deliver you to Heard Island tracking facility."

"Well, don't do anything just because some guy flying a desk back in Washington thinks it's possible, okay? I mean, don't put yourself out on my account."

But the kid wasn't listening. Instead seemed to be counting backwards as if towards a blastoff of some kind. "Ready, sir?"

It was a rhetorical question. August sat up straight, clutching the cheap suitcase already bulging at the zipper. Lena had taken the good set. Along with just about everything else that wasn't bolted down.

"You'll have to jump quick, I'm afraid. No time to hang around. Radio control's just said that the weather's closing in. I'll have to dump you fast and get back to Desolation."

The gleaming ice had given way to a thin strip of grey sand that had yet to ever see a sunbather. Some gritty plants and

strands of tussock grass had dragged themselves from the punished driftwood onto a scrubby dune. Just beyond stood the
tracking station, its severe lines dutifully whitewashed every
year. Behind the station, as if trying to scoop in the sky, stood
the massive tracking dishes. Picking his way carefully down to
the shore was a figure dressed in neon orange overalls.

The copter hovered over a clear area at the edge of the
beach. "This is it, sir."

August gripped the suitcase and zipped his coat to his neck.
He slid the heavy door open and stared down at a row of thin
rounded stones jutting out of the crabgrass beyond the sand.
"What's that?"

The pilot followed his gaze. "Oh, that's the graveyard."
August thought the guy actually smiled for the first time. "All the
sealers and whalers who died of cold — or misery — out here."

"Right." August flipped the pathetically thin nylon ladder
over the side of the copter and tossed his suitcase out. Weaving
in the wind, hail stinging his face, he groped down the ladder,
feeling the press of the huge machine whirring above him and
the pull of the dark island.

ULURU
January 19

*Red dust swirled from behind a blinding crimson cloud. Choking.
Searing his raw throat. Sprawled in the dirt gasping for breath. Larry
Fisher snap . . . snap . . . snapping photographs of his agony. Larry
tossing the prints into the sand. Thick, bloody snakes sliding from
beneath them. Crawling over Charles. More and more of them slith-
ering up his legs. Across his chest. Towards his throat.*

Charles woke up gagging, pawing at his throat.

There was a sharp knock at the door. "Are you all right?" a
woman called.

Charles opened his eyes, the feeling of overdose he'd inher-
ited thirty years ago starting his day with a pall as usual. He

walked slowly to the door and opened it, staring in surprise at his daughter. "What are you doing here?"

She walked to the window and snapped the shade up, releasing a red neon flood of light into the cramped room. Larry Fisher groaned from the other twin bed and pushed his head farther into the pillow.

"I got a chance for a flight last night. Some bigwigs from Canberra wanted to see the Rock." Emma went to the tiny bathroom and ran some warm water onto a facecloth. She offered it to her father and he daubed it against his throat. She'd never adjusted to the sight of that raw wound. She never would. She looked away from the thin white legs flung over the side of the bed and ignored the quickly repressed groan of pain as he heaved himself into a sitting position. He shouldn't be going today. Indulging the likes of that British twit, Larry Fisher.

Standing over Larry she clapped her hands briskly. "Rise and shine!" A quick, tight smile as he winced.

A trail of saliva had dried on his stubbled cheek. Larry opened his eyes, and his face twisted in what might have been a cocky grin twenty years before. Now it translated into a leer. "Well, now . . . not every day a sweetie gets me out of bed. Charles, you old devil, you never told me!"

"This is my daughter," Charles snapped.

Larry's inspection of Emma trampled the advances of feminism. Wispy blonde hair danced around her broad, not quite pretty, face, and although her cheekbones were high, they were too round to fit any classic sculpture. But the deep blue of her eyes almost overcame the neutrality of her other features. She was dressed in a crisp white blouse and pleated skirt — the overall effect an old-fashioned primness. She had what Larry called a tidy figure, and good legs above the high heels, which seemed slightly incongruous in the middle of the outback.

Emma dismissed Larry with a look that could cool the Australian sun and turned back to Charles, who sat hunched on the edge of the bed. "I don't think you should go on this climb today. It's far too hot and you're getting too old for this kind of nonsense."

"Hey! What is this? A bloody conspiracy?" Larry climbed out of the bed, his diamond-patterned pyjamas assaulting her eyes. "Charlie promised that if I showed for this reunion thing he'd show me some good Aussie climbing." He shoved his feet into a pair of new velveteen slippers and walked to the window. He squinted at the landscape. "The only bloody climbing in this god-forsaken frying pan. I might not have beat Everest but I've tackled one mountain on every continent." He snorted contemptuously. "And these little old rump roasts aren't going to stop me."

Charles was watching Emma. She was straightening the razor and shaving cream on top of the bureau. "Are you going back to the Base this morning?" He didn't want his daughter here. Not today, of all days.

"Well, *excuse me* — don't mind me at all," Larry said sarcastically, squeezing deliberately close to Emma in the narrow space between the bureau and the bathroom. "Got to perform my morning ablutions."

"They're sending a plane for me," Emma said. "I have to get back to Pine Gap. Something's come up." She put her hands on his shoulders, kneading them. "You're awfully tight."

"Didn't sleep well. Bad dreams." The massage reached deep, penetrated the muscle. Emma's expert fingers dug along his spine and molded the length of his back. She had surprising strength for such a small woman.

"Why did you invite this horrible man here? What's so special about him? Besides his bad breath and worse manners, I mean?" She worked the gnarled area between his shoulder blades.

Emory rubbed his forehead as if a great weariness were tracking him. "Just wanted to see Larry again."

She snorted. "Oh! Of course! You've always been so sentimental about Maralinga and the good old days!" Her hands rested lightly on his shoulders. "What is it? Unfinished business? Maybe the nightmares will stop when you clear it up?"

"*My* business," he said forcefully, raising his head, a clear coldness defining his expression as he looked in the bureau mirror, letting his eyes meet hers. "*My* business," he repeated.

She picked up a comb on the night table and drew it through

her hair. She avoided looking directly at her image. She knew she'd see a tired woman who appeared older than her thirty-four years despite her wispy light hair and small stature. But she did look at the man reflected there. A man with too little flesh on his wide shoulders, ribs too apparent and skin too white. Whenever she saw him through a stranger's eyes, through the maudlin, pitying gaze of people like Larry Fisher, the reality of what was happening to him hit her all over again.

Charles sighed and walked up behind her. "Don't take offence, old girl." He patted her arm. "It's no use you getting involved. It's ancient history, Emma. A young woman like you shouldn't be concerning herself with," he studied himself in the mirror, "well, with . . .," he tried on a narrow smile, "horrors of the past."

She squeezed the comb in her hand until the teeth left dark imprints on her palm. But she held back the tears. Her father didn't like tears. He saw them as a weakness. "Tears give the opponent an advantage," he was fond of saying.

"So," he said, the cheerful tone sounding hollow, "what's this dash back to the Base all about?"

Emma glanced towards the bathroom. The shower was hissing and Larry Fisher was crooning a remarkably passable "Black Magic." "David Taylor is down on Heard on a routine maintenance inspection, and some reconnaissance expert from America has shown up. There's a rumour that he'll be flying in to the Gap any day to make sure we've all blown our noses and tied our shoelaces tight."

Charles sought her eyes in the mirror but she was fiddling with the razor and comb. "What does he really want?" he asked.

She smiled tightly. "You know I can't tell you that."

He put his hand over hers. "You need a holiday, Em. Why don't you take a couple of weeks and go to Tonga for a little R&R?"

"Can't be done at the moment, Dad. I'm head of security, remember?"

"You'll have some breakfast though before you leave? Help me endure Larry and his snapshots?"

She shook her head and walked across the room quickly, as if she might change her mind if she lingered. "I shouldn't have come here anyway. It was just an impulse. To see how you were doing." She opened the door and then hesitated, "Don't take any chances up there today, all right?"

But he was at the window, lost in the crimson flood that signalled dawn in the dead centre of Australia.

Noon

"You're a heartless bugger, Charles. Jesus, I must've lost ten pounds in sweat already. I stink to high heaven." Larry heaved himself onto the ledge, scraping his hands along the dark red rock. They'd been climbing all morning and he'd barely been able to keep up with Charles even though the man looked like a walking skeleton.

"Stop your bellyaching, Larry. You said you wanted a good workout. That's what you're getting."

"Are we nearly there?" Larry whined as he collapsed on the rock floor, unloading a small packsack from his shoulders.

Charles shaded his eyes and peered up at the smooth face of stone looming above. "Another couple of hours."

Larry crawled into the shade of the small cave gouged by some geological spasm a million years before. Its rock was cool against his sweat-caked face. "Ah," he sighed. "Where's that water, mate?" He reached towards Charles. The other man's features were obscured but his figure was outlined by the glare of the sun behind him as it tried to reach into the cave. Charles held the canteen towards Larry. And then suddenly swung it away and gulped a mouthful.

"Hold on, now. Guests first," Larry tried to laugh, licking his lips.

"Oh, I think I've held on long enough," Charles's voice seemed loud in the cave. Beyond it lay only the silence of the noon heat.

Larry laughed uncomfortably. He'd heard that temperatures

like this could do funny things to people. But Charles had surely lived in this hole long enough to know that? He pushed himself up, pulling his packsack with him, resisting the cool floor of the cave. "Well, how about a spot of lunch then?" He flipped open the buckle on his pack.

"You didn't remember Johnnie Tjilkamata at all, did you?"

Larry plunged a hand into the knapsack. "You're not still on about that, are you?" His fingers closed around his own canteen.

"In fact, Maralinga never kept you awake many nights, did it?"

"Why should it?" Larry shrugged. "I was just doing a job. The whole bloody thing was exaggerated anyway. I'm still healthy as a horse." He unscrewed the canteen top.

"You made sure you got back home to London and some first-class medical treatment. You had your drinking buddy Stahel sign all the right papers for you. The rest of us weren't quite so lucky. Or influential."

Larry stopped with the canteen midway to his mouth. "How'd you know about that?"

"David Taylor went back with you. He went on a mechanic's course, remember? You introduced him to the pleasures of gambling. Or don't you remember that either, Larry? You were pleased as punch when the quacks gave you a clean bill of health."

"Oh, Taylor. That little weasel. Never did like the man. But he was useful." Larry rolled his eyes. "He lost a fortune on that trip, silly devil." He raised the water to his lips.

Charles swept the canteen from Larry's hand. It bounced across the dry floor of the cave. "Why didn't you tell the rest of us about the treatment?"

Larry stared after the canteen, at the water slowly staining the dry floor of the cave, and then back at Charles, whose lean face had angled into the brash light now. His eyes looked black. "It was a . . . an experiment, Charles," he stuttered. "Could've . . . could've gone either way, old boy." His lips felt parched.

Charles stepped around Larry, so that the cave's interior was behind him. Larry was forced to turn. The open sky was now to his back, the sun flaying his shoulders. His breath was faintly rancid.

"But we never got the chance to find out, did we, Larry? My boy never got the chance to find out, did he?"

Oh Christ! Emory's kid! Larry remembered now. Of course. Born pickled or something. Lived a week. Or was it a month? They'd sent old Charlie away on an extended R&R — it was coming back to him now. He glanced over the lip of the cave. Like a fool he'd insisted on climbing on the far side of the damned rock. The less popular side. He glanced over his shoulder. Below and at a distance he could see some dots on the horizon which might be people. Then again they could be one of those odd animals they had down here. Oh Jesus! Yes! The kid.

"You know we all felt bad about that, Charles."

"Not bad enough to send flowers."

Larry suddenly felt like vomiting. His lips were parched dry and he could feel the sun sizzling a brand on the back of his neck. The rock beneath his feet was slippery dry.

"You helped him die." Charles's voice was cool, as if he'd rehearsed the words a hundred times.

"Hold on now, old boy! That's not fair." Charles's rage was pummelling him harder than the sun. Larry stepped back.

Charles laughed. A harsh sound. "Not fair! Well, you've finally said something sensible!"

Larry felt his lower lip trembling and his insides heaving. The tall man's palm was flat against his chest. "You'll not take as long to die as my boy."

The pressure through Larry's shirt seemed horribly slow. But as solid and inevitable as if Charles's fist was around his heart.

No one heard the sound of Larry Fisher's body hitting the red earth two hundred feet below.

NPIC
WASHINGTON, DC

A few isolated street lamps flickered against the oncoming dusk. They made the six-storey cement facade of the NPIC appear even more cheerless than usual. Jamie Watts flashed his ID at a guard armed with a semiautomatic and was waved through the main gate. He lifted a hand to Jack Andrews who manned the night desk, hunched over a crossword puzzle as usual. As the elevator door closed behind him, Jamie unbuttoned the heavy overcoat he'd worn as protection against the chilly Washington night. He didn't want to waste a moment upstairs. Something big was brewing. And Jamie Watts, kid from the Chicago Projects, scholarship grad, University of Chicago, 1988, was going to be in on it. A sour twist had distorted Laine's face when he'd informed Jamie that he'd been requisitioned for this assignment. But August Riley had asked specifically for him.

He stepped from the elevator into the corridor that ran the length of the top floor. A janitor pushed a floor polisher along the corridor's uninspiring beige and grey tile. He glanced at Jamie, an unwelcome intruder into his routine, before increasing the speed of his machine.

Wendell Laine was sitting with his back to Jamie, hands steepled under his chin, staring at an oil painting, a still life of a waxy-looking apple and an anemic pear in what looked to Jamie like a very tarnished bowl. The room was decorated in a poor imitation of an English gentleman's study somewhere at the turn of the century.

"Sir?"

Laine didn't respond. His fingers moved slowly together in small circles and Jamie noticed for the first time that Laine grew his very thin hair long on one side so that he could comb it over his bald skull. The strangely vulnerable-looking pink skin was revealed clearly beneath the unflattering light of the Tiffany lamp on his desk.

"Sir?" Jamie repeated, a little nervously now. Laine was known as a bit of an eccentric. Jamie had as much respect for individuality as the next guy but sometimes . . .

"Sir," he repeated, with a little more force.

And then he noticed the earphones. Wendell Laine had a Walkman clamped around his head! Jamie smiled to himself. He doubted the man was listening to rap.

He reached forward and tapped the rigid shoulder. Hey — shoulder pads as well! Only time he'd actually touched the boss, aside from the briefest, coolest of glancing skin at his initial interview.

Laine jerked in his seat and whipped the earphones from his head. Jamie could hear what sounded like some kind of angry classical tome pounding from the set.

"What's wrong with you, Watts? You could give a person a heart attack!"

"Sorry, sir," Jamie waved ineffectively behind him. "Your door was open. You did tell me to come right over."

"Yes. Right." Laine seemed to have recovered. "Sit down, sit down." The man sounded impatient, irritable. What else was new?

Jamie arranged himself in the leather chair opposite the desk. He noticed a silver-framed photo of what looked like a collie dog and a crystal rendition of Rodin's *The Kiss* on one corner of the desk. The uncompromising sensuality of the embracing couple tugged at Jamie's eye and contrasted unfavourably with the dour-faced man across from him.

"As I said on the telephone, August Riley wants a special assignment carried out from our end. It's to track the leak that you . . .," Laine ducked his head as the words came out reluctantly, "so cleverly pointed out to us."

"Yes?" Jamie wanted to loosen his collar in the worst way.

"We want to redirect the Lacrosse satellite material coming in from over the Middle East to Heard Island."

"Heard Island? Isn't that . . .?"

"Yes." Laine was pressing his fingertips hard together. "Yes. It's our station in the middle of nowhere. Some chip of rock off Antarctica."

"But why . . .?"

"Riley is going to doctor the images from there. Send them on." He glanced from beneath his brows with a look of such condescension that Jamie wanted to slap him. "I can't impress on you enough the need for discretion in this matter. August Riley insisted on reclassifying your security clearance. You might as well know that I didn't approve. But . . .," Laine pushed a pen around on his desk, "well, Mr. Riley went over my head." He looked up, the sourness tightening his face again. "In any case, this way Riley believes he can eliminate certain suspects. We'll start by letting Mr. Hussein think the Coalition forces are going to try for an amphibious landing."

Jamie loosened his collar. "But isn't it . . . well, a bit dangerous? Because as you say, it's very isolated down there. At Heard, I mean. This is war we're talking about now. And if the word . . ."

Laine leaned across his desk. He actually wore cufflinks. Pure gold, it looked like. Jamie didn't think anyone wore cufflinks anymore. "Mr. Watts, if the word, as you say, gets out, it means that *one* of us is having very naughty conversations with someone we shouldn't be now, doesn't it?"

Jamie flushed at the memory of the one indiscreet lazy chat he'd had with Nellie the night they'd first made love. But Laine couldn't possibly know about that. Besides they were getting married. Sometime. He glanced at the Rodin sculpture and the shot of the dog. Hell, old Laine probably told Lassie there all about his hard day at the office every night.

"Yes, I suppose so, sir." He thought his dutiful tone successfully covered his embarrassment.

Laine's hands were tightly clasped. Jamie noticed how white the fingernails were. The guy must have poor circulation. "Now then, Mr. Watts, can you, or can you not, provide a doctored file of photographs of the Middle East?"

Jamie stood up. He could do this job. Not for Laine. But he'd do it for Riley. "When do we start, sir?"

For once Laine looked half-pleased. He stood up and walked to another ugly oil painting against one wall, this time of a rigid stag poised between two evergreens. Sliding the painting aside to reveal a safe embedded in the wall, he flicked the dial, reached inside, and retrieved a file. He passed it to Jamie. "These are the need-to-know codes. We start right now, Mr. Watts."

3

HEARD ISLAND
January 19

The black cat was curled in the big man's lap. David Taylor's cheerful head of curly orange hair and thick beard contrasted with the bleakness of the surroundings. He scratched behind the cat's pointed ears, a little roughly, August thought. The cat obviously disagreed. Its thick purr almost offset the wail of the wind outside the glorified shack that served as so-called living quarters for the tracking station. The computers blipping in a roughly partitioned corner seemed out of place with the sparsely furnished rooms, the chipped mug of stewed coffee in August's hand, and the plants struggling in cloudy specimen jars.

"How long you been here, Taylor?" August asked, trying not to appear too interested.

The other man offered the cat a sliver of the half-frozen cherry Danish he was chewing. The animal sniffed it and then rejected the offer, climbing its way carefully down his leg. "Oh," David licked each finger carefully, "not long. They don't send you down to a place like this for long."

You didn't answer the question, August thought. "They tell me Pine Gap is quite a place. Very sophisticated stuff."

David Taylor stretched and stood up, pulling a heavy sweater over his ample belly. "Like anywhere else, I suppose. You get used to anything after awhile." He glanced around the chilly room. "It's a damned sight better than this hole anyway." He wiped a hand against the windowpane and peered at the rain that had begun to punish the open ground outside. "You coming?" he asked.

August took another sip of thick coffee. "Think I'll stay in and do my homework."

Taylor shrugged. "Suit yourself." He stepped into the bright orange overalls August had spotted from the air and flipped the hood over his head, pulling the strings tight around his chin. His face was round, almost comical, peering from the weather-proof clothes. "Well, I'm not going to tell you the fresh air would be good for you, mate." He chuckled to himself. "Least you can do is put some fresh coffee on for me before I get back, though. Be an hour or two. That damned hail yesterday pelted the dishes pretty bad. Size of bloody golf balls. Got to get up there and check out the damage."

August watched Taylor walk down the narrow scratch of path that wound through the sparse vegetation surviving on this bit of land. The cat jumped onto the windowsill and squeezed itself between August and the cold panes. Behind Taylor the island's incredible glacier, looking as harmlessly thrilling as the Matterhorn at Disneyland, pushed against the sky, no hint of the dormant volcano simmering inside. August squinted and shielded his eyes against the window. A tiny speck was outlined against the smooth white shell of the receiving dish. He picked up the binoculars sitting on the windowsill.

His instinct had been right. A hawk. A very small, very fast specimen. It was hovering now. He adjusted the lens. The bird blurred in his vision and then soared and disappeared before he could identify it.

The computer beeped, calling him back to the screen. He swung the binoculars once more across the horizon and watched as Taylor's neon orange suit disappeared. Washington had slipped up not telling him about this guy. August sighed and turned to the computer. Well, an hour or two might be enough, it was the right time of day. And he'd received Jamie Watts's doctored download safely four hours ago when Taylor was still asleep. The sooner he got this over with the better.

He sat down in front of the screen and for the first time in twenty-two months lit a cigarette. One phony amphibious landing coming up.

Two Hours Later

August leaned back and rubbed his eyes. God, he'd forgotten how tiring working these screens could be. He punched in one last command, waited for it to clear, double-checked Jamie's acknowledgement code, and signed off. This assignment was risky, a new wrinkle in an old game. But then again, that was precisely how they'd suckered him into taking it on. He couldn't go belly up now. If he pulled this one off he could dictate his own terms next time. Like maybe a log cabin some-where inaccessible by road — or by damned float plane!

The cat was meowing and weaving around his legs. August rubbed its head. "Hungry, old fella? What's for chow in this deli anyway?" He searched the fridge, pushing aside the packet of overripe cheese, three bottles of ketchup, a Danish with one bite out of it, until he found an opened can of pinkish cat food. He sniffed it and flipped it onto a saucer. "This'll have to do. I don't think it's gourmet but there's no running to the corner store for something else. So love it or leave it, guy." The ani-mal hunched over the dish, purring.

As he moved away from the tiny kitchen area and the green-ish light emitted by the fridge, August noticed the deepening shadow. The only light in the rest of the quarters came from a battery-operated Minnie Mouse clock, her pupils pinpoints of light and her arms splayed out to show the hour. At the win-dow the receiving dish was barely visible through the thick fog that had crept around the station while August was working. Taylor was overdue. How far could he have gone without any food or a vehicle? A slight ripple of alarm touched August. The last thing he needed was complications on this job. But Taylor hadn't seemed the type to take any stupid risks.

August picked up the binoculars and scanned the horizon. No orange suit signalling the other man's presence. He scanned once again. Unmelted by the weak sun, hail covered the ground in crystal pockets. Odd shades of light seemed to be calling sunset in quickly. He replaced the binoculars and stared out the window for a long moment. The place was so barren. Even the wind's howl seemed to decry the lack of a tree or bush to pummel.

As he pulled on the boots he'd left by the door August was glad that Supply Section had insisted on outfitting him with some rugged footwear. Their tight grip would guarantee a decent grip on the rocky ground. He shrugged on his coat, pulling a toque over his head, and grabbed a heavy flashlight as he left.

The cat watched him go and then flicked its pink tongue and rubbed a paw contentedly over its face.

Taylor was slumped against the back of a small shed at the end of the rough pier that edged tentatively into the sea beyond the satellite dishes. The pier's wood was rotting and the winter waves ate more of its pilings every year. Washington thought it would look too suspicious to keep the joint spic and span. Whitewashed, as Wendell had punned in one of his better jokes, so the place had been allowed to deteriorate. Besides, they always used the copters, didn't really need the pier, or so the official explanation went.

"That you, mate?" David called, exhaustion cracking his voice.

August bent beside him. His colour looked okay but his breathing was laboured. Saliva speckled the red beard. "Where do you hurt?"

David groaned and tried to prop himself up on one elbow. "Should've brought the damn radio with me. Them's the rules." He managed half a grin. "Not the first time I've got myself in deep shit by ignoring the rules." He moaned loudly as he adjusted his position.

"Take it easy. Where does it hurt?"

"I think I've cracked my leg. God!" He winced as August placed one hand on his shin. "Take my word for it, mate. From where I'm sitting it's broken. I knew I'd never make it back. Figured you'd come for me eventually. My company isn't all that bad."

"Can't splint you here. We'll have to get back to the station before nightfall. It'll be twice as bad trying to cover this ground after dark."

Taylor tried for a grin. "My hot toddy won't wait that long either."

"If you can do it, I can."

August hauled the big man's arm over his shoulders and lodged his hip against Taylor's. They swayed like a couple of drunks for a moment before August could adjust his balance. The twisted leg gradually looked more human as it straightened beneath Taylor. He squinted up at the satellite dish silhouetted against the evening sky. "Damned hail had frozen in clumps and I missed my footing. Lucky I didn't break my bloody stupid neck."

"You said it, I didn't."

David winced as his foot grazed the ground. "You'll have to get me out of here."

"There's some painkillers in the First Aid box. We'll radio for them to send a copter first thing in the morning."

"Sorry to leave you in this beauty spot by yourself. It's not a place to wake up to alone in the wee hours of the morning."

August glanced around at the sky. It was knitting itself into an elaborate pattern of storm clouds.

"Guess I'll find out."

TEN MILES OUTSIDE ALICE SPRINGS
AUSTRALIA
January 21

Dr. Ahmed Maher placed the plastic cup of water in the chimpanzee's bony fingers and let it grasp the cup's gnarled edge.

The animal, its limbs trembling, gulped the tepid water. Maher strolled along the narrow aisle, dragging his hand along the bars of the cramped cages. Behind them several apes rolled rhythmically. A solitary beagle crouched in a corner. Maher reached the air lock at the end of the pens and pressed a red button. The heavy door slid open, releasing him, and the compartment in his mind where he kept the sights and sounds of the laboratory shut down with habitual relief.

He walked briskly past the long, low building squatting behind the handsome Spanish-style house he'd built a decade before. In his office at the rear of the house he opened a desk drawer and uncurled the map, smoothing and tacking it across one wall. He'd been lucky to get this. The woman at the bookstore had announced quite proudly that it was the last in stock. War was good business for everybody it seemed.

It amused Ahmed, the way his homeland was always painted in blank expanses of yellow and numbing browns. They knew nothing of the desert, nothing of the life it could sustain there, nothing of the skills it took to survive its harsh demands. He tossed the tacks he held in his hand. Well, they'd soon be learning. Fifty years too late. But this time they would finally learn.

The fates were turning his way. At last a chance to transmute his years of dedication into hard concrete action. The thousands and thousands of hours of research over obscure books, sleepless nights in the laboratory, collating, testing, checking over and over again for the error, the carelessness that might discredit all his work. A chance to see results beyond the artificial shelter of the laboratory. His father's bountiful legacy put to good use, not squandered like his brother Zaid's fortune. Ahmed had feared that he might also become jaded, a cloistered academic, his goals muddled by years in the West. But he was tasting the future again, enthusiasm reinvigorating him: the end to his exile was in sight. Ahmed was ready to go home.

He gazed at the map, one finger following its artificial lines over and around Saudi Arabia, across Iraq, and finally west. To Jordan. His country, squeezed for its lifeblood between the awesome power of the American military and the fanatical dedication of Hussein. But Maher could turn them both to his advantage. And the time had come to do so. He had something that Hussein wanted. Something more deadly, more valuable, than all his modern equipment — and the Americans would give plenty for it as well. But this time no amount of money would buy them victory.

Maher loosened his tie and tapped out one of the two cigarettes he allowed himself each day. He unlocked another drawer in the cedar desk, pulled out a file, and removed the plastic folder holding the photographs. The close-ups of the animals' bodies were graphic, but Ahmed Maher looked at the results of his work with cold detachment.

Yes, the pictures were enough. Enough to convince him that his goal had been achieved.

Zuleika didn't bother to knock before striding into the room.

Ahmed scowled at his wife and shoved the photos and notes back into the drawer. "How many times must I ask you not to come in here unannounced?" He looked with sad resignation at her wild mass of thick hair, the sloppy jeans and sweater she wore, her bare feet and tight mouth. The only colour about her person was the chipped crimson paint on her toenails and the brilliant ruby set in a deep wave of gold glittering on her right hand.

"I'm going to London," she said, her voice defiant, but her eyes searching his face. "To see Khalaf."

Ahmed sighed. "We agreed . . ."

She cut him off. "There was no 'we' about it, Ahmed. You decided!" Zuleika pushed her tangled hair from her face as if wanting no distractions as she spoke, then modified her tone, the effort pinching the corners of her eyes and mouth. "I can change my mind, can't I? You know that I was weak when I agreed. Surely . . . surely you can see that, Ahmed?"

"It's too dangerous to travel at the moment." Ahmed picked up a sheaf of papers and thumbed through them.

"Ah," Zuleika threw up her hands, the ruby glittering at him. "Don't talk such nonsense, Ahmed Maher! You don't care what danger I'm in. You just want to keep me away from Khalaf."

"Can you blame me? Look at you! You would be such a wonderful influence on him, I'm sure," he said sarcastically.

But he tolerated her hand on his arm. "Please, can't we put this anger behind us — for Khalaf's sake? It's been six months. That's a long time, Ahmed. Please. His birthday is soon."

"I told you — I don't want him to see you like this," he forced the words from his mouth. He couldn't delude himself any longer. He had loved her more than he thought he ever would. And she had given him great joy in his son. But his wife was a liability now. "Look at the way you dress. You make no effort, Zuleika. Moping around here. Playing with those birds." She started to protest, but he raised a hand to silence her. "It's bad enough that Khalaf spent his first six years in this decadent place. But I got him out in time. He'll get a good education in England and then be raised with my family as a good Muslim. He will not live the foolish, pointless life of people in this part of the world." He looked at her. "And he will not be corrupted by the idleness of his mother."

Hating the gesture, but forcing herself, Zuleika bowed her head, still gripping his sleeve. "I promised you that I would raise him as a good man. A devout Muslim if you insisted."

"How could you?" he shot back with a bitterness she hadn't heard in his voice for years. "A weak woman who didn't have the discipline to resist drugs. Drugs!" His words dripped with contempt. "You expect me to leave Khalaf here with that?"

She twisted his sleeve in her hand. "In heaven's name, Ahmed! I lost my way for a little while. We're all entitled. I came to this place — in the middle of nowhere — because we were starting a life together. But you thought only of your work. And these people — they treated me like an ignorant chattel! I couldn't stand it. After you sent Khalaf away I thought I would die. He was what I lived for here. You knew that!

"Please! Don't be a hypocrite. You've taken a drink on occasion when it suited you. This was no worse. A little marijuana.

And I stopped. You know I did. You brought Khalaf back to me — and I stopped." She looked at her husband's stony, hard face. A handsome face which seldom smiled, although she remembered when it did. The brief summer of their courtship. "Why don't you just divorce me?" she asked suddenly, as if it were a new idea.

He licked his thumb and pulled a sheet from the middle of the pile he was examining. "I will — when it suits me."

"Perhaps I'll divorce you," she said defiantly.

He flipped the sheet of paper to the bottom of the pile. "You will never see Khalaf again. You know that."

"And you will never forgive me for disgracing you, will you?" she said softly.

For a moment her voice was touched with that golden dip that had so entranced him when he'd first met her. He glanced towards her, but her face and its expression were shadowed in the quiet light of the office. Her figure had thickened since the birth of Khalaf, a reflection of a generous, eager nature that had pulled her husband towards an intimacy that he didn't really want. She had been his beautiful, educated bride who would do him proud in the West. Who encompassed all the virtues of womanhood but who understood the demands of a man who had made his way in this alien culture. Maher had married late and thought he had chosen the mother of his sons well. It was a sad mistake. "If Zaid hadn't told me I never would have discovered your filthy habits."

"Your brother is not entitled to point the finger." Her eyes drifted to the map on the wall.

"I trust my brother. More than I trust you. If it wasn't for him you might have been arrested. You know how the Americans are about security around Pine Gap. You and your useless friends would have been thrown into jail as a security risk if I hadn't forced you away from them. And a lifetime of work would have been ruined."

She rolled her eyes. "Ah yes. Of course. The work. The precious," the word was a hiss on her lips, "work. Well, I hate it! I hate everything about it. I hate what goes on in there!"

She waved her hands towards the corridor and the far wing of the building. "I hate whatever it is that you do to those creatures! And I hate you, Ahmed!" She slapped the papers from his hand and ran to the door.

He didn't like this. He'd seen her angry before but this reference to the work . . . he didn't like it. "Zuleika. Wait. I'm planning a visit to London soon."

She turned to him, her eyes narrowing skeptically.

"If you'd like — I'll take a letter," he said roughly. He mustn't overdo it.

Impulsively she darted towards him, her face bright. She started to speak. And then thought better of it. "Thank you."

He nodded and motioned her towards the door. False hope was better than no hope at all. Then he locked the door of his study behind his wife and turned back to the new map on his wall.

LONDON
ENGLAND

Margaret Haden-Brown's calf leather boots held a poor grip on London's winter pavement. They'd been tooled for stepping gracefully from a limo onto red carpet, not quivering across several feet of ice. Her coat, on the other hand, black mink with a wide collar, was definitely cut for weather like this. Although she really should have worn the pale fur — the one with the flattering hood. But boots or no boots, Margaret wasn't about to sacrifice her weekly trip to the yellow stone building on Threadneedle Street. She loved to descend the creaky metal staircase to the bowels of the bank, leaving the shove and push of London's financial district roaring above her.

Margaret's beauty queen days were long behind her but she still knew how to make a graceful entrance. She held herself erect, even while negotiating the awkward stairs. Nodding to Phil, the security man, a fixture who'd been at his post since the first day she'd visited almost a decade ago, she made sure she offered him her brightest smile as he took her hand for the lower steps. They'd both gathered some crowsfeet and an extra chin during the past ten years, although Phil hadn't benefited from the expert scalpel of a Harley Street plastic surgeon.

He escorted her to the third aisle of safety deposit boxes, each religiously divided from the others by an iron gate which creaked open for them. The sanctuary guarded many a family fortune and was lit by a series of low wattage naked bulbs casting a greenish light over the aging metal. Phil slid the heavy box from its high slot, hefted it to his shoulder, and carried it to the cubicle Margaret pointed out.

Inside the claustrophobic space she carefully opened the lid of the box and surveyed the meticulously packed treasure she'd gathered over thirty years of marriage to a wealthy man. The jewels, a few bars of gold, two dozen rings (some more valuable than others), the deed to the house in Switzerland, a respectable collection of stocks and bonds. There was something faintly wicked about knowing Peter's office was only a block away as she stood over the scratched box in this grubby little cubicle. But in this place a certain privacy never available at the estate in Sussex or the Hampstead flat enveloped her and brought the world back within her control. Here she could sort and touch or just look at her wonderful things. The diamond the man from Johannesburg had given her when he was trying to influence Peter to sell him a part of the company. The quaint antique cameo, not her style really, but lovely, that the young student who'd apprenticed with Peter had tucked into her hand one dawn. He said she'd broken his heart. Sometimes she wondered where he was now.

Peter had never guessed her little secret. He hadn't been interested in her secrets or anything else about her for awhile. And this wonderful collection, so delicious to feel, was part of her security against the day her husband announced, as he surely would, that he was divorcing her. Divorcing her to start a family with Ms. Wright, the new, liberated, "bright" (the word he so often used) executive assistant he'd hired a year ago.

She kept her favourite things near the bottom. The best for last. Here it was, her most recent acquisition. The leopard pin was indeed a coup, a bribe from Peter really, soon after he'd started the affair. She'd known the time was right to pressure him for it while his guilt and infatuation with the other woman were fresh and his affection for his wife not too stale. She just liked to look at the pretty little thing and run a finger over its delicate features, across the bumps where the tiny chips of black diamonds spotted its coat. She smoothed the soft cushion of fabric around the pin and tucked it snugly against the side of the safety deposit box. Her hand brushed hard steel. She'd forgotten about the revolver with its ivory handle and smoothly polished barrel. London was getting to be a much more dangerous city than it used to be. And Peter was away so much. Especially at night. He'd given her the revolver during the heyday of their first years when he'd been convinced every crook in England was about to kidnap her. The first years when he'd loved her.

Margaret picked up the gun.

4

ALICE SPRINGS
January 22

Dr. Ahmed Maher pulled the jeep in behind a tour bus and watched as it spilled a load of Japanese tourists from its air-conditioned interior. Neither the crushing heat nor the dull strip of souvenir shops and restaurants that made up Alice's main street seemed to deter their enthusiasm as they surged across the sidewalk. Expensive sunglasses were quickly wrapped around a dozen pair of eyes as the numbness of five hundred monotonous miles of outback dropped from their limbs. A lone harassed guide herded them into the art gallery specializing in Aboriginal work. Ahmed was just as glad to follow in the wake of their small wave. The more people clustered in the gallery this afternoon, the better.

A wide tinted glass just inside the door displayed a single painting that drew Ahmed's eye past his own expressionless reflection. He knew he'd see no uncombed hair or unbuttoned shirt there. He always wore a tie and polished his shoes every day — no detail of his outward appearance escaped his attention.

The spare painting was cleverly displayed, the bright wide brushstrokes surrounded by a red mat immediately drawing the attention of the visitors. Ahmed glanced over their heads, looking about the spacious gallery, nodding to a few familiar faces.

Over the years he'd come into Alice only when necessary, and since his work consumed most of his time it hadn't been that often. But even *he* had to get out of the lab's claustrophobic atmosphere sometimes. The endless desert surrounding it made the building seem worse somehow, offering not a respite of space but an extended prison. Almost every leave he returned to Jordan. But that wasn't always possible. And Zuleika's silent resentment, which got so much worse after Khalaf was sent away, forced Ahmed into town more often. He could browse in the fairly decent bookstore, sip a coffee and eat a slice of pie in the good cafe hidden behind the tourist strip, or even take in a film. He'd sometimes indulge in a small purchase in one of the shops, a cassette or some perfume for Zuleika, a small watercolour or box of cards from the gallery, but never anything too expensive. He didn't want to stand out. He needed these places: he needed to be familiar enough to them that his arrival caused no particular comment.

And he'd been careful to cultivate a nodding acquaintance with some of the locals. He'd been content to let the stereotypical cloak of the mysterious Arab fall around him. The locals considered Ahmed Maher as not unfriendly, but not really a mate, "that's fer certain." Ahmed knew that Zuleika had paid for his attitude in her isolation but there was nothing he could do about that. She had made her own choices.

He spotted his contact, code-named Kestrel, after a few minutes, standing in front of a wide canvas covering most of one wall. The artist had depicted a Dreamtime myth in which a solitary gum tree, its trunk blackened by thirst or fire, strained under a blazing sun to seduce a germ of moisture from the air. It was called "Song of Survival." Ahmed preferred photographs to paintings — they were more precise, more real, and less open to misinterpretation.

"Rather bleak, don't you think?" he said, one eye on the

small cluster of tourists at the far end of the canvas who were leaning towards the depiction as if the world indeed might be found in a grain of sand.

Kestrel didn't look at him. "On the contrary, it reflects the present situation precisely, I'd say. Whether that's a bleak prospect or not depends entirely on where you're standing."

"And what would you say that situation is?"

Kestrel looked at the painting, the brittle roots jutting beneath the thin soil. "I would say that the tree has a slim chance of survival in the desert until a storm, or other disaster, sweeps it away."

Ahmed thought he saw a thin smile flicker over Kestrel's lips. He restrained the beat of anger that so often penetrated his dealings with his precious mole, a mole so well placed to serve his ultimate end that it was worth his while to indulge these eccentricities. Even after all the years, years of clandestine meetings in innocuous places like this or beside a dark, dry well on the periphery of Pine Gap, Ahmed had never quite penetrated Kestrel's drive. But the information was always reliable, if sporadic. And Kestrel went where few others did inside the nearby Pine Gap satellite ground control station, nineteen kilometres from Alice.

Pine Gap, an installation categorized by the CIA as "deep black," the most secret of secret categories, had been protected and cloistered since its inception by even the most left-leaning Australian government. Each new prime minister dutifully wrinkled his brow and mouthed the appropriate phrases about American military activities on Aussie soil. Each one in turn was taken by the elbow by the military men, treated to a personal tour, and emerged curiously mute on the subject for the rest of his term.

Yes, Ahmed Maher could afford to mollify Kestrel a little longer. His mission had started thirty years ago. Soon it would end. Soon he would go home — back to Jordan for good. A little patience was in order now.

"How can you be so certain the tree will be destroyed? Its roots grow very deep."

Kestrel looked at him this time. "Not deep enough."

"What do you mean?"

Two teenagers slouched into place beside them. The boy tossing his hair from his eyes as he screwed up his face in exaggerated criticism of the painting, the girl clutching at him.

"Let's move," Kestrel demanded with the edge that had been the source of the code name in the first place.

Ahmed had seen a kestrel on the day he'd first noticed Zuleika. She had been a shy figure on the periphery of his vision who had been raised by his sister. They both had been at her father's aviary. The old man had been boasting of his latest prize, a martial eagle, newly caged but uncowed, perched defiantly in one corner of his prison. Zuleika had come home from university. She'd been standing at the edge of the enclosure as he drove in, a long blue dress swirling at her ankles, a white shawl covering her marvellous hair, and a tame kestrel on her arm. Their first conversation had been about the bird. The most easily domesticated of the raptors, she'd told him, excitement carrying her rich voice on a wave. A compact, keen hunter that could turn abruptly to kill when necessary. A tame creature that could flit from confinement to freedom in the blink of an eye. A bird that from its birth was more mature than others of its fierce family, declining the protection of its youthful downy feathers and instead growing almost immediately the stronger, more mature covering of an older bird. The kestrel sought out wide spaces, could thrive in the desert.

Ahmed and Kestrel pushed through a side door into a narrow street that was artificially shaded by a blue plastic awning decorated with a bouquet of silver tinsel still undisturbed from Christmas. A few Aborigines sat in the dust beyond the awning, some pencil and crayon sketches beneath their feet. Ahmed and Kestrel stepped around them. They walked in silence past the tarted-up little shops, stale byways now elevated to tourist attractions by no other virtue except that they were literally in the middle of nowhere.

Ahmed and Kestrel crossed over a block. Behind the main street lay the dry bed of the Todd River where regattas were held on the waterless ravine every year. Another Australian joke at British expense. Bottomless boats were propelled by a dozen pair of galloping legs in an annual sendup of the much more discreet event in the old country. It never failed to elicit hoots and whistles of approval from the throng of spectators.

Ahmed didn't like the sudden silence, as if the town had dropped off the edge of the earth somewhere behind them. "We shouldn't have come here. The gallery's different. We could easily meet there by chance, or even at the cafe. This looks more like . . ."

Kestrel kicked a tin can, sending the white dust at their feet into paroxysms. "Don't worry, we're not likely to run into anyone. Activity at the Base is intense right now. People aren't getting any time off — everyone's on overtime and standby. I said I had a doctor's appointment. Which is true. In fact, I'm due there in twenty minutes so let's get on with it."

"I can't stay long today. I need the latest you're sending to Riyadh."

"It doesn't go directly there. The route is Colorado Springs, then Washington. They decide what they want Riyadh to get from there."

"I know, I know," Ahmed shook his head impatiently. "But sooner or later . . . sooner . . . Schwarzkopf gets it. And we all know that the satellites are what he's really using to run this thing. And what he will continue to use."

Kestrel's hands were long and thin and blue-veined. They tapped slowly against one sleeve. "The clampdown is tight now. I have to be very careful. Washington knows there's a leak. They've sent a man to Heard Island to check something out. That's the only reason a Yank would be there. We usually cover routine maintenance and all the rest of it. Someone's down there keeping an eye on him, but it's not easy. The Americans only tell us what they want us to know. Their man's next stop is here — Pine Gap."

Maher's head jerked up. "Are you a suspect?"

Kestrel smiled slowly. "Everyone's a suspect. That's to be assumed."

"Who's this man from Washington?"

Kestrel shrugged. "Let's put it this way. His name just didn't happen to be next up on the Duty Roster. Not for this job. This fellow knows exactly what he's doing and what he's looking for."

One ash white gum tottered on the river bank as if hungering after the nourishment that once flowed there. They moved into the tree's thin slice of shade.

Kestrel stopped. The sly, unblinking eyes locked on Ahmed's. "The price will be higher this time."

Ahmed sighed. "We doubled the money when the air war started."

Kestrel squinted up at the sky. A tumble of clouds moved beyond the horizon. "Washington's decided on their strategy. The satellite run sent down the evidence this morning."

Ahmed licked his lips. But chose silence.

They stepped over the exposed roots of a fallen tree.

"You know, it might even rain," Kestrel said. "Wouldn't that be something?"

"How much do you want?"

Kestrel turned from examining the sky. "Triple last time."

Ahmed thought about the money he'd need to get his equipment — the new labs. And he should leave Zuleika with something. After all, he was never coming back.

On the other hand . . . once he reached home . . . once his mission was accomplished . . . money and committees and self-righteous citizens' groups would never be a problem for him again. And Kestrel was the code to the combination lock on his future.

He pulled a thin wine-coloured wallet from his inside pocket and counted out the money.

Glancing around to make sure no vagrant emerging from an alcoholic haze was watching, Kestrel tucked the bills into a hand-tooled money belt. The price could have quadrupled. But triple was enough.

Kestrel leaned against the gum tree. It seemed to shudder under the extra weight. "When the Atlantis shuttle went up in

November it launched a satellite carrying the most sophisticated camera yet. Lacrosse. Nobody's been able to get their hands on a crumb of information about it. But we know — because we have to — that it takes close-ups that make the KH-12 and previous Birds look like something from Edison's day. It combines photographic reconnaissance with heat sensitivity and electronic capability. They're working overtime at NPIC in Washington just to sort through the tons of stuff it's sending back every day. It's picking out every safety pin Hussein's got lying around down there. He doesn't stand a chance."

Ahmed felt himself bristle. No glamorous camera would be able to fight what he had in store. But knowing what the Americans knew, that would be precious gold to barter when he got home. He licked his lips. The question had to be asked. His last chance. But Kestrel had been unpredictable in what was told, what was held back. No amount of money could ever determine what would be offered at a particular meeting. It depended on Kestrel's mood, the degree of anger still simmering. And today's mood was very hard to read. Kestrel seemed a little worried, more defensive than usual.

But he had to ask. "It must work both ways. The KH-12 must also reveal where Schwarzkopf has placed his troops?"

Kestrel smiled, a surprisingly warm smile. "Took you long enough to ask."

Ahmed didn't like to be teased. His face clamped shut.

Kestrel laughed. "Well, Dr. Maher, it seems that General Schwarzkopf would like to play Ike for awhile."

Maher wrinkled his brow, puzzled. "Eisenhower?"

"Remember D-Day?" Kestrel prompted. "It's to be an amphibious landing, Dr. Maher. Off the Kuwaiti coast. It'll all be over soon."

Kestrel kicked a tin can. It echoed in the dusty space of the parched river bed as the mole walked back towards Alice.

5

SUSSEX
ENGLAND
January 22

Margaret's pinky finger trembled as she steadied it on her chin to outline her lips in the new shade of peach she'd picked up yesterday. The girl at Harrod's cosmetic counter had suggested it as most suiting her "spring" complexion. Margaret could see that the girl was right. She sat back on the cushioned stool that matched the dressing table she'd bought the year she met Peter — the same year her mother had presented her with the oak hope chest, now home for generations of spiders somewhere in the attic of this country mausoleum she and Peter had called their weekend home for twenty years. She straightened the fringe of hair that fell over her forehead. In this light it still held its shine and swung as easily as it had when she was twenty. One thing to be grateful for, her hairdresser was a marvel.

She adjusted the ceramic figurine that held pride of place on the dressing table. Aside from a tiny chip in the arm it looked as fresh and appealing as the day she'd received it. A sturdy-figured farm girl wearing a wide straw hat decorated in tiny rosebuds and carrying a straw basket. Parting gift from the girls she worked with, the only job she'd ever held. Two years of boring typing but lots of laughing and giggling before Peter, to the swooning envy of the others, swept her away.

The girls must have had to contribute several pounds each to afford it. Margaret smiled sadly. She'd made the mistake of inviting Susan, her favourite of the four, to dinner five years ago. She'd pined for the atmosphere of casual laughter. But Susie had been grey and dour-faced, monosyllabic and bitter. She still worked in the same law office.

Margaret had been glad to see her go.

She didn't hear Peter come in. Suddenly he was behind her.

"Darling, you startled me!" Her hand went automatically to her throat. She didn't like him to see the mottling that had gathered there recently. "I wasn't expecting you for an hour yet. Dinner won't be ready."

"No dinner tonight, Margaret." His hands were in his pockets. He didn't look at her as he sat down on the edge of the bed.

Her chest tightened. It was coming.

She turned on the stool to face him. "What is it?" she asked quietly. And then she found the courage from somewhere to add, "as if I don't know . . ."

He looked at her, his eyes bloodshot and watery.

"You're having an affair with Sara," she stated flatly.

Peter drew in his breath sharply. "How long have you known?"

Every organ in her body rolled into a tight, hard steel ball that she knew would never entirely dissipate. Somehow, now that he'd admitted it, it was worse than all her worst imaginings. She found herself saying what she knew she'd despise herself for tomorrow. "Please, Peter, don't leave me. We can sort it out. Every marriage goes through this kind of thing. Lots of men have affairs."

"No, Margaret. Not me. Never before. You know that."

Margaret bit her lip. Ten months' worth of tears stung her eyes. She knew the mascara would run and that she'd look uglier than ever to him. She nodded. "Yes. I know." She had to give him that. Her voice was a hoarse whisper.

He reached across the space between them and took her hand. At the cost of her pride she let him. He stroked the wide wedding band, the skin on both sides squeezed against it now. "It's been a good marriage, Margaret. I don't regret it. Not the first years especially. But life happens only once. I haven't felt alive for ages."

"And now you do, I suppose?" she challenged him, some surge of anger at last propelling her. "God, Peter, I never thought you a man of such inane clichés! You can't have a middle-aged crisis like every other male fool in England. Oh no, you have to have seen God!"

He stood up. Reaching into his pocket he pulled out a jeweller's box, a gesture she'd seen many times. But every other time it had precipitated a wave of anticipation, a realization of how far she'd come from filing in the office of Abercrombie and Jarvis. "I wanted you to have this," he said stiffly. "I know it might be in poor taste, but on every other significant occasion in our lives I've given you something. I hope you'll accept it in the spirit intended." He opened the honey-coloured box. Inside was a delicate pin, fashioned in the shape of an emerald crescent moon.

She swept it from his hand. "How dare you?" she cried. "After thirty years you offer me a bribe?" Her voice rose in a shriek. "How dare you? Get out of my sight!"

He walked quickly to the door. Eager to obey her command.

Blinded by her tears she groped for the figurine on her dressing table and hurled it against the door. The delicate girl smashed into a hundred pieces.

LONDON
Two Days Later

The rain had revived the bank's old yellow stone facade, cutting wide streams through centuries of grime before spilling out into the gutter. Zaid Maher looked up at the rain and let it run in rivulets against his freshly shaven face. It would stain his new suede jacket but it wasn't the first time the English weather had ruined his clothes. His brother Ahmed thought he was perverse and wasteful. But then again, his older brother had always been a prisoner of his own rigidity. Even when they were younger he'd been the correct one, the driven one, happy to fulfill whatever duties their father dictated.

Zaid, on the other hand, believed that only a fool let the pleasures of life slip through his fingers because he was blinded by duty. Ah well, it was one of the few advantages of being the brother-in-waiting. Fifteen years younger than Ahmed, child of a third wife, after eight daughters, Zaid had perhaps not been respected by his father, but he was indulged and allowed to run without rein. And Ahmed, even now, years after their father's death, seemed to feel the bit between his teeth.

Zaid pulled up his collar and trotted a little faster over the last few yards to the bank. A taxi swished past, sending a spray of mud over his new jeans. His brother had never appreciated the advantages of the West. How could he? Living in that great desert of a country where he had chosen to stay. He'd shown little interest in Europe, in the cities. Except for his lecture tours about his endless microbes and experiments, Ahmed may as well have stayed in Jordan.

But Zaid had adapted well to the West — the clothes, the weather, the freedom — but he knew it wasn't meant to last forever. He might be able to carry some of these privileges back to Jordan with him, but only some. And when they returned home, Ahmed would enforce not only the appearance, but also the reality of respectability. And Zaid told himself each time he awoke yet again with a bloated hangover that he would be ready when the time came.

He took the wide stairs outside the bank two at a time. He'd retrieve the gold monogrammed tie clip from his safety deposit box for the reception tonight and then dash over to Harrod's for a new shirt. Maybe a tie. It would be nice to have company. But he wasn't in the mood for the kind of woman he usually paid for — one way or the other — and little Lisa Mason . . . or Jason . . . whatever her name was . . . was getting nervous about her husband. He knew she'd come if he insisted. But he was in a generous mood tonight. Let her have an evening of domestic bliss in front of the television set; it always guaranteed her passion the next time they met.

The woman almost took his eye out with the sharp end of her huge, waving umbrella.

"Watch out!" he shouted, rubbing his hand across the welt he could already feel forming across his brow. Wouldn't that be lovely tonight? He pushed the weapon away. "Please, madam, watch where you are going!"

"Oh! I'm sorry! Terribly sorry!" She swung the umbrella away from him, allowing the rain to stream down on what was obviously her hairdresser's very recent effort. He liked her immediately for that. One leather-gloved hand fluttered towards his head and then to her mouth. "It's cut. How utterly clumsy of me!"

That wonderful British reticence and overreaction to the slightest inconvenience to others. How typical of a society that had sprung from this lush, green land and well-stocked sea. Advantage made people generous, Zaid always thought, generous with everything — even sympathy.

He grinned at her distress as the rain mingled with his blood and slipped into his eye. "Please don't worry. It could happen to anyone." He leaned towards her. Diamonds sparkled at her ears and a subtle perfume misted from her throat. A pleasant change from Lisa's ruder intoxication. Zaid studied the woman. A distraction might suit him at the moment.

"But . . . really . . . I," Margaret stammered. She normally took pride in her articulation. She fumbled in her purse for the tissue she kept there. Seizing one from a side pocket she raised it to his face. "I must . . . can I do anything?"

Gently, he took her wrist. "Never mind. It will make an amusing story to tell at the party I'm forced to attend this evening. I shall tell them that I fell while rescuing a lady in distress. What do you think?"

Margaret knew she was blushing. The rain felt exhilarating as it slipped down her neck against her silk blouse. "Well, I . . ." He was still holding her wrist. "I really must . . ."

"I need a partner for my engagement tonight," he interrupted. "Would you consider accompanying me? I assure you that I am completely respectable. The party is being held at the Jordanian Embassy. You can check with them. I'm on the guest list."

Margaret licked her lips. He was too young. And he was definitely too good-looking. And she had trusted Peter all her life.

She nodded.

Zaid smiled. "Would you do one thing for me?"

"Of course." Mortified, she saw the bulb of a definite bruise emerging above his eye.

Zaid nodded towards the umbrella. "Could you close that thing? I've saved my eyesight once. I'd hate to be blinded by that colour." Mischief danced across his face.

Margaret looked down at the shocking pink fabric, bought years before to match a long discarded raincoat. The last two days she'd barely had the strength to emerge from her misery to dress herself, let alone coordinate her clothes. The umbrella rolled on the pavement like a clownish reminder of the past.

She laughed. A laugh that started in her diaphragm and burst from her throat in a healthy chortle. A great, real laugh like she hadn't enjoyed in a year.

COALITION COMMAND HEADQUARTERS
SAUDI ARABIA

The General leaned against the edge of a wide desk that ran half the length of the War Room. The battery of phones standing in formation along it were ringing intermittently as usual. But all eyes, including Norman Schwarzkopf's, were riveted to the television monitor suspended from a corner of the ceiling. Schwarzkopf's thick arms formed a barricade across his chest. "The bastards," he muttered, echoing the thought of everyone else in the room. His thin lips drew back in a tight grimace as the stretch of water depicted on the screen was gradually and irretrievably stained and blackened by the oil spewing from wide open valves far up the Gulf. A doomed cormorant, eyes dulled, was slowly suffocating in the dark sea. Schwarzkopf dropped his head, the high forehead gleaming beneath the thinning hair, and leaned the heel of his hands into the sharp desk. "Senseless . . . mindless . . . why?"

"This makes the Exxon Valdez look like a hiccup," an officer said quietly at the back of the room.

A murmur of agreement.

The familiar crease that had begun to occupy a permanent position between his brows over the past few months buried Schwarzkopf's small eyes even deeper into his face. "I just don't understand it . . .," the thick voice that seemed to struggle a bit through his sinuses underscored his words. "What possible advantage is there in drowning the ocean in oil? Damned stupid! Damned stupid waste."

A few of the men in the room tensed. Anger had clarified Schwarzkopf's tone, pointing the General towards some hard direction on his personal compass. They waited to find out where.

"Sir?" A young soldier saluted at the door. "Message for you, sir." He walked briskly to the front of the room, past the detailed maps and desks with their neat in and out trays, just like any other office, except that there were very few pending items. He handed Schwarzkopf a slip of paper. Behind them the image of the once bright stretch of shore that had been transformed into a nightmare of black sludge still flickered against the ceiling.

The General read the message and then followed the soldier out of the War Room into the long institutional hallway. Four heavily armed bodyguards, two Americans, two Saudis, surrounded him for the brief trip to his living quarters, stopping only when they were outside the door.

Secretary of Defense Dick Cheney was waiting, looking vaguely uncomfortable in the cramped room. It was not the atmosphere he was accustomed to for a high-level meeting. He was staring at the caricature of Norman Schwarzkopf framed on one wall, a tiny Saddam Hussein squeezed in his fist.

"Pretty good, isn't it?" Schwarzkopf managed a genuine smile for the first time in two days.

Cheney nodded, his highly polished glasses partly obscuring his pale eyes. But that was it for the social niceties. "You've heard about the oil spill?"

The General's smooth, relatively unlined face fell back into a grim demeanour. "What do you mean spill? That was no spill. It was a deluge! A damned, deliberate release! They turned on the taps and cheered! Serves no purpose. No damned military purpose at all!" Schwarzkopf sat down behind his cluttered desk. His right knee jerked slightly, the only indication of anger still chasing him. He raised one big hand towards Cheney as if trying to seize some invisible weapon from the air. "How do we fight that?"

"We don't."

"What do you mean?"

"Hussein was trying to fight us by releasing that stuff."

"But our guys aren't even out there."

"Exactly. But he thought they were. He thought we had an entire amphibious assault force just waiting to swarm across Kuwait and wipe him out. And he had evidence that the amphibious landing was going to happen. Soon."

"What evidence? How could he have any damned evidence? It isn't going to happen!"

Cheney sat down in the hard-backed chair across from Schwarzkopf. The cotton shirt he'd put on that morning had already outlived its coolness. "We've suspected a spy at one of the satellite receiving stations. Of course, we presume them to be attempting to infiltrate all the time — and things have tightened up considerably since the Christopher Boyce fiasco — selling a KH-11 manual to the Russians," Cheney shook his head at the memory of it. "But right now we especially can't afford anything to get out. Any leak would be disastrous to the whole effort here." His eyes slid over the maps covering one wall.

"Excuse me, but with all due respect, Mr. Secretary, you aren't trying to be funny, are you?" The General stood up and leaned towards Cheney, his bulk seeming too large for this squat room. "But you know as well as I do — this whole effort depends on that real time satellite juice that I get. If that's tainted —," his head ducked like an angry bull, "if that's even slightly tainted, let alone spoiled — we stand to drag this thing on for a mighty long time. Once Saddam starts poisoning that well he gets an even hand. We can't allow that. We just can't allow it."

Dick Cheney lifted one hand, as if to hold back the rising heat from Schwarzkopf, palpable even through the recycled, air-conditioned atmosphere in the underground bunker. "Slow down now. It's not that bad," he looked over the top of his glasses, "we hope. No real damage yet. We've got one of our best men tracking this thing. It might take a little time, but like I say — he's the best. Riley's done the desk work side of things at NPIC for years and he's also had some experience in Operations. As of this morning, his guess is that the mole is working out of our station in Australia. He's been trying to smoke the mole out by sending phony information to Pine Gap from an intermediate station on Heard Island."

"Phony info?" A flicker of recognition darted over Schwarzkopf's face, "you mean . . . ?"

Cheney nodded. "We doctored the images to show a massive amphibious landing force gathered, poised and ready to go."

Schwarzkopf's face widened into a rare grin. "And Saddam couldn't wait to dump the oil to stop us."

Cheney nodded. "It worked."

The General's grin disappeared as suddenly as it came. "Does this mean I can't rely on any of the stuff we're getting from the Big Bird now? In case your people are fooling with it before I get it?"

Cheney shook his head vigorously. "Don't worry about that. We'll make sure you know what the real thing is."

"But it's not totally reliable, right? Not until you plug that leak?"

The Secretary of Defense stood up, eager to go. "As I said, don't worry about that. We're working on it as fast as we can. When Riley gives the all clear you'll know thirty seconds after we do." He picked up his blazer and glanced at his watch. "Well, General . . ."

"And the oil — the destruction? Did we predict Hussein would react that way?"

Cheney looked disconcerted. "Well," he said, "it had to be considered . . ."

"So we're responsible. Indirectly responsible. It wasn't just Saddam throwing a convenient fit of defiance?"

"Had to be tried, General." Cheney buttoned his jacket.

Schwarzkopf glanced at the collection of framed family photos on his desk. He held out a hand to Cheney. "Thanks for telling me in person. End justified the means, in this case. A little like Hiroshima, wouldn't you say? One horror to avoid a long extended tragedy. At least that's what we'll tell ourselves, right Mr. Secretary?"

After the Secretary of Defense was escorted down the narrow runway of a hall by the young security guards, General Schwarzkopf closed the door tightly and punched on his tape deck. Beethoven bounced off the concrete walls. He turned up the volume and picked up the stuffed toy bear that sat on his desk, a thin yellow ribbon tied in a neat bow around its neck, and twisted the key that projected from its side, then put the toy down on the bare desk. He watched as it crawled rigidly away from him, coughing its funny, braying call.

For once, it didn't draw a smile from the General.

MARALINGA

Squadron Leader Charles Emory stood on the Bridge of Sighs at the point where it arched primly over the chipped shell of a dry ornamental pool. This spot had welcomed hundreds of soldiers to Maralinga in the fifties. Myth held that the servicemen paused here to gaze into the water before starting their sentence of a twelve-month tour of duty in the outback. Lingering here as they entered, or so the story went, they offered a sigh of agony. And a sigh of relief on the way out.

"Premature relief," Charles thought. "Very premature relief indeed." He should have assigned one of the boys to throw a coat of paint on the bridge and fill up the barren pool. But it would be a futile effort. The water would curdle, lily pads shrivel, within days. And the life expectancy of any goldfish would be briefer than that of its ancestor in a twenties college fraternity. Besides, somehow he liked the pool's battered, neglected air. It was like the rest of the Maralinga survivors. The fact that it was here at all, battered and neglected, represented a small victory over the place. A very small victory.

Tony Lawson handed the invitation to the serious woman standing at the entrance to the old aircraft hangar. David Taylor hung over his shoulder. "I'd like you to meet Tony Lawson," David said.

"Corporal Lawson, welcome back," Emma said. Her voice reined a strong Australian twang. "David!" she added with real delight, brushing her cheek against his.

"Hello, Em. How's this shindig going then?"

Emma pinned a plastic identity card to Tony's sport shirt with her red-splashed nails. A halo of light hair wisped around her face and dust swirled at her high-heeled feet. Behind them the tin sides of an aircraft hangar clanged like an off-tune cymbal.

She smiled at David, her expression changing from bland to almost attractive. She shrugged. "Oh, you know, he —," she gestured towards Charles, who was making his way across the Bridge, " — he did insist on this reunion. I have to do my share. Otherwise he'd exhaust himself. But what about you? We were told you'd cracked a leg down on Heard? Where's the crutches?"

David reached down and pulled the leg of the corduroy trousers he was wearing up to the knee. An ugly gash discoloured the lower part of his calf.

"Taylor! For heaven's sake!" Tony muttered, licking his lips in distaste.

"Beaut, isn't it?" David said proudly. "Thought I was done for. But turns out it was just a damned awful bruising. Feels like it's been beaten by a cricket bat, I must say. Never mind, though," he winked at Emma, "got me out of that paradise, didn't it?"

"Tony! Tony Lawson!" Charles Emory's voice rasped at his shoulder. "Well, you haven't changed a bit." Charles grasped his hand and then stepped back to look him up and down. "The only sixty-year-old I know who still has freckles." He laughed harshly, the sound exaggerated by the small plastic tube protruding from his throat. "Nice to see you, David," he nodded towards Taylor before turning his attention exclusively to the other man.

Tony laughed uncomfortably. It was a shame what had happened to Charles. He'd had a long chat about it with Larry Fisher, poor devil, when they'd been deciding whether to come to this macabre reunion or not. "Clever idea this do, Charles," he finally stammered. "Clever idea. Most of the boys coming, are they?"

Charles's fingers whipped to his throat, startling Tony a little. He gulped and plugged the hole, while Tony tried not to watch. "Those who are left. More arriving next couple of days. Coming from all over, you know."

"Awful bad luck about Larry, wasn't it? I just heard. Funny, the way things work out, isn't it? There he was swaggering about as usual, healthy as a bloody horse — and wham, steps the wrong way off a cliff!" To Emma's surprise Tony actually laughed. "Just like that!" He jabbed Charles in the chest. "Hey! Sure you didn't give the irritating little bastard a nudge, Charlie? I felt like stepping on him often enough myself." He hooted with laughter. "Good thing you're so bloody respectable, Charles."

"It's not the first time it's happened to an amateur climber," Emma said defensively. "The police will decide if there's reason to investigate."

Tony snorted. "Well, old Larry always figured he was cleverer than the rest of us. Funny the way things turn out, isn't it?"

"Yes, it's funny the way things turn out," Charles answered, studying Tony as if it was the first time they'd met. "How's the family? Boy and girl I think you had?"

"All grown now." Tony was wondering whether there might be a few kegs of brew on tap inside that cavernous hangar.

Emory never had been the most stimulating company and the man's height made it necessary for Tony to practically stare at the wound in his throat every time he said anything. "Don't see much of them you know. Left home the minute they could." He glanced around, searching for more familiar faces. The girl still hovered somewhere behind Emory's shoulder, clutching identity pins. She had a very nice mouth even if it was pinched tightly in an expression between irritation and concentration as she marked off the new arrivals against a list pinned to a large clipboard. "You know the way kids are these days. Can't wait to spit in your eye." He forced himself to look at Emory again. Another few minutes of chitchat should do it for manners. "How about you? How's the fam . . ." Tony's white skin turned beet red beneath the freckles. "Oh . . . sorry. Of course . . ."

He couldn't tell if it was a smile or grimace that punched Emory's mouth. "Phyllis and I were divorced ten years ago."

"Oh yes . . . yes . . ." Tony snatched for words. God! He should have remembered. Emory's kids . . . David Taylor had mentioned something. Twins . . . the boy dead years ago. The girl . . . ? Oh hell! The girl — she worked with him now. Damn! The pale one with the identity pins! Well, he couldn't be expected to remember all the gossip. They all had their problems. His own son was a bloody coke addict and his daughter had joined a cult in Idaho. In between writing home for money she spent her time communing with some warrior spirit from the second century. Yeah, they all had their problems. And Emory must be used to having people forget by now. They all just wanted to forget, really. He'd only come here himself as a good excuse to get away from Nancy for awhile. "All the same," he managed. "Divorce — it happens a lot now."

"Does it?"

Tony couldn't tell from Charles's monotone if his reply held any sarcasm. But he was waving them away now, like some royal potentate tired of their company. Tony was just as glad. "Why don't you go on and see who you can see?" Charles asked cheerfully. "It's much cooler inside — we've rigged up some fans in there." Tugging at the collar of his sport shirt, Tony hurried towards the looming space of the old air hangar, David Taylor limping behind him.

"Was he part of the original tests?" Emma asked. She balanced carefully on her spike heels as they crossed the Bridge of Sighs.

Charles looked after Tony as he flung open the wide door of the hangar, his loud voice hooting into the interior. "Oh yes," he said. "He was part of it, all right. He was definitely a part of it. Lawson came along to do the paperwork. He was the clerk attached to the unit. Afterwards there was a shortage of typists. Tony processed all the compensation claims. They always said Corporal Lawson was good at his job. He followed the rules to the t. No blind spots for Tony. If every i wasn't dotted you kept going back, and going back . . ." A vein near Emory's eye flickered briefly. He shook his head as if emerging from a daze. "We should start back to Alice soon. They'll be kicking us out in another couple of hours anyway. The limit is five hours. After that they don't offer any guarantees about the radiation that's floating around here. Not like they did in the old days." A weak gurgle from his throat meant half a laugh.

She studied him. "You don't look well. And you don't really seem to be enjoying this."

His hand flew to his throat. "You aren't my head doctor, Emma. Keep your amateur analysis to yourself."

She glanced around at the featureless, grey-painted square buildings, at the ruts of dust connecting them. A large crimson sign welcoming Maralinga Vets in hand-lettered printing hung from the small hut that had once served as the airfield's reception area. She ignored his outburst. "It always did strike me as a bit of a morbid idea in the first place. I mean," she glanced around the desolate scene, "well, who really wants to celebrate anything at a nuclear testing site?"

"You're far too sensitive, Emma. People like Tony Lawson . . . and Larry Fisher . . . remember only the beer and the sand. If that. This is just an excuse to fly halfway round the world and get drunk."

Emma hugged the clipboard tight to her chest. "Don't you think it's a bit much, though?"

Charles smoothed his uniform and touched the four medals along his chest before sweeping his hand to his throat. "Oh yes. It's a bit much, dear." His eyes swept the bare, gritty scene, the bright bunting and painted signs somehow making it look all the more dismal, like an old woman with too much makeup. "It's a bit much all right."

NEAR PINE GAP
That Night
9:00 p.m.

Slipping from the jeep's sweat-stained seat, Dr. Ahmed Maher climbed the crumbling porch stairs that still clung to the abandoned station house. It had taken him all day to find this place. But it was safe. No chance of anybody, he glanced around the barren place, except perhaps some restless ghost, certainly not any busybody local gossip, overhearing what he had to say. And tonight he wanted to be able to speak clearly, and loudly, if necessary. Dr. Maher was not a man to lose his temper. But tonight he was angry — and he didn't intend to hide it.

Dust rose to his nostrils and the sound of his feet hitting rotten wood echoed in the stifling late afternoon air. A verandah completely encircled the remnants of the house as if shielding it from the onslaught of time. The front door hung from one hinge. Vandals or a violent winter had torn holes in its rusting screen.

Pulling his straw hat down over his eyes, missing the sensible, cooling headdress of his home country, he squinted across the sparse sun-eaten saltbush and packed dust that passed for earth in these parts. Twisted strands of barbed wire, erected to protect some optimistic woman's stunted vegetables from hungry wildlife, squirmed across the horizon. The only other relief in the stark landscape was the skeletal remains of a dead ghost gum and the black joists of a drained well jutting into the sky.

The hope of the pioneer family who had lived here had evaporated with its last drop of water.

Maher dabbed a spotless white handkerchief around his neck and across his dripping forehead. He folded it carefully and tucked it back into his pocket before stepping into the house.

10:00 p.m.

The lone figure flipped an identification card towards the security guard and stepped through Gate 1 onto the road leading to Alice. The heat of the day was still trapped in the pavement and throbbed against the soles of Kestrel's shoes. Blazing strobe lights lit the road and the steady hum of electronic equipment pushed at the night like the buzz of a thousand moribund insects.

The outback gathered quickly as Kestrel strode away from the base.

Kestrel's pace quickened. There was no leaving behind the eerie shape of the white radomes dominating the Pine Gap site. They were its reason for existing. The gigantic Perspex shells protected the most advanced antennae available. But as Kestrel moved farther towards the outskirts of the seven-square-mile buffer zone, the wide dark space of the outback gathered around and night sounds of small cold-blooded creatures began to move within the sand.

The moon rose, silhouetting a few stripped ghost gums against the bruised sky. The light glanced off their bone white arms, pushing the thin trunks into shadow. Very little in the landscape differentiated one spot from another to a newcomer. But to the Aborigines this place illuminated the magic of the Dreamtime, the time when their ancestors strode across the brown earth, forging a God's trail of rough low hills and winding desert. Each tuck and swell of the land was a Braille map of the past to the natives. A possible bonanza lode to the white man.

A dingo barked against the darkness. Kestrel sensed that a sudden turn might catch a glimpse of a force silently shifting and changing the world, while the clumsy humans blundered along, oblivious to the magic around them. A light shiver pressed against the mole's spine as the moon slid behind a streak of night cloud. It wasn't a good night for stars.

A patch of rough bush protected the overgrown garden behind the abandoned station house. Not ordinarily superstitious, Kestrel was nagged by the rumours of bad luck that had pursued the family who had once lived here. It always seemed a little disrespectful to scuff over the dry earth of their pitiful garden and dead dreams.

The flashlight, blinding in its intensity, jerked Kestrel to the present. It came from an upper window.

Maher flashed the light again.

So typical of him, Kestrel thought, so typical. He must have the power, the control, from the first moment.

Kestrel walked slowly through the house. A child's motheaten sweater still hung from a hook in the hallway. In one room a handsome, woodburning stove stood against the wall. Great holes gaped in the faded wallpaper. Upstairs, the doors to three small bedrooms stood open, stripped even more thoroughly of their contents than downstairs. The moon was high now and it washed the house in a strange electric blue light, similar to some of the night vision shots sent back by Big Bird.

Ahmed was waiting in what had been the master bedroom. Talk around Alice was that the father of the family had hanged himself in this room. A lamp covered in the remnants of some delicate, blue material sat on the ledge of a crumbling fireplace. Against another wall sagged an old mattress, home to more than one family of lizards. The leg of a wooden chair could be glimpsed just behind it. Kestrel wondered if that was the anchor to life that the father had kicked free.

"Sorry I'm late," Kestrel said, "couldn't get away."

"What amphibious landing?" Ahmed demanded. He was standing at the window, flashlight still in his hand. He swirled around, flashing the light once again. "What damned amphibious landing?"

Kestrel's hand flew up. "Jesus! Turn that thing off!"

"Ah . . . you Westerners . . . always so blasphemous." Ahmed walked towards Kestrel, the flashlight a weapon in his hand. The moonlight accentuated the strength of his frame. Not even the comical hat, so at odds with the tailor-made suit and well-polished shoes, distracted from his natural authority. "Now then, what happened to the thousands of amphibious craft poised to land in Kuwait?" He jerked the flashlight up, flicking the beam and flushing Kestrel in a brief, harsh light.

"I did mention the man who's been sent to Heard Island?"

"What's that got to do with it?"

"Well, apparently he didn't want to wait until he arrived here to display his abilities. He planted false data. A non-existent armada poised and ready to go. When Hussein released the oil that was the obvious sign that the false information had been received. The Americans know the mole is here, Dr. Maher."

Air hissed through Ahmed's teeth, ruffling the meticulously trimmed moustache. "And you were stupid enough to fall for it? You've been around longer than that!"

"So have you."

Ahmed slapped the light against his thigh. "All right. We've both been stupid. But now what? That means he must be closing in."

"Not necessarily. I'm well protected. There's time yet. There are other possibilities for the CIA's little sheriff to chase down."

"But if there's even a chance? I need you — especially now."

Kestrel laughed. "Nice to be wanted. But you're the one with the influence with the movers and shakers, my friend. I just pass on the information, take the money, and you decide what you want to do with it. Always has been that way."

"He'll have to go," Ahmed muttered. "He'll have to go. I can't afford anything to be jeopardized now. Not now. Not after all this time."

Kestrel leaned against the windowpane and rubbed a circle in the dirt encrusted there. "Getting rid of him won't stop the problem. Washington knows there's a leak — they won't rest until they plug it." Outside a rusted clothesline creaked in a slight wind. A dingo sang just beyond the horizon.

"Getting rid of him will delay it. Maybe even enough. Enough for you to get some more good information to me." Ahmed hit his palm with the flashlight. "He has to go. Every day that he's alive increases the danger."

Kestrel shrugged as if they were discussing where to have dinner. "I suppose." The dingo howled again. The animal might be alone now, Kestrel thought. But tonight it would join its pack. Slink back into its proper place in the universe.

For Kestrel that place was forever lost.

6

LONDON
January 24

Newsprint had smudged his freshly manicured hands and his linen trousers were drenched but Zaid Maher didn't care. He perched on the edge of the Rodin statue outside the Houses of Parliament and, hunching forward, spread the newspapers across the wet grass. The screaming tabloid headline, *Bombs Away*, churned Zaid's innards but his eyes were drawn back to the photo that dominated another paper. A photo of a crying Palestinian woman caught in the glare of the camera, struggling in the choke of refugees fleeing Kuwait. Unwanted at any border.

Depression pushed against Zaid. He was ashamed of the man he had become over the past decade, the partying playboy who spread his wealth and charm freely. His occasional courier services for Ahmed had not been enough to disguise his brother's contempt for his lifestyle. And there had been moments over these past ten years when Zaid had wondered if that facade had become the real thing.

He kicked at the newspapers and stood up. An elderly man in peaked cap grumbled disapprovingly about litter. Zaid reached inside his pocket and unfolded the damp letter he'd received that morning, rereading it for what must have been the tenth time. He shook the rain from his thick, dark hair and pursed his lips over the words. He didn't really see them. He had the message memorized.

Ra'ad was dead. His friend was dead. Another bloated body spit up on the bank of the Jordan River, barely recognizable from the beatings and bullets it had taken. The letter was from Ra'ad's wife, Haya, begging Zaid to help them. He knew what the plea had cost her. She and Ra'ad had never asked him for anything in all their long friendship. They had gratefully accepted the gifts he gave, but had never asked. Now Haya was alone. And her pride had to submit to the necessities of four children.

Zaid pulled the money order from his top pocket. It was significant. But not enough, he knew — it could never be enough to buy Haya's dignity back. Rain splashed onto the stark numbers printed on the cheque.

His last visit, two months before, had been uncomfortable. Brief. He'd tossed them a scrap of his time and a handful of dinars. He'd been so busy celebrating his mother's birthday, renewing old amusing acquaintances in Amman. And Ra'ad had grown so intense, so haggard since Zaid had last seen him, crouched in a corner, pounding Zaid with bitter rhetoric as he watched his children clamber over his friend. Zaid had teased the older girl, a skinny elf of eleven, and made her blush. Haya had found some meat and cooked it carefully in his honour. Inwardly, Zaid cringed at the noise and the dirt around his friend's home. The memory of their childhood twenty-three years before, especially that one spring day, was vanishing from his memory. And it frightened him. Frightened and shamed him. Because that was the day that he'd understood something about loss and innocence: his friend's loss and his own innocence.

They were both ten years old. Wandering over the crest of a hill, returning with stragglers from the herd, to Ra'ad's encampment, they'd found the rest of the family gathering the tents, the women crying, the men urging the animals ahead of them. They were being driven by the Israelis into the dregs of the land. It had eaten a small hole into Zaid's soul to watch Ra'ad cry. He'd never seen such tears before.

Since then that hole had grown into a yawning pit filled with drink and gambling and women. A pit he'd refused to look into.

At the end of the last visit they'd sat outside the hut together as they had so often before, their backs pressed against the cool cement wall. Ra'ad hinted of a mission — across the river. Zaid tried to dissuade him, but Ra'ad accused him of turning his face away. "It is so easy not to see," he'd cried. Zaid defended himself, clumsily, but the bond between them had frayed, and their parting words were harsh.

Puddles of rain were pooling in the newspapers at his feet, obscuring the headlines. It was time to do something. Time to stop pretending that the role of messenger boy that Ahmed had assigned him was enough. He would say good-bye to this life sooner than he'd expected. But not soon enough. It was time to be a man. Time to take on a man's fight.

HEARD ISLAND

"Joe? Where are ya, Joe? Come on. Dinner time." August made mewing noises and bent down to check under the couch. "Come on, guy. My company's not that bad. Besides, we're stuck with each other."

He slid the plate he was holding back onto the counter. His own uneaten meal, a congealing stew fresh from the can, sat beside it. He walked back to the work area and sat down in front of the blinking computer screen. After punching in a few commands the digits were swimming before him. God, now his eyes were going. He'd been prescribed some mild glasses last year, but the order slip had disappeared amidst the chaos of his apartment and he'd never bothered to get another one. A headache was lurking just behind his right eye. No more work would be done tonight.

At least there wasn't much left to do. One more piece of mole bait sent down the line to eliminate personnel working the midnight to eight shift at Pine Gap and he could pack it all in at this end. He'd be damned glad to get out of this place. Everything had gone like clockwork. Saddam had been getting the phony messages all right. He'd proven that by throwing the guts of those oil wells into the Gulf. But August had a nagging feeling that something wasn't quite right. It was going too well.

He rubbed his eyes and slipped the image of the foul blanket of oil into what he called his Scarlett O'Hara compartment, his "think about it tomorrow" department. Seemed that compartment was pretty well stocked. He'd managed to shove just about his whole life into it. He pushed back the chair and went to the sink. Cupping his hands, he filled them with freezing water from the spitting faucet and splashed it on his face, sending every cell into overdrive. Couldn't call the water tepid in this place. It could've come right out of Burnt Paw Lake. August was at the stage where he had to concentrate on whatever advantages this assignment did happen to have. Maybe he'd been alone too long. The only relief since they'd carted the Taylor guy away on a stretcher four days ago was the daily calls to Washington. If he was lucky he got through on Jamie Watts's shift instead of Laine's. But good old Wendell usually made a point of being there on the other end of the line.

Still, not long to go. And he hadn't quite exhausted the station's small library, stocked with the tastes of the many changing crews over the past five years. Everything from Louis L'Amour to a morbidly explicit account of Scott's Antarctic expedition. August found himself lingering a little too long over the gaunt faces of stubborn Scott and noble Evans, standing dejected beside the British flag or huddled over their rations, dark beards staining their hollow cheeks. It was around then that the tinned stew wouldn't go down his throat anymore. He'd turned back to L'Amour and the fictional fights more easily won.

August had just successfully conquered Dead Horse Pass with

a wagon train of settlers when a sudden wild clang followed by what sounded like a bark pushed his blood pressure up a couple of points. He put the book aside. He'd already fastened down the inner and outer shutters of the building, trying to save himself some aggravation later in the night. A ferocious wind would often rise with the moon, and, unrestrained by any trees or strong shrub, it would rattle the house and his nerves, robbing him of sleep into the early hours of the morning.

He unbolted the door and stuck his head outside, the cold threatening to separate the top layer of his skin from his face. That strained, harsh bark again. A dog? Jesus, had some bastard abandoned the animal in this place? It must be starving to death. Joe better watch himself. This cat might not be king of this particular territory after all.

"Joe! Joe! Get your fat ass in here!" He didn't like the way his voice bounced back at him. The wind sliced through his sweater and flipped the door from his hand, smashing it against the wall.

That unmistakable clang again, an eerie church bell, something like the Hunchback of Notre Dame might use to tune up, followed by the weird, dry bark. Nothing like he'd heard here before. And August had become intimate with every tone of the wind, every loose and rattly piece of equipment, the protests of every wild bird. The erratic noise had been a kind of company, a reassurance that he wasn't the only living thing in some kind of a dream at the end of the earth. These sounds had become almost more real to him than Wendell Laine's pompous tones or even Jamie's disembodied, restrained excitement beamed from that airless building in DC.

He pulled on his coat and zipped it to his chin. As he grabbed the flashlight and bolted the door he thought of Scott marching into the Antarctic void, so confident. Hesitating, he stepped back inside and pulled the 9 mm Browning from the ledge beside the door.

Walking slowly around the small building, he checked the shutters, stopping to scrape the crud from his boots against the stone step. If he fell it might take them days to discover him with this storm building up. But he had to check out those satellite dishes. Taylor hadn't finished the job and if one of those suckers went, August would be in real trouble.

As he stepped off the rock path, the sky was split by a bolt of lightning. He froze in instinctive respect as it branded the sky, silencing even the wind.

And then the bark again. And the relentless clang, the petty sounds of civilization reasserting itself. August picked his way towards the dishes, looming over him now, whitish-grey sweeps of magnet pulling him forward.

He climbed up the ladder to the belly of the dish, and his flashlight beam picked up the problem right away. Taylor had left a huge wrench dangling from the joist. The wind was tossing it against the side of the dish, sending a crescendo of wild sound across the island. August stretched, using the length of the flashlight to sweep the wrench to the ground. He was totally exposed to the wind up here — and lightning. He allowed one brief thought of what might happen if the gods decided to throw another tantrum before he jumped to the ground.

He was picking up the wrench when he heard the bark again. It sounded like it was only a few yards away. Such a strangled sound, maybe the animal was wounded? He hesitated. Years of Alaskan visits had made him wary. What if it wasn't a dog? The wind started up again, lashing his eyes. He pulled the hood of his jacket forward to protect his face as he moved towards the shore, robbing himself of peripheral vision. The sea was close now. He could hear it bashing the rock below. Spray salted his lips. Again the barking sound.

A black shape was moving against the rock. Big black shape. No dog this.

He slowly pulled the Browning from his inner pocket and backed off a little. A pungent odour attacked his nostrils. He gagged. The shadow moved at the sound. Black against black. The sky split again. Sulphur mingling with the scent of what-ever was waiting for him.

The shape swung around, roaring.

August staggered and fell backwards, into the barbed-wire brush.

The sea lion reared up, its soaked fur rolling over its solid frame, and tossed its massive head towards August. And then with a great flap of its belly, the huge beast flopped against the steep black rock and slid into the sea.

August gasped and hauled himself to his feet, the flashlight bouncing its surreal light off sheets of rain and shining rock. Christ! His heart's rhythm had pounded into overdrive. The satellite domes pulsated above him, droning on whether he was dead or alive.

He'd never felt so alone. What the hell was he doing in this awful place? Fiddling with machines, juggling computer time — an intellectual challenge devoid of emotion, that about summed up a lot of his attitude. Lena had more than once accused him of rushing to his work because it had clear answers and solid feedback. Information he could pick at and manipulate until one way or another he got what he wanted. Unlike marriage.

But August had seen it as a way of holding onto the world with both hands so that there was energy left over for the unpredictability of intimacy. The unending demand and counterdemand, roller coaster and flat plain of a relationship. All the unique pressures of caring for Katy, their daughter, injured in that blinding December blizzard nine years ago. It seemed like yesterday. Lena had never forgiven him for stopping his visits to the sunny, white building, its lawn never less than freshly clipped, where his daughter sat with a frozen smile in a too-tidy room, her toys the toys of a two-year-old, untouched since the day she'd arrived. In fact, he sometimes thought Lena hated him for that. He knew he hated himself. And so, half-relieved, he'd watched his wife pack and leave him after fifteen years of seeing it through.

Waves smashed the cliffs and ground back out to sea, pulverizing the cliffs and punching at his thoughts. August wiped a hand over his face, touching it like a blind man reading Braille as if he might find some answer there. He'd always believed in his work and his fascination with the technology had never waned. Even when, hungry for concrete action, he'd talked the powers-that-be into transferring him to Operations, he'd never succumbed to the sneering "dirty work but some-one's gotta do it" philosophy.

But now? Now he just didn't know . . .

The sea salt and wind seemed to find newly created crevices to burrow into his face. He wiped his eyes and nose with the back of his hand and hauled himself towards the station house. He didn't want to think about Lena. And he didn't want to think about Katy, his heart churning and pushing the pain of her through him, accelerating as he climbed the narrow path.

He had a job to do.

LONDON
January 25

Zaid groped along the night table to try to stop the telephone's harsh ringing. He groaned and rolled over, rubbing his gritty eyes. He raised his lids far enough to look at the digital clock — it had just turned 7:00 a.m. Had to be a wrong number. Anyone who knew him would never be calling at this hour. He sat up, naked, letting the duvet slide from his body, bent over to lift the receiver, and then deliberately slammed it down again. Whoever had the nerve to call at this ridiculous hour deserved no courtesy.

Falling back against the pillow he licked his lips and pulled the quilt back up around his shoulders. He snuggled up against Margaret's full body. What she'd lost in youth she'd more than made up for in enthusiasm, even if she had been a little shy at first. It had been a fine farewell. An irresistible surrender to create a last memory to take into his new life. She was lost in a small deep snore, her face buried deep in the pillow. A smear of makeup had turned orange against the silk sheet. He lifted the hair from her ear and licked the lobe. The tiny diamond still glinted there. He liked the taste of it. She stirred a little. His hand slid around her waist to cup her breast.

The phone screeched again.

He scooped it from the floor and barked his phone number into the receiver.

"Collect call for a Mr. Zaid Maher from . . ."

"Collect call . . . you must be joking!"

"Call from Australia, sir. From Dr. Ahmed Maher."

"Oh . . . Oh! Yes. Go ahead, operator." Ahmed calling him collect? What on earth . . .? Margaret moaned and rolled towards him, trailing her fingers down his back. He stroked her thigh.

"Zaid? What are you playing at? Why don't you answer your telephone?"

"Ahmed, it's seven in the morning here, you know. And I was . . .," he glanced at Margaret and smiled, "up late last night. Why on earth are you telephoning collect? You are many things, my brother — but never cheap," he laughed.

Margaret pressed herself against Zaid's back, kissing his neck. He reached around and pulled her closer against him.

A wheeze of impatience came down the line. "Never mind. I'm calling from a public phone box. Do you understand?"

Zaid frowned and ran a hand over his chest. "Zaid, listen to me," Ahmed hissed. "I have to ask you to do something for me. Something important. More important than anything you've done before. Something that will do father's memory proud."

Zaid straightened and unwound Margaret's arms from around his neck. She sank back on the bed, rebuffed. "What is it?" He leaned forward, replacing the telephone carefully on the night table and pushing the receiver tight against his ear. The time had come. His brother would give him his chance to redeem the last wasted decade, the decade he had played while Ra'ad fought.

"I want you on the next flight to Sydney. Charter a small plane from there to Alice. You must come immediately. Zaid, I've never asked anything of such importance. Do you understand me?"

"Of course, Ahmed. Of course I understand. I'll see you within twenty-four hours." He hung the receiver up softly, staring at it in the early morning silence.

"Zaid?" Margaret whispered, suddenly self-conscious of her nakedness.

"Yes?" He turned and looked at her as if he'd never seen her before.

"What is it? Where are you going? You said we'd spend the day together." She touched the bruise above his eye.

He pushed his hands through his hair and suddenly was grinning that same charming grin, the first light seeking his skin. "It just won't be possible today." He picked up her hand and kissed the tips of her fingers. "Business, you know. When I get back we'll make up for it." He kissed her, a lingering, deep kiss. "Besides, I thought you were going to the Riviera?"

She pulled him towards her, running her hands over his shoulders, arching herself towards him. "I don't care about that. I'd rather be with you." He laughed and pulled her hands from him. "Next time, Margaret, next time."

There was a firmness in his voice that made her pull back to study his expression. But he wasn't looking at her. He pushed himself from the bed and walked to the bathroom, closing the door firmly behind him.

ALICE SPRINGS
January 26

The hawk allowed Zuleika to trail her fingers along his back. His feathers rose slowly, as if in silent disapproval of the intimacy, and then he shook himself gently, dismissing her touch, before settling back against her hand. The silver bells attached to his legs tinkled as the curved talons moved against the leather glove. She tightened the leash dangling from the jesses around the hawk's legs.

She was still in control of something in her life. The sky lay open and unlimited above them. She'd left Gawain unhooded today, and his bright eyes moved in accord with her own as she followed the dust cloud of her husband's car wending towards the house.

So Zaid had arrived after all. As usual, without forewarning. She didn't relish her brother-in-law's visit. For awhile not long after her marriage, they'd actually been amiable companions. They'd shared a fascination with this new culture. She liked Zaid's laughter. His humour was so quick compared to Ahmed, who seemed increasingly to take any levity as a trivial luxury, a challenge to the cloak of intense seriousness that he draped around himself.

But her attraction to Zaid's casualness had been short-lived. She'd soon understood that his life drifted from indulgence to indulgence, guided by no central principle or even half-baked purpose. He was a dilettante who used even his religion as protective colouring behind which he could retreat whenever criticism or the consequences of his actions veered too close to home. Zuleika had developed a taste for freedom in the West; her brother-in-law had become drunk on licence.

Zaid had resented her retreat from him and baited her with it. She'd been young and distressed at losing one of her few friends, but in the end she'd preferred her husband's commitment to Zaid's laughter. And Khalaf had been born, which made the choice easier. At the time she'd felt that Ahmed's influence was the most important for their son.

What a fool she had been.

She stood far above the road, a speck on a ledge of one hill in the McDonnell Range. This ridge cradled Alice Springs and provided the illusion of mountain, the dream of a relief from the desert. Gawain swivelled his compact head to look at her. Not the most beautiful bird she'd ever owned. Not even the most intelligent. Or fastest. But the most courageous by far. A gift from her father at her wedding feast. Slowly trained in hour after hour of solitary exploration in these stunted mountains.

Today's hunt had been unsuccessful, but the light had been clear and the cradle of the mountain cool. They had walked for miles, the hawk alert and secure, gripping the thick glove, the power of his talons always there, inches from the thin flesh of her hand. But Gawain's reward would be great today, nevertheless. For she had found him a mate. A beautiful tawny female bought from a grasping little man who'd driven from Darwin on the promise of $30,000 in cash, for a good bird, mere interest on the money deposited faithfully by her father every month in a London bank. The creature had been dehydrated and moulting in distress when he'd hauled her, covered in dust, from the cramped carrying case shoved in the back seat of his tiny car. She was a passager, a young but independent hawk, captured during her first migration, so she had lost the docility of extreme youth but was still inexperienced and full of angry protest.

Zuleika would introduce her to Gawain tonight. And soon she could anticipate the difficult, time-consuming task of raising their young. She would teach this continent and these clumsy Westerners the beauty and pleasures of these creatures. Now that her Khalaf was gone, this could be a way to pass the endless months between visits with him. Zuleika clucked to the bird and squinted under the shade of the broad-rimmed hat protecting her face.

Suddenly Gawain stiffened on her hand. She felt it before she saw his rigid position, his spine thrown back as if hit by some shock. The *yarak* position: ready to kill. She followed his tight stare, her hand loosening on the leash. Some small bird, obscured to her poor human vision, swung near the dust released by the car. Gawain's wings were hunching forward now, like some thick cave concealing his malevolent intent. Quickly she flicked the jesses from his ankles and clucked twice.

He lifted from her hand and swooped into the valley, his whole body a quivering arrow direct to the prey. Zuleika watched until unable to track him any longer.

Her gaze returned to the car, engulfed now in a dust cloud, and followed it as it headed towards her home.

"How do you stand it, Ahmed? I mean," Zaid raised himself from the water, propped one elbow on the edge of the pool, and blinked the chlorine from his eyes, "the house is fine. But what a country, my brother! With your qualifications — if you must work, and that's just foolish pride, Zuleika would keep you. You could travel — see so many wonderful places." Zaid pulled himself from the water, grabbing a thick towel. He stood dripping and shivering in front of Ahmed who sat beneath a wide umbrella sipping ice water.

"Australia grants me a great deal of privacy. I began my career here. It suited me to continue. But I will leave soon." He studied his brother. He'd always been a strong child. A strong man. But full of hollow rebellion. "How old are you now, Zaid?" he asked abruptly.

Zaid stopped rubbing the towel across his shoulders, unconsciously flexing the biceps won the hard way at a London gym four times a week. "If you must know — thirty-two. Thirty-three next month. Why?" He winked at his brother. "You worried about an appropriate gift?" He licked his lips. "It's parched out here. Where's that pretty wife of yours? Get her to bring me something to drink." He took Ahmed's glass.

Ahmed seized his wrist before he could drink. "You were initiated long ago, Zaid. It's time our real partnership was begun."

Zaid released his arm from Ahmed's grip, water spilling over his fingers. His heart was beating faster. It was what he wanted. What he was ready for. But he knew the test might be fierce. "Cheers!" he said, a sudden fear grasping at his old image. He lifted the glass and gulped back the water. The ice clicked against his teeth.

Ahmed glanced back to the house. He could see the blind at Zuleika's window pulled tightly to the ledge. Gardenias crowded against the sill. She'd gone straight to the aviary when she'd come in, barely greeting Zaid. He'd have a word with her later about her inhospitality, though it would scarcely be important for much longer. She'd be free to entertain whomever she chose — any of the rude tribe who occupied this land.

He pulled the photograph of August Riley he'd obtained from Kestrel from the pocket of his shirt and tossed it on the table. "I want you to kill this man."

The reaction was what Ahmed was looking for.

Zaid placed his glass down gently on the table and pulled the towel around his neck, letting it drape over his shoulders as if keeping out a chill. His dark eyes passed from the photo to his brother. No wild gleam there now, just a keen interest. Ahmed had never doubted his brother's character. And he loved him with a reluctant admiration for his daring, misguided gambling. But the boy's sense of adventure had been squandered, scattered like all his other gifts wherever his attention happened to be at the moment. Zaid was like an animal, living too much in the present. Ahmed had lived his own life for the future. It was time his brother learned. And Ahmed could trust him like he could trust no one else. He had hoped not to have to use him quite so soon, but it was necessary.

Zaid pulled up the deck chair opposite and sat down, picking up the photograph with his damp fingers. His legs dripped water onto the tile beneath their feet. "Why?" he said.

Ahmed folded his hands on the table, flexing his fingers. "This man jeopardizes everything that I've worked towards for thirty years. Just as it is about to reach fruition."

Zaid picked up the photo again. It was unusual for his brother to speak so directly. He usually sweetened his chores with some flattery. "Where is he?"

"You must take a plane from here to a place called Desolation Island. From there you charter a boat to Heard Island. It's not approachable by plane except with a special clearance. On Heard Island you will find him," Ahmed flicked the back of the photo, "August Riley."

"Who is he?"

Ahmed took a slow sip of his drink and then leaned forward. "Zaid, my work has two arms that I hope to use to surround our enemies. This man is trying to amputate one of those arms. For years I have been obtaining information from a source within Pine Gap, the American base near here. You have often carried that information to our contact in France."

Zaid nodded. The sun swam across the wet circles on the glass table. It was coming.

"Well, for years I thought that this . . . information would be my only contribution. But now the time and place for my real work have become clear. The gains I've made in my field, my research, can finally be put to use."

Zaid had never seen his brother so animated.

"Kill August Riley and you give me the time I need to carry home the weapon that will win this war."

Zaid lay the photograph of the rough, friendly-looking face down on the table. The edges curled away from his wet fingers.

"When do you want me to leave?"

Gawain's beautiful mate was dying. Her thick plumage lay in tufts around the pen. She had fallen from her perch in front of Zuleika and now lay helpless, her smooth beak opening and closing in small silent breaths. Her bright eyes were dulled and losing the struggle to hold onto the light as her lids dropped lower and lower. Until they closed for the last time.

The bird had been in shock when she arrived, but was basically healthy. Zuleika was sure of it, much as she'd like to blame the nasty little man from Darwin. She knew all the signs of disease — the apathy, the moulting, the rot of beak and talon. None of these had lurked in this bird. She'd been adjusting to her fate. Had her captivity been bad enough to die for?

Zuleika bent and lifted the creature to her breast, cradling it against her. The body was warm and totally still. She fingered the thin band that she'd affixed to the hawk's ankle just this morning. It felt hard and unyielding around the thin leg. The delicate feet flexed softly once and then curled in a last slow spasm. It wasn't the first bird she'd lost. She hated it every time. But this one was special. This one had been her new start, her attempt to adjust to her own fate.

She peered through a crack into the adjoining pen. Gawain sat on his perch preening each feather with meticulous care. He didn't know what he'd missed. But Zuleika did. She laid the dead bird in a bed of straw and lifted a soft cloth from a hook. Slowly she began to polish the incubator flown in especially from Los Angeles in case the anticipated eggs had needed help. She switched on the warming light inside the machine. Her hand moved in wide circles over its sterile, empty interior, pushing the cloth wider and wider, faster and faster around the artificial womb that would have protected and nurtured the ayesses as they grew into fine adults. Protected and nurtured them in a way that she'd not been able to protect her own son. Tears spilled onto the Plexiglas. She wiped them away as quickly as they fell.

Ahmed watched her from the other side of the wire mesh that led to the narrow run between the pens. "I warned you not to continue to bring attention to this place with your criminal dealings, Zuleika. I warned you months ago. And granted you many opportunities. Falcon smuggling is not approved. Even in this barbaric country."

Tears streamed down her face. "It's none of your business. You agreed to leave me alone. I have no friends now because of you. No son. This is my pleasure now. You have no right to interfere, Ahmed. You promised."

"I promised on the condition that you would do nothing to disgrace me or bring the authorities into our life. I've told you a hundred times — my funding, my work, my reputation depends on my respectability. Ludicrous as it may sound, it is a fact. And you told me you had accepted that. I have left you alone to pursue your interests. You could visit Khalaf three times a year. More often whenever it could be arranged — and this is how you reward me? Dealing with men who engage in illegal smuggling and trading in rare birds. Hardly designed to sustain our low profile, Zuleika, is it now?"

She bit her lip and, picking up a broom, began to violently sweep the straw and excrement that dotted the floor. Her gold bracelets jangled in the evening air.

Ahmed stepped back from the rising dust, clearing his throat. "And I think it's time you paid your proper respects to my brother. I don't want him relaying stories about your rudeness when he returns to Jordan. I don't think you want him revealing that Khalaf's mother has forgotten how to exhibit common courtesy to a guest. Even towards his father's brother." He calmly unlatched the gate and opened it, stepping back cautiously as if she were some wild captured animal.

"You bastard," she whispered. "You would tell them that,

wouldn't you? What are you planning in the end, Ahmed? Tell me! You are planning to take him away altogether, aren't you?" she shouted, jabbing the broom at him like a weapon.

"Hey! Hey now!" It was Zaid, striding across the patch of sparse grass between the house and the aviary. "What's this? Attacking poor old Ahmed, are you, woman?" He laughed and seized the broom from her.

Zuleika's head dropped. She didn't have the strength for both of them. She looked at him through a veil of tears and dark hair. "Get out of here. This is my private place."

Bowing mockingly, he laughed. "Lovely to see you again as well!"

"Leave her, Zaid." It was Ahmed, his voice a low command. "Zuleika — make us a meal. Zaid has had a long journey. He needs some food." Ahmed reached into the aviary and picked up the dead hawk by its legs. The wings swung loosely from its body and Zuleika remembered the gruesome photos she'd seen of tortured birds hung from poles in mediaeval times. "I will dispose of this for you." Holding the hawk away from him he walked towards the back of the house and his laboratory.

Zuleika watched with stony eyes.

A certain compassion shifted through Zaid's veins. They'd shared many a good laugh in the old days. She'd been a kindred spirit of a sort. And he'd been disappointed when her affection had curdled on him. Not that he wasn't used to that with women — the very qualities that attracted them so often were used as poisoned barbs against him when the time came. But he could afford to be generous. His brother had accepted him into the inner circle, had anointed him with a Holy Mission. In his exhilaration he could be generous with Zuleika who, after all, had done little more than lose her way. Just as he had himself.

She tried to push past him. She smelled of sand and an old familiar perfume. Her smooth brown skin was free of makeup, the wild dark hair barely brushed into some semblance of order. She'd put on weight since the last time he'd seen her. It suited her, unlike the dark circles beneath her eyes.

He touched her arm, but immediately withdrew it as she

glanced at his hand with contempt. Despite their years of Westernization, some of the old rules still dogged them. It was still taboo for him to touch her in so deliberate a manner. "Zuleika — I have something for you. It's from Khalaf. A note. My sister let the boy write it when he was in Jordan for my mother's birthday."

She grabbed the paper from him like a lost traveller reaching a well, drinking without pause. The childish scrawl was surrounded with colourful drawings of palm trees and at the bottom of the sheet a rough depiction of a tiny hawk, the pet he'd taken with him back to Jordan. She read it three times.

Zaid leaned against the wire pens, still tingling from his conversation with Ahmed. He was filled with tense anticipation. He smiled indulgently as Zuleika brushed the hair from her eyes, her lips moving as she caressed each word. "Hofa's always liked you," he said gently. "She wanted you to have something."

She looked up, smiling at him as she hadn't for years. "When did you see Khalaf?" she asked, trying not to reveal her eagerness.

"Two months ago. It was mother's birthday. I took a gift from London. Quite a celebration. I gave her a solid gold . . ." He raised his brows, impressed with the memory, and tried to erase that other memory of his trip, the sights and sounds of Ra'ad's home in the refugee camp outside Amman. "A solid gold serving dish," he said. "She used it at every meal."

"But Khalaf. Did you see him?"

"Oh yes. He asked me to give you a kiss." Zaid smiled and winked. "But I don't think that would be appropriate, my dear sister-in-law."

Zuleika smiled and ducked her head. The fool had always imagined she was taken with him. Let him think so just a little while longer if it would suit her purpose. "Will you be seeing him again soon?"

Zaid hesitated. Careful now. Mustn't reveal too much about his plans. But mustn't let her think anything was out of the ordinary, either.

"Perhaps."

She stepped surprisingly close to him, her thick lashes revealing a hint of coyness. "Would you take something to Khalaf for me, Zaid?"

"I don't know — really, Zuleika . . ."

"Please," her hand barely brushed his chest. Not actually touching. "His birthday is next month. You remember," the old mischievous look lit her face for a moment, "it's the day before yours. Please, I would like to give him a gift. A boy can have a gift from his mother, can't he? You just told me — you took one yourself — to your own mother . . ."

"What is it?"

She'd reached him.

Pulling a thick gold chain from around her neck she unfastened a delicate ring from it. He saw that her nails were bitten down. The tiny ruby and perfect emerald glinted in the late slanting sun of the aviary. "My father gave it to me on my tenth birthday. I told Khalaf he would have it one day."

Zaid fingered the ring. It was lovely. "All right." He put a hand up to stop her excited exclamation. "But I can't promise when it will be delivered." He slipped it into his pocket. "Ahmed and I have important business," he said smugly.

She was smiling again. "Thank you." She had to resist kissing him. "Thank you."

The sound of Ahmed's footsteps crunching over the hard earth interrupted them. "Ah, there he is," Zaid said, a quick apologetic glance at her before turning to join his brother.

Zuleika lifted the cool paper of the note to her cheek and rested it there. Contact. Colourful, bright, bold-lettered contact from her boy. She was still in his mind somewhere. Still part of the small stock of memories he held of this place. She carefully folded the note and pushed it deep into the wide pocket of her cotton dress.

Behind her Gawain keened once. She locked the pen and walked slowly back to the house and her duties of hospitality, her hand deep in her pocket, her fingers caressing the thin paper.

7

DESOLATION ISLAND
SOUTH INDIAN OCEAN
January 27

It wasn't as Zaid had pictured. He'd picked it out on the map, of course. No tropical jewel of the South Seas, not even a "diamond in the rough," this place. He stood on the dock, hunched against the wind, the dark basalt shore jagged around him. Desolation Island — so aptly named. As barren as the desert in its own way. The ground cover consisted of patches of wild cabbage that scratched a living from the hard earth, the low plant a sickly green, as if its true shade had been squeezed from it long ago.

Well, if Ahmed was testing him, he'd chosen the right place. And he'd made it very clear that this was where the mission must start. Zaid eyed the motley array of vessels bobbing against the edge of the dock. Most were working boats that looked as if they weren't earning a very good living. Paint rubbed raw from their sides, punished by brutal weather into a splintery grey uniformity, they creaked in protest as another swell reached under the dock's pylons to punch at them. Only two looked as if they'd hold up all the way to Heard Island. One was a luxury vessel, surely docked for repairs. Far too obvious in any case. Gleaming and no doubt locked up tight from bow to stern, it would be too difficult to handle without a crew. As he watched, three men came from below, one older, two barely out of their teens, and began to tune the sail, methodically twisting and turning. It looked like they'd done it a hundred times. Zaid knew he wouldn't be able to handle all three of them.

His gaze turned to the other boat, a small vessel docked at the far end. It was old, no sophisticated aerial scanning the sky, only a fresh coat of bright red paint to distinguish it. The pert bow and scrubbed teak deck announced a vessel with a purpose, merely passing through this sad port. Looked after, probably kept in good repair, somebody's expensive hobby, or dream. CALIFORNIA GIRL was painted in gold letters along the side. The skipper was bent over a curled rope on the deck, a rain slicker flapping loosely around salt-rimmed boots.

"Hello! Hello there!" Zaid called from the dock, putting on his best, hail fellow voice.

He was surprised to see a woman's serious face, most of her features hidden by a wide hood, turn to greet him. "You talking to me?" Her voice was gravelly.

"Just wondering if you'd know of anyone with a boat to rent — or sell?"

Her brown nut face wrinkled into puzzlement. "You've come a long way without a boat to be looking for one now." Her voice held a certain suspicious disapproval. She stood squarely in front of him, a thick rope twisting from her hands. The yellow slicker was too big for her and ballooned around her feet. Black rubber boots with thick red soles made her look like some exotic flat-footed bird.

He shrugged. Might be time to play up the city slicker angle. Not that it would take much acting on his part. He punched at the pack he carried over his shoulder. "Came down from University of London. I'm a biologist. I'm trying to collect specimens, but I developed a pump problem on my boat and got a lift this far. My grant runs out in a month. Not likely to be getting the chance to be dropping in at Heard Island again very soon."

"Heard?" She dropped the rope and rubbed her hands together. "That's no hop, skip, and jump, you know. It's a bit of a run." The hood fell from her head to reveal faded hair pulled back tight against her head with an old-fashioned scarlet barrette like only very young girls ever seemed to wear anymore. Earrings in the shape of tiny, kicking red and white horses dangled from her pierced ears. Her eyes were colourless slits lost in her sun-punished face.

"Pierre Gagnon," Zaid said in his best French accent — all those drops in Paris for Ahmed might as well count for everything they could. He extended his hand.

She stepped smoothly from the gently rocking deck of the boat to the pier, wiping the palm of her hand on the slicker before taking his. Her hand was small, blistered, and feverishly hot. "Jill," she said, making it clear that her first name was all she was offering, and even that reluctantly.

Close up, he could see that her thick sweater was faded from many washings and the slicker was covered in several places with those patches you could buy to fix leaks in canvas tents. The boots were new but the paint on the inside surface of the craft was thin. The bucket that lay next to her feet was bent and worn and the plastic of the small guiding seat was torn.

He met her eyes, which hadn't missed his examination. "I'll pay you two thousand American dollars to take me to Heard Island." He had twenty thousand cash on him and could go any amount higher if it meant buying a boat to get there. But he couldn't appear too eager, he was supposed to be a student, after all.

She chewed the inside of her cheek. "Rough journey," she said doubtfully.

"Three thousand. This research is for my thesis. It'll be another year before I get back down here."

She scuffed at the dock with the toe of her boot. "I was planning to head to Crozet tomorrow."

Liar, he thought. But a shrewd liar. How far should he go? Not likely many other boats would be docking soon. He might wait. Something would come along eventually. But how long would Riley stay on Heard? "Thirty-five hundred. Every penny I've got. Fifteen hundred now — two thousand when we get there. That only leaves me with return air fare."

A flick of triumph traced her mouth, revealing a set of very bad teeth. "When do you want to leave?"

You'll pay for that smile, Zaid thought. He grinned back, his widest, most charming grin. "Whenever you're ready."

The living quarters were cramped and smelled of too many days at sea. Zaid sat in one corner, squeezed between a tight little table and its padded seat, a bowl of soup slopping in front of him with the rhythm of the waves. He'd spent the last hour hunched over the side vomiting his insides into the Indian Ocean and swearing he'd never set foot on a boat again. But he'd managed to keep the pack containing the money and the gun on him at all times. He wouldn't put anything past this rough little one. She sat across from him, puffing nauseating smoke into the air from some kind of foul hand-rolled tobacco. In between slurping spoonfuls of soup and mugs of muddy coffee she chewed her filthy nails. She barely disguised her amusement at his condition. At the same time his evident vulnerability had loosened her tongue.

"Yeah, I'm from California — the original California girl, right?" she laughed, choking on her cigarette smoke. "Well, the Beach Boys sure as hell weren't singin' about me!" She chewed a hangnail at the edge of her thumb and sucked in another arc of smoke. "Northern California — not the same thing at all, you know." She shook her head emphatically, the dancing horses at her ears, exclamation points. "Nope. Not the same thing at all. They all think it's LA and surf and jags. But up in my part of the country," she sighed and flicked the ash from the cigarette into a tin saucer in front of them, "there's a bit of room up there. Real trees. Can't see the sky through 'em. I mean," she laughed roughly, "have you ever seen what they call the California National Forest down there? It's a friggin' joke! Those little stumps! A cactus has more character and doesn't have the nerve to call itself a tree! You ever seen a redwood?" she demanded, leaning towards him skeptically. "You haven't seen a tree till you've seen one a those," she insisted. "You ever see one?"

"No. No, I don't think so."

She screeched with laughter. "You don't think so! Believe me, buddy, you'd know if you'd seen one!"

Zaid was starting to feel claustrophobic.

"Eat your soup. Made it from scratch. Good stuff."

He picked up his spoon obediently. At least she was off the trees, seemed to be a bit of a manic subject for her.

"So why did you leave California, Jill?"

She studied him intensely, as if looking for a threat behind his question. "My first old man dumped me for a woman ten years older than me. The second took every penny I had. And the last was picked up for molesting little girls. It was what you might call the last straw," she said, a sudden clear ring of sanity in her voice. Even her face had cleared of confusion, as if the memory of why she was floating on the Indian Ocean with a complete stranger had offered her a certain peace. She patted the wooden seat beside her. "Been around the world twice in this old tub. Alone," she said, raising her thick brows as if expecting a challenge.

A sudden swell lifted Zaid's bowl towards him and slurped its contents into his lap. He jumped up suddenly, his head hitting the low ceiling. She giggled excitedly.

"What are you laughing at?" he snapped, rubbing violently at the spreading stain on his trousers.

She stood up. Her face had closed back in. "We'll be there in a half hour or so. You're lucky the weather's just closing in now. This trip woulda taken twice as long otherwise."

He followed her up the stairs. She was strong — a fighter he guessed. But small-boned. Fragile underneath.

On deck the sky was lanced with jags of violent purple, wild reminders of how far south they were. She took the wheel, steadying it expertly. "Got that other two thou?"

"We're not there yet, Jill."

"Just about. There it is straight ahead," she said proudly.

Heard Island, a black formless shape, lay about fifteen minutes ahead. Some kind of beacon flashed at the summit of a mountain above it.

"Bet ya thought no woman could really do it, didn't ya? Only took me cause ya had no choice." She laughed her rough, proud laugh into the night air.

In the end he didn't need the gun and Zaid hated it. But as he walked up behind Jill from Northern California, he thought of Ra'ad. His friend had been forced to worse while Zaid danced and drank and embraced the West.

Her neck snapped as she twisted back, surprising him, clawing with her raw, blistered hands.

The yellow rain slicker bobbed on the black ocean and then disappeared.

August was completing the last rounds of the night. Despite his distaste for it, he'd discovered that imposing a certain military regulation on the day prevented being eaten alive by boredom. His assignment was complete, Wendell had guaranteed a flight to pick him up as soon as the weather cleared, whenever that might be, and he'd be dropped at Pine Gap to partake of whatever dubious pleasures of civilization that place had to offer. He found himself missing David Taylor's cheerful presence. But he'd finish the L'Amour tonight and move on to the Agatha Christie. The tinned stew and dry shortbread biscuits were beginning to get a bit tedious but he had to start another diet anyway.

He'd climbed the damned slippery ladder, making a note to himself to recommend some foot grips for that deadly thing when he got off this place, and checked the receiving dishes. The heavy battery-operated lantern he'd hauled up was threatening to die on him. Its glow would vibrate for thirty seconds and then gradually ebb, leaving a pinprick of light to see by before flaring again as if snatching one last effort at utility. He pulled a knife from the leather sheath he'd strapped around his waist and cut into the thick, fibrous branch the wind had clamped around one of the satellite's metal tendrils. The huge dishes stood anonymous and blank, that steady buzz sucking in electronic signals, translating the wavelengths into something understandable for the stick figures far below.

This place made him feel small, not part of it like Burnt Paw Lake, which always seemed willing to take him in. Heard Island seemed fiercely jealous of its bare rock and thin grasses, as if conscious that its stingy resources couldn't be shared. Speckles of cold rain blew against his face and the old bull sea lion that had scared the shit out of him still loomed in its well-rubbed cave just below the cliff edge. August was about to turn back to the elementary comfort of the hut when he saw the light. He'd rarely glimpsed any boat traffic — the occasional freighter, its cold lights spotting the horizon, and sometimes the odd cruiser, the jaded passengers looking for some new "unspoiled" Eden. But inevitably, as soon as they drew closer to the stripped land they turned away. But this was a steady red flash, pricking the blackness like a neon needle stitching the sky.

August moved closer, the sea lion's smell and grunt almost familiar to him now. He raised the lantern. Its fading light barely penetrated the rain skating across the night.

The flashing stopped. Then resumed again. Three short bursts. Three long.

Three short.

Three long.

S.O.S.

Quickly he lifted the lantern again, covering and opening the light in the universal distress signal. It offered a weak halo of illumination, casting only a few yards from where August stood. No boat pitching in that cauldron would ever spot it. He could hear the motor chugging towards him now. Sounded healthy enough. But the building wind made it hard to tell.

Zaid squinted through the streaked windscreen, his hands clutching the rudder. He flashed the red emergency beam again.

Then bent to light the flare. There were only a few left. He had to be sure and use them at the right time.

It hissed and streamed into the sky, an ominous firework. Under its brief light he pulled the photograph of August Riley from his pocket and then checked the gun and the pack. It was time to do it. Move on. Get back to the airport at Desolation. London within twenty-four hours. And back into Ahmed's good graces for the rest of his life. And it wouldn't be long until his brother, one way or another, made it known to the rest of the family that Zaid had performed a great service. And then Zaid could demand that he write his own role in the drama Ahmed was about to play out. This August Riley would not be allowed to destroy it all.

The path's bare rock, slicked down like a clean black plate, was treacherous underfoot as August hurried towards the glowing window of the hut. He shook himself like a dog and stepped inside, splattering cold rain over the kitchen. He grabbed the flashlight from the sill and flicked it off and on, shining it into the rain, slashing now against the stone sides of the building. Damn! Batteries were almost dead. The heat from the stoked stove seemed enormous and inviting as he rushed to the cramped storeroom at the rear to collect a pair of fresh batteries. Water dripped from his rain slicker and his boots embedded giant tread marks across the floor.

The enforced tenant before David Taylor had had a low threshold for boredom and a high aptitude for organization. The batteries were under "B" right before "Beans" and right after "Barbecue Sauce" (spicy). August silently blessed the guy's neuroses and punched four batteries into the large flashlight, the model used by big city cops and nervous explorers everywhere.

By the time he slipped and scraped his way back down to the dock, the path seemed twice as steep as it had in daylight. Handfuls of dirt crumbled and eroded around his feet, undermining the already fragile structure of the path. No sign of a light, or the boat. He flicked the flashlight anyway and was rewarded with a healthy light that beamed onto the dark sea like a spotlight at Wrigley Field.

From the boat a flare sparked brilliantly against the night and then just as quickly fizzled.

He tracked the boat as it lurched towards land and sputtered up to the dock. August stepped back while the man came ashore. A landlubber for sure. White slacks, brand new windbreaker, running shoes, no less. Only the thickly knitted black pullover made any sense. "You all right? Engine problems?" August shouted against the rising wind.

"No," a disarming smile, "think I'm lost. Where is this?" The guy was adjusting a big pack over his shoulder.

"Heard Island."

"Oh," he waved his hands in relief and pulled off his glove. A hand was jutted towards August. Some kind of expensive ring on the little finger. Gold ID bracelet dangling over the wrist. "Pierre Gagnon. Biologist."

August slowly took his hand. Very cold. "They never told me about you." He declined to introduce himself.

"Wasn't due till next week. But — had a chance to catch this boat. Owner rented it to me. Thought I'd try it on my own. Done a little sailing, you know." He rolled his eyes. "But the waters off Nice aren't exactly like this."

August nodded.

"Listen — do you have anything resembling a hot drink — or a cold one — in that place?" He nodded towards the hut. The photograph was pretty accurate, even with Riley's features distorted against the weather. No taller, a bit heavier than Zaid. Still he couldn't underestimate him.

August reached for the pack.

Zaid arched his shoulder back. "It's all right. I've carried it halfway around the world." He glanced at August. "Bit fussy, that's all. You know how it is. My special tools. Specimens, etc. Has to be handled just right."

"Sure. I'm kinda fussy that way myself. Come on, I'll put the kettle on. Hope you like stale shortbread," he said with forced joviality.

Zaid laughed, but he could hear the blood pounding in his ears. Despite the slashing rain, he was hot. His face felt flushed.

Riley moved directly ahead of him along the dock, his back broad and wide, a perfect target. The hood of his parka pushed stiffly out from his head. But a head shot wouldn't be necessary. Straight through the back. Finish him off afterwards. Better out here than in the hut — less evidence.

Do it now. Get it done. Over with.

He was drained. The Jill woman had been terrified. All the cynicism and anger fleeing from her as she screamed into the wind.

He thought of Ra'ad. Would he have flinched and whined against what he had to do?

Now. Do it now. No more conversation. All night to get away.

Zaid shrugged the pack down his shoulder. It shook against his trembling body.

"Sure you don't need some help with that?" August called back, his big feet clomping along the rotting planks of the dock.

"No thanks." The gun was right on top of his clothes. The zipper seemed to screech his intention into the night as he opened the pack. The hut glowed just beyond them. His fingertips brushed the gun. The Jill woman had bothered him more than he'd thought she would. Much more. He could still feel the sting of her deep scratches along his arm.

Ahmed had warned him that bystanders might get inadvertently involved. Warned him not to let anything distract him. Warned him how much depended on the successful completion of his task. And reminded him of how little he'd ever asked of Zaid.

He gripped the butt of the gun, eyes glued to August's back. He was moving a little faster now. Despite the four times a week workout, Zaid felt his breath come short. He had to do it before they reached that hut. Blood, fibres, carelessness, so much harder to erase in there. Out here this devil's weather would clear up half the job for him. He might even persuade the ocean to swallow the body again.

The gun was out of the satchel, cocked.

He raised it. The heat and flush in his head was suddenly replaced with a cold certainty.

The trigger was an easy pressure against his finger . . .

"Hey! What're you doing!" August swooped towards the ground, grabbing a cat slinking around his ankles.

Zaid tumbled over him, the bullet pinging in a benign sound against the dock.

The cat yowled somewhere.

August heaved the flashlight at Zaid, the heavy plastic casing hitting him square in the temple. Zaid fell, the weight of his body sending a shudder through the dock. But he had the gun. His hand tight around it as he scrambled to find his feet.

August hit the water as heavily as if already encased in the death Zaid had planned for him. Plummeting straight down into the black, cold hell, his lungs screaming that he would never come up. The barnacle-encrusted posts were like a hundred razors taken to his cheek. Warm blood oozed from his skin, cauterized immediately by the icy, salt water.

He seized a pylon and used it to launch himself forward, blinking and flailing blindly with his hands, unable to seize even a fraction of light to orientate himself. His lungs were held to his body with serrated ribbons of steel. Impossible to endure. Impossible to release. Forcing his palms straight up in a gesture for mercy he pushed towards air.

His fist hit the underside of the pier, ripping the skin from his knuckles. Air! Some vestige of energy transformed his blood to rocket fuel and propelled him upwards. He pressed his face against the few inches of space between the underside of the dock and the waterline, gulping the tangy, foul air trapped there. Slimy and pungent in his nostrils. But sweet. Saliva and the vomit dregs of fear seeped from his mouth. But it was air.

Silver flicked across the blackness ahead of him like the erratic lighting at some perverse rock concert. Jumping and darting and sliding in and around the pillars.

The stranger had the flashlight! And the gun . . .

August pushed himself around a wooden post supporting the pier and hit the surface gasping, heaving oxygen into his lungs, gurgling.

A bullet sliced the water beside his head. He ducked back down, his eyes ice metal balls rotating in his skull.

The boat's bow waved above his head. He managed an awkward breast stroke over, up and up towards it. Forcing his shoulders into the narrow space between the bow and the dock, he pressed his nose and mouth upwards like some huge sea animal trolling the surface for air. He could hear the man's footfall swinging back and forth along the dock. The light stabbed and swept the water, chasing him like a dog on the verge of a trail. His clothes were dragging him towards the bottom an inch at a time. But he couldn't discard them. Hypothermia was stalking him.

He felt his way along the boat and dipped beneath the ropes that had been swung onto the wharf to secure it. They were too highly arched for August to stretch and unhinge. Fumbling at his waist he pulled the knife from its sheath. The cold was paralyzing, screaming at him to shed this place before his system shut down. The nylon ropes were tough and fibrous, gritty with salt and stiff as years of sea punishment could make them. He sawed clumsily. And then ducked back beneath the surface, bobbing against the hard floor of the boat, as the other man marched, methodically now, above him.

Surfacing again, he forced his hands to bend and loosen the rope, some old instinct urging him to tear at it with his teeth. Instead he sawed steadily, trying to give his reason some advantage in its uneven struggle with his panic. Slowly, very slowly, the rope shredded away. He swam to the other one and sliced and hacked at it, finally nudging the boat towards the end of the dock.

Zaid had jumped to the beach, searching for his prey along the edge of the tide, certain that August would be struggling towards land by now.

The boat lifted naturally as it slid into its element, responding easily to August's urging. As he crawled towards the sea, a wave flew at his head, choking him. He pushed his soaked sleeve against his mouth, praying that the man wouldn't hear him sputter through the violent rain that was adding its din to the night.

He could hear the old sea lion bellowing fresh indignities from the depth of his cave.

The cave. If he could ease the boat that far he might be able to climb up the sides and pull himself onto the deck. He pushed a little harder, thrashing his legs behind him. His limbs were disembodied weights.

The sea lion snorted angrily as the boat tipped against the tiny stone island. August found a foothold on a narrow ledge and pulled himself onto the boat's deck. He groped his way to the wheelhouse, the craft lurching beneath him, and twisted the ignition.

The engine sputtered and caught. This thing would never make it in these seas. He could already hear the fizz and glug of some small leak designing a catastrophe below. But five minutes, even four, of distraction was all he needed. He flicked the ignition, heard the propeller jump, and eased himself back onto the lava rock, pushing the boat with one long, last burst of energy out into the night's harsh arms. It dived and jumped with deceptive lightness, punched side to side by the waves.

The flashlight swept past August crouched in the dank space between the slippery rocks, zeroing in on the boat, its beam probing and sliding between the deck and wheelhouse. A shout, immediately smothered by the wind. Another gunshot. Too wild, zinging past the windscreen. The boat puttered out to sea. A blind vessel.

The other man's footsteps pounded along the shore, dodging the rocks. Now and then, there was a brief enraged cry as he veered towards the boat as if tempted to plunge after it.

August breathed deeply, salt stinging his throat. He reined a gag as he faced the next step. Easing himself down the side of the rock face, penguin droppings sliding beneath his raw palms, he forced himself back into the water.

He gasped. His knees and the ankle broken on that day with Sam a lifetime ago locked as the waves gnawed at his flesh. Not far . . . not far . . . he muttered over and over like a mantra. A few yards and he could pass the rock and come up on the other side with a clear run to the hut. And the radio. And warmth. He beat down the groan that clambered up his throat and cut through the ice water, gunning the acceleration of his heart and lungs, deaf to any sound but his own breathing churning over and over above the waves.

The dank beach was welcome grit beneath his hands and face but he didn't allow himself the luxury of lingering there. Staggering, he lurched along the stony ground, weaving through black charcoal gravestones that tilted through the thin topsoil, using them as a pivot to push himself forward. A sharp, wild crack and one of the stones split beneath his hand, tumbling to the ground, the wind crackling through its shredded epitaph.

He couldn't make it.

The path was too steep. It was too far to the hut. Blinding sheets of rain rose and fell across his vision. The thin-skinned balloon of his lungs would burst before he could get there. His teeth launched into a chattering dance. His gums felt frozen in his jaw.

This guy was probably waiting there right now. Gun cradled in his lap. Just waiting for August to stagger through the door.

He'd never make it.

The shot grazed his upper arm, tearing away the fabric of his rainslicker and the outer layer of skin. Anger pumped the blood back through his veins and spilled adrenalin back into his will. August pulled himself down behind another headstone, the harsh grasses scratching at his face, water streaming from his clothes.

The stranger's thin white coat and slacks were plastered against his body. August could hear his running shoes squishing through the deep puddles fomenting around the shallow graves. He rolled, the wound stinging him, and heaved himself behind a double set of headstones, which were a little less deteriorated than the others, as if their carver had intended them to defy this place for as long as possible.

Sarah Harwood and the Infant Harwood, Jonathan. Another headstone hugged close to it, marking the resting place of one Dr. Matthew Harwood, dated two months later.

August slammed his foot against the thin depression in the ground. Falling on it, he scrabbled at the consumptive earth, his nails ripping as he scraped it aside. He kicked again and the grave suddenly yawned open, dirt and rain rushing into it. He crouched into its shallow shelter, feeling the tentative wood of the coffin beneath his boots. He ducked further, catching the beam of the hunter's flashlight dodging the gravestones just ahead. The light cast long shadows around him, making his thin legs, the trousers plastered against them, look like the limbs of a zombie escaped from some horror film. August's shuddering threatened to cast him into a seizure.

The stranger had swung around now, casting the light along the winding path up towards the hut. Its powerful beam picked out the chinks in the rocks that had been placed together to form a rough footstep.

August crawled out of the grave and stepped carefully around the headstone, hearing the slide of water down his coat like a torrential downpour, his footsteps the pounding tread of a giant.

His mind was blank. The hours, days, weeks of martial arts training sieving through his brain like the rain into the porous earth. But he had to move. To act.

He rushed across the last few yards of open ground.

Behind the gunman now. Fingers plunging into the vagus nerve behind his jutting shoulder blade. The neck strangely warm and thin beneath his hand. The other hand sliding along his arm to the wrist that held the gun. The satisfying choking, astonished sound of the other man, arms jerking like a wireless puppet into the air.

The explosive sound of the bullet escaping.

August wheezed. The guy had ten years on him. Don't stop now!

Pressing his body into the killer's back, he felt the man's spine contract. Thick clothes restrained the hold. He tightened his grip on the man's wrist and wrenched it up. The gun was black steel in the night. Small sounds of dark rage from the other man.

Surge of energy. The gunman's body heaved against him, sending August backwards. Don't let go! Don't let go!

He felt himself losing the grip. Stumbling. The other falling as well, leaning into him as if they were champion ice skaters dancing a finale. He heard a grunt from the pit of the killer's guts as the man heaved once more, shoving himself backwards, trying to flick August from him like a fly at a picnic.

The gun still pointed somewhere out of there. August was spinning. Toeing backwards. Slipping on the side of the grave and swinging a wide, wide arc.

The Academy instructor making them practise over and over . . . over and over . . . the wide, wide arc.

The wheel . . . the wheel . . . the wheel . . . he would intone in that high, feminine voice that the younger ones mocked.

"The wheel . . . the wheel . . .," August whispered, sweeping the killer into the ground, his head bouncing on the headstone, his feet tangling beneath him into the grave with Sarah, Jonathan, and Matthew Harwood.

The gun spun at August's feet, flashing wildly in the light's beam.

8

JOINT DEFENSE FACILITY PINE GAP (CIA CODE NAME: MERINO)
January 28

"Going down now," the pilot lifted one finger and spoke around his headphone.

August nodded and tightened his feet against the case between his legs which held the cat. He could feel the prisoner tense in the seat beside him. It probably isn't through any fear of flying, August thought. More likely fear of what was going to come later as August had made clear to him as he held the gun at him through the night. He'd reluctantly admired the prisoner's resilience as they'd sat with the wind howling around them and the smell of stale cat food filling the air. The guy was scared, very scared. But resolute. August was afraid he had a martyr on his hands. And martyrs always worried him. People who didn't give a damn about their own lives were usually more than ready to sacrifice others.

Beneath them, sprouting in the pale valley between the McDonnell Range, were eight huge, bizarre mushrooms. The monster domes curved over the sensitive equipment, ensuring that no inquisitive foreign satellite could peer into the electronic guts of the West's most sophisticated tracking nuts and bolts. Twenty-four hours a day the dishes sucked in information bounced to earth by the powerful reconnaissance satellites circling above. The Big Birds were spectacular pieces of space hardware, capable, through a precise dance of interacting mirrors, telescopes, and lenses, of guiding missiles to a dictator's bunker or reading a licence plate on a Serbian dirt road. The high-resolution pictures were classified "deep black"; the precise capabilities of the satellites' microscopic view was one of the deepest secrets in a very secret world.

August was here to find out what the Birds had done for him lately. And which two-faced voyeur was peeking where he shouldn't.

The helicopter blades chewed up the air and sent the dry earth beneath them into a spin. August held onto his stomach and nerves as the pilot lowered the machine exactly onto the centre of the landing pad. Zaid's handcuffed fists bounced on his lap.

August peered into the carrying case on the floor. He stuck a finger inside to be answered by a loud hiss. "I know exactly how you feel, Joe, old boy."

The blades spun lazily now. August picked up the cat and jumped from his cramped bucket seat onto the narrow metal stairs that had been tucked up against the copter. "Get out," he ordered Zaid, whose bruised face peered tentatively around the helicopter's door. He balanced on the stairs, stumbling as he neared the ground.

A woman's hand stretched out to steady him. "Careful now. One step at a time."

Zaid pulled his arm away and spit on the ground.

August seized Zaid's collar with his free hand and pinned him against the side of the helicopter. Joe protested vigorously. The vibrating engine throbbed against them and magnified the heat of the blazing tarmac. "Enough of that, buddy," August growled. "You're about to learn the benefits of cooperation." He shoved him forward.

The woman's curiously blank face studied August. "No need for that, Mr. Riley. We carry on things in a civilized way here."

August stood close to her, wincing against the blinding sunlight reflecting off the runway. Sounded like she'd taken lessons on condescension at some second-rate private school. "Look, Miss — number one — where I come from we introduce ourselves . . . you know my name, what's yours?"

"Emma, Emma Cowen," she answered calmly. "Head of security."

"Number two, Ms. Cowen, generally speaking I don't subscribe to the Miss Manners school of etiquette when dealing with guys who try to kill me. That all right with you?" She watched his face impassively. "And third, I'd expect the head of security at a place like this to be just a tad more appreciative of those types of facts."

"Of course." She pulled herself up straighter. She was quite short if you subtracted the high heels. "My apologies."

She didn't sound very apologetic.

They strode towards the small flat-roofed box that seemed to serve as the air terminal, Emma quickly covering a surprising length of the blistering runway. Zaid slouched next to August, his eyes darting everywhere. A tall, very thin man dressed in a squadron leader's uniform stepped forward from the shade of a transport plane nosed up against a hangar. Three armed MPs trailed him. They smoothly encapsulated Zaid, who shrank even further into his black sweater and flimsy windbreaker, torn and soiled after his late-night encounter on Heard.

"Pleased to see you arrived safely after all, Riley." The long hand was flaky dry. "Squadron Leader Emory. Charles Emory. We were sorry to hear about the . . .," he looked Zaid up and down as if he were some expensive cargo newly unloaded, ". . . incident. I had hoped to welcome you to Australia under more friendly circumstances." His voice was halting and harsh. August could see the plastic nub indicating the guy's voice box was in trouble or gone. He vaguely remembered the file. He'd gone through hundreds of them — present employees, past employees, employees with a grudge, a denied promotion, a discipline problem . . . The photograph attached to Charles Emory's file had depicted a much healthier guy. He was hardly recognizable. Emory had risen through the ranks. He had a reputation as a hard taskmaster and ox of a worker, doing paperwork from a hospital bed when necessary. Better man than I am, Gunga Din, August thought.

"Thanks," he said, gripping Emory's hand. Hell, it was a better welcome than he'd received so far. "How's Taylor doing? That leg get set all right?"

"David's fine," Emma offered curtly. "His leg wasn't broken after all."

"Good." August held up the carrying case. "I brought his cat with me. Nobody down there to take care of the old devil. And Taylor seemed attached to him."

"He'll appreciate that, Mr. Riley," Charles said. "Taylor was sorry about what happened. He felt a bit responsible that he hadn't been there to help you out."

Emma stopped in mid-stride and looked at the older man. "Do you really think that was wise? Telling David about . . .," she glanced back at Zaid who was busy trying to erase a stain from the front of his shirt with saliva, ". . . subsequent events?"

Emory frowned. "Taylor is your deputy after all, Emma. He would find out one way or another. Besides, David's a good man. I've known him a long time, don't forget."

"So have I. And I wouldn't have informed him of a breakdown in security like this."

"Well then — we disagree don't we, my dear? Put your complaint in writing."

August watched her breach her temper. Very controlled lady. She stalked ahead of them, her pleated skirt swirling around her.

He allowed himself a quick glance around as they covered the distance across the tarmac to the terminal, the carrying case bumping against his legs. His eyes were gritty from exhaustion, his hot clothes were chafing him in all the wrong places, and the sound of revving engines was deafening. Aside from the huge mushroom-shaped radomes dominating the horizon, the place looked like a baking two-bit airport in a dying African republic.

They marched through the tiny waiting room. Not many sleepless passengers lingered here over cold coffee and stale cigarettes. The plastic seats were torturously rounded in a shape guaranteed to make some chiropractor rich. A uniformed woman, shaped like a guard in a maximum security pen, was punishing some bread into sandwiches behind a narrow counter.

They all squeezed into a silent elevator, which plunged immediately to the bowels of the earth. Zaid and the three guards stood in front of August, Charles, and Emma. August thought he heard a tiny whimper from Zaid as his own stomach skipped a few floors. He stared at the back of the prisoner's head. No blinking numbers indicated in what particular void the elevator was suspended. There were only two anonymous buttons, which Emory had pressed when they entered. The Squadron Leader stood now, swaying slightly, next to the wall. He had a sour, medicinal smell about him — the same smell that had dusted August's Uncle Olsen before he'd capitulated to the infection caused by the fumbling doctor, twelve days hostage to a hospital room before he died. A pasty yellow box of a place completely alien from the cabin where he'd found his refuge fifty years before. It was during those twelve days that August had cut the idea of justice from his mind.

Charles offered him a sickly, dry smile. His teeth looked soft and yellow. Two were missing from the upper palate.

Emma Cowen held herself rigidly away from August's other shoulder. No chance of a smile there, sickly or otherwise. There was something off about her face, something he couldn't quite put his finger on. She was carefully made up. Didn't need as much as she'd applied. The lips were primly outlined in pink and August glimpsed a beige streak beneath her chin where the foundation hadn't quite blended. This woman had been too busy to abuse her skin with the Australian sun. Her features were neatly arranged as if she'd lifted them from the same drawer as the starched blouse she wore. Its pattern of tiny blue flowers didn't distract from the uncompromising air of the stiff cotton.

"Some dirt on my face is there, Mr. Riley?"

August cleared his throat. "Ah . . . no . . . ah . . . just

admiring your earrings." He hadn't actually until that moment noticed them. Small silver hoops.

Her hands were clasped in front of her. Not looking at him, she said sarcastically, "Yes, I'm sure you are very interested. Well, if you get into Alice before Saturday they are on sale for $10.95. Regular $15.95."

Charles laughed. It was a hard, raspy sound. "Don't mind Emma, Mr. Riley. She tends to be a little direct sometimes. Diplomacy is not her strong suit."

She turned to look at August again. A disconcertingly clear look. Deep blue eyes. "A job like mine tends to make one cynical, Mr. Riley. I'm sure you find that in your line of work as well." She blinked slowly as if erasing him from her sight and turned away. It was then that he realized what had been bothering him about her face: she didn't have any eyelashes. Her eyelids were smooth and bald, giving her a slightly alien appearance. She wasn't the type to glue on those spidery false lashes that some women still insisted on wearing. Emma Cowen had much more important ways to spend her time.

The elevator bumped to a soft stop somewhere in the depths of the building. The door opened to a long, bare corridor. Jesus, August thought, am I never going to escape these damned narrow places that squeeze out the sky and trees?

The walls and floor of the tunnel were a blazing white-washed cement that demanded your attention. The white ceiling magnified the unrelenting beat of fluorescent lighting strung along the length of the corridor. Here and there a passage flanked to the side, leading to what seemed just another narrow opening. The blank white doors they passed offered no escape. They were making their way through a nest of underground passages and rooms.

From the air Pine Gap looked like a scrappy gathering of squat buildings dominated by the huge Perspex radomes, but here, carved into the cool shelter of the earth, lay the brain of the place. A stockpile of food and water, spare parts, communications systems, even air-conditioning, ensured that this labyrinth would offer the Base a second chance in the face of any attack.

Charles stopped abruptly and opened one of the anonymous doors. Inside, a guard sat in front of a computer screen and two telephones. Another sat with his chair tipped against the wall drinking coffee, deep into a rugby magazine. A grid of iron bars, painted pale blue, something like a new mother would pick to decorate a nursery, ran along the far wall. A poster from an amateur Alice Springs production of *Gypsy* enlivened one wall and a Van Gogh calendar, this month depicting one of the artist's more manic wheat fields, splashed against another. A tape deck blasted heavy metal. The first guard reached over and snapped it off as the second guy dropped his magazine, jumped to his feet, and saluted.

Charles gestured for him to relax before turning to August. "Well, Mr. Riley, our facility doesn't normally entertain such guests. It's usually reserved for the occasional drunk. Every few months, someone in one of the more lively Alice bars dares the fellow on the next stool to drive a jeep through the restricted zone looking for aliens. Or we sometimes welcome a screamingly righteous protester trying to crucify himself on the barbed wire on the east side. Ned here likes those the best, don't you, Ned?"

Ned laughed. "They might as well come in with a Bible and pulpit. They sit in there," he jerked one thumb over his shoulder, "and try to make me see the wickedness of my ways. An Aussie working for the Yanks. Last one in here talked for two hours straight. Didn't really want me to talk back." He laughed and shook his head.

"Put him in a cell," Charles said, unlocking Zaid's cuffs. "We'll complete the paperwork later."

"There isn't much paperwork to complete, is there?" Emma asked. "You weren't able to get much out of him on Heard, were you, Mr. Riley?" she said condescendingly. "We don't have the slightest idea who he is."

Perspiration dribbled from Zaid's brow, but August didn't like the defiant look in his eye as their gaze met. He put the carrying case on the desk. Joe's mottled nose and whiskers peered out at them. "He had ID — but it's most certainly phony. We're trying to trace the boat now. He could have picked it up anywhere," he glanced at Zaid who was rubbing his wrists sulkily as the second guard guided him into the sterile cell. "I don't want him to sleep tonight."

The guard glanced at Charles, who nodded. "Mr. Riley's in charge of this prisoner."

"I must protest." Emma raised herself to her full five foot three. "As head of security . . ."

"This is a special case, Emma. We've promised Washington that Mr. Riley will have our full cooperation. Due to the unique aspects of this case, his investigation must take priority."

"I still object."

"Put it in writing with your other complaints." Charles turned to August. "Now then, I imagine you might like a shower, a hot meal, and a comfortable bed."

"That's the best offer I've had in quite awhile."

August grinned at Zaid who was standing in the middle of the cell examining his new world with horror.

AYERS ROCK CAMPSITE
January 29

In the flickering light of the barbecue pit, campers chatted as they chugged beer and flipped steaks. Someone strummed a guitar halfheartedly. A lot of families, a few singles. Ahmed Maher and Kestrel had both been careful to dress casually — sweatshirts, running shoes, loose slacks. Ahmed hadn't been able to bring himself to wear jeans. He sat forward on the seat of the heavy wooden picnic table and retrieved a pack of cigarettes from his back pocket. He needed one of his daily ration for this meeting.

Kestrel had phoned, the calm voice edged with anxiety, insisting they meet somewhere outside of Alice. Not at one of their regular spots. Ahmed had agreed. He couldn't take any chances right now. He probed the tissue inside the cigarette pack. Empty. Damn! He'd warned Zuleika a dozen times about helping herself. He crushed the package in his fist and tossed it to the ground.

"You have the money?" Kestrel demanded.

Ahmed slipped an envelope from his inside pocket and placed it on the scarred picnic table next to Kestrel's. "No one noticed you were gone?"

"No. A prisoner has been brought in from Heard Island and has been taking up most of their attention."

Ahmed sucked in his breath. "From Heard Island?"

Kestrel smiled. "Thought you'd be interested. You sent him to get the CIA man, didn't you?" The mole ran one finger along the seal of the envelope. "Should have sent a professional, Dr. Maher."

Pungent smoke drifted towards them and the smell of charcoal tinged the air. Someone struck a light to a gas lantern in a tent a few yards away. A baby cried inside the tent and a woman clucked comfort to it. Ahmed lowered his voice, trying to keep the panic from it. "Has he said anything?"

"Not yet. But Riley hasn't had a real chance to get at him. He will soon." The firelight cast the mole's face into grotesque shadows. "The prisoner doesn't look like the type who could stand up to much interrogation, if you know what I mean."

Ahmed clenched his teeth. "He's my brother. If Riley breaks him, he breaks us." The baby's cry reached a crescendo pitch. A man's voice muttered angrily and the woman's soothing grew more frantic.

"Us?" Kestrel's face was hard. "No one knows about me."

Ahmed's face was harder. "It's you they're looking for, remember?"

"But your brother doesn't know my identity." Kestrel pinned him with a look. "Does he?"

"Of course not. But can we get him out?"

Kestrel shrugged. "Maybe. He's holding up well so far. We have a little time." The mole fingered the money. "*I'm* getting out. This August Riley is serious. Washington is serious. They're all jumpy, worried that their much ballyhooed Desert Storm might prove to be all hot air. The amount of arms and men and money pouring into Saudi Arabia — the investment is far too high to lose. The Americans and their British lapdogs are gung ho right now. But give them six months and fifty thousand casualties and see how long they can drape the coffins in gung ho. No — they're scared to death someone is going to blow this one."

"And is someone?" Ahmed tried not to sound too eager. He'd always had the advantage in these encounters. Kestrel could never afford to be revealed. And Ahmed could always afford to disappear if he had to. But now Kestrel held a lot of the cards. He could see that the mole was high, on edge and he didn't like this sense of having to tiptoe around a strange volatility. Things were too critical right now for any radical deviation from their usual routine. This was the time. Time for years of cultivation to pay off.

Kestrel nodded and looked at him. "Oh yes. You and I are going to tear that Desert Shield wide open and let Mr. Hussein drive right through it."

The lantern inside the tent flickered, throwing giant shadows over the canvas walls. The baby screeched and a man swore. The door flap was thrown back and the father, still cursing under his breath, pushed his way out, pulling his jeans over his hips. He stared angrily at Ahmed and Kestrel.

"Feel like a walk?" Ahmed said with sudden forced conviviality.

Kestrel nodded. They eased themselves from the picnic table and walked away from the circle of the campfire. Steaks spit over metal racks. The guitar player had picked up energy now and an enthusiastic singsong had begun. They stepped over the flimsy wooden barrier separating the communal circle from the desert. So typical of the Westerner, Ahmed thought, to try to divide and conquer the elements in this way. Determinedly hammering yet another fence, another house, another barrier to nature. And all the while the sand slowly, inexorably, drifted around their feet and crept through the cracks of whatever artificial fortress they erected.

"And the invasion plans?" Ahmed couldn't hold back any longer. "What about the invasion plans?"

"They're calling it the Hail Mary play," Kestrel said to the ghost gums, gleaming in the moonlight.

Maher stopped walking. "What?"

Kestrel laughed. "Don't worry — I had to get it explained to me as well."

Ahmed's impatience was rising. He was capable of waiting a long time to get what he wanted. He had waited for years. Decades. But this — he wanted to know this now. "What are you talking about?"

Kestrel leaned against the peeling bark of an old tree. "It's an American football term. Hail Mary. You know anything about American football, Dr. Maher?"

"I understand that a dozen or so mutantly huge men on each team periodically charge into each other, inflicting maximum injuries. They evidently spend three hours or so in this fashion making their way to one end or another of the playing field."

"Yes. Well, there is a ball involved. The huge men have to carry it safely to the opponent's end. The Hail Mary play is used when all the members of Team A unexpectedly veer to one side. Team A's quarterback throws the ball in that direction, giving Team A the advantage."

"How is that?"

"Team B expects the ball to be thrown straight down the field instead of . . .," Kestrel looked at him, "instead of to the east or west."

Ahmed frowned. "There's no amphibious landing? But Schwarzkopf isn't going straight through Kuwait either?"

Kestrel nodded. "Correct the first time."

Ahmed was instantly skeptical. "How do you know? That amphibious landing information you gave me was rubbish."

"The Lacrosse went up on the Atlantis shuttle in November. That Bird's eye is so keen that it shows us when the marines are picking their noses and its heat sensors are primed to break out in a rash if a GI even lights up a cigarette. They've been working the KH-12 overtime ever since it went up. Been diverting its usual spying chores from China to the Gulf for months now. And Lacrosse shows the tanks and supply lines set up like men on a chess board."

"How do you know this Riley character hasn't just messed

with the images again. Falsifying them? Leading us up another wild path?"

"Not this time. He hasn't been near the reconnaissance room since he left Heard Island. Hasn't had time. Been preoccupied with your brother. Figures he can get his answers there."

Ahmed ran his hand over his face. "Where is Schwarzkopf going with this Hail Mary plan?"

"Where is there to go?"

Ahmed remembered the map pinned to his wall. "If it isn't Kuwait," he turned to Kestrel. "It has to be . . . a sweep to the west! Through Iraq itself. Hussein has all his forces on the Kuwaiti-Saudi border. There's nothing left."

"Correct again."

The folk song around the campfire reached a crescendo. A chorus of toneless voices joined in the last verse, ending on a high, giggly note of drunken self-congratulation.

ALICE SPRINGS
The Next Day

Charles Emory glanced at Tony Lawson's well-remembered profile, the sunburnt nose and deep creases around his eyes. They were driving through Alice's residential area, tidy homes huddled together as if crouching from the desert gnawing at their back. "You've aged well," Charles remarked, turning his attention back to the road.

"Clean living, Charlie. Clean living," Tony laughed.

"Must be all those Hawaiian beaches and bikinis."

"Well, if you're going to flog real estate for a living you might as well do it in Hawaii. Throw in a little development," he winked at Charles and drummed his fingers on his knee, "sell some folks an eight-hundred-square-foot condo with a Jacuzzi and a fresh coat of paint and they think they've died and gone to heaven. And they'll dish out heavenly prices too, I can tell you. Yep, it was the best move I ever made going to Waikiki in '60. Never looked back. I mean," he ran a tidily manicured hand over his face, "where would I have gone in the army? Posted from one dump to another like this?" He gestured over the milky-white streets and thirsty lawns.

Charles nodded and fiddled with the radio controls. He hated the pressure. He'd planned this for so long. He'd always thought that when the moment for revenge arrived he'd be able to take his sweet time over it. But time had been stalking him ever since the final diagnosis. Charles had thought he'd be rid of the sense of important deeds undone once Larry was gone. Instead it was worse. And time was still biting at his heels. And August Riley's appearance, his questions, his skeptical eyes, had accelerated everything.

Tony added hastily, "No offence. But it just isn't for me." He glanced nervously at Charles who stared straight ahead at the road. "Obviously the right move for you, though. Army did all right by you. Involved with all the hush-hush, wink-wink stuff, right? Very important too, I bet," he added patronizingly.

"Had no choice, Tony. Benefits. Couldn't very well risk losing them. My girl needed them."

"Oh yeah." Tony's Cockney accent had been muted by a hybrid American strain over his thirty years in Hawaii. "Sure." He wiped a piece of grit from his eye and examined it. "Expensive stuff, I suppose."

"You ought to know. You were on the Appeal Board when I launched the claim."

Tony looked at him, puzzled. "Appeal Board?"

"June 8, 1959. You were one of the committee who turned me down for the extended claim. Nixed the supplementary benefits."

There was something about Charles's tone that Tony didn't like. It held the same edge that certain municipal counsellors had adopted when they found out he'd gotten around the zoning bylaws for that condo on the north side. "Wasn't allowable, old man. You never proved that the kids . . . well, that their . . . problems . . . were Army related."

Charles remembered Tony's white face, the exploding red

splotch of freckles across the nose, the gap between the front teeth. The kid who'd dismissed him with a flourish of a cheap ballpoint as Charles begged for his children's health. The kid who wanted to buy him a drink in the PX an hour later. Charles had taken the drink and swallowed the cheap apologies. And vowed never to forget.

"Tell me. You believe in an eye for an eye? That philosophy of things?"

A hot wind blew through the open windows. Tony ran his hands through his newly trimmed hair, a skim of grit covering it now, and moistened his parched lips. He gripped the edge of the seat as Charles swung around a sudden curve. Fumbling in his shirt pocket he pulled out a handkerchief and wiped it across his dripping forehead. "Well, I figure if some guy punches you in the head he'll get the message that you don't like it if you punch him back. I mean, a bloke would be dead if he waited for the legal system to dish out justice. Most of these bleeding heart judges don't know the difference between a good wallop and a slap on the wrist."

"Exactly." Charles shifted the car into a lower gear as they climbed through a subdivision. Tidy spaces of lawn separated the houses and large shade trees lined the sidewalks.

Relieved at this semblance of agreement and the chance to change the subject, Tony babbled. "Good of you to invite me to stay at your place, Charles. That hotel in lovely downtown Alice isn't exactly the Ritz. But I'll be out of your way tomorrow," he added, a little too hastily.

"Still swim, do you?" Charles asked. He punched a button on the dashboard which released a blue liquid to clear the windscreen of dead insects.

"Ha! Does the Pope pray?" His chest visibly expanded as he spoke. "Came fourth in the '60 Olympics, you know."

Charles nodded. As if Tony would ever let anyone forget.

"One hundred metres. Oh yes. Could have done the two hundred. I qualified for that event, you know!" He glanced at Charles as if expecting a challenge. But he was concentrating on steering the car around a boy weaving along the street, a heavy bag of papers slung over his shoulder and a Labrador loping along beside him. "But that Nigel Lloyd got my place. He was sleeping with the coach. Everyone knew. But I drew the line at certain things, no matter how much I wanted the gold, huh, Charlie!" He laughed and shouted out the window, "Get off the road, you little bugger!"

The car swung heavily around a curve and lurched to a halt outside a pastel-painted bungalow set well back on a closely trimmed lawn. A mailbox, painted in the same flamingo pink as the house, was propped on the other side of the driveway. Tony jumped from the car in relief, wiping his perspiration drenched brow.

Charles followed him into the house.

Tony dived and weaved in the water, executing elaborate twirls and imitating the synchronized swimmers he'd seen on television. Bobbing above the water line he clenched an imaginary rose between his teeth and then with a mincing movement dived below, sticking his rear high into the air. Suddenly swooping back into sight, he sputtered, "Great place you've got here, Charles!"

The sun glinted off the pale water reflecting into his eyes. He could see Charles in the lounge by the pool, his white face and arms vulnerable in the late afternoon sun. Wide reflector sunglasses hid most of his face and he sat absolutely still, his legs straight and stiff in front of him, dressed in the same shirt and slacks he'd worn in the car. The man had just never learned how to relax. "Come on in. Water's great." The chlorine stung Tony's eyes. He cleared them and snorted something out of his nostrils. This was great. He felt sixteen years old whenever he got back in a pool. And he could still compete with any buck half his age. Poor old Charles probably felt self-conscious about climbing in with him. Poor bugger didn't look very fit. And that was certainly an understatement.

"Charles! Come on in! Cool you right off!" Tony had swum almost a full length underwater. He felt like a porpoise, diving and swooping through the clear pale water. This end of the pool was shaded by some limp palms, and their yellowing leaves dotted the surface of the water. Several clung to Tony's back as he swam up under them. "Charles. It's no fun on my own," he shouted. A lie. But it was, after all, the old stick-in-a-mud's pool. Tony knew how to play the gracious guest.

He floated on his back in the deep end. "Charles?" A breeze shifted net curtains across the French windows. It was definitely a lot cooler down at this end. Surprising that Charles had been able to coax this much foliage to thrive in this godawful country. Tony shaded his eyes with his hand, propping his back against the hard edge of the pool.

And then he saw Charles.

Jesus! This sickness, whatever it was, must have started rotting the poor devil's brain. Charles was standing at the edge of the pool. Dressed in full scuba gear, for God's sake!

"Charles?" Tony laughed nervously. The shiny wet suit looked too big for him, like an ill-fitting, wrinkly second skin. The face mask darkened his features and he looked like he would collapse under the weight of the heavy oxygen tank. Even flippers. Sticking grotesquely straight out in front of him.

All of a sudden Tony couldn't wait to go home. This Maralinga Reunion thing had been a bad idea. He'd rather tolerate an extra few days with Nancy than handle this. He'd never been very good with cripples or sickies — especially mental ones.

Charles sat down slowly on the edge of the pool, moving as if it cost him a great effort. Suddenly he somersaulted forward. As if he were diving from a bloody boat in the middle of the ocean, for heaven's sake!

Tony paddled backwards quickly, rocked by the impact of Charles hitting the surface.

Charles's body hit him like a load of concrete, pulling him smoothly beneath the water's surface like one of those trained seals scooping a ball from a hoop. Tony gasped and struggled back up. But Charles's one thin arm, now a black octopus tentacle, gripped him. Clamping his mouth shut, Tony kicked frantically, trying to unleash a cry as he momentarily felt air on his face. And then stinging water was rushing into his eyes. Choking, he rolled over and brought his teeth down hard on Emory's arm, his jaws rigid as a bull terrier's.

The octopus sprung its grip.

But Charles managed to buoy himself up, pressing Tony's shoulders back into the water. Dragging him silently down. Tony's feet brushed the concrete bottom of the pool. His lungs tightened, an iron press around his heart. Emory's hands dug deeper into his shoulders. The eyes were brimming with ancient rage. Tony's breath bubbled into the pool.

He found one last wave of energy. Bringing his knee up, he jammed it into the concave spot beneath Charles's ribs. He wrenched the breathing apparatus from Charles's mouth and a cascade of bubbles rushed from the hole in his throat to the surface.

Tony's lungs were screaming against his rib cage. He shoved the breathing tube into his own mouth.

Charles doubled over in agony, clutching blindly at the water. The awful hole at his throat gaping and sucking for air. The blue eyes turned inky black as he clawed at the side of the pool.

Tony seized him, pressing him farther down. Charles kicked once, his face contorted in a silent cry before a last spasm crushed him. He slumped, gurgling, a grotesque black shape in the clear, pale water.

Tony collapsed onto the bright, cool tiles surrounding the pool. The hot air and yellowing foliage dropping from the thirsty trees seemed very, very sweet.

Tony felt a hundred years old.

9

PINE GAP
January 30

The prisoner sat huddled at the far end of the cell, his hands cupped over his ears, his tight curls matted against his head. His legs were drawn up. A small tear corrugated the knee of his expensive slacks and his shoes were crusted with mud.

August had bluffed or bullied nothing out of him. He was still waiting for the results from the mug shot and prints sent to DC. In the meantime, Babyface had proven tougher than August would have guessed.

At least he'd gotten rid of Emma Cowen. She'd left an hour before after a brief phone call, her face folded into an accordion of worry. At the interview she'd been distracted, interjecting irrelevant questions. August was sure the prisoner could smell her desperation for answers. He wondered how such an inadequate interrogator had made it as head of security at Pine Gap. He'd restrained the impulse to challenge her, hoping the prisoner would interpret the tension between them as the good cop, bad cop act. He might have to demand Washington get Emma

Cowen off his back if she kept it up, but he wanted to avoid that. The Aussies were sensitive about being pushed around on their own territory.

Emma had insisted on flicking on a tape recorder before she left. August flipped it off now.

Zaid looked up, his eyes liquid black and defiant.

"Nice ring you've got there," August said, leaning against the cell wall, his gaze focusing on the ruby on Zaid's pinky. "Real, is it?" he asked, taking a deep drag from his cigarette. There was something about a guy trying to kill you that opened your nerves like someone had taken a scalpel to them.

"How would you know?" Zaid sneered, looking August up and down, the faded jeans and fake leather belt, the unstyled hair and plaid shirt.

August laughed, choking a little on the unfamiliar smoke. "You're right about that. Maybe you can educate me." He stepped towards Zaid.

Zaid stood up, his back sliding up the wall. He didn't want this man looming over him. He hadn't slept for three days. But nothing would make him betray his brother. Not now. If he had to die he would die a Holy Martyr. Ahmed would see to that.

The white room swam a little around him. He'd like to sit down at the small table, better yet lie down, but the cot had been folded into the wall. And they wouldn't take it down. Just ten minutes sleep was all he needed. And a shower would be nice.

He steadied himself against the wall. Say nothing. That's all he had to remember. Say nothing.

The phone on the guard's desk jangled into the silence, jolting Zaid from his haze. He blinked. Warm liquid bathed his raw, red eyes.

August cursed to himself. He'd have to get that damned phone taken out of here.

"It's for you, sir," Ned offered him the receiver.

August raised a hand indicating he needed a minute and turned back to Zaid. "Let's have a look, shall we?" August held his hand out.

Zaid spit.

"Give it to me. Now."

Zaid twisted the ring off his finger and held it. Smiling, he dropped it to the tile floor. It rolled beneath the table.

August shrugged and indicated to the guard to open the lock. He puffed on his cigarette and coughed as the cell door slid behind him.

"Smoking will kill you!" Zaid sneered.

August smashed the butt into a tin ashtray on the guard's desk. "Just so long as you don't, sonny boy. Just so long as you don't."

ALICE SPRINGS
That Night

The bar was a bleak box of a place, its darkness only relieved whenever the door swung open and drenched the dark walls in dust-mottled light. The heat seemed to have been carried inside in blocks. August was working on his second beer and still felt dehydrated.

David Taylor was very late. He'd been monosyllabic and stilted on the phone. But something about his tone had made August capitulate to his insistence on a meeting. He needed a break from the little worm in the prison cell anyway. Besides, he'd been summoned to too many strange places under too many strange circumstances over the years to casually refuse any invitation. Some of them turned out to be the lead he needed. And Taylor could know a lot. He'd been hanging around this neck of the woods for a long time. Maybe too long from the sound of his voice over the phone.

The bar's clientele seemed to run to alcoholic prospectors and exhausted tourists. The few scrapings of gold that the prospectors ever found soon disappeared into the bar's cash register. And the tourists carried their gullibility strapped to them like their $300 walking shoes. The music squawking from the antique jukebox was loud and the records skipped over well-worn grooves. Dean Martin moaning about pizza and *amore* . . . and *amore* . . . and *amore* . . . and the moon in the sky. An old-timer who looked welded to the bar stool was singing along, using his beer bottle as a microphone. A woman perched two stools away from him dressed in a snug flower-patterned dress and bright pink stockings, her skin long ago overbaked by the Australian sun, winked at August. He looked away. There was something pathetic about the pink stockings.

The door released a blanket of white light and David Taylor walked in. His wiry beard obscured his mouth and wisps of hair chased each other across the wide space of his scalp. He seemed a lot less bulky than he had in the confined space of Heard Island. He was carrying a broad-rimmed hat. Another man trotted beside him, glancing nervously from side to side.

"Good of you to come," Taylor said, pressing his sidekick into one of the red plastic chairs opposite. "Tony, this is August Riley — the man I was telling you about. August, Tony Lawson."

"Yes indeed. Good of you to come," Lawson said nervously, sticking his hand towards August. "Couldn't talk to just any-one you know. Not just anyone."

"Well, I hope it's important. I'm in the middle of something right now."

A heavy waitress in a clinging fuzzy sweater rested one thigh against their table. She was balancing a tray of glasses and tinned beer. "What you want, mates?" She sounded like a transplant from some Eastern European country. August won-dered how attractive the new soil on the other side of the Wall had turned out to be for this particular escapee.

"The same," August said, studying Lawson whose red freck-led face seemed incongruous on his lanky body.

"My usual," David said. "A Coke," he gestured towards Lawson.

"Whatever you've got," Tony said quickly.

She laughed sarcastically. "Well now, you don't ask for much." She dumped three glasses and two beer in the middle of the table, sweeping up August's empties in an expert move-ment that testified to many long shifts.

David placed a bill in her hand. "Keep the change."

She laughed again at some private joke and slouched to the next table where a shining couple with freshly pressed slacks and shirts and heavy German accents leaned over a map.

"Yes. Well, I've explained to Tony that you are a busy man, August. But you see, he doesn't trust anyone right now. Not even the police. He . . . well, we thought that perhaps you being an outsider here — an outsider with some authority — that you might be able to help him."

The waitress sauntered back to them and slid a soft drink across the table.

"What's your connection?" August asked.

David looked vaguely uncomfortable. He pulled the tab from his can and took a slurp of pop. Over the jukebox the Four Tops launched into a tune with a lot of choruses. "Tony and I go back a long way."

August returned his gaze to Tony. He could practically see the heat rash rising along the poor guy's collar line. Big purple splotches, some kind of bruise, were sprouting right alongside it. "Look, Mr. Lawson. Nothing personal. But I'm in Pine Gap on business. So, if you've got a problem, this part of Australia probably has more so-called authorities crawling over it per square mile than any place in the country. I'm sure one of them could help you."

Tony's long neck jerked forward. His face was gleaming white even in the gloom of the bar, and splatters of freckles stood out like uneven birthmarks across his nose and cheek-bones. His eyes were unnaturally bright. "Charles Emory tried to kill me!" He released a little gasp at the end of his words as if the shock had just hit him again.

August frowned and took a sip of beer. He pursed his lips against its sourness. "When?"

"This afternoon. Mind you, the bugger's been acting strange ever since I got here. Always was a bit off his head. Never could . . . well," Tony glanced at David, as if for confirmation, "the man never could socialize properly. Too intense. I always said that about Charles Emory. Too bloody intense! But this is just over the top!" His hand was shaking as he tipped his beer into the grubby glass.

"Why would Charles Emory want to kill you?"

"Why?" There was an edge of hysteria to Tony Lawson's voice. "Why? Who the hell knows? But he's been into all this top secret stuff for years now. He might have been imagining all sorts of stuff about me. Tried to drown me! All decked out in a damned monkey suit! Tried to bloody well drown me, I tell you!" Tony's eyes were bulging at the memory, his Cockney accent back in full dress uniform and his small head jerking up and down as if controlled by a puppeteer.

David leaned forward on the table. "Tony was taking a swim in Charles's pool. Apparently Charles, dressed in scuba gear, jumped in and tried to pull Tony under." Tony shuddered in agreement. "We've been worried about Charles for awhile now. He was always a bit of . . . well, a loner, I guess. But over the past year he's seemed to . . . it's hard to put a finger on it . . ."

"You'd better try to put a finger on it or you're wasting my time," August interjected.

"Larry Fisher. Tell him about Larry Fisher," Tony insisted.

David sighed, as if wishing he were somewhere else. "Fisher came down for the Maralinga Reunion. He died on a hike up Ayers Rock with Charles last weekend. There'll be an investigation but that'll take months."

"Maralinga?" August didn't recognize the name.

"It's south of here," David answered. "Nuclear testing site in the fifties. Now and then a few of us get together. Don't ask me why. The tests must have fried our brains, after all."

"And what about Bob Stahel last year?" Tony said excitedly, the big vein in his neck starting to throb. "What about Bob?" August thought Tony was going to burst into tears.

David put a hand on Tony's shoulder. "Hold on. Hold on now. No use getting all overexcited." He glanced at August. "Bob was killed while he was visiting Charles last year. Coroner ruled it an accident."

"Accident!" Tony's voice was a quiet shriek. "They find the man down a bloody well! David here tells me that they didn't find his body for a month! And the well was on Charles's property! Some big spread of his in Queensland."

"What was the connection?" August asked.

A beat of silence. Lawson glanced at Taylor as if seeking permission. Taylor took a long drink.

August leaned back. "What aren't you telling me?"

Lawson drew in his breath. "Bob was on Emory's Appeal Board. When he tried to get compensation . . .," he shrugged dismissively but his eyes were darting somewhere in the past. "They turned Charles down." He laughed lamely. "Guess he's still mad at me as well. I was on the same Appeal Board."

David Taylor drew the back of his hand across his mouth.

"What do you want me to do about it?" August didn't like this. A distraction right now could ruin everything. "Go to the police. The civvies if you don't trust the MPs."

Tony licked his lips and lowered his voice. "I don't want that bastard to get away with this. He's a big wheel around here. The military — and the civilians for that matter — will cover it up. Anything that gets the press nosing around Pine Gap makes them nervous. They'll do anything to keep them out. Including covering up attempted murder!" His voice was reaching the shriek level again.

"Why not take it to Emma Cowen? She's head of security. That's her job, looking after this kind of thing."

Tony glanced at David, astonishment lifting his features, and then back to August. "She's his daughter, for God's sake!" he almost sobbed, the suggestion of tears glistening in his eyes. "She's probably been protecting him for years! She won't help me."

August looked at David Taylor. "His daughter?"

Taylor nodded. "Cowen's her married name."

A subliminal alarm jumped in August's throat. All those files. Had he missed something? He'd been punch-drunk and worried about Katy. During his weekly duty phone call, the quacks had told him there might be signs of diabetes. That was the same night he'd done the senior Pine Gap personnel files. Why did something suddenly seem funny? Why did something tell him it was going to be a long night?

He glanced over at the woman with the pink stockings. He couldn't tell if she was still looking at him or had just fallen into a semi-drunken coma, her elbow cocked on the bar, one fist folded under her chin. If she winked at him again he might just be tempted to get up from that cramped table covered in filthy imitation velvet and follow her.

ALICE SPRINGS HOSPITAL

Emma Cowen, née Emory, paced back and forth across the waiting room floor, her high heels tap, tap, tapping incessantly. August watched her from the vinyl-covered couch and cursed the No Smoking sign someone had printed in pencil and tacked next to the machine that dispensed regular doses of caffeine. How much longer could the woman keep up that damned pacing? A harried intern, his eyes puffy from lack of sleep, had told her twice now that they were doing "the best they could" for her father. She'd locked onto that intern's arm like it was a lifeline.

"Want a coffee?" he asked. Anything to stop the damned pacing.

She stood in front of the beverage machine and studied the gaudy pictures of steaming cups and thick sandwiches bearing no resemblance to the counterfeits inside. Then she fumbled in her purse. Coins scattered to the floor. Biting her lip and rubbing her hands along her legs, she watched them roll around her feet.

August sighed and pulled himself off the couch. He scooped the change from the floor and pushed some of it into the coin slot. "What do you want?"

She reluctantly punched one of the squares and a paper cup fell crookedly into the opening, followed by foul-looking streams of dark chocolate that managed to hit the container only half the time. Her hand shook as she tried to lift the cup out, spilling even more of it in the process. She emitted a little cry of frustration.

August reached around her and tugged the cup through the opening.

Suddenly she hit his wrist and sent the drink flying against the wall where it dribbled to the floor in a sticky brown trail guaranteed to infuriate the next cleaning shift. "Get out! Just get out of here!" she sobbed. She dropped to her knees, sopping at the liquid with her skirt. "Oh, I'm sorry. Please . . . just leave me alone . . ."

August watched as this meticulous, organized woman came apart in front of him. He started to accept her apology and then hesitated. Taking advantage of vulnerable people was just one of the many stinking perks of this job. He offered her a hand and pulled her to her feet. He couldn't afford any words of comfort right now. They might prove to be too expensive later. "What was your father doing in a swimming pool in full scuba gear?"

She preoccupied herself with finding a tissue in her purse and took her time carefully wiping the tears from her cheeks. Again August noticed the strange vulnerable look of her face, tears pooled in her unprotected eyes. Her chin jutted defiantly towards him. "Dad is an expert diver. He likes to practise. Living here he can't get to the ocean very often." Calmly, she pushed some more coins into the machine and punched another button. The cup slid down easily this time and filled precisely to a half inch below the brim. "I hate hospitals," she said. "I spent four months in this place when I was sixteen years old. Dad was due to be admitted again next month."

August studied the lines of her carefully neutral face. "Your father never mentioned that he still needed treatment. He's ill?"

She laughed, the bitterness of its sound camouflaged by its rarity, and stirred her tea. "Ill is a bit of an understatement. But then again — he's a master of that particular art. Probably how he kept his sanity in his job." She sipped her drink and then looked directly at him. "My father has cancer. He's been fighting it for years. I'm just worried that this . . . this accident . . . might take all his strength too soon. Take his fight."

August felt a sudden nausea creep over him. Christ! This

sparrow-like woman was scraping under his skin more than all the men he'd shoved against mental and physical brick walls over the years. All the men whose pride he'd seen piss down their legs as they begged for mercy, caught in the mesh of interrogation. Maybe it had been a mistake taking on this job. Maybe he didn't have the backbone anymore to do what he had to do.

"Did you know your father tried to drown Tony Lawson this afternoon?"

A glimpse of the shrewd professional flashed in her eyes. "He wouldn't."

"I spoke to Lawson less than an hour ago."

"Yes . . .?" She feigned disinterest.

"You know better than anyone the job I was sent here to do. There have been leaks from Pine Gap for months now. Serious, irretrievable leaks that I have to plug. How long have you been protecting your father? How long has he been a spy?" he hammered at her. "Why did he think Tony Lawson was onto him? Did Larry Fisher know as well?"

He was startled to see the frozen cynicism on her face. The soft raw vulnerability of her swollen eyes contradicted the solid set of her jaw, the sudden rigidity of her posture. "My father is a patriot, Mr. Riley. Always has been. Look up his war record. I suggest you check out your sources a little more carefully. My department has been watching David Taylor, for example, for some time now. If you'd taken the trouble to check the documents I had sent to your quarters you would have noted that."

A doctor came through the door. No exhausted intern, this man walked with an erect posture that belied the three hours he'd just spent with a human brain under his knife. August noticed that he'd taken the time to change into a fresh smock. No bloodstains and crumpled linen. Good sign or bad?

"We did what we could, Ms. Cowen." They must print a glossary of those inane expressions in the back of medical texts, August thought. "The amount of time under water." The doctor shook his head. "It brought on a stroke. Too much damage. Combined with the general state of his health . . . well, it was just too much."

Emma opened her mouth in one long, silent wail. August reached out but couldn't find the hypocrisy to put his arms around her.

She jerked violently away from him, clutching her purse to her chest as if it offered a shield from the news. "You just couldn't wait to tidy things up, could you? Find a scapegoat and pin everything on him. Well, you're wrong. But he can't defend himself now. So no doubt you'll just go about your dirty little business as usual!"

"Look, I . . ."

She branded August with a look of pure hatred that silenced him. "He might have had another six months. Six months to do whatever he had to do. But you had to come poking around here. Putting him under more and more pressure. Suggesting that he hadn't done his job properly. All the years he gave this place. All the years," she spit the words out.

And then she was walking away, the high heels a little wobbly but her back like iron.

Her look still seared him.

PINE GAP
January 31

David winced as August shoved the file like a weapon across the bare metal table. The folder was black. A neat typewritten label across the top spelled out: Atomic Test Sites. Beneath it in smaller print: Maralinga — 1956–1957 — Procedures.

"It's a copy, so don't get any funny ideas about lighting any matches," August warned. "I sweated blood to get this. Only a select few have had access."

Perspiration dotted David's upper lip but his eyes were cool, his hands folded on top of the table. He didn't touch the folder. "I know what's in it."

August sighed and rubbed a hand across his eyes. This was going to be another hard one. He hated this part of the job. His technique had always left a lot to be desired and now rusting holes in his interrogation skills might just let too much information escape. He wished Cowen was available — but she had gone to ground, mourning her father, refusing to see August, let alone speak to him.

"By rights you should be sharing a cell with the charmer I brought in from Heard," August gestured over his shoulder to the hall and the other underground caves surrounding them, "you know, the gentleman who tried to kill me. Accessory, I believe the technical term for it is." August sat down on the edge of the table. "Ah yes, a fine triad — Charles Emory to lift the material, the cretin next door to spill the blood, and you . . . what about you, David? Are you the stooge?"

"I never tried to kill anyone," David said suddenly. "Charles was sick. He'd been sick for a long time. He didn't know what he was doing."

"Look, Emory's dead. And your buddy next door has spilled his guts," he bluffed. So, there's no point trying to protect anyone — or any grand cause for that matter. This particular battle is over."

"I never tried to kill anyone," David repeated, his face expressionless.

"No. You just made sure that your hit man knew that I was alone on Heard Island." August gave a mock light salute to him. "Excuse me for suggesting that you actually got your lily whites dirty in the process." He tapped David's knuckles with the pen he was holding.

David's head jerked up. Finally — a reaction. The man's joviality had dissolved over the past few hours into a muted fear, which had then hardened into stonewalling. "I know nothing about what happened on Heard. Only what Emma told me."

August sighed. It was cool down here burrowed beneath the desert. Too cool. Neither had removed their jackets. August felt like he was suspended in some kind of surreal aquarium. The walls, ceiling, and floors were all painted the same pale blue as the iron bars in the cell next door where the prisoner was being held. Some shrink's idea of "soothing," August thought. Some shrink who, as usual, had taken a half-baked theory and shoved it down some bureaucrat's throat. Every government institution between here and Tasmania was probably drenched in the stuff.

"Well, Ms. Cowen has some other ideas about you, Taylor. You are her deputy. As such you could gain access, legit or otherwise, to everything she does. Right?"

David's hands were still folded in front of him.

August leaned forward, "I said, isn't that right, Mr. Taylor?"

"I've known Emma since she was born. She has reasons for what she says."

"Reasons which add up to a life sentence for you. It was on your shift, the shift that you rushed back from Heard Island for, with your broken leg," he pulled his mouth down in mock sympathy, "that the phony amphibious assault stuff was leaked."

August leaned back to let the information penetrate. "Life, Taylor. Maximum security isn't a pleasant place so they tell me. I understand the other inmates treat traitors just a mite above child abusers and rapists. And as I said, your friend next door is not half the gentleman you are as far as protecting his sources goes."

"He's a liar," David said.

"I think I'm looking at the liar."

"No." David shook his head. His nails were white where he was pressing them into his palm. "I don't know what you're talking about."

"You'd like to lay the whole thing on Charles Emory, wouldn't you? You knew he was on the way out, I was sniffing a bit close, so when Tony Lawson came running to you with his story you saw the perfect chance to close the books. A few nasty coincidental deaths, Emory claiming his revenge, and you had your patsy all ready to fry. But Emma Cowen wasn't going to let her father's reputation die with him. You hadn't counted on that, had you?"

"I would never hurt Emma — or Charles. Never."

"Please. Don't play the sentimentalist, Taylor. The role doesn't suit you. Because you have already hurt them, haven't you?"

August flipped open the black folder and pulled out a piece of onionskin. His eyes ran down the page before he placed it on the table and turned it towards David.

David stared blankly at the sheet. He bit his lip and blinked. "I won't even be there when Emma buries Charles," he whispered. "Charles didn't want any fuss. Emma won't waste any time on ceremony."

"Where exactly were you on October 4, 1956?"

"You know damned well where I was." David was still staring at the paper.

August stood up. "I know where you were supposed to be." He picked up the paper and read from it, "Corporal David Michael Taylor: Assigned to Road Barrier 2-C." He replaced it between them. "The brass ordered you to sound the alarm after the disastrous wind shift, didn't they? You were supposed to drive out to all the stations along the route of the wind. Evacuate the residents. Why didn't you make it to Charles Emory's home that day, Taylor? You were supposed to warn his wife that the radiation might get that far. Why didn't you make it? And what about the Aborigines who wandered through Barrier 2-C? Straight into a radioactive minefield? You weren't at your post then either, were you?"

A trickle of spit was running down David's chin. He was chewing at his lips.

"I was drunk," he whispered to his clenched hands. "Passed out in the front seat of an army pickup. It was a long drive to Charles and Phyllis's place. I just needed a couple of hours sleep." He finally looked at August, thirty years of muted despair veiling his eyes. "Tony Lawson found me eight hours later."

August sat down. The victory tasted stale.

David's hands were clenched into fists now.

"Charles Emory and his wife were good friends of yours," August said quietly. "You were best man at their wedding. Godfather to the kids. You never wanted him to find out that you hadn't warned his wife, did you? Who did find out, David? Who blackmailed you? Tony must have told someone. Did that someone tell someone else? Until one day you found yourself in a side street in Canberra giving secrets to little men with funny accents and cheap suits. Was that the way it happened?"

"Something like that."

August leaned back and closed his eyes, his hands folded behind his head. At last. He opened his eyes. "Why didn't the brass nail you at the beginning? Dereliction of duty and all that?"

"Charles put in a compensation claim. They didn't want any evidence coming forward to justify it. If it came out that I'd been ordered to warn people about the miscalculation of the wind factor then it would help his case."

"Compensation claim?"

David wiped a hand across his chin, smearing the spittle. "The twins were born prematurely, six months after the nuke test. March 19. The boy was blind. And the doctors figured he'd be severely retarded." He blinked back the tears and gazed at the ceiling. "They called him David, after me." He looked at August, undisguised agony on his face.

August picked at the edge of the folder. A sudden vision of the hawk sweeping across the plain, seizing the rabbit, flashed at him.

"He died on May 1," David said, his voice low.

"Why didn't you tell Emory? It would have been better than the alternatives."

"I was going to. But at first, well, he was like a crazy man with grief. And I thought he might kill me if I said anything. Sometimes I wish he had. Then I thought we might be able to forget it. That it might fade away. Eventually Charles did seem to forget. He never spoke of it. And then one day they called me. It was blackmail."

"Who contacted you?"

"I don't know."

"Taylor, don't make it harder on yourself than it already is — who contacted you?"

"I never knew a name or a face. We used dead letter drops. But I swear I never told them anything critical! It was usually just stuff from the personnel files. Weaknesses — drugs, gambling, sex, that kind of thing. That was my main beat in security. Not the big time stuff. I swear it!"

"What about Tony Lawson? Could it have been him? He stayed around Pine Gap for a few years after the tests. Regular trips back here?"

"No. Tony's not a bad guy. He just wanted a quiet life. He sobered me up that day. Made me promise to never take another drink. And I didn't. Not for years. Not until . . .," he shook his head and continued, "besides, it wasn't in Tony's interest to squawk either."

"Why not?"

"He was on the Appeal Board. He'd been promoted by then. Tony was always an expert paper pusher. If Charles had succeeded in getting his claim established, it might have meant hundreds more veterans coming forward. He knew the brass didn't want that. Tony was strictly a yes man. And he just wanted an easy route out of the army."

August leaned back, scraping the metal nub of the ballpoint along his teeth. "I want you to do something for me, Taylor," he said. "Something that will keep you out of jail for a little while longer."

"What?"

"Take me to meet Phyllis Emory."

"Phyllis?" David's face was white. "You're not going to tell . . .?"

"No. Not yet. Not if you cooperate. I want to see what she has to say."

"But Phyll and Charles were divorced eleven years ago. Charles has always looked after her but . . ."

"That might be for the best. Long enough to be over the bitterness. But she was married to him for a long time. Long enough to have a vested stake during the time he started spying."

David shook his head and moaned a little, "I don't know. Phyllis . . . I don't know . . ."

August seized the big man by his shirt. A button popped onto the table and rolled to the spotless floor. "I don't know if you tried to kill me or not, Taylor. But we're going to see

Phyllis Emory. You are going to introduce me as an old friend. And you're going to be convincing. If you don't think you can quite manage that you can say good-bye now and join someone who I do know tried to kill me." He shoved him back down into the metal chair.

David dropped his head between his hands, his knuckles white and thick, pressing like a vise. August turned away and fought to stay erect. He felt nauseated. He wanted to collapse into the other chair and drop his head in the exact same gesture. Instead, he punched on the bars to signal the guard. The privilege of self-reflection was a distant luxury he'd traded in several years ago. He couldn't remember exactly what he'd bartered it for.

10

DR. AHMED MAHER'S LABORATORY
February 1

The hissing always bothered Ahmed. Perhaps in a few years technology would mute the sound of oxygen pressing into the mask. He squinted against the reflection of the laboratory's overhead lights. The plastic eyeshield exaggerated the glare as he concentrated on transferring the lethal toxin from the culture dishes and Plexiglas tubes to the alternative containers he'd brought with him. In the years of working legally with those deadly substances, Dr. Ahmed Maher had never had an accident or even been cited for a marginal safety violation. The habits gained then held him steady now.

Ever since Ahmed had recognized where the new pioneering science lay, he'd been meticulous and properly paranoid about the devastating effects of the materials he manipulated every day. He was one of a handful who had the courage to buck public opinion and push the work wherever it would go, delving into the mysteries of the biological magic that could be plucked from the earth. He'd abandoned the radiation field fairly early, turning away from his more conventional colleagues in disgust, and rediscovered the heart of the explorer and true scientist in the researchers who were willing to spend years gathering the cobra's venom drop by drop or patiently collecting and grinding thousands and thousands of shellfish to gain a few grams of the deadly poison saxitoxin.

His hands, encased in a second skin of surgical gloves, were steady as he carefully filled the three vials held immobile behind a glass partition. Almost done. Yes, three vials for Desert Storm ought to do it. The toxin in them would be enough to cover the battlefield in corpses. Enough to force the imperialists to think twice before carrying their wars and enforced borders into the twenty-first century. They weren't dealing with illiterate tribesmen anymore.

Ahmed painstakingly retrieved the vials and moved slowly towards the exit, stepping carefully across the spotless floor in his rubber boots. The heavy urethane suit that encased him was awkward and uncomfortable. The hissing from the spring-coiled tube that hung from the ceiling to supply oxygen followed him towards the door. It was getting hot under the mask. Just another few minutes and he could remove it.

Ahmed poured the drops of the powerful toxin into the small thermos-like containers. Every drop was worth a fortune. One drop could infect a thousand victims with a twentieth-century version of the plague. Half a cup could infect New York City. Or Tokyo. Or London. It was a weapon more lethal than any sword or gun. Less precise, perhaps. But precision was not the virtue needed for this task. Numbers were what counted.

Slowly, he screwed on the tops of each canister, tightly ensuring that no microgram could escape. The containers had been molded from one clean line of metal — he'd managed to secure a prototype during his last visit to Fort Detrick, Maryland. The U.S. Army's Medical Research Institute of Infectious Diseases provided its staff with the best.

The next step was tricky. The two casings had to be attached to the cans perfectly. But the copies made from his stolen prototype were exquisite. They'd been crafted by a fine artisan Ahmed had met in Hong Kong; the man had known the value of his work and had charged accordingly. Ahmed hadn't objected. He would have paid much more.

The last thermos slipped into its casing.

Secure now, Ahmed let his breath slip a little. The hiss filled his mask. Slowly, he carried each container through the rubber door leading from the experimental area, working in slow motion. Now was not the time to rush. He changed his latex gloves before pulling the toxins through the last section.

He studied each can, holding it up to the light, as if it were fine crystal: the two tins — Black Knight Shaving Cream (for sensitive skin) and Casino Deodorant — and finally the tin of perfume encased by smoky glass made from the same material as the space shuttle's windshield, Fatal Attraction, the latest scent pushed by the latest over-madeup, underdressed actress.

He'd see to Zaid's suitcase himself. If there was a way to get him out of that prison cell, Kestrel would find it. The customs man, or hopefully woman, would take one look at his brother and find it more than likely that he'd be carrying an expensive bottle of perfume as a gift for some paramour. And as for his shaving cream and deodorant, a suitably exclusive brand.

Ahmed pressed a cap tightly over each container. Done. He placed each into a basket hanging from a hook in the centre of the room. The basket was lined with cotton wool and had an elongated handle, which he placed around his neck, cradling the containers against his chest. He stepped carefully towards Air Lock 1 and punched a code into the control panel. The door opened with an abrupt sucking sound. He punched another command into a side nodule and, taking the canisters out of the basket, pushed them through to the next air lock. Lifting the basket from his neck, he stepped out of the urethane suit and stripped naked.

He picked up each discarded latex glove in turn and blew into them. To his relief the gloves stayed almost comically puffed up. No leaks. He stepped into a small cubicle that locked automatically behind him. The shower felt good, erasing the exposure from him.

One more task left.

His hair still damp, Ahmed pulled on a one-piece overall and a pair of cloth slippers over his feet just to be sure. No point in taking chances at this stage. He zipped the overall up to his neck and placed a surgical mask over his nose and mouth before punching a command to pass through the last air lock into the holding area.

He always hated the smell in here. A tight automatic bark from one of the newer dogs as he stepped inside. They usually learned within a few weeks that barking would never be relevant again.

It took Dr. Maher less than five minutes. The last was the big ape in the far cage. He'd existed in that corner for three years. Ahmed had gained a grudging respect for the creature. None of the others had survived that long. It turned its grey grizzled face away from him as it held its pockmarked arm out for the syringe. For one last time.

RHAPSODY STATION
TWO HUNDRED MILES EAST OF ALICE
SPRINGS

Rock hard sand crumpled under the plane's wheels as David Taylor guided it to a rough landing. The afternoon sun slammed into August as he pulled himself out of the cramped passenger seat. Dust stung his eyes. David climbed from the cockpit and led the way towards a large wooden house that seemed to sit reluctantly in the midst of the dry grassland surrounding it. Hydrangeas covered by a film of grit were lined up in low tubs crouched around the sprawling verandah. A few had already choked to a premature death during the last sandstorm, their husks scattered over an otherwise spotless wooden floor.

The middle-aged nurse who peered through the screen door studied the two men as if to measure exactly what amount of harm their visit would cause her patient. "Mrs. Emory is not at her best. It's been a difficult few days."

"Don't you worry, Maureen," David assured her. "We'll keep it as short as possible."

Inside, the hydrangeas' perfume was replaced by the sickly sweet odour of antiseptics and old medicine. Dust-collecting china — delicate ballerinas, clowns, poodles — covered every surface. But dominating the cluttered room was a portrait of a tall soldier in an Australian Air Force uniform standing proudly behind a seated woman in a flowing blue gown. White blonde hair curled to her shoulders and her head was tilted coquettishly.

"That you, Charles?" a shrill voice penetrated the drowsiness of the afternoon. "Maureen! Did I hear Charles come in?"

August and Taylor exchanged quick glances. "Does she know about Emory?" August whispered.

David looked worried. "They buried him yesterday. But Phyllis gets things mixed up sometimes."

The nurse frowned as if all her worst suspicions had already been confirmed. "No, Mrs. Emory," she called. "It's Mr. Taylor come to see you." The smell of disinfectant was overwhelming as she opened the door into another room.

"I know. I know." A giggle came from the fragile figure seated in a chair by the window. "I've been watching them, haven't I?" Phyllis Emory gestured outside. The makeshift landing strip and small plane could be glimpsed through a jungle of plastic plants that crowded the window ledge. She held an empty watering can in her lap. "I knew it was David, didn't I then?" And in a gesture of surprising elegance she offered her hand to David, who even more surprisingly, lifted it and brushed his lips against the blue-veined fingers. She waved the nurse away with her other hand.

"Hello Phyllis, dear," David said heartily. "Got someone here who wants to meet you. Friend of mine. August Riley."

The startling blue eyes turned on August. With a shock he recognized the now raked features of the girl in the portrait. "Very pleased to meet you, Mrs. Emory."

Her face clouded over with sudden suspicion. "What do you want?"

Taylor pulled a chair up next to her, sat down, and placed a hand gently on her shoulder.

"They all want something!" she snapped at him.

"Phyll, Mr. Riley wanted to meet you."

"I might not want to meet him. Did that ever occur to you?" With one arthritic hand she pulled a tightly knit shawl roughly around her shoulders.

"May I sit down, Mrs. Emory?" August gestured towards the other chair.

She shrugged and placed the watering can carefully on the window ledge, muttering as she stroked the broad leaf of a wilting plant that sat amongst its plastic imitators.

August sat down and offered her a cigarette. He'd noticed the yellow stain fouling one of her fingers. She glanced tentatively at him and withdrew one delicately from the package. "Those quacks in Sydney try to tell me that these things are killing Charlie," she said indignantly. "But I know better. I know better," she clucked.

A tingle of anticipation chased across the back of August's neck. The sun beat through the open window onto the bare wooden floor. Years of its relentless heat had bleached a wide patch in the wood. The room was silent. "What *is* killing him, Mrs. Emory?" he asked gently.

"Bloody Brits . . . bloody, blood Brits . . ." A tear fell onto her paper dry cheeks. August had an impulse to stroke it away. "Are you a Brit?" she demanded accusingly. And then the flash of anger dissipated and she jutted her chin forward for August to light the cigarette.

He obliged.

"Charlie was a volunteer for that nasty business. I warned him not to go." She pursed her lips carefully around the cigarette. "I said to him — what's the point of volunteering for things you don't know what they're all about? That's what I said to him." She inhaled deeply and looked at August as if expecting an answer.

"What exactly did your husband volunteer for, Mrs. Emory?"

She sighed impatiently. "I just said, didn't I? The tests? Away out in the desert they were. Maralinga." She shook her head. "Pretty name for such dreadful things. Maralinga . . . means field of thunder, you know. That's what the Abos called it. Quite right too." She nodded vigorously. Her hand shook as she puffed furiously on the cigarette. "But Charles was a grown man. He could take his own chances. But he had no right to risk me. Me and the babies. No right!"

"Don't fret yourself, Phyll," David patted her gnarled hand.

She pulled her fist away and tossed him a look of total contempt. Leaning towards August she hissed, "Don't fret yourself, he says! Don't fret yourself! When your babies . . . their own father risks them." Tears were streaming down her cheeks now. "Two months later little Davie was in a white coffin! Natural causes the quacks said." She snorted. "Natural causes! I don't believe it. And neither does Charlie. I'll say that for him, Charlie doesn't believe it either." She stubbed the cigarette out violently on the arm of her chair. The armrest was covered with burns.

Suddenly, she looked straight at August. "Charles would never admit it. But the same thing got him in the end, didn't it? Didn't it?" The sour smell of the butted cigarette hung in the air. Her face was a map of deep ravines. But her eyes were blazing. "The Brits got Charles in the end as well. That fancy Sydney doctor told him he has six, maybe eight months. I knew Maralinga would catch him. It just took longer to get him than our baby, that's all." Her words were fading as if she could only sustain short powerful volts of anger.

"What do you think killed . . . is killing your husband, Mrs. Emory?"

"Evil's killing him. Evil, evil things. That radiation . . . living in us for all these years." She shivered and scratched at her arms. And then her eyes were calmly sane. "After awhile I knew that it was better that my boy went so fast." She coughed harshly. "But we only wanted the Army to admit it," she said, years of resignation in her voice. "That's all we ever wanted. Just for someone to admit it. Some peace of mind for Charlie. It was too big a burden of guilt for him to carry alone. Someone else was guilty as well. They never apologized. They never told him what really happened. They never told any of us."

Taylor stood up suddenly. "You're getting tired, Phyll, old girl. We'd better go now."

"Yes." August stood as well. Not much point in torturing an old woman any further with her memories. He could get all she had to tell him out of a dry, black file with no tears.

"You're a nice-looking man," Phyllis said to August. "Not as handsome as Charles in his prime, though. Oh, not now, of course. Oh no. Not now. All skin and bones now. You're not as tall either. But handsome . . .," she drifted off. Again August caught a glimpse of the girl in the portrait. "David," her head jerked up suddenly, command in her voice.

"What is it, Phyll?"

"Pass me my handbag. It's on the mantel there."

Taylor retrieved a creased leather bag from between an over-sized porcelain poodle and two brass candlesticks. She rummaged through it before lifting out two photographs wrapped in yellowing tissue. Her face creased in a smile as she peeled back the paper. "Would you like to see my children, Mr. Riley?" she asked, rubbing a thumb over and over the images.

"Yes. Very much."

She squeezed his hand as she passed him the pictures.

One was of an infant, tufts of blonde hair sprouting across his skull, eyes squeezed shut, fists clenched tight, a stuffed koala tucked next to him. "That's Davie," she said, glancing with affection at David. He nodded halfheartedly, a sickly smile contorting his face. "We named him after David." The other photo was of a girl about three. Serious looking for a toddler. Her mother's curling white hair. "And that's Button. She doesn't like it when I call her that now. But I had to give her another name, you know. Emma was a silly name. Emma Emory. But, you see, I wasn't thinking clearly then — at the christening, I mean." She pointed carefully at the photo. "That's Button."

"Beautiful children, Mrs. Emory."

She took the pictures back and studied them as if she'd never seen them before. "Charlie doesn't like me keeping this picture of Davie. Bad memories he would always say. Bad times, he said." She carefully tucked the photos back into her purse. "I have one of Charlie here in his prime. You'll see what a handsome man he was."

David looked desperately at August. "Phyllis, I think we'd better be going . . ."

Still ignoring him she pawed through the bag and thrust another photo towards August. "See what a fine figure of a man my Charlie was?"

August took the faded photograph from her. The man she pointed to was exceptionally tall, arms folded across a wide chest, his face creased by a smile, and a thick crop of hair pushing out from beneath a narrow cap. He was leaning against what looked like the verandah of this same house.

"Oh God, look at me!" David laughed. "And look at Tony. Damn it — I think he looks better now than he did then!" An almost unrecognizable Tony Lawson leaned against David. Several other men smiled self-consciously into the camera. Sand drifted at their feet. Phyllis was holding her daughter on one hip, jutting her other hip provocatively towards the lens and smiling vaguely.

"The day of the barbecue," Phyllis said, pointing at the picture. "Charlie smiled a lot that day. I remember because it was the first time I'd heard him laugh a nice big laugh since Davie died. He had a marvellous . . ."

"Christ . . .," August muttered.

"What is it?" Taylor said.

"Please. Mrs. Emory. May I?" August eased the photo from her hand. A small protest passed her lips.

He jabbed at the picture. "There . . . that guy there. It's the goddamned prisoner I'm holding at Pine Gap. The creep who tried to kill me!"

David furrowed his brow. "What are you talking about, Riley? This was taken thirty years ago."

"There!" August jutted his finger at the picture. "Him!"

Taylor looked at August. "Can't be. That's Ahmed Maher, chief biologist on the Maralinga project. Studied the effects of radiation on insects and crawlies in general. Spent most of the time with his eye glued to the end of a microscope safely behind the trenches as far as I can remember.

"That's him, I tell you! I spent five hours cooped up with the guy yesterday. Do you think I wouldn't recognize him?"

"But the man is nearly sixty now! It's either a ghost or his son. And as far as I know he married for the first time quite late. They had a boy about four years ago the last I heard from the gossip mill. So that's certainly not his son you've been looking at."

August stared at the photo. "Maybe not. But this man could be a twin to the guy sitting in that cell in Pine Gap." He tapped the picture. "It's got to be a relative," he whispered.

"Like I said, Maher kept himself to himself. Settled for awhile in the States and then opened up his own consultancy on civvie street. Never was much on reunions or anything. But he did come from a large family. The wedding was quite a do. Must have cost the wife's relations a fortune. Over in the Mid-East somewhere I think."

"Where in the Middle East?"

Taylor shrugged. "Don't know." He peered closer at the picture. "Listen here — you're not saying . . .?"

"Yes. I'm saying that this Maher — whoever he is — sent his double to kill me. Probably because he realized that I was closing in on Emory." August snapped his fingers. "And now I have a key to that little creep I've got rotting in Pine Gap. A key I can turn and turn until he tells me all his contacts."

"You mean Ahmed Maher — and Emory."

"And probably you as well, Taylor. You are most likely looking at your Control. The man who has milked you for information for the past thirty years."

Taylor nodded, a great weariness aging him in front of August.

Phyllis Emory suddenly lunged towards them. "Give me my picture back!" she shouted.

A brief rap at the door. Emma Cowen strode into the room. "What's going on here?"

August turned and found himself looking into Emma Cowen's hard, blue eyes.

THE MAHER RESIDENCE
The Same Day

Zuleika lifted Gawain to his perch, unfastened the hawk's jesses, and lifted his hood. Today's hunt had been disappointing. He'd lost interest after one kill, flying listlessly from her arm, taking freedom reluctantly as if aware that his brief flight would only result in return to this comfortable cage. They'd come home early. Usually they stayed away until dark, losing time and memories in the stony neutrality of the hills and desert sand. She had no sentimental attachment to this dry, unforgiving terrain. But it held the echo of her girlhood. Running with her hawks. Exploring for hours on end. No future worries and no past responsibilities to curb her. Her father had been an indulgent man who had, much to his later sorrow, cultivated his child's spirit, never imagining how far from his heart it would take his daughter. He cursed the day he'd allowed her to attend an American university. She'd returned unrecognizable to him.

Zuleika laid the carcass of the bloodied pigeon on the wide feeding perch she had made. Gawain poked at it once and then withdrew. The hawk's eyes followed her apathetically as she removed the thick leather glove that covered her left hand to the elbow. She took a fresh cloth from the pile folded in a corner and moistened it in a pail of stagnant water. Stroking Gawain's thick dark talons, she inspected them carefully for the minute signs of disease. Her hands were darkened from hours in the Australian sun, her palms scratched and bruised from following her hawks amongst the thornbush, clamouring up cliffs and into hollows after prey. Catching sight of her nails, bitten to the quick, she remembered the manicures, the gold bracelets, and the rich rings, the softness of life in her father's home. Her life before Ahmed, before Khalaf. Her life before they had given it purpose. Now she had come full circle. Drifting in whatever valley of air lifted her, carrying her without design through the long days.

Gawain allowed her to stroke his feathers, indifferent to her touch. The hay and sawdust beneath her feet rustled in the still afternoon air and the bird keened softly. The air was thick with dust mites as the late sun slid through the open door. Zuleika sneezed. Gawain blinked lazily.

A scratching sound drew her gaze to the arcing glass roof she'd had installed to increase the light in the aviary, add some illusion of free space. But the pane was streaked with dried dust, only adding to the gloom inside. Squinting, she could see something rubbing against the grimy glass. A rustle above. Gawain moved restlessly on his perch. A peregrine falcon was moving above them. Zuleika raised her hand to shade her eyes. A shadow crossed them. The falcon was gone.

She offered Gawain some water, but he turned his head away. She prodded the dead pigeon towards him again. He shuffled farther down his perch. She moved the water around in the bowl. The stuff from the pipes out here had looked a little rusty lately. She'd go to the house and get some fresh from the kitchen, maybe lie down for an hour. She hated this time of day. It had been one of Khalaf's play times. They would always have a swimming lesson and then sit by the pool snuggled in a big towel and she would read to him. Maybe she'd pack up some of his books tomorrow.

The kitchen was cool and dark. Khalaf's clumsy sketch of an eagle was still taped to the fridge. Zuleika had left it there in the hope that if she confronted her pain every day it might gradually diminish. So far it hadn't worked.

The house was quiet. Too quiet. Something was different.

She turned her head from side to side, listening.

The generator. It was the generator. The one that fed all the outbuildings and Ahmed's laboratory. He must have turned it off, plunging the house into this thick silence.

She moved through the quiet rooms. The drapes in the living room were drawn tightly against the afternoon sun. The green blue water of a large aquarium bubbled softly. The door to Ahmed's room was open. She walked in slowly. It was a long time since she'd been close to her husband. A long time since she'd entered the room where he slept.

A suitcase lay open on the bed. An empty frame that had contained a picture of herself and Khalaf, taken on his third birthday, was the only item left on the top of the cleared dresser. Her heart flip-flopped. She closed the door and searched the suitcase. Three tickets to London were wedged between Ahmed's carefully folded shirts. Zuleika picked them up. Stamped February 4. One in Ahmed's name. One in Zaid's. The third, a name she didn't recognize. Puzzled, Zuleika studied the tickets before tucking them back into the suitcase.

Her hand brushed paper beneath a light sweater. She pulled out the picture that had been in the silver frame. Her own image had been carefully cut from it, leaving only Khalaf's smiling face looking into the camera. She stared at the mutilated photo for a long moment. Very carefully, trying to control her shaking hands, she replaced the torn picture exactly where she'd found it.

RHAPSODY STATION

"Shit!" August muttered.

"May I help you, Mr. Riley?" The nurse wrinkled her nose and pressed her square, white hands against her spotless shift. She was standing in the doorway of the converted pantry, which served as the isolated station's radio room. She held herself slightly away from him as if he might be one of her contagious patients.

"This damned thing! Is it missing a battery or what?" August bent over the radio, the receiver clamped to his head. "All I'm getting is static."

"Is this your outgoing call number?" She looked at the paper where he'd scribbled the code.

"Yes. The International operator keeps interrupting — squawking at me to dial again."

The nurse reached past him, careful not to touch him. "You haven't tuned in your station properly," she admonished, superiority emanating from her like a sixth sense. "One has to know what one is doing with these machines. You must appreciate that they aren't toys." He hadn't noticed the forced British accent before, the affectation of a woman who didn't really know where she belonged. "We don't usually get a lot of interference, you know."

August knew. One of the reasons Pine Gap had been built in the middle of nowhere was because of the outback's ideal receiving conditions for any radio, satellite, and for all he knew, UFO signals that were being tossed around up there.

The nurse twirled the dial expertly and mixed and matched several knobs. Static and a wailing country and western ballad scraped the air.

The red on-call signal suddenly went into overdrive. August raised his hand as the familiar code of NPIC dotted the air waves. "Thanks. Thank you. I owe you one, nurse," he said abruptly, dismissing her.

Disinclined to spend any more time with him than necessary, she hurried from the room, muttering about the rudeness of "some people." She nodded to poor Miss Emory as she came into the hall. The girl's eyes were red-rimmed and puffy. This family was cursed. But Maureen had stayed as long as she had, although she'd die before admitting it, partly because these people made her own life look a little less futile. Maureen eased past Emma. Sympathy was not really well received in this house. Besides, she had the supper to start, since Mrs. Emory had invited these vulgar men to stay for a meal. They'd accepted, David Taylor reluctantly, the American a little more graciously, his eyes darting intrusively around the house.

Emma leaned against the wall, watching August as he bent over the radio.

It took him ten minutes of shouting into the line to convince Jack Andrews, the graveyard shift switchboard operator at NPIC, that he was who he said he was. And another five for Jack to figure out that Jamie Watts was at home, still in bed.

August didn't waste much time on long-distance apologies to Jamie. The kid was up anyway, pouring a fresh round of sunflower seeds into the bird feeder. And as far as Jamie was concerned, if August Riley wanted to send him on a drive up the highway to check out some dude named Ahmed Maher, that was okay with him. He had the choice of that or an enforced visit with Nellie's mother.

He picked up the phone to make his excuses to Nellie.

11

RHAPSODY STATION
February 1

"Won't you let us even grieve in peace?" Emma watched him, her eyes narrowed. "I buried my father this morning."

"After what Taylor told me, I had to find out if your mother could confirm anything he said about the Maralinga tests." August glanced around the room. The wallpaper was the faded choice of a young girl — pink roses and lilac butterflies. A small reproduction of the portrait of Charles and Phyllis Emory that August had admired in the living room was hung above the bed. Current affairs magazines spilled from the side table and the pine bureau in one corner was curiously free of feminine clutter. A few sticks of makeup, an old-fashioned matching brush and mirror backed with tiny grey and pink shells, and next to them an odd-shaped piece of Styrofoam. A formal photograph of a graduating student with a boyish face was pushed to one side.

She was watching him now. "Your curiosity satisfied is it, Mr. Riley?" He started to protest and she waved away his explanation. "This is my mother's home. The place where I grew up. I resent your intrusion at this time. As you have discovered for yourself, my mother is mentally ill. She's tolerating your presence because she doesn't know any better. But I don't have to. We aren't on working hours now."

At the far side of the house a canary warbled unconvincingly and the muted sound of the nurse's soap opera drifted from her room next door. "Look, you know I was sent to Pine Gap on a job. A critical job — one that I intend to complete." August shifted the file he was carrying from one hand to the other.

Emma sat down on the bed. "Even if it means harassing a man's family before he's cold in his grave?"

"Yes."

She pulled the shapeless sweater that hung around her shoulders closer. "God! You people are disgusting!" He didn't like the slick whiteness of her skin and the barely perceptible trembling beneath the starched collar of her pale blouse.

August tapped the file. "If I turn this mess about your father over to Washington now they'll have every big cheese down here on the next flight. You'll have some politician nosing around trying to make the evening news. Then before you know it, he'll be chairing a goddamned committee and that means everyone from the director of the CIA to the office assistant who fetched your father a cup of coffee in 1980 will know that he was a spy! People who are bound by oaths of secrecy love to wallow in gossip. I don't have to tell you that."

She was picking at a loose button on the sweater. "That's the way it's going to be in any case. Sooner or later," her voice was rough and the cords in her neck stiffened like restraining devices for her anger.

"It doesn't have to be. Do you think anyone wants these leaks revealed now, with a war being fought? If you tell me what I have to know we can bury it, maybe permanently. Your father's dead. The leak is plugged. But I have to make a report. And I have to know where, when, and why. If I take that back with me I can satisfy Washington. I can go camping again and you can get on with your life." He looked into her tired, wary eyes. "Tell me or tell a Congressional Committee."

She twirled the loose button on a single thread.

August despised himself for the realization that immediately gripped him. This was a moment he'd never get back, the optimum moment to mine her. In an hour she'd hate him and regret every word she'd said. "You can hand in a quick resignation. Give your version of events, your regrets, and so on."

The button fell into her lap. "I didn't know what he was doing until recently." Her eyes were hard, challenging August to deny it. Something about her primly folded hands and the wisps of hair at her neck touched him. He said nothing.

She stood up, walked to the bureau, and tugged open the bottom drawer. She pulled out some pale silky material and tugged it roughly over the Styrofoam block sitting on the dresser. Its featureless round face stared back at them from beneath the wig's long waves. "This is a souvenir, Mr. Riley. A souvenir from a time before I was born." She pressed her own thin hair back against her skull as she turned to look at him. "My hair used to be my vanity. It was down to my waist. My father brushed it every night when I was a girl. It grew back after the treatments, of course," she laughed roughly. "Just like they said it would." She curled her fingers around the wig. "Real hair, you know. Only the best.

"Sometimes I think that's when it really ended for him. The day he came in here unexpectedly and saw me without my wig for the first time. I think of all the shocks he'd had in his life that might have been the worst. He even fought the throat cancer. But this," she looked at herself in the mirror and reached out to curl one golden wisp of the wig around her blue-veined finger, "this really did get my father down."

"Did the illness . . . the hair . . . have anything to do with Maralinga? With the death of your brother?"

"My mother was pregnant when they detonated at Maralinga. The wind took an unexpected shift and dumped the radiation directly on our Station. My brother died when he was six weeks old. My father never talked about it. Over the years I gradually got the story from Mother. Sometimes she thinks she's still there.

On the porch, in the outback, the day of the test. You see, poor mother is a perfectionist. She could never accept bringing less than a perfect child into this world. I suppose we all look for reasons outside ourselves for our little tragedies." She turned her faded blue eyes on August and he was struck by the hint of guarded cynicism he glimpsed there. "But reason usually doesn't have much to do with life — or death, I suppose."

She picked up the photo on the bureau. With one finger she tenderly traced the outline of the student's mouth. "Scott E. Cowen," she said, holding the picture away from her as if examining it for the first time. The sweater fell from her shoulders. "We were married for five years. He left me when I finally got up the nerve to tell him that I'd had a complete hysterectomy when I was sixteen."

She put the photo back. "Scottie sells real estate in Nevada now. He's got three children." She turned to August. "After he left, the effects of my father's illness really started to show. I had to watch him even more closely. He never trusted the Base doctors."

"That must have been difficult," August didn't have to force the sympathy into his voice.

She shrugged. "It gave my day a structure. A reason to get up in the morning. He needed me." She looked at August. "But people like you wouldn't understand that. You know exactly why you are getting up in the morning, don't you?"

"Not always," August said softly, picking up the sweater and placing it back around her shoulders, "not always."

She hesitated. "His work at Pine Gap had just been show for a long time. They didn't want to discharge him because they knew, being Dad, he'd make a hell of a stink. He'd kicked up a fuss when they wouldn't cough up any compensation and he'd continued to kick up a fuss every chance he could over the years. I kept Dad quiet and let him feel important by sharing some of my work." She smiled to herself. "But I guess the old devil was cleverer than I thought. He was helping himself to stuff behind my back while playing the eccentric. He had his revenge in the end."

"Not really."

She looked at him.

"It's over now. The leak was caught before he could do any real damage."

"Yes. I suppose you're right."

August quickly filed his relief away from her eyes. "Who was your father's contact?"

She frowned. "How would I know that?"

"Weren't you watching him?"

"I told you — I only just realized what was going on myself. I hadn't sorted out what to do yet."

"But you said it had been going on for years?"

"I thought it was David Taylor. I knew he was weak. A gambler. I kept him from the top-secret information, the really black stuff. I thought he might make a good decoy. And David was easy to mislead with misinformation."

August rubbed his hands over his eyes. "Why did your father try to kill Tony Lawson?"

"The same reason that he killed Larry Fisher. They were all connected to the committee that put him on his knees begging for funds to get us through the years after my brother died. They kept our misery stoked. He must have thought they were sadists. I don't. I think they just didn't want to spend the time — or the effort." Her voice was flat. "And then a year ago the specialists told me that things weren't getting any better. They were sharpening their scalpels for me when I walked in for the checkup. I didn't usually discuss it with Dad but I was in the hospital for three weeks and he found out. That's when he saw me without the wig. He changed after that. Stahel was found in the well a month later. I suspected Dad but didn't want to believe it. Then when Fisher was killed last week I was certain."

"Why didn't you stop him?"

"I didn't want to." She looked at August, a hint of defiance in her eyes. "They deserved it."

"You could be charged as an accomplice."

"Prove it."

August tossed the file on her bed. "Some reading material there for you. You might be interested." He walked to the door. "I want an official statement before you resign."

She shrugged and picked up the shell-backed brush and drew it through the wig. "You know where to find me."

August closed the door behind him. The soap opera was silenced and the canary had stopped singing.

Emma crouched at her father's grave, her hands wrapped around her knees. There was no marker yet. As usual she'd have to take care of it. Her mother had remained in the house with Maureen during the funeral, watching a Lawrence Welk rerun. Her off-key humming of an old waltz had drifted over the chaplain's intonation. The ceremony had been short and unadorned as she'd promised him. She used her influence to claim his body immediately and called in a favour to fly the Base chaplain and two commandeered gravediggers to her mother's home. Phyllis had fed the chaplain coffee and pancakes and only her brief glances towards the window betrayed that she might know that a grave was being dug.

But Emma wouldn't have time now to order the stone. Her father would have understood. He didn't put much credence in the so-called afterlife anyway. That was why he'd decided to take the bastards with him. If only she'd known. She would have helped him. Her father's revenge had burned with a clean fire. Her own was so abstract, so cold. Who was it who said, revenge is a dish best served cold? It wasn't quite true. The taste had soured after awhile. But by then Ahmed Maher had her. And she could never let him know. But she still needed him. Just awhile longer. She would make one more phone call to keep him close and ensure their reluctant partnership.

Ahmed Maher. All this time. The silent dealer as he'd been even at Maralinga. Using them all as experimental animals, living data banks for his research. He'd taken the guinea pigs of Maralinga and built a career on them. He'd taken her angry naivete and built a library of secrets on it.

And David. Her convenient scapegoat. Sweet, harmless David. The Santa Claus of her girlhood, smiling and stumbling through their lives. His betrayal neatly typed out in August Riley's stark file. Her friend from childhood directly responsible for the pain, the loss of everything that might have been. For more than thirty years eating at their table, taking their confidences, and even once, Emma knew, just after the divorce, sleeping in her mother's bed. David. This tore away what was left of her soul.

The single white rose she'd left on the grave lay crushed by another heavier bouquet. She pulled the bud from the dirt and smoothed its petals. There was still time to strike one big bonfire for her father — and for her family, the family which had never really existed because of a mistake the British made thirty years ago. They'd never even apologized. But she still had time.

Now they were strutting arrogantly into yet another distant country. Ready to push and shove their vision of the right way. Understanding nothing about where they were going or who the people they sought to dominate really were. Her father had understood. She'd learned her history at his knee.

Emma ran her nail along the flower's stem. Milky foam spilled onto her fingers. She'd worked her life away for ten years trying to make him proud. And he had been. Although he'd never said, she knew he had been. She could never replace the son he missed so much. Never Davie and all he might have been. But a good second best.

And now this American. This August Riley. Sweeping down here ready to organize them all to death. Ready to take over just when everything should be finished. He saw her only as the victim; it didn't occur to him that she might fight back. It was her great advantage. The reason she was an expert in martial arts. Her size, her manner, her hidden attitude. She'd broken the arm of a drunk who attacked her in the cells one night. The look of surprise as she'd pinned him with her one-hundred-pound frame, sick as she was, had been totally satisfying.

She placed the crushed rose carefully back on top of the tulips and carnations. A handful of plastic ferns jutted from a bouquet of heather. The sight of the stiff plastic jutting from the sandy earth rose like gall in the back of her throat. She stood up and wrenched it from the grave, bending it between her hands over and over again.

★ ★ ★

"Let me take mother's supper in tonight." Emma lifted the tray from Maureen's arms.

The nurse straightened the linen napkin next to the plate and placed three small prescription bottles beside the glass of milk. "Make sure she takes two of those." She pointed to each bottle in turn. "And one each of those, or she won't sleep tonight. Not more than one though, mind you. That Dr. Wyatt gave her far too strong a dosage this time in my opinion. Although far be it from me to have an opinion," she sniffed.

"Potent are they?"

"Yes, too potent, if you ask me. But as I said, Dr. Wyatt doesn't seem to think it necessary to ask me very much." She wiped her hands on a tea towel as if she could wipe out the doctor and his malpractice. "And your mother will insist on dispensing them herself." She smiled indulgently. "She doesn't like to be babied, Miss Emory."

"But she is a baby now in many ways, Maureen, isn't she?"

The nurse shook her head sadly and turned back to scraping the skim from a caramel pudding cooling on the counter.

Emma stopped at the door. "Why don't you take the rest of the evening off, Maureen? I'll see to our guests. You've already made the dinner. All I have to do is serve it up."

"Well . . . there is a Command Performance on television tonight. From London. Julio Iglesias."

Emma smiled. "Enjoy it, Maureen. I appreciate all you've done over the past few days. Don't worry about Mr. Riley. I'll take care of him."

Maureen turned from the stove, one hand catching a drip from the ladle, "If you really don't mind?"

But Emma was gone.

THE MAHER RESIDENCE

Ahmed stepped out into the blazing light of the afternoon. The deceptively light aerosols were cradled in the basket, shaded by the brim of a large straw hat. One of the hawks keened as he approached the aviary. They were probably getting hungry. But he'd made sure Zuleika would be off on one of her expeditions today. She'd taken the jeep early that morning, her favourite hawk in the back seat. He suspected she'd gone to contact that man in Darwin, the illegal smuggler, despite his warning. Ah well, it didn't really matter anymore.

"Ahmed?" His wife stepped from the shade of the aviary, her eyes questioning, hooded with anger. She took a step towards him, peering into the basket, and then searched his face. "Where are you going?"

Dr. Maher looked at his wife. He had loved her once. She was still a beautiful woman, despite the way she dressed and held herself so defiantly from him. A tender nature easily obscured by the quick, angry words that came so easily to her now. She knew nothing about his work. She cared only for her son and her birds. He'd planned to leave her with plenty of money and the property.

She knew nothing. So she could tell nothing. But that was yesterday.

He wished she hadn't come back so early.

Later, Zuleika never knew what made her reach out and grab one of the metal containers. But the look on her husband's face told her she'd found a weapon. The sun was dropping fast and she could feel the cold metal of the container as her fist tightened around it. "What is this?" she demanded.

One hand reached towards her while he tried to balance the other containers. "Zuleika," his voice was low, cajoling, "my work, Zuleika. Leave it."

She backed towards the aviary, pressing against the hatch door. "Where are you going? Why have you taken that picture of Khalaf? That's all I want to know. And then you can have your precious tin can back." She pulled the canister against her body. Ahmed's eyes followed it. A streak of fear raced through her but desperation leapfrogged it and transformed it into determination. Straw rustled beneath her feet. She pushed the hair from her eyes. It was almost dark in the aviary. But she knew every splinter in its wood, the crack in the mesh wire of each cage, the beam that needed sanding in the end enclosure.

Ahmed removed the basket from around his neck and placed it slowly on the ground, his eyes never leaving her. His calm threatened to overwhelm her. Frighten her into submission. She rushed to fill the silence. "Just tell me," she appealed to her husband. "Just tell me why you are leaving now. Tell me about Khalaf. That's all I want to know." She reached behind her with one hand and undid the bottom hatch door, bumping it inward with her hip.

"I go away all the time, Zuleika," his voice was caressing as he walked towards her. "This is just another trip." He shrugged. "I admit it's a spur of the moment thing. But I would have told you."

She fumbled at the upper latch. It was unlocked. She pushed it open and stood in the gaping doorway, the aviary lost in twilight shadow behind her. Gawain twittered in alarm from his perch. "You liar," she cursed the tremble in her voice. To compensate for it she thrust the can towards him.

Ahmed jerked back, pulling his hands towards his chest, clenching and unclenching his fists. "Zuleika, please, understand. That material you are holding . . . it is . . .," he hesitated and then held his palms outward, open as if offering up all he knew. "It's dangerous, my dear."

She broke into a sweat.

Ahmed took another step.

She moved quickly behind the hutch door, swinging the lower half back as a crude barrier between them.

"You shouldn't be near it," he said. "I was transferring them to the toxic disposal area."

"Why was my picture cut from the photo?" The trembling slithered into her chest, and she wound the fingers of her free hand around the mesh of Gawain's cage for support. Ahmed was standing on the other side of the hutch door, his eyes hidden in the gloom.

"Ah, Zuleika," he seemed resigned. "I used to admire your curiosity about the world. But it can be a very bad thing for a woman. And now it has led you down a dangerous road. You really shouldn't have gone through my private things. It isn't like you." The low monotone turned to a growl. "You really shouldn't have."

And then he had pushed the hutch open and was plunging through the aviary after her, Gawain screeching in protest as Zuleika's fingers tore at the mesh of his cage.

U.S. ARMY MEDICAL RESEARCH INSTITUTE OF INFECTIOUS DISEASES FORT DETRICK, MARYLAND

Jamie was surprised at the benign look of the place as he drove along the streets. All red brick and genuine antique — a town where he might have taken Nellie for a stroll any Sunday afternoon. The sun had come out, coaxing the vines that curled around several of the buildings into a few false spring shoots. He rolled down the window as he drove. The Appalachians lay in a hazy mist cradling the town. He loosened his tie. Didn't seem much like a home for biological warfare research — more like a fifties time warp. He half expected Beaver Cleaver to come strolling down Main Street.

But he recognized Fort Detrick when he saw it. The cluster of new houses at the edge of the stark subdivision jutted abruptly up against a cold chain-link fence crowned with barbed wire. Jamie eased off the accelerator as a small girl, legs pumping furiously, pedalled a tricycle along the sidewalk beside the road. A dog had poked his nose through the fence, ears cocked towards the crows foraging in the fallow fields on the other side, fields in which crops were planted and nurtured, only to be destroyed with experimental agents.

They were expecting him but it still took twenty minutes for the military police to snap a photo ID and stick an official pass to his windshield. The sun seemed colder by the time they'd finished. He'd had a chance to notice the fenced-off areas that could only be animal pens and corrals, empty in the fading afternoon light. A group of plain buildings ran alongside them, their plainness bizarrely abated by the convoluted maze of pipes and ventilation ducts twisted around them. Pipes and smoke-stacks protruded into the air like the skyline in a futuristic movie.

He took a deep breath as he parked in the spot pointed out by the artificially pleasant MP. His smile seemed as out of place as the insanely grinning Garfield toy clinging to the window of the guardhouse. This building looked like a three-storey bunker choked up from beneath the ground. Its sandy surface couldn't hide the fact that it was constructed from concrete, and its few windows looked like machine gun slits from World War Two bunkers. No catastrophic leak was going to escape this nest if the ants who'd constructed it had anything to do with it.

Jamie tightened his tie again and tried not to hold his breath as he entered the building. He kept repeating to himself the litany of how reliable these joints were, how safety measures were built in. All that stuff. They couldn't run them if they weren't safe? Could they? He pushed back the four hundred instances of accidental infection in the past fifty years or the two litres of some weirdly horrible African virus that had dis-appeared. He tried not to think about the fact that this research facility contained a laboratory which had been designated BL-4 — Biosafety Level 4, maximum containment facility. There were only four of them in the United States, and any-one working in the bowels of those places did so dressed in a getup suitable for a walk on the moon.

The guy who'd known Ahmed Maher obviously wished he hadn't. But then he looked like he wished a lot of things hadn't. Dr. Grey stayed scowling over a file on his desk for a full minute after Jamie announced himself. When he did acknowledge Jamie's presence, it was only to wave him into the chair opposite, still scowling. His face was one of those that had looked old since he was ten. Jowly and pale, with the kind of skin that has to be shaved every few hours, and black hair slicked back with some kind of smelly gel. His white coat bris-tled as he moved. A tape recorder was rolling next to the in-basket.

Jamie reached over and turned it off. "Sorry, Dr. Grey. This conversation cannot be recorded."

The other man's features fell deeper into the scowl. "I'm required to tape all transactions in this office. This is sensitive work we're doing here you know, Mr. . . .?" He raised his thick brows skeptically as if doubting any identity Jamie might claim and reached to switch the recorder back on.

Jamie was quicker. He covered the buttons first and met the doctor's eyes. "Sorry, sir. No can do." He reached inside his top pocket. The doctor jerked back.

God! The fool thought he was going to pull a gun! Jamie flipped his identification onto the desk along with the phone number he'd scribbled on a piece of paper after August had dictated it to him. He leaned back into his chair. "If you call that number Dr. Grey, you'll get the office of the Secretary of Defense." He nodded towards the silent machine. "Someone there will confirm the confidentiality of our discussion."

"Well then," Dr. Grey thrust a moist lower lip outward and glanced over the top of his bifocals at Jamie's ID. "Of course, I will tell you what I can. But it isn't much. I haven't seen Dr. Maher for . . .," he chewed on his lower lip, "must be five years."

Jamie pulled out a notebook and lifted one of the doctor's pens from the brass mug on his desk. Grey's eyes followed his move. "Why did Maher leave here?"

"He didn't follow protocol."

"Protocol?"

"Yes. We have enough trouble with public relations as it is. Maher was brilliant but he was always going too fast, too soon. He was an impatient man."

"What was he working on?"

Grey looked suspicious again. "Toxins," he finally said reluctantly.

"Toxins?"

The older man pursed his lips in disapproval and leaned forward, hands clasped on his desk, and spoke slowly, emitting each word carefully as if Jamie had to lip-read. "Yes, toxins.

Poisons. Usually produced by bacteria but also found in natural substances like snake venom. Red Tide, for example. Manifests itself in certain shellfish favoured by trendy West Coast types."

Jamie wrinkled his nose. There was nothing he liked better than a good clam chowder. He bit on the end of the pen. Grey watched distastefully. "Shellfish?" Jamie repeated the word as if he hoped he hadn't heard right.

Dr. Grey tapped the desk. He was starting to enjoy this. Not often he got to show off. Amongst the airy-fairy crowd his wife liked to wine-and-cheese or barbecue with, it was definitely not socially acceptable to discuss biological and chemical weapons over the canapés. "Oh yes. One gram from the Alaskan butter clam's little arsenal will kill five thousand people." He was rewarded with a nervous gulp from Jamie followed by some hurried scribbling on the notepad. Dr. Grey continued. "Francis Gary Powers — the U-2 pilot shot down over Russia . . .?" Jamie nodded. "Had that stuff in his suicide pill, you know."

"No, I didn't know."

"Oh yes," Dr. Grey was warming up now. "At one time this lab gathered together more saxitoxin than has ever been in one place. Mind you, quite a few Alaskan butter clams had to sacrifice themselves for the cause." He actually chuckled.

Jamie wondered if this was like that black humour supposedly indulged in by medical students during dissections and the like. "And Dr. Maher was working on these . . . these toxins, was he?"

Grey drew back as if disappointed to be turned from his subject. "Yes. Mainly the aerosol applications."

"Aerosol?"

"Yes. You know there's no defence against the tiniest microbe of a deadly germ. The general public is quite right to be scared witless about it. One spray could wipe out hundreds of people. Nasty sort of death too, I can tell you."

Jamie thought he'd rather the doctor didn't tell him. "And you don't do that kind of work here?"

Grey's soft little face looked like a potato too long in the back of the cupboard as he rolled his fat lips upwards and held a pudgy hand in the air. "Strictly defensive research here — have to know how to defend ourselves. We're what you might call the Star Wars of biochemical warfare. Misunderstood but critical," his tone had taken on tinges of self-righteousness. "But we wouldn't mind half the funding they get. Star Wars, that is."

"So Dr. Maher didn't want to stick to the defensive stuff?"

"I wouldn't say that, exactly. He was ahead of the government, that's all. People couldn't keep up with him. Like I said, he was impatient. I tried to talk him into going out to Dugway, in Utah. They've got a good setup there. But by then he was so discouraged with the bureaucracy that he just wanted out. Left honourably, no problem there. Very nice party we had for him actually. Pretty wife. Younger than him, mind you. I danced with her."

"Where did he go then?"

Grey stared at the ceiling and pursed his lips. "Well, he didn't really keep in touch. Not much of one for sending Christmas cards or anything. But then neither am I . . ." Jamie tried to keep from leaping out of his chair while Grey chewed his lip and smoothed the front of his already smooth white coat.

One finger pointed slowly to the ceiling as if tracing a pattern there. "Yes. I do believe he went to Australia. Someone told me he'd pulled some strings and got a government grant to do more research. Of course, he might have arranged a private deal for all I know. Lots of odd types interested in our work," he said reluctantly.

Jamie was clicking the pen nib in and out. "Where in Australia? Do you know?"

"Not really sure. Think his wife was pregnant. They wanted to set up house somewhere — get away from it all type of thing. Seems he'd done some important work years ago, right after the war I think it was, down there. Might have been Alice Springs?"

Jamie was on his feet, still clicking the ball-point pen, other hand extended. "Thank you, Dr. Grey. Appreciate your time."

Before Dr. Grey was out of his chair, Jamie was marching down the tight long hall to the exit. The scientist mumbled discontentedly and fell back into his chair. The so-and-so still had his pen.

12

THE MAHER RESIDENCE
February 1

The wire mesh stung Zuleika's fingers as Ahmed pulled them from Gawain's cage. She jerked away from him and bolted down the length of the aviary, the empty cages flashing in light and shadow as she fled towards the rear door.

Ahmed was behind her, his feet slipping on patches of straw scattered over the cement aisle.

She gripped the canister as if rigor mortis had set in. Punching the door open, she ran into the stifling outside air, speeding from the aviary around the back of the house, past the pool, tripping over the bamboo furniture. Her loose sandals slipped in the water that had slopped over the side of the pool. She stumbled across the patio and through the open French windows into the living room, almost tipping over the aquarium. The fish swam in tight, frantic circles.

Ahmed was crossing the patio now. The unnatural tap, tap of his leather-soled shoes moving across the tiles coming closer and closer. The long, thick drapes at the patio windows, especially designed to shield the room from the afternoon sun, were pulled partially closed over another set of decorative lace curtains. She ducked behind them, resisting the impulse to pull them close around her. The drapes swung across her body in a brief breeze. She held her breath, the canister still tight at her chest, and flattened herself against the wall, praying that the dance of the wind wouldn't betray her.

She glimpsed Ahmed standing at the patio door, one arm resting on the door frame, staring into the darkened room. His breathing sounded harsh and angry. His eyes swept the still rolling water of the aquarium and then dropped to the floor. Zuleika bit her tongue to rein in a cry as she watched his eyes follow the trail of her damp footprints across the white carpet, to the edge of the drapes.

A roar rushed from her lungs and she wrenched the drapes from their railing, heaving them over Ahmed. Clawing the net curtains from her face, she ran back across the patio, past the change room and towards the garage, remembering with horror that her keys were still in the house. She dashed around the far wing.

And then she saw it.

The treehouse! Khalaf's treehouse! It sat in an old eucalyptus that shaded the guest bedroom, neat and freshly painted green as he'd wanted, tucked into the high branches of the old tree. A galah flew in a flash of pink from the roughly cut window.

Her feet slipped on the wooden ladder, designed for a child's feet. The tree trunk seemed maliciously smooth, denying her any hold as she clung to it with one hand, the other still cradling the canister. She pulled herself up to the level of the treehouse's miniature door. The step cracked and swayed under her weight. It would never hold her all the way to the top.

She could hear Ahmed's footsteps coming across the wet tile of the pool, the dry bricks.

She'd need two hands to pull herself in.

Slowly she eased the canister up and over the lip of the doorstep. And then the step buckled, sending her sliding down the tree, her cheek burning against the bark.

And then she was running, tripping into the unfamiliar

territory behind the garage, the far wing of the house that had never been used. Ahmed had demanded the area be left undecorated for privacy's sake. The trail ended abruptly at a solid metal door leaning into the ground, and the earth behind it sloped away into some kind of an underground bunker. She'd been out here once or twice during construction. Ahmed had pointed out the advantages of underground rooms in this climate — the improved temperature control for his work, the quietness, fewer distractions. But it was unrecognizable now since the days when the dust of construction and stench of welding tools had sent her back to the house as quickly as possible. Dark weed and stringy grass had gradually grown over the building welts and from an aircraft the area would seem no more than a minor rise in the earth.

She pushed against the door. It was locked. She flung herself against it, pounding with her fist.

"Where's the canister, Zuleika?"

She backed against the steel door. It was unforgiving. "I dropped it. Back there. By the pool. I was frightened." Her voice touched close enough to hysteria to camouflage the lie.

"You've always been curious. Now's your chance." She could feel his breath on her neck. He pulled out a key and unlocked the door. It swung open. Almost gently, he pressed her forward. She felt her feet moving beneath her like automatons. There was nowhere to go.

It was over quickly.

One more push, not gentle this time, and she was inside the black cave. A pungent odour of wild and dark things and then she was sliding down the cold wall, descending into tears and the black silence.

The phone started to ring as Ahmed was walking around the far side of the pool, the shaded side where he could see into its depths a little easier.

His first impulse had been to plunge in and grope along the bottom of the pool for the canister. But he had to stay calm. Do this methodically. The container might already be eroding. It was very strong. But not designed for a chlorine filled swimming pool. Besides, he couldn't risk the irony of contaminating himself.

He tried to shake off the sound of the phone jarring through the hot afternoon air. Crouching down, shading his eyes. Nothing.

He straightened up and started towards the house. The phone stopped its irritating insistence. As he started towards the shed where some long poles were kept that might be used to sweep the bottom of the pool the ringing split the air again.

He got it on the second ring.

It was Kestrel.

The time had come.

RHAPSODY STATION
February 2
5:00 a.m.

"I shouldn't be doing this. Even for you Emma, my girl." David Taylor shifted the throttle on the plane and hauled them into the sky.

"I thought your loyalty lay with the family, David?"

"Yes. But this . . . this is different. That August Riley. When this gets out . . . when he gets back to Washington . . ." David's head was pounding. He cursed himself for that first long drink. He hated wine anyway. Why had he allowed himself to be coaxed into it? He could never refuse Emma anything. His guilt had always carried a heavy price.

As they circled Emma watched the small blanket of shadowed flowers that marked her father's grave. "Mr. Riley won't be getting back to Washington. If he isn't dead now he will be within a couple of hours."

"Dead?" The blood abandoned David's face. "Oh God! Emma . . . oh God . . ."

"He knew." She glanced at David with contempt and tightened the black scarf she'd tied around her head. "Don't worry.

He never felt a thing. His caramel pudding — the glutton helped himself to a second helping — was topped up with a dozen of Mother's more potent pills. He simply won't wake up tomorrow." She went back to studying the view from the window and chewing one nail. "Oh yes, he played the sympathizer all right, but he knew." She turned towards David. "You never should have brought him here. It wasn't good for Mother and look where it's led me. Not to mention where it's led you. Four glasses of wine last night. And all that babbling at the table. You really did embarrass us, David. Mother went to her room in tears." She twisted her head to watch the station house disappear from view, its sprawling outbuildings suddenly dwarfed as the plane gained altitude.

"Babbling?" David risked a glance at his passenger and saw the disapproval he was dreading there. "What did I say?" He wasn't used to seeing her without makeup. Emma was usually so meticulously turned out. Even at Emory's funeral she'd been pressed and primped, the lips neatly outlined, the nails carefully manicured. Now she looked pale and even smaller than usual, the blue-tinged skin under her eyes like thin paper. He suddenly felt a wave of tenderness towards her. She'd shyly offered him her dolls to play with when she was a girl. He'd held her hand in the hospital when she was sixteen and they'd ripped her apart. He'd hugged her when that no good husband had flown the coop. She'd been like the daughter he'd never had. He'd loved her mother more than a little when Phyllis's blonde curls had fallen over her forehead and Charles had been his idol. Emma, Phyllis, and Charles — these ravaged people had been his family.

"All drunks babble," she said cruelly. "What can you expect with your first drink in . . . how many years?" The little muscles at the edge of her mouth were twitching. "More years than I've known you," she answered for him. "But I understand. The pressure must have been unbearable having to jump to Riley's every command. A stronger man than you would have broken."

"But good God . . . Emma . . . I mean killing . . . actually killing . . ."

"Don't be a fool, David," she said, clutching at her seat as the plane bounced through turbulence. "As soon as he got back to Pine Gap he would have had us both arrested."

"Us?" David's eyes widened as he rode the craft over another gust of wind. Only the desert outback stretched below them now. An endless road wound somewhere far off to the left, quickly drowning in dunes of crabgrass and grit.

"Yes, us. Did you think that I didn't know what you've been up to all these years? And now he's caught me as well. The best lawyer in the world won't get us off. You know that. We'll have to get out of the country."

"Maher had you in his pocket as well?" David whispered, blinking hard to concentrate on keeping the plane level as each shock wave hit him.

"Who had who in the pocket is debatable but irrelevant at this point. The main thing is, we still have something that Ahmed Maher wants badly enough to oversee our freedom."

"What? We're useless to him now that Riley has stopped us. Even if he's dead, sooner or later word will get back to his masters."

"We have Maher's brother sitting safe and sound in a jail cell." She looked at David. "Worth his weight in gold, wouldn't you say?"

"We'll need more than money," David said, trying to beat down the hope that was rising in him.

"The passports are ready. One of the advantages of my job, David. Only trouble is your choice of destination is Brazil — or Brazil."

David allowed himself a shred of hope. Maybe, just maybe, he could do it. Do what he should have done when he was a young man. Leave this damned country and the past behind him. He'd served his penance and served it well. "What about Phyllis?"

David didn't see her face crumble. "Maureen will see to her. She loves my mother. She's been with her for twelve years. Half the time mother thinks she's me anyway. I'm sure Maureen knows her better than I do."

"How will we get Maher's brother off the Base?"

"Don't worry about that. As far as anyone else is concerned, I'm still in charge of security at Pine Gap. We're returning early from my father's funeral, that's all."

"What about Riley? He'll have told someone by now." David's head was starting to pound again.

"No, I don't think so. The man had a streak of arrogance he tried very hard to hide behind that modest manner. I don't think August Riley is the type to announce his coup until he was sure. And he wasn't sure until tonight."

"Well, I'm not sure. Not sure at all," David said.

Emma watched the desert brightening in the early light and smiled slightly as a kangaroo, flushed from the scrub by the churning of the plane's engines, leaped away from them, its joey wobbling in its pouch.

February 2
9:00 a.m.

The gold-rimmed eye, unblinking and bold despite the human's dangerous proximity, stared at August. He hesitated. The climb had been hard. Harder than he'd expected when he'd taken Sam's dare. But now he could see the falcon chicks. Only a movement away.

A deep flutter of alarm shivered across the gyrfalcon's body as she rose slowly from her protective position, still following his nervous gaze with her clear, dark one. She was snow white except for the coal black streaks slashing the tips of her wings. August had never been this close to wildness before. The gyr's winter plumage was so full it seemed his hand would sink to the wrist if he plunged it into her breast. But the talons jutting beneath the stout, muscular legs were the well-honed weapons of some mediaeval warrior, sharpened by season after season of survival on the lip of the Arctic.

The nest smelled of fresh kill.

"Hurry up, August! Move your ass — or we're in big trouble with my dad!" Sam yelled from below.

"Shut up!" His foot slipped on the barren rock and August scrambled

to regain a hold on the narrow cleft. Stones dislodged from under his feet and tumbled to meet the plain.

"It's gettin' cold," Sam moaned.

August's eyes shifted from the gyrfalcon's bold gaze to its offspring. The two chicks were huddled together. Feathers sticking from their bodies at strange angles made them look like victims of a high-voltage shock. Their embryonic wings shivered, and one chick started to chatter. The falcon spread her wings, feathers fluttering in nervous anticipation. She still hadn't sent a warning into the cold high air around them. Instead, her energy seemed concentrated in the deceptively gentle movement of her great talons, in and out on the hard bed of the rock shelf.

"Come on down," Sam's voice was a whine now. "We're in big trouble. My dad's gonna kill us if we don't get back before dark." He jumped up and down, his round, red face peering up at August from beneath the baseball cap pulled down low on his forehead.

The cliff face scratched against August's cheek and the smell of moldy excrement rubbed his nostrils. His lips were dry in the cold air as his fingers inched towards the closest chick, pushing aside the limp carcass of a freshly killed squirrel. The bird opened her thick beak and let out a low, harsh cry. The hard muscle of her legs contracted as she rose slightly over the aerie, her wings almost a burden as she hovered, her shriek gaining in intensity now.

The flesh of August's hand suddenly seemed terribly vulnerable. The first chick squawked and scuttled away from him, dancing perilously close to the ledge, its stubby wings pumping impotently. He reached for the other one. It was more passive, but still a few inches from his grasp. The female hovered above, the beat of her wings churning the darkening air.

His hand closed around the chick's fragile body. Bones brittle as fine china. Tufts of silky feather spotted his fingers.

The female screamed and dived.

August jerked back, his feet slipping beneath him, scrambling to retain his narrow perch. But his toes in the thin city shoes had lost their edge. He clawed at the rock.

Nothing.

The hard earth rushed to meet him.

The screeching gyrfalcon rose and dove over her violated nest.

"*Jeez! August! August! You okay?*" *Sam scurried to his friend, stumbling over his untied laces.* "*Answer me!*" *His flushed, moon-shaped face stared down at August.*

August groaned and rolled against the rock.

"*Oh shit,*" *Sam moaned.* "*Shit! Talk to me!*" *His friend's body rolled like a rag doll as he shook him by the shoulders.* "*Don't be dead. Please . . . don't be dead! You can have my Davy Crockett rifle. Just don't be dead!*" *His voice threatened to strike a wail and his plump lower lip was trembling violently.*

"*I won the bet, bullethead!*" *August was grinning, one eye wide open.* "*I got up there. You owe me a buck.*" *He rolled over on one elbow, ignoring the way his ankle splayed at such an odd angle.* "*Pay up. A buck or the Crockett rifle.*"

Sam groaned and punched him in the arm. "*You never got an egg. That was the deal.*" *He leaned back on his heels, embarrassed now.* "*That was the deal,*" *he repeated defiantly.*

August slowly opened his scratched, bruised hand.

The chick lay, paper thin and tender in his dirty palm.

They both stared at the ball of white fluff, the pink skin still obvious beneath the down.

"*That's a gyp.*" *Sam's lower lip trembled.* "*That's a real cheat. It's gone and died on us.*"

The bird's fragile neck rolled against August's fingers. He stroked a needle thin blue vein, a strange new emotion rising in his chest. "*It was me that did it. It was me that killed it, Sam.*"

August came to choking on his own vomit, a bullhorn pounding his name in his ear. "Mr. Riley! Wake up. Wake up now, Mr. Riley! Now, I say!"

He retched again. "Good! Very good!" Someone was lifting his neck and thrusting a bowl under his chin. "That's all right. Get it out! Get it all out!" He rode the systolic wave of his guts and thought he was going to turn inside out as he heaved over the edge of the bed and tumbled to the floor into his own muck. He rolled over and lay on his back, weak as a baby, sweat pouring down his face, the vomit trickling into the corner of his ears. He didn't have the strength to even wipe it away.

And then a coolness was soothing his humanity back over him. His eyes began to focus on Maureen who was crouched beside him, her thick stockings brushing his face, one hand under his neck, the other wiping his mouth. He felt like burying his head at her breast and begging her to rock him to sleep. Instead, he groaned. "Jesus. What happened to me?" His brain felt like it had achieved total separation from his body.

"Come on, get up. Get up. Now!" she ordered.

He collapsed back to the floor. "I said now, Mr. Riley! I don't want to put my back out lifting you. Get yourself up." Her voice was devoid of whatever sympathy he'd been looking for. He groaned again. "You have to get up immediately. Miss Emory and Mr. Taylor have gone. The radio's destroyed. The distributor caps from the car and the truck are missing. So you better get up and do something about it. I can't get a doctor for you. And if Mrs. Emory has some kind of emergency I have to be able to reach him. So come on now. Get up!"

This time she nudged his leg with her foot. It felt numb. Her words rolled around his head like cue balls on a pool table. It was serious. He knew what she was saying was serious.

"In a minute, Maureen. Just give me a minute," he whispered, his throat unbearably sore.

She dumped the pail of water over his head.

It was lukewarm. But he jumped to his feet, cursing and shaking himself like a dog.

She reached out to steady him. "All right now?" she asked gently. "Sorry. Had to do it, Mr. Riley."

He pushed the hair from his eyes and tried to dredge up some remnants of his shredded dignity. "Yes, well, forgive me if I don't thank you." The inside of his mouth felt like he'd just staggered out of a bungling dentist's office. He wiped his sleeve across his face. "What the hell happened to me?"

She looked shamefaced, as if she was responsible. "It seems you must have taken . . . been given . . . some drugs. Mrs. Emory's supply has been tampered with. Must have been in your supper last night, Mr. Riley." She shook her head. "I'm awful worried. Mr. Taylor, well, I've always liked him. But now . . .

he's fallen off the wagon. I could hear him last night crying and carrying on so loud he disturbed my program. All those terrible things he was saying at dinner got Mrs. Emory in such a state. And now he's taken Miss Emory." Tears pushed at the corners of her eyes. "He's kidnapped her. I just know it."

"What's this about the radio?" August asked abruptly. He didn't have time to debate David Taylor's character.

She led him from the room. Wires hung from the radio's innards like colourful spaghetti. He fell into the chair in front of it. "And the car — the truck? Out of commission as well?"

"Yes. I'm afraid so," she said regretfully.

Sudden hope jerked August's features into an eager question. "When do your suppliers deliver? The mail, food, fuel, that kind of thing?"

She bit her lip and nervously smoothed the flowered shift she wore. "Next week. Bobby Harmon brings the bulk food order next Wednesday."

August picked up one of the dangling wires. It had been sliced straight through. Its copper jagged out at him. He turned it around, over and over again, against his finger, until it started to tear a red patch in his skin.

PINE GAP
9:30 a.m.

David waited in the jeep outside the jail, his hat pulled down over his eyes, praying that he wouldn't see anyone he knew.

She'd gone in alone. They both recognized it was for the best. He knew he'd never be able to pull it off. Ned Durand was on duty today. If he looked at David the wrong way it would all be over. He'd be inside that cell next to Zaid Maher spilling everything they could drain out of him. But the price he'd paid for his lack of nerve was to be handcuffed to the steering wheel. Emma said she had to make it look good. After all, he'd been a prisoner of August Riley the last time he'd left here. The hair on his arms stood up even though it was sweltering outside. Damn it! How much longer was she going to be? Was she talking the latest football scores with Ned or what? He couldn't stand it a minute longer.

Emma had barely spoken to him since they'd landed the plane. But she'd had a lot of shocks lately. He could understand it. He kept telling himself he could understand everything. He just had to do the smart thing for once in his life. Another few hours and he'd be out from under Maher. A new life. Enough money. Never set foot on this lousy continent again. Emma might come with him. Not impossible. She didn't really have family now either. Maybe? He allowed himself to swim in the thought a little longer as he felt the heat prickle on his neck.

The door to the jail was pushed open and Emma came out. David's heart skipped when he saw the huge guard behind her, dwarfing her tiny frame. They knew. They were coming for him now. He started to whimper.

And then he saw Zaid. Behind Emma. Handcuffed. Shadowed by the guard.

Emma strode to the jeep. Not looking to either side. Or at David. She swung open the door. Zaid climbed awkwardly into the back seat, a look of frightened anticipation tracing his features.

"Thank you, Corporal Richmond," Emma said briskly, as she climbed into the driver's seat. "I can deal with the prisoners now. They're needed over at Admin." She released David's cuffs from the steering wheel, still not looking at him.

The guard saluted and she turned the key. They drove silently from the compound, only the sound of sizzling tarmac and Zaid's jangling cuffs disturbing David's racing thoughts as he pressed a hundred questions back down his throat.

PLENTY HIGHWAY

August's feet felt like one big blister, the fiery road eating through the soles of his boots. He'd tramped the five miles from the Station to the main road leading to Alice at a quick march and was paying for it now. The rim on his hat was molten iron squeezing him into unconsciousness at any moment. But he couldn't chance removing it and inviting heatstroke. He'd passed the entry gate to Rhapsody Station, a plain wooden sign, two names, Phyllis and Charles, burned into it with some kind of branding iron, hanging still as death.

The tarmac held a meaner heat than the dirt and gravel side road from the Station. August shoved his hat back and cleared the sweat released from the dam around his eyes and hairline. Some sporadic relief was offered where low dunes of sand and scrub drifted over the road's boundaries. The evidence of smooth tarmac meant that vehicles were travelling through here regularly. At least that's how he would like to interpret it. Otherwise, he was facing two hundred miles of baking heat and an unmerciful sun shimmering against the horizon.

He unsnapped the canteen of water he'd slung into a pack and forced himself to sip on it. Rationing was a necessity. He had no way of knowing how long he'd be out here. He wiped his streaming head and the back of his neck again, adjusted his hat and sunglasses and stared down the road. Its monotony taunted him with glimpses of mirages to come.

He began to walk, a deliberate pace this time. Trying to wipe his mind clean, trying to forget that he was somewhere smack dab in the middle of a wild continent that civilization had tentatively prodded before pulling out in a hurry. He passed the abandoned shells of two vehicles beside the road, one, the remnants of an early model Honda, looking like the carcass of some mutant ladybug, gouges of dark rust all over its roof and sides, the other, a van, its side door hanging at an angle. They were nose to nose just off the road. Both windscreens glinted with jagged edges, and chunks of glass lay in heaps around the bare tire rims. Spinifax grass sliced through the empty space between the window frames. As August passed, watching from the side of his eyes, he half expected to see a skeleton sprawled across the interior of the van. But instead only the rags of a blue sleeping bag, haven for snakes and insects, and a rusted camping stove tipped on its side met his gaze.

He adjusted the pack and strode on, feeling a monotonous ache getting ready to settle into his long-ago broken ankle.

He heard the radio blasting Van Halen before he heard the car's motor. A roar and sputter. He turned around, walking quickly backwards. "Please," he muttered, jutting his thumb out. "Please!" If he got a ride now he'd make it back to Alice before dark. A Chevy jounced over the horizon, four teenage boys hanging out of all four windows. Including the driver's. They waved and hooted at him, leaning on the horn. The one in the front passenger seat was leaning towards him like a mediaeval knight on a charge waving what looked like a jousting stick.

But it was no goddamn jousting stick.

The kid had a rifle!

August hit the ditch, rolling into its shallow shelter just as the .22 went off. An echo of shots ricocheted along the dirt. Puffs of sand rose in the air above him and fell on his shoulders and neck.

Screeching laughter as the car bounced ahead.

Sand was slipping into August's mouth and the pack pressed against his back. What seemed like a thousand camouflaged insects started crawling from the sand. He forced himself to press his chest closer to the ditch. And then he heard the radio again, a screaming guitar electrifying the air. Sweat seared the side of his face into the ground. Four against one. No matter how amateur they were — if they were amateurs — he was no match. Not four against one. Maybe his fear of the skeleton had been a premonition . . . it was his own bones he'd seen scattered amongst the rags in the van.

He could hear the Chevy weaving back and forth above him. "Hey mate!" one called drunkenly. "Didn't mean to scare the piss out 'a you. Thought you was a 'roo!"

Two others joined in the chorus. "Thought you was a kangaroo!" they screeched, laughing hysterically.

The heavy metal music was pounding in his ears now. The car throbbed exhaust into his nostrils. A door slammed. That heavy, solid thump of an older model.

August shoved his knuckles into his mouth. He remembered a ditch on the Czechoslovak border in 1968 when he'd been a young and very naive student, a cheap guidebook tucked under his arm. And in the right place at the wrong time to guide a defector across the frontier. He remembered the cold. The taste of stagnant water as a guard stood over him. The warm wetness of his bladder surrendering his dignity. Wondering if he was going to die before he was twenty. They'd shot the defector right there in that stinking ditch. A physicist who'd survived Dachau and loved jazz and wanted most of all to see New Orleans.

August had reminded the guard of his son. And so he had spared him and instead lectured him about the error of his ways as August watched the snow fall into the physicist's vacant eyes. And the guard, with pointing finger, like a mother telling her son to dress warmly, had instructed August to carry the message of what happened to defectors who tried to avoid "official channels." He'd left August to stare at the button from the physicist's coat which lay in the mud after they'd dragged the body away. He'd crouched in that ditch for two days and one interminable night. August hadn't forgotten the message. He'd distrusted "official channels" ever since. And he still carried the button.

The punk was standing over him, scratching his crotch and dragging the rifle butt in the dirt. A boy in the back seat pounded his fist against the side of the car. "Come on, Jacko! Let's go! Quit wasting time."

"Hey mate!"

August forced himself to look up.

Scuffed boots, untied laces spilling to the ground. Scratched muscular legs. Torn shorts. Bare chest, ten years' worth of sun branded over the skin. A dusty, dirty face. Bright eyes. Not more than sixteen.

"Hey you!" the kid prodded him with the gun. A boyish grin. "Hey mate! Just joking. Lighten up! Come on, you want a lift?"

August dragged himself to a standing position. All eyes were on him now. It felt like every bone in his body had been chewed up and spit out by a combine harvester.

"Yes. Thanks." His voice was surprisingly steady. His knees unbuckled. They felt as if the marrow had melted.

"Hey! A fucking Yank!" someone shouted from the back. "A goddamned fucking Yankee! No wonder he's wandering around here like a fucking loser in the middle of nowhere!" A hoot of derision.

The bright-eyed youth jumped into the passenger seat. The dashboard vibrated from the impact of the booming speakers. The back door swung open, and the smell of too many beers and a lot of vomit and stale chips fell over him. August hoped he wouldn't upchuck the rest of whatever pills Emma Cowen had pumped into him. Mind you, that might just be the initiation rite that would prove his manliness to them. "Bloody well jump in then, fucking Yank," the rough voice from the back called.

"Yeah, we haven't got all fucking day!" A chorus of indignant agreement.

August swung the pack over his shoulder and wiped his brow with the back of his hand as he walked towards them. The open door swung violently on its hinges. Four wild laughs and a deafening roar from the dead muffler as the driver stepped on the gas.

The Chevy swung wildly up the road, leaving a trail of black rubber branded across the pavement and August by the side of the road choking in a veil of hot exhaust.

NEAR PINE GAP

The lizard jerked its head back inside the angry ruffle of scales at its neck and flicked its tongue at Zaid. He pulled his bare feet from the floor and curled back on the sagging mattress, resting his head on the stained wall. It had been a long time since he'd seen a desert lizard. The mattress creaked. The woman's head swung towards him. He drew back further. Last thing Zaid wanted to do was draw attention to himself. The lizard blinked at him and then with an abrupt, erect march disappeared through a torn piece of plaster in the wall.

The other man muttered something to get the woman's attention. Zaid squirmed. Why here? He tried to tell himself that this must be a government safe house, a place to carry out more intensive interrogation. But the peeling walls, the rat droppings, the saltbush scratching at the steps when he'd stumbled up the verandah, all denied his frantic optimism. And there was no electricity.

They had brought him here to kill him.

"How do you know Maher will go for it?" David glanced nervously at Zaid huddled on the bed. The man seemed explosive to him. Docile and cooperative on the surface. Ready to lash out at any time. He wished Emma had kept the handcuffs on him.

"He has no choice."

"But Maher might just say go to hell! Keep my brother!"

"Would you?"

David shrugged. He was exhausted. But Emma had a bright, manic look as if she could stay up for days. Her hair stood out in a bizarre halo around her head, and her eyes were clear, focused somewhere beyond his shoulder.

"Maher's family is important to him. It's one of the things we had in common."

"In common?" David felt a very real prickle of the hair on the back of his neck.

"Oh yes. Over the years we talked about family a lot. His ambition was to return permanently to Jordan and bind the family of the Middle East together. And to achieve that he'll need to get the Hail Mary plan out of Australia. I intend to help him do that. My interests have always been less grand, of course. I just wanted a couple of people to be happy." She watched a red ant totter across the scarred wooden table under the burden of an acacia seed. "And what about you David? Who do you want to make happy?"

"Myself!" he said, glad for the chance at a feeble joke.

She nodded, her index finger right behind the ant. "My mother and father. You didn't think it would make them very happy if you told them about your dereliction of duty on the day of the nuclear test?"

"Pardon me?" His voice was hollow and too high.

"You shouldn't go near the booze, David. It's poison to you. You should have remembered that," she said sadly.

"Did I . . . did I . . .?"

"After the third glass, I think it was. You don't even remember Mother slapping you, do you?"

He cleared his throat. "No . . . I, well . . . I," he turned to her, sorrow creasing his features, tears in his eyes. "Emma . . . please . . . listen to me . . . I am so sorry. So very sorry. You'll never know how I've paid . . ."

She put a small, soft hand over his mouth, her strange alien eyes near his. "It's long ago, David. We have the future to deal with now. Other problems to look to." She motioned towards Zaid.

David nodded eagerly, grateful for the distraction from his own sins. "Yes. Well, he's not going anywhere, is he? We just keep him here until Maher helps us out of the country. And then we let him know where his brother is. Right?"

"Something like that. I want to move him first."

"Move him?"

"Yes. This place isn't isolated enough. I don't want any stupid, lost tourist stumbling over him. There's a shearing shed out back. We'll put him in there."

"If you say so, Emma."

They had Zaid handcuffed and moving to the prod of the tidy, light gun Emma had retrieved from the folds of her tailored pants. David walked tentatively beside the prisoner, listening for lizards and hearing only the gains of an afternoon wind. A red gum tree jutted into the moonlight and Zaid stumbled over a metal garbage can someone had used for target practice. David pulled him to his feet and kept a hand at his elbow. Zaid kept jerking his head back to stare at the gun.

The outback hadn't obeyed the dictates of the dingo fence that surrounded the abandoned station yard. It had begun to reclaim its rights long ago, burying the wire fence under a slow onslaught of dirt and sand.

They stopped abruptly at the dry well on the edge of the old garden.

"Can't see any shearing shed, Emma, old girl. Sure you've got the right place?"

Tears gleamed in her eyes but her arm was steady as Emma swung the gun around in one smooth gesture and pulled the trigger.

The blood splattered onto her blouse and face as David fell in a heap at her feet. "That's for my mother," she whispered. "And for my brother."

Zaid was making crying animal noises, cowering against the well, his handcuffed arms raised over his head.

She swung towards him, the gun high again, her arm trembling this time. "And that's for you as well, Zaid Maher. I have an offer to make you, but if you don't cooperate I will kill you as easily as him." She looked at David's crumpled form, the ebbing blood staining his face, and then looked back at Zaid, "more easily," she said.

Zaid dropped to his knees, murmuring a thankful prayer to Allah.

13

PLENTY HIGHWAY
February 2

The wave of heat rolled down the road like surf. The straps of August's backpack dug into his shoulders as the sun tightened its harness around him. He'd been walking about an hour, with imaginary cars, trucks, planes, drunken howling teenagers, lecturing guards periodically preying on him. He'd vomited twice, the lining of his stomach surely tossed somewhere along the side of this hellish tarmac.

Slowly, the sun was forced into narrow bands of light beyond the mulga bushes. At first he thought the steady roar behind him was a storm gathering strength from the darkened sky. But when the drone didn't stop, August turned. He tripped, stumbling over his own feet as the monster drummed towards him over a slight rise of earth, swallowing the road whole.

A road train. Belting towards Alice carrying cargo the length of a city block. More efficient and cheaper than traditional trains tied to a track, these Leviathans ploughed constantly back and forth across Australia.

August waved desperately, jumping up and down as he identified the blur of a human face high in the cockpit of the massive cab. Lightning bolts painted across the grinning face of the hood screamed down on him and he heard the grind of gears that belonged in a 747. And then the road train obliterated the sky as a deranged fog horn lifted him from his feet.

August's arm flew up to cover his face and erase the sight of wheels as tall as two men hurtling past him. Spattering grit and rock barely left him his outer layer of skin. The blast beat a roll against his eardrums. A groan escaped him as the road train carried the heat wave with it.

And then a sound like a prehistoric animal in pain, as some gigantic brake locked into action and the hurtling cars slowed, a clumsy plane jerking onto a runway.

It was stopping! The huge mirrors jutting from each side of the truck winked back at him. He started to run. No telling how long this guy would wait. It didn't seem like he was on a schedule that allowed for too many pit stops.

The pack bounced against his spine. His skin was raw against the straps. A face peered from the four-foot-high rearview mirror. Please God, not another sadist, August prayed as he reached the passenger side and stared up at the cab.

The sound of some kind of hydraulic release. The door swung smoothly open above his head. "Make it quick, mate. 'Aven't got all day."

August pulled himself up the metal staircase welded to the side of the truck, the smell of the baking rubber wheels and the heat sizzling off the engine almost overwhelming him. He dared not let his hand slip against the burning metal. He tossed his pack inside and fell into a seat designed for a giant. A very comfortable giant. A very comfortable, very cool giant. August sighed and let the air-conditioning penetrate him.

The driver stared. "What you doing out here in Perisher Land, man?" The tone was rough, disbelieving, but not unsympathetic. He was a young Aborigine already heaving one of the two dozen gears back into place.

August was suddenly acutely conscious of his frayed boots,

which had begun to curl at the toes, his torn trousers, and the ragged knuckles he'd shoved in his mouth as he lay in the ditch. He blinked away the sweat streaming into his eyes. "Let's just say that hitchhiking across Australia wasn't one of my better ideas."

The driver studied him intently, judging if he was the victim of some bad joke. And then his face contorted with laughter and he stuck his hand out. "Daniel's me name. Headin' to Alice. That where you headin'?"

August gratefully gripped the offered hand. "I am now."

Another roar of laughter and the road train eased forward into full flight.

"You been driving long?" August asked, anxious to make conversation, anything to pass the next few hours.

"Since I was fifteen." He looked maybe thirty. A handsome profile marred by rough, pockmarked skin. His hair was tucked into a neat trim from which wild curls sprung intermittently over his head. "Best fucking driver this damned company ever had. Do this trip faster than any other bloke. Twice a week as well," he said aggressively, as if expecting August to challenge him.

"What you carrying?"

"Everythin'. Furniture, couple a cars this time," he raised his brows, "a jag — some hotshot on municipal council thinks he's prime minister — twenty tons a tinned goods, three freezer cars fulla meat, coupla tons bananas, and melons. That's why I gotta really hit it this time. Like that stuff to stay fresh. You're lucky I stopped for you, fella."

August said sincerely, "I know." He looked around the cab. The vast windscreen was covered with dead bugs. Periodically, Daniel pressed a button to release a spray of orange liquid and wash the bodies away with a pair of huge wipers. The dashboard had been polished to a gleam. A small plastic vase of artificial daisies was attached to it next to a picture of a cheerful-looking girl with a slightly bucktoothed grin. A tape deck and a row of big band cassettes sat neatly alphabetized in a rack beside the deck. A picture, carefully clipped, of Indiana Jones, whip in hand, was taped to the upper corner of the driver's window. An elaborate radio with headsets and microphone hung just next to the steering wheel. August studied it, but what he had to say to Washington couldn't be said over the airwaves while every trucker between here and Sydney eavesdropped. "Quite a rig you've got here."

"Gotta live in it. Might as well keep it decent s'what I say," he said defensively, flipping on the tape deck. Some silky-voiced crooner edged into "When I Fall in Love." Daniel sang along with him in a more than passable baritone.

"Think we could stop at the next diner?"

Daniel looked at him skeptically, as if he'd asked to drive. "Got a schedule to keep, man."

"It's an emergency." August silently counted to ten. He didn't want to have to try and take on this guy. He might possibly win a round with Daniel. But in a wrestling match with that steering wheel August didn't stand a chance.

Daniel stared through the windscreen, eyes judging the sky. "Suppose I could make an early pit stop." He flicked his hands against the gears in a series of quick, intricate movements, manipulating switches on the dashboard like a pilot.

August didn't bother to say "thank you." He could see that Daniel was already regretting taking him on. Instead, he watched the heat shimmer against the window, the desert chasing their heels, threatening to smother them. I never want to see another goddamned desert, he thought. Closing his eyes he dosed and dreamt of the green depths of Burnt Paw Lake. The sensation of sliding through the cold water. The icy wells as his body dropped deeper, deeper into its clarity.

The cinder block building with attached motel sprung out of the dusk at them. No sign identified it. Just the square white box with two wretched gas pumps in front and a sad camel tethered to the side. "Camel Rides" was printed on a cardboard sign nailed to the wall beside its head.

The phone booth had been vandalized and rude graffiti covered what remained of its steel fittings. But he got the sweet sound of a dial tone. The camel looked on through thick lashes in mild curiosity, chewing fitfully on nothing. August tried desperately to calculate the time change and prayed that Jamie Watts was in a position to accept a collect call.

Jamie's calm, when August finally got through to him, covered a simmering excitement. The line crackled and August pressed his hand against his open ear to cover the noise coming from the cafe. "What do you mean Maher's a biggie? What kind of language is that, Jamie?"

"He knows everything there is to know about biological warfare," Jamie shouted. "And I mean everything. He might have some kind of a private setup out there near Pine Gap."

"Near Pine Gap?"

"Yep. Apparently he's lived in that neck of the woods on and off since the fifties. Brilliant man they say."

"Jamie — get Wendell onto the head man at Pine Gap. Tell them to arrest Ahmed Maher and not to let Emma Cowen near the place. Got it?"

"Sure. But what . . .?"

"No time to talk now." He glanced at his watch. The dye from the cheap wrist band had started to seep into his damp skin. "A man named David Taylor might be with one of them. Get him taken into custody as well."

"August! Wait! Don't hang up! Wendell's been going nuts trying to get ahold of you. He'll have my ass if I don't tell him where you are! Where the hell are you?"

"About fifty miles out of Alice, I think. It'll be easier to stay on the road with this guy than to try and get a copter down here. By the time they organize the red tape I could probably have driven there and back three times. Okay, Jamie?"

"Sure, okay. But, August . . .?"

The line was dead.

NEAR PINE GAP
February 3

Emma drove ten miles off the main road, bouncing and jutting over the dark wells gouged into the trail by the last big rain.

The outback stretched under the sky's dark cape. In daylight an occasional dry creek bed or slash of brush was a welcome relief to the monotonous horizon, but not so in the anonymity of night. The jeep jerked violently across a deep hole, nearly throwing her from her seat.

It seemed an intolerable length of time before she recognized the rough shape of the old farmhouse looming out of the darkness.

She left the headlamps on. Taking a flashlight from the glove compartment she flicked it tentatively over the grounds and outbuildings, although there were no other vehicles in sight and only a madman or lost soul — or spy — would come on foot to this place. Shadows from gaping windows followed the flashlight's beam as she moved it from doorway to doorway. The flashlight tripped over empty corners and dust-filled cavities of the past.

"Where's my brother?"

She pulled back as Ahmed appeared suddenly from the far side of the house, his feet scuffing through the dust. How like him to linger until you were unprepared. Well, let him enjoy his illusions of control a little longer. She blinked back the image of those coldly typed pages in the file August Riley had given her pulled from the archives in Washington. Line after line delineating Ahmed Maher's complicity in the radiation experiments at Maralinga. His careful, complete series of blood tests. His meticulous measurements of each man present on that blinding, seamless plain on that October day in 1956.

"Not far from here," she said, covering her brief lapse of concentration.

"Where?" Ahmed insisted, leaning across the hood of the car as if his gaze alone could force her to answer.

"Not so fast — we have some arrangements . . . to arrange."

Ahmed shoved his clenched fists into his pockets and tried to think. "What did Zaid tell Riley?"

"Not much. He held out quite well during the initial interrogation. But then again, Riley didn't really get the chance to get at him. And now that Riley and David are dead it will take

Washington awhile to figure out where Zaid fits into the picture. Riley started to put two and two together when he saw that photo of you taken thirty years ago with my father." She studied his face dispassionately. "It's true, the resemblance is remarkable."

"What do you want?" Ahmed ran his hand along the dark hood of the jeep. He knew a plane ticket to London wouldn't rid him of her.

A sharp pain suddenly asserted itself against her chest. She pulled herself upright and spoke quickly to cover its bite. "Zaid stays with me for the next twenty-four hours. We go our own way once we get to London. That's all. Let's just say I'd like to teach the British a lesson. You can help me do that. But I want him with me for the next twenty-four hours to ensure you don't pull any clever deals with anyone to try to get him back. Deals that might just involve sacrificing me."

Ahmed drew back a little from the pasty-skinned woman, whose growing anger and disillusionment he'd watched eat her alive for nearly a decade. Like a corkscrew it wound around and around inside her until her humanity lay in shreds. Her rage had drawn her down to the bottom of that corkscrew, deeper and deeper inside herself, until her sight had been clouded forever. She was dangerous. But finely tuned to her target.

"But you must see that three people are so much more of a risk for me than two? And I can't possibly be as certain of you as I am of my own brother?"

"You've been certain of me for ten years, Dr. Maher. And . . .," she drew in her breath and then aimed a look like a cold laser at him. "This will be my last trip anywhere. Oh, I might well gasp out another year. Maybe two," she curled her lip and shook her head, "with all the right radiation." She pressed her arms against her chest as if conserving what energy she had left. "I don't want it," she said defiantly. "But I'll tell you what I do want," she shoved her angular body over the hood of the car towards him. If she could get Ahmed Maher and his brother together in London she could accomplish all she wanted. "I want to take some of them with me."

He pushed down his shock. He couldn't afford to have this conversation spin out of control. He had to find a way to get Zaid back. "What happens if I say no?"

She shrugged. "I eventually get arrested and die in some prison hospital all carefully doped and washed and diapered like a baby. Or I die when and how I want to."

"And what about . . ."

"Zaid? Well, if I don't go back he either walks his way across the outback barefoot and handcuffed," her mouth jerked in a wry smile, "or through some miracle somebody might stumble upon him. He'll then be arrested for trying to kill a CIA agent during the Gulf War. A future marginally more palatable than facing the rigours of the outback, I would guess. Take your pick. It's up to you."

"I see." He studied the deep scratches along the side of the jeep.

"I have passports. Identification," she offered, refusing to sound eager.

"Why London? Why don't you go straight to South America?"

Carefully she pinned one strand of hair back behind her ear in a strangely girlish gesture. "No, London will do quite well for my purposes. The British need to have this issue switched from an academic exercise debated by the fossils in the House of Commons to a real exercise carried out by real people. They've been waiting for thirty years for all us uppity Maralinga Aussies to die out. And they've just about succeeded. I want some uncomfortable questions raised," she said vehemently. "Questions my father never had answered."

"Questions?"

"Questions about using the colonies to test their poison. What is it they say, dying tends to concentrate the mind? Well, my mind is concentrated quite nicely."

Ahmed drew his nail along the line of a deep scratch from a thorn bush that had caught the edge of the headlight. He drew in his breath and then exhaled it as if it might be his last. "What do you really want, Emma?"

"One vial primed with toxin."

Ahmed drew in his breath. "Zaid told you . . .?"

"He had the choice of falling headfirst down a very empty well and keeping David Taylor company — or telling me what he knew about your plans. Zaid is a clever man. It didn't take him long to realize that I wasn't playing by any Roberts Rules of Order. He decided that spilling his guts was the better part of valour."

"I see." Ahmed kicked the jeep's dusty wheel. He made the only choice he could. "Where shall we meet?"

"Darwin Airport. For our flight tomorrow. You have the tickets. We make the exchange on board, after takeoff. You give me the vial. And you see Zaid. That way neither of us goes anywhere in a hurry."

Ahmed ran his hands through his hair. "All right. You'll be there?"

She tapped his shoulder. "We'll be right behind you. No worries, mate. No worries at all."

There was nothing reassuring about the high pitch of her voice or the bleak whiteness of her face in the reflection of the headlights.

ALICE SPRINGS

It was sometime during the second day that Zuleika realized that the air was getting thin. Until then she'd willed herself to stay sane against the suffocating blanket of darkness. The dwindling oxygen had been hidden in the unfamiliar smells and the waves of fear ebbing and flowing over her as she groped her way around the narrow space. Her eyes clawed at the blackness, searching out some form to latch onto, some shape that her mind could read for reassurance. There were shapes and forms — but nothing vaguely resembling assurance rested in this place.

She felt the bars, their cold rejection of her touch. But the sound of her fingers trailing along them was almost a comfort.

Her hand fell on rough animal hair. She drew back instinctively, but its stiff limbs offered no threat. Her trembling fingers searched out its silky ears and gaping muzzle, a dry tongue lolled to the side. The dog lay in a pungent bed of hay and feces. She plunged her hand into the water in the tin bowl by its head.

Her struggle now was to conserve breath. She had to rein her instinct to suck the air and try to take small, rationed breaths instead. She savoured the air. But was scared of it as well — dreading whatever it might be she was forced to inhale to live.

The wall behind her was stark and ungiving, scraping her bare shoulder as she slid against it towards the concrete floor. She forced herself up again, stamping her feet, pushing her eyes open against the blindness. Refusing the fantasies that dogged her now: her son's chubby arms around her neck, Gawain's powerful talons clutching her arm as they stood in the thick wind of a hunting afternoon. She shook her head. That way lay delirium. She forced herself to think of mathematical exercises, the rituals of calculus that had so intrigued her in school. And the Koran. She tried to remember why she'd rejected her old life, all the safety and advantages in which her culture had cradled her. She had turned her back on it. *Spit in her father's eye,* that's what he'd said the last time she'd seen him. Quiet and patient as always, the sadness on his face and one small ring, his only legacy to her. Where had her so-called freedom taken her? How great did the punishment have to be for succumbing to the temptation to live another life, for indulging in the exploration of her own will? And where had that maze led her?

Only to this end.

It was getting warm. She must have been here for awhile if the earth's natural coolness was starting to dissipate. She was thirsty. Her tongue felt swollen and dry. She groped towards the cage that held the dog's carcass and gripped the bars, easing herself down towards the floor of the cage. With one hand she pulled the bowl towards her. It spilled warm and wet over her wrist. She pressed her face to the bars. If she pushed her tongue through them she could lap at the water like an animal.

Like an animal. Like the dead creature inches away. Her mouth screamed in parched desire as she hit the bowl to the back of the cage and fell back against the wall. No. She might die. But she would not commit suicide. She clamped her mouth shut and pulled small snorts of air through her nostrils.

The craving for the water wrestled with her reason, luring her back to the cage again and the tepid bowl she'd so foolishly flung away. She remembered the stories of men at sea who drank salt water and didn't live to regret it. The stories of desert explorers who made a sip of moisture last a day. Who drank a camel's blood to survive.

She might sit down. Rest for a minute. Just sit down. Not sleep. Not lie down. No surrender to the ground where the ruthless air and pungent pain of this place would gradually suck the life from her. No, just rest awhile. Regain her strength.

The wall felt softer as she eased down it, bracing herself with her hands. Pushing the opposite wall back with her legs so that it didn't move. Wouldn't catch her unawares and crush her.

Just for awhile . . .

Two Hours Later

August stood amongst the carnage. The sound of his own breathing was laboured and harsh in his ears, trampled every few seconds by the pounding of the blood drumming through his body. The protective suit made his limbs feel like solid steel. His tongue was heavy in his head and his vision swam behind the clear plastic mask, as if he'd been transported to a grim underwater hell. But the suit kept his sanity pressed against him. A fissure, a leak anywhere and it might escape, curling into the dead air like a genie from a bottle.

The grisly photos of the pain-ridden creatures that they'd found on Maher's desk hadn't prepared him. The immaculate cleanliness was an obscenity amongst the emaciated animals and bright white iron bars. The technicians from Pine Gap milled around him, moving reluctantly, trying to translate theory mouthed in well-lit classrooms on bio/chem warfare into this grim practice. They worked in silence.

Eyes burning dry as if the tears had been sucked forever from them, August walked down the whitewashed aisle between the cages. He wanted to see all that this man had done. All that he was capable of. Forcing himself to look from side to side, he moved towards the darkness at the far end.

A desert rat scratched at the inside of her mouth. Scratching, scratching. Sucking her saliva, pulling the blood from her gums. The sun scorched her head. Seared her eyes. Black ash from the burnt-out sun branded her flesh. She was on another planet. A planet built of bricks of heat whirling through the black universe. She would be spun off it soon, thrown into the void. A dark, cool void that waited to nurse her pain . . .

A space man had come to take her there. To guide her to the next planet in the emptiness. A place of streams and shade. Water and air. Long, deep drowning gasps of air.

The space man leaned over her. His aqua green eyes were like a cool bottomless lake inviting her to dive through the funny bubble mask he had to wear on this hot planet. He was very white, floating in the dark pit. He had a clumsy, bulky body but she could feel tenderness through his thick gloves like the ones she used for the falcons, but smooth and silky and soothing. Fresh air blowing on her face. Her mouth still a desert.

And then the sun screaming down at her.

Zuleika moaned and jerked away, her hands clawing at her eyes.

"All right. It's all right now." He was shading her eyes. The big gloves were gone. He had large brown hands, fingernails bitten, fingers bruised and scratched. "Breathe this. Calm down. Just breathe. You'll be all right. Here — hold it." He was offering an oxygen mask, placing it gently over her nose, guiding her hand to it. She gulped, too quickly at first. And then slowly, very slowly, inhaled the sweet mixture.

After a moment he eased the mask away and offered her water in a plastic cup. Eagerly she pushed it against her lips, not wanting to lose a precious drop. She chewed at the rim of the cup as she drained it. The sun stabbed her eyes.

He lifted the cup and wiped the spittle from the edge of her lips. "Whoa, now! Not too fast!" For the first time the large golden brown eyes seemed to focus on him. August supported her neck with his hand. "You're all right. You're all right now."

Zuleika struggled to prop herself on one elbow. "Inside . . .," she thought she was screaming.

Her voice was a whisper. He leaned closer.

"Inside . . ."

"Yes. We know. It's been sealed off. We know what it is. We know what was going on in there."

She collapsed again. "I touched . . ."

He smoothed the wet hair back from her forehead. "You weren't in the contaminated area. The animals had been dead for some time. We don't think you were exposed, but we'll do some tests. The air ambulance will be here any minute."

"Gawain . . . have you seen Gawain?" repressed hysteria stretched her voice.

The sound of rotating blades beat the air into a stifling wind and churned the dust around them.

"Gawain? I'm sorry, but . . ."

The paramedics were a cool relief, efficient and quick — a boy who looked barely out of high school, starched shirt and spit-polished shoes, and an older guy, peppered sideburns a decade out of style and hairy arms, but moving just as fast as the youngster.

August squeezed himself into the ridiculously small seat behind the pilot and watched the golden-skinned woman ministered to by a series of smoothly pumping machines. The paramedics' automatic and expressionless faces moved above her.

And then her eyes lifted in a look of such despair and panic that August eased forward. Groping along the low-slung cot where she lay, he found her hand.

"Sir, I'm sorry, sir, but . . .," the fresh-faced paramedic protested.

"Shut up," August growled.

The older guy glanced over the swinging IV and shook his head.

Her hand was squeezing the blood from his. But the panic ebbed from her eyes, leaving the despair more naked than ever.

"It's all right now," August said, wondering if she could hear him over the engine's rising scream.

Slowly, her grip loosened and her hand fell to the side of the sling as the juice in her veins took over. The young paramedic picked up her hand and placed it tidily over her chest, tossing August a dirty look.

August hated helicopters.

She was sitting on the edge of the high hospital bed, long, brown legs stretching over the side towards the tiled floor, thick black hair tumbling erratically to her shoulders, the ugly green hospital gown covering her body. She gripped the edge of the mattress and stretched her feet out further.

"I think that's a no-no!"

Zuleika glanced up. The man was big, his shoulders dwarfed the door. Rough and untidy looking, he looked like he hadn't slept for a week or shaved in about that time either. His shirt hung from his jeans. But something about his bulk and untidiness was more reassuring than the stark antiseptics of this room. His eyes were lost in sleepless dark pouches, his chin too big and his long hair thinning. But as he walked tentatively closer she recognized the warmth of the space man's aqua green eyes.

As she swung her head August noticed the heavy silver pendants dangling at her ears. Her mouth still held the raw, parched look of her ordeal. But the despair in her eyes had been hooded by curiosity.

"Mr. Riley?" her voice was a husky gold.

"You're feeling better, I see?" He hardly recognized the stilted formality of his own voice.

She nodded and held her hand out to him. "I was just about to try to find a telephone. I have to see to some things."

"You won't be using a telephone quite yet, I'm afraid."

Her hand rested in his. She looked at him, puzzled.

He let her hand drop. "Let's not waste your time or mine. Where are your husband and his brother?"

"In England. London, I believe."

So easy? He'd expected the first evasion to be the roughest to drag out. He'd deliberately come while she was still confined to hospital to take whatever advantage he could. He didn't have time for the niceties. "How do you know?"

"I saw the tickets."

"Why London?"

She thought for a moment, chewing her lip.

This is it, August thought. The manipulation. The determination of which story sounds best. "Our son is there. At school. It's his birthday and I think Ahmed may be going to visit him."

"Uh, huh . . ."

She drew her legs up onto the bed and sat back against the pillow, sensing his antagonism. The earrings made a small tinkling sound against her neck.

He leaned over the bed. "Don't play stupid with me. I dragged you out of that lab, remember? You trying to tell me you didn't have any idea what he was doing in there?"

"My husband has always been involved in dangerous work. I didn't know how dangerous. But I knew it wasn't . . . conventional."

"Or legal?"

Confusion flashed across her features. "The work was funded by legitimate businesses. Perhaps a few private donors."

"How about Saddam Hussein as a private donor?"

A steel trap winced her chest. "What do you mean?"

August hesitated. Genuine surprise had ricocheted across her face. Just a good actress? Or a wife really unaware? He'd read her file. Intelligent woman. Grew up near Amman, Jordan. Went to UCLA during the liberal seventies before the Arabs cracked down on women putting two and two together. A stint at the University of London. Degree in mathematics. Daddy pulled her back home when she was caught playing the piano in a jazz club in downtown LA for fun and seven bucks an hour. Taught math in Amman for awhile. Got out again by latching onto Maher. Reading between the lines, the marriage had been an arranged one. Though August wondered if Daddy and Maher had been wrong as to who had really arranged what. So far, this lady had gotten most of what she wanted out of life, or so it appeared. A minor drug bust five years ago. In with the wrong crowd out at the Base. Maher was respected enough to cover up the record. And pay the bail.

But August figured he'd found a weak spot — both in her file and in the too casual answers she'd offered him. "If you think your husband has flown out of here to order the ice cream and cake for your boy's birthday party, you're not as smart as your file would indicate. Dr. Maher was manufacturing what we suspect are lethal biological toxins in that little playpen of his."

He saw her stiffen, swallow quickly. He resisted the impulse to encircle her bare ankle with his hand. The impulse to reassure her, to cradle her again as he had at the lab, to tell her, to tell himself, that it was all going to be all right. Instead he said, "Help me. And I'll help you. It's that simple."

She pulled a blanket up over her legs and sat with her arms clutching her knees, rocking slowly. August prayed that no damned interfering doctor or the bossy nurse he'd met in the hall would come waltzing in right now.

"What do you want?" she asked, her voice weary.

"What do *you* want?"

"My son. Ahmed has taken him from me. I want him back." Her voice cracked but she recovered quickly. "He's only six. I haven't seen him for six months."

"If we can find your husband, we can find your son. That makes sense, doesn't it?"

"Perhaps." She turned her brown eyes on him and he had the uncomfortable feeling that she was reading him like some kind of map of her future. "And what do you want, Mr. Riley?"

"Everything you know. Everything you think you might know."

She nodded and reached for the water beside the bed. "There's a canister hidden in my son's treehouse." She tried to pour the water but her hands were shaking. "I think it contains the poison you are talking about." August took the pitcher from her. "Ahmed had three of them." Her fingers were ice cold.

February 4

The hawk was huddled on the far side of the pen. He moved nervously as August opened the hatch gate. He'd found the glove by the door where Zuleika had dropped it. He slipped it over his own hand. The hawk was hungry. Best to do it now. August clucked and offered his arm. The hawk moved back on the perch, pressing against the wall. August could see his golden eyes regarding him in the gloom of the pen. The hay beneath his feet was stale and dirty and there was nothing in the feeding pen. August clucked again, "Come on, fella." The bird looked at him like the intruding stranger he was and keened arrogantly. "That's it — you tell me all about it."

The curved, hard beak pecked once at his glove as if checking its validity and then the hawk tentatively put one thick black talon against the leather. August stayed rigidly still.

And then drawing himself to his full dignity, Gawain stepped onto the glove. August eased the bird slowly through the dark aviary and out into the sun. It blinked and swivelled its head, turning again to examine August as if he wanted to see his abductor in full daylight, then shifted his delicately balanced weight against August's arm.

They moved to a small rise behind the pen. Cicadas hissed at them in the baking afternoon sun. The view was confined by a copse of straddling ghost gums and thick thornbush, but a small field divided by fence posts erupted beyond the trees.

Gawain sat lethargically on his fist. "Come on, boy," August said. "Go for it. It doesn't look like much. But it's freedom. Take it."

A movement in the bush. August felt the hawk's blood revive in its veins. It fluttered and stiffened its body against his hand, the talons pressuring the glove now.

"He's afraid, Mr. Riley. The world out there is too big — and too dangerous for timid souls such as Gawain." Zuleika moved out from the shelter of the path that led from the main house.

The hawk keened to her.

August held the bird up and away from him, admiring the sleek lines of his body. "Oh, I don't know. I suspect he probably just doesn't know what he's missing." The hawk's beak arched towards the sky.

"We can't all survive those conditions. Someone like you would find it hard to understand, I'm sure. But sometimes protection and security are more important than freedom."

"Not for a creature with wings."

She cocked her head at him. He'd answered with no hesitancy. So certain. "He might die if you let him go. If I don't feed him."

"There are enough prisons around," August said, suddenly impatient with her rationalizations, feeling some challenge in her words. "Enough human ones, without caging everything else in sight."

She felt herself drawn to his obvious passion for the hawk. She could almost feel the magnetism pinning Gawain to August Riley's thick arm. She'd never thought of the birds that way before. She'd been around them ever since she could remember. They were pampered, indulged creatures, catered to as the expensive hobby they were. She watched Gawain's wings rise slightly and fall again as if rehearsing some dream.

August Riley looked like he belonged here, in her territory, her sanctuary.

"In any case," she found herself demanding, "who gave you the right to release my property? I asked that someone check on them. Not release them!" Her voice was suddenly hard and practical.

"I didn't think it was wise to keep them around under the circumstances. The vet's given them a clean bill of health. And I . . ."

"And you just took it upon yourself to decide what was best

for my birds?" She hated the power he had over her. The way he'd strode into that hospital room and squeezed every drop of cooperation from her. It was all she'd been able to do to hang onto the few bargaining chips she had left.

"Look," August sighed in irritation. He didn't like her anger, it bothered him more than it should and veiled all his intentions with a vague guilt. He had a job to do. "You told me that you are only interested in one thing. Getting your boy back. You wanted safe passage to London to try to find him. Well, you've got it. In exchange for whatever you can feed us about Ahmed Maher. We'll be out of here in four hours. I didn't think you'd be worrying about the birds. I thought they might starve to death."

He turned away from her, dismissing the liquid brown of her eyes and the complexity he suspected lurked there. Things had to stay simple right now. Things had to stay straightforward.

She reached towards the hawk. August lifted his arm. And then Gawain was gone, shooting into the sky and hovering over the pinched, dry field.

"Go for it," August whispered, suddenly wishing for a transfusion of the hawk's blood into his own veins.

He pulled off the glove and rubbed his hand. The mark of the talon was still imprinted on his skin.

14

FLIGHT QF 061
QANTAS AIRLINES
February 4

The air in the plane was stale. The film was some dry comedy Zaid lost interest in three minutes into the scene where the hero devastated a room of sophisticates with his wit. Emma had fallen into a fitful sleep in the seat next to his, her head rolling against the porthole window. He was constantly aware of her at his elbow although she barely spoke to him. It was going to be a long flight. He got up to prowl the length of the cabin, feeling Ahmed's eyes following him.

Zaid had failed his brother. And he'd failed Ra'ad.

He pressed past an air attendant. First important flight, maybe, eager to please. She smiled at him. He nodded and moved on. The washrooms were full. He turned back to search out the facilities at the opposite end of the cabin. It wasn't as if he didn't have plenty of time. They were four hours into a thirteen-hour flight and the atmosphere had settled into a numbing neutrality. A lot of people were dosing, arms and legs flopping into the aisle, earplugs trying to perpetuate the illusion of a decent rest under the murky spots of light.

He felt Ahmed behind him, his breath hot in Zaid's ear. "Turn around. As if we are just waiting to get into the toilets." He jabbed Zaid in the back. "Turn around, I said."

Zaid obeyed, as he always had.

"You have to get rid of that woman when we get to London. She knows too much. And she's off her head. For the moment she thinks we're a reluctant team. Let her keep thinking that — and get rid of her at the first opportunity."

Zaid stared at the sliding tab on the washroom door. Occupied. "How?"

Ahmed sucked in his breath, that familiar impatient sound. "That's up to you. It's a big city. And you know a lot of people. But first, I want you to get Khalaf out of that school."

The cute attendant squeezed past them carrying a handful of miniature liquor bottles. She didn't smile this time.

"You still have faith in me, Ahmed? You believe I can do this?"

"You must do it," his brother hissed.

The little tab slipped to vacant and the bathroom door swung open releasing the stench of cigarette smoke and a skinny teenage boy who smiled guiltily.

LONDON
February 5

Peter wouldn't meet her eyes across the burnished oak conference table. And so it should be. Shame was an emotion that had dropped out of style but sometimes, she reflected, it was still apt. The barristers did most of the talking for them, and Margaret tried to concentrate on the tidy disposition of their material goods. Peter was being generous as she knew he would. She'd made old Mr. Abercrombie ask for the flat and the villa and twice the cash settlement that Peter had offered. Abercrombie had muttered incomprehensibly, disapprovingly, but agreed in the end. She'd wanted to push Peter, make him fight her, make him react, make him look at her as a worthy adversary at least.

But he'd acquiesced to everything. His lawyer, a forceful jolly type who seemed almost pleased to be handing over so much of Peter's assets, must have received strict orders to cooperate. Quiet, friendly instructions, but orders nonetheless. Everyone followed Peter's orders sooner or later. Just as she had, in the end, obeyed his command to get out of his life without a fuss. The painful thought erupted in her mind as she sat in the lush, thick-carpeted offices of Abercrombie and Fraser that Peter might very well turn over everything he owned just to get rid of her. He wanted her to go quietly — and quickly.

She smoothed her leather skirt and took some satisfaction from the fact that she'd lost several pounds since he'd walked out of their home. On an impulse she'd instructed her hairdresser to dye her hair black. Zaid had let it slip that he liked brunettes. The leather skirt was stylishly short, her legs were still good, her makeup was brighter and more colourful than she'd ever dared, and her heels were two inches higher. She'd seen old Fraser's eyes widen as she'd swept through the reception area. But Peter had barely glanced at her when she entered the conference room, just a polite acknowledgement.

She plucked a bud from the bouquet of yellow roses in the middle of the table and smiled to herself, thinking of the lush armful of flowers Zaid had sent her before he'd left. The delivery boy had peered over the huge box, barely able to see her as he confirmed the address. She'd treat herself to a couple of days in New York, and when Zaid returned she would ask him to come to Monaco with her. She refused to spend the rest of her years moping and jumping from plastic surgeon to plastic surgeon like so many of her friends.

Peter was signing the papers. His familiar smooth hands rushing his name. His ring finger was bare. She twisted her own. A new ring, platinum, plain, encircled the third finger of his right hand. He was speaking. Looking at her for the first time. "Margaret, I do appreciate that you cut short your holiday in order to come back for this meeting. But I have to leave for America and I don't know how long I'll be away. I thought it was best to deal with this paperwork as soon as possible."

She twirled the rosebud between her fingers. "It was rather inconvenient. But I'd like to tie things up as well." She gathered her coldness to her and looked at him. Abercrombie shuffled uncomfortably.

"I do have one more thing to ask," Peter was saying, as if her bitter look hadn't penetrated at all. "Could I possibly come to the house tonight and collect some papers from my study? I'm sorry, I did think that I'd taken everything. But there were a few things . . ."

"Of course." She was proud of her cool tone.

"Yes. All right, then." Fussy Abercrombie picked up a pen and handed it to her with the sheaf of papers. "Just sign at the bottom of each page, Margaret, and then we can all go home." She'd fire him when this was over. He still spoke to her like she was his little secretary from the country.

She hardly recognized her own signature beneath the shaking hand which distorted it. The others were gracious enough to look away. She had received everything she wanted and more.

"The decree will be official in three months," Abercrombie was saying. His voice seemed to be coming from a great distance as she watched Peter pick a piece of lint from his jacket.

"We'd appreciate if it could be put on the docket as soon as possible," her husband said.

With his words a wave of pain broke through the dam Margaret had carefully constructed, threatening to drown her. She was horrified at the certainty that she would fall to the floor here in a final humiliation. Instead, she found herself saying, her voice harsh, "Yes, let's just get this over with."

Three sets of eyes watched as she gathered her purse and tossed her coat over her arm. She turned and prayed the unfamiliar heels wouldn't wobble on the thick carpet as she walked to the door.

The downstairs lobby was all marble, exquisite vague paintings, and cold inaccessibility. Her footsteps tapped loudly against the floor. She leaned against a wall to catch her breath, bending into the telephone cubicle for the relief of its cold metal against her forehead. She lifted the receiver and dialled Zaid's number. She knew he wouldn't be home. Maybe though . . . just a chance. She would love so much to just walk with him through the park. He was a good listener. He'd indulged all her tales of woe.

Maybe . . . maybe through some miracle he'd come back to London early. Her horoscope today had said to expect the totally unexpected. Just the sound of his voice would be enough right now. She rested the receiver between her shoulder and chin and pulled some coins from her change purse.

One. Two. Three rings. She knew the routine. His answering machine clicked on. The purr of his voice.

Peter stepped from the lift with his solicitor. Margaret hung up the phone without speaking. She'd send Zaid a present — something special to keep her on his mind. Peter looked straight ahead as he walked past her. There had been a time when they were both always at the periphery of each other's vision. A time when they could spot each other within a block on Oxford Street during January sales. A time when they'd meant that much to each other.

The solicitor looked jovial as ever. Peter was grim around the mouth but there was no denying the relief in his eyes.

A woman came through the revolving doors. She looked out of place in jeans and a crumpled white blouse tailing under a baggy green mackintosh, dark hair that hung in a wet braid over one shoulder. Margaret saw the solicitor frown in disapproval as the woman ran towards them.

And she saw Peter's face smiling with delight as she swept into his arms and kissed him.

Margaret hadn't recognized Sara Wright out of her office uniform of tailored suits and tidily bunned hair.

"Is it over?" Sara was asking eagerly. "Is it over?"

Peter's arm slipped easily around her waist. Peter, Margaret's self-conscious, always socially prim husband, seemed unembarrassed by his new love's exuberance. "Yes," he said. "It's all over."

SWISS COTTAGE
LONDON
February 7

The flat was smaller than he'd expected and the goddamned English plumbing was as eccentric as ever. August coaxed a dribble of lukewarm water from the tap and sank back in the tub with the washcloth draped over his face, slowly turning his sore ankle. He'd given up on the prospect of a shower. They'd be tripping over each other in this place. MI5 must be having real budget troubles if this was the best they could do by way of a safe house.

Ward — *Commander* Ward, as he'd pointed out — sounded like a real tightass on the phone. Despite all his pleadings from a crackling embassy safe line in Canberra, Wendell Laine had insisted that the British be brought in. It was their territory, their foreign national, and potentially their great big fucking problem, as Wendell pointed out through teeth August could hear grinding over the line. But August wanted this Maher bastard himself. Maybe then he'd be able to erase the smell of agony that lingered around him from that place, from that hole in the ground where Dr. Ahmed Maher carried on his meticulously cruel research.

Wendell had pointed out that if Maher or his brother pulled the tab on one of those canisters the British would, after all, be the ones doing all the explaining.

August had countered that he was one of the millions sitting potentially downwind from Maher's latest toy.

Wendell sucked in his breath and said, with exquisite patience, as if it were the ultimate test, that he'd gone to school with Ward.

"Oh well!" August replied, "you should have told me at the start and I wouldn't have bothered you with these details." Wendell's sputter was interrupted when August hung up.

And so he and Zuleika had trailed, both of them bug-eyed after a sixteen-hour flight, from a decent three-bedroom setup over in Mayfair with central heating and coffee already jumping, to this chilly dump with a three-bar electric heater, two kinds of tasteless tea that had been there since Day One, and, he noticed as he lifted one corner of the wash cloth, what looked suspiciously like rising damp crawling up the walls. God, the Brits were masochists.

He heaved himself from the tub and released the water, ignoring the nasty-looking stain ringing the enamel. At least this arrangement might give him a chance to get closer to Zuleika Maher — and her real intentions. She'd hidden behind a set of headphones during the flight from Sydney, barely asking him to pass the salt during what seemed like a dozen bland meals. He'd actually wondered if she might bolt at Heathrow, but she'd only strode ahead as if she didn't know him, a resigned set to her shoulders.

He sniffed at his shirt, crumpled it into a ball along with his pants, and pulled on a terrycloth robe that dangled from a hook on the back of the door. It was a size too small. Wondering whether the poor devil who had last worn it was dead or alive now, he padded out to the other room.

Zuleika was sitting in an overstuffed chair next to the electric fire, her feet pulled up under her like some snug little animal, thick hair obscuring her face as always. The scent of a musky perfume hung in the air. Raw light from the heater provided the only mean warmth and a cup of murky tea was balanced on the chair's arm.

August pulled the robe closer around him. "Any of that still hot?" he said, gesturing towards the cup.

She looked up at him through her veil of hair. He wanted to reach down and sweep it from her face so that he could have a real good look at her. See if exhaustion or doubt had cracked that mask. "Help yourself. I made a pot," she said.

He went into the small kitchen. Seemed MI5 wasn't dishing out much for cleaning ladies, either. A layer of spattered grease had built up on the wall next to the stove and the tiled floor looked like it didn't have much memory of a mop. No doubt MI5 was so distrustful of outside contractors that stuff like this was left for months while someone tried to push the right piece of paper, in triplicate, into the right basket. He examined a stained mug and then reluctantly rinsed it out. He was antsy. A strange sensation had dogged him since they'd dragged themselves into this place a few hours back, pulled the curtains, and locked the door behind them. A sensation of being sucked into a deep vortex of uncertainty. He had a goal. And he knew what it was. But it was starting to cloud around the edges, obscuring his view. He didn't like it.

He poured himself some of the greyish tea and walked back to the other room. He caught a sigh from her. "Something wrong?" he asked, an edge to his voice. The responsibility for her was starting to seem heavy.

"Just tired."

"We'll both be a lot more damned tired before this is over." He held the dusty curtain back from the window and stared through the rain-streaked panes onto the narrow patch of garden.

"Who is this man coming to see us?" she asked.

"Name's Ward." August sipped at the hot, foul tea, his breath forming circles against the thin windowpane. Black clouds tumbled beyond the roofs bringing an early night.

"What does he want?"

August rubbed his hand against the fog he'd created on the window. "Same thing I do." He turned to look at her.

"To use me to hunt down my husband." She was stretching her hands towards the weak fire. "I'd forgotten how cold it is in this country. Especially in February."

"What did you expect? Your husband manufactures a deadly toxin in his cute little underground bunker. We find you in there. For the first twenty-hour hours you ration out information to us like it's your personal property — and now you're Miss Discreet."

She traced the lip of her cup with one finger. He noticed how solid and brown her hands looked. Worn-looking hands for a woman who'd been pretty well indulged all her life. Ragged at the nails and a long scar from thumb to wrist where a hawk had seized it bare. "The information is my personal property," she said quietly.

"Grow up!" His voice was hard. He saw her shoulders

hunch and felt briefly the bully. But he knew better than to be lured by appearances. Innocence didn't exist beyond the age of ten these days. "The guy's carrying around enough poison to wipe all of us out at any time. This whole city, you understand that? It's just a question of figuring out when and where he and that little bastard of a brother of his are planning to do it. And while you sit around here playing games with me it might already be too late."

"Why do you insist I'm lying?" she said it with no anger, just a puzzled curiosity.

"How about lying by omission?"

"Why should I trust you? Give you the only weapon I have — what I know?"

He sat down and leaned towards her. "Had it occurred to you that the winds might blow Khalaf's way? He's in London. You have to tell me. You have no choice."

She drained the cup and then leaned back in the lumpy chair, tilting her head like an elegant bird. His eyes followed the line of her neck, along her jaw to her wide mouth. She pulled her hair from her face as if she wanted to see him more clearly. Her eyes were dark with exhaustion but clear in expression. Determination. "Ah . . . but Mr. Riley, I discovered when I was twenty that there is always a choice. In fact, it was your country that taught me that. When I discovered that it was my own hand that pulled the veil over my face every day, my own mind that bowed to every opinion but my own. When I discovered that, I couldn't wait to strip those blindfolds away. And then, like every rebel before me, I discovered that there were many advantages, protections, securities that went with the old ways. But by then, you see, it was too late. There was never any security again," she said clearly. "In any case, Mr. Riley, your argument is flawed. I don't accept your basic premise. There is always a choice." She smiled ruefully. "I may not be a shining example, but there's always a choice."

"Fine. Play the Queen of Existentialism! We'll sit here and rot while you debate which way you're going to jump." The electric heater flickered as a lightning bolt short-circuited a pole somewhere. August reached down and cranked up the heat. "Perhaps you're in this thing with your husband? Maybe this is all just a way to keep me off guard. After all, you're in the thick of it now. He knows exactly where we are if you choose to tell him — and how much we know."

He felt the heat of her sudden anger fall over him. "Yes. Indeed. Lock myself in that laboratory! Make myself your prisoner! Put myself in a position where I am totally reliant on your good graces from moment to moment. Please. I took you for a cleverer man than that!"

August leaned back in his chair, studying her. "Very pretty speech. Very self-righteous and indignant. But there's just one little problem there, Zuleika." It was the first time he'd used her name and with a pang of regret he saw her lock her shoulders against him. "There's at least one thing you aren't telling us. Where your brother-in-law lives. Oh, they'll track him down soon enough. That kind of thing only takes a few hours. But an hour could make the difference. And if your son is still in this country that hour could be the difference to him as well. Had you thought of that?"

He saw her stiffen. He'd caught her. She'd stumbled over one of his trip wires. He decided to press the advantage. It might not come again. "You ever seen pictures of how people die in biological warfare, Zuleika? Just about as pretty as the chemicals. Remember Mr. Saddam's Kurds? These weapons don't discriminate, you know. Every living thing in their way. Surely," his voice softened, "surely, you weren't really so ignorant of your husband's work? Did you see what he did to those dogs, those apes?"

Even in the red glow from the electric fire he could see that the blood had drained from her face. "I chose not to know," she whispered. She unfolded herself from the chair and walked to a small desk by the window and scribbled on a piece of paper. She held it towards him. "Zaid's address," she said flatly. "He's lived in that block for ten years. I lived there myself when I went to university here."

August stood up. The comforting warmth of the bath had

begun to ebb and his ankle had started to throb again. He tried not to limp as he walked towards her. He took the paper. "Thank you."

Tears glimmered behind her lashes. He pushed the hair from her eyes and cupped her cheek, turning her face towards him.

His hands felt cool against her skin. Rain slashed against the high, narrow windows. She wished that the light was brighter. His face was in shadows. She couldn't give in now. There might be a time when she could afford this weakness. But not now. Not now.

He gathered her towards him, his hands pushing gently — roughly — through her hair.

She let herself fall against him and surrendered to a sweet sense of safety as his arms wove around her. The desire to lean on him stung her. His mouth found hers and she fell into his heat. She pulled him closer, tighter against her. "What do you really want?" she murmured, half regretting the words as they escaped her. But there was too much at risk. Too much to let a kiss and a glimpse of tenderness confuse her.

He stepped back, holding her away from him. Maybe he had been alone too long. He'd always been half proud of his tolerance for solitude, his preference for it. Most encounters with the human race just sent him head down, back to the wilderness every chance he got. Now, like a novice he'd blundered into the oldest con in the book. "Look," he said, "we're stuck in this together whether we like each other or not. I need you to get any hint of where your husband or his brother might be. You need me to help you get your kid. It's not very complicated!"

She shook off his grip and twirled to face the window, her head hunched between her shoulders. The shadows of rain reflected in her face.

August threw up his hands. "Hey — forget what just happened. Just one of those things. We're both exhausted. We're both under terrible pressure." He laughed roughly. "We're both human, I think."

She smiled and his heart churned unexpectedly. "Perhaps we can agree on something, after all," she said.

He stepped towards her. The rain threatened the old window-panes. She wanted to lean into the curve of his arm again. Just for a moment.

A key turned in the lock.

August jerked around, acutely aware that the gun was in the bathroom.

Commander Ward stood, poker-faced and disapproving, in the entryway, bringing a rush of cold air with him. He flicked on the overhead light. His narrow eyes trailed from August's bare legs and robe to Zuleika's dishevelled hair and rigid figure.

"Well, well, I realize you Americans believe in making yourselves comfortable, but isn't this rather pushing it a bit, Mr. Riley?"

"And so much for the great British reputation for courtesy," August pulled the robe tighter around him. "You ever hear of knocking?"

"I did." His eyes made a cold slide across Zuleika. "You must have been preoccupied." He raised his hand as if she were a servant to dismiss. "We have to talk alone."

August glanced at Zuleika and saw the stony mask descend across her face. She stared at Ward for one long moment and then tossed a look at August that he couldn't translate. He felt she was waiting for him to say something. But the search for Maher had to take priority now. Ward had to take priority. Surely, she could understand that?

She pushed past them into the bedroom.

"Don't you think it would be more comfortable for both of us if you got dressed?" Ward asked dryly, raising one thin brow.

August marked Commander Ward as one of those little twerps who liked his daily dose of power, however diluted. "What's the matter? Am I too knock-kneed for your tastes?" August had the satisfaction of spotting a faint flush cross Ward's face before he headed for the bathroom and his crumpled clothes.

At Ward's irritated invitation August sat down in the bright light next to the fire. He could hear Zuleika moving around in the next room. Hangers clinking together in the closet. The creak of the bed. Applause from the portable television set.

Some game show. He was sitting in her chair. The cup of tea was quickly cooling on the floor beside his feet. Her perfume still lingered in the air.

Ward crossed one leg high on the other, his coat was folded neatly over his legs and the umbrella dripped over the carpet. August noticed how the Commander's nostrils always seemed to be twitching at the air like some animal scent was just escaping him. Still, the guy was supposed to know what he was doing. If Wendell Laine was going to dump him with anyone, it might as well be good old Commander Ward.

"It's been decided that she be taken into custody," he said matter-of-factly.

August sat up straight. It wasn't a time for temper. "It has, has it? And who exactly decided?"

"I have." Ward smoothed the lines of the raincoat as if it had a pedigree. "Too dangerous to keep her here. Security not good enough."

"Well, I'm the security."

"Exactly." Ward raised his hand to stem August's objections. "Nothing personal. But you are only one man, after all. For all we know, her husband and brother-in-law could be planning to snatch her from here. There could be a whole ring of them. You could have been followed."

"That's why I wanted to stay in Mayfair. My people had the Watchers and security all set up. It was your idea to bring us over here."

"You will have access to her. At any time."

August leaned forward, hoping the vein in his forehead wouldn't throb the way it did when he started to lose it. "That's not really the point is it, Commander Ward? The point is, she won't trust anyone if you put her in a place that's obviously first cousin to a prison, then hook her up to a poly and shine a strobe light in her eyes, will she?"

"Despite American opinions to the contrary, our methods are marginally more sophisticated than that, Mr. Riley."

"You know what I'm getting at. We don't have time to go through all that. If she's trained at all she'll be up on those methods and able to resist them indefinitely. The atmosphere here is more conducive to getting something out of her." He touched the piece of paper with Zaid's address that sat next to the chair on a rickety table. "She still needs help getting to the boy. She knows our resources are a hell of a lot more extensive than anything she can do on her own."

Ward smoothed his moustache in a gesture August decided would eventually lead any spouse to murder. And if he was on the jury he wouldn't convict. "I believe the son is already gone — out of the country — a ploy to delay us. A decoy, so to speak."

"What about her exposure at the lab? Why would she risk that? She was in pretty bad shape when I got there."

"She wasn't infected though, after all, was she?" Ward said smugly. "Not a thing wrong with her when all was said and done — apart from a bit of so-called shock. Anyone can fabricate that."

"Did she fabricate the aerosol toxin she had?" August demanded.

"That's still with our own lab boys," Ward said, trying not to let his nerves show.

"Of course." August picked up the scrap of paper and tossed it onto Ward's lap. It slipped to the floor. "She gave me this just before you came in. Zaid Maher's address."

Ward picked it daintily off the floor and smoothed out the paper, studying it closely. "We've already got that far. Zaid Maher moved from there a couple of years ago." He nodded his head sadly. "From your record I didn't get the impression that you were the type to be distracted by a woman, Mr. Riley." He stood up. "No, I'm sorry. But I'm in charge on this side of the Atlantic. As I said, you'll have complete access. But it's my professional opinion that this woman must be removed to a more secure environment immediately."

August dropped his head between his hands. "Shit," he cursed, looking up at Ward through fanned fingers, "you're so sure of yourself, aren't you?"

Letting himself out, Ward said, "Certainty isn't a luxury I have come to know in my job, Mr. Riley."

★ ★ ★

Zuleika winced as the window sash slid clumsily against its rotting frame. The wind shifted the rusting fire escape over its weak hinges and it clanged against the brick building. It glistened with puddles of moisture in the quickly disappearing day. Zuleika forced herself to move slowly, the television still pushing the high shrieks of the game show into the room behind her. The rain slashed at her face as she groped for a footing on the small platform outside her window before jump-ing to the ground.

15

NEAR CHELMSFORD
February 7
5:45 p.m.

The Headmaster was polite but clearly puzzled. "I'm sorry, madam. But your son was discharged . . . ah . . . let's see," he studied his wristwatch, "less than an hour ago. His uncle paid all outstanding expenses," he couldn't resist a slight grunt of satisfaction. "He took Khalaf to the station to catch the six o'clock train, I believe." He leaned forward, studying her over the edge of his shining bifocals. He'd never met the mother before, an attractive woman but rather untidy. Stanley Harris didn't think himself a snob, but who wouldn't have noticed the mud-stained shoes and sloppy shirt? She hadn't even bothered to comb her hair. It was plastered against her head from the downpour that she'd brought with her. He knew he was old-fashioned but a touch of lipstick never did a woman any harm in his opinion. Her striking face was bare except for the anxiety woven between her brows.

He touched up his reassuring smile that usually relaxed these foreign types. "Don't you worry. If I do say so myself, young Khalaf looked particularly pleased to be off with his uncle and the young lady." Zuleika was immediately alert. "Not much compliment to us, I'm sure." He shelved the smile. It didn't seem to be working. "I did explain to your brother-in-law about the seriousness of removing a student during mid-term. We don't approve. But your husband had called and spoken to me so, of course, the family's wishes always prevail." He wished she'd say something. Amanda was cooking steak and kidney tonight and he was late as it was. "Madam?"

She'd stood up and was looking at him with that particularly vacant stare as if there was something just beyond his left shoulder mesmerizing her. Her long coat dripped rain water onto the Persian carpet the Board had finally bought him last month. "The six o'clock train?" she asked in a monotone.

"Yes. But . . ." Something in her face stopped him. Maybe he didn't want to question this situation too closely, after all. He had spoken directly to Dr. Maher. He knew his voice well. And as a matter of fact, a written note of permission to release the boy to his uncle's care was right here in his top tray. Stanley pushed through the pile of papers in the metal file, a vision of the tabloid headlines accelerating his perpetual indigestion. Arab Boy Disappears from Exclusive Public School. Headmaster says he had "no idea" anything was wrong! Accompanied by some unflattering Polaroid of Stanley in his bathing trunks at Bournemouth last year. He swallowed. "Anything further I can do for you?" he asked softly. If he was lucky she wouldn't even hear him.

"Where is the station?"

"Straight through the village. Just beyond the grocer's at the end of the road. You can't miss it. Post office is right next door." He started to wave the note from Maher, which he'd finally found, but she had disappeared. He watched her through the leaded windows. Khalaf Maher's mother was running across the soggy playing field, her coat flapping in the wind behind her.

She could hear the train's engine throbbing as she hurtled her rented car into the parking lot. As she ran through the empty waiting room, a fat woman in a cubbyhole plastered with flyers for London musicals screeched at her. Zuleika threw herself against the turnstile. One bar caught her sleeve as she tried to climb over it. Heat rose from the train into the damp air. A few pairs of curious eyes turned towards her from clouded windows as the conductor marched along the platform methodically slamming doors, shouting the traditional All Aboard!

Two children ran beside the train, dressed in the dark blue uniform accented with yellow piping of Khalaf's school. Her heart bounced. They climbed through an open door, pushing and shoving each other. She could see then that they were older than Khalaf.

The fat woman was behind her now, squeezing herself across the turnstile, shouting about tickets.

Zuleika ran to a compartment door and seized its cold handle. Reaching high to wrench it open. The train pumped and grumbled under her.

And then she saw Khalaf, his round face smiling down at her. There was a tiredness in his black eyes she'd never seen before. A woman leaned over him. A small and fair and pale woman. Khalaf's chubby palms were pressed against the windowpane as if trying to touch his mother. His mouth opened in a wide "oh" of astonishment. Zaid was leaning over him, his expression shocked. He darted away from the window, the pale woman shouting after him. A door at the end of the car tilted open. Zaid jumped to the ground. The engine lurched and then the train started sliding away. Zuleika clutched at the smooth, merciless steel, her nails raking against it.

But she was slipping down, falling away. The train gathered speed. She couldn't hold on. Not even for Khalaf.

And then hands seized her, wrenching her down. "Very dangerous trick that, luv. Very dangerous, indeed," the conductor clucked. "If you'd like to just get yourself a ticket there's another one coming through in fifteen minutes. We'll get you on that." He patted her shoulder awkwardly, as if afraid she might be violent.

"It's all right. My sister is a little upset. I'll take care of her."

Zuleika turned and looked into Zaid's eyes. Somewhere behind her the train was passing around a curve of leaning linden trees. The fat woman was grumbling to the conductor who was muttering back.

"What are you doing here?" Shock was chopping at Zaid's voice. He was pulling her down the platform towards the wooded area beyond the parking lot. "What's wrong with you, woman? Don't you realize what you're doing?"

She seized his lapels. "Tell me where he's gone! For heaven's sake, Zaid, tell me!"

Zaid, a quick regret softening his features, looked after the train. She followed his gaze. And then turned on him, her voice bitter. "Where have you sent him? To Ahmed?"

Zaid shook his head.

She stepped back. "It's kidnapping, you know. I can telephone the police right now and have Khalaf taken from the train at the next station. You will be arrested," she added desperately.

"Ahmed is his father, Zuleika. The court system in this country is not as we are used to. Khalaf will be in college before the paperwork is completed to even start to look for him. You must prove Ahmed took him. You must prove he took him without your permission. And don't forget — Ahmed is Khalaf's registered guardian when he is in school here."

"The police might be quite happy to have you instead then," she bartered.

Zaid thought quickly. He'd never seen her like this. She was desperate and angry. It was shock enough to find her here. Ahmed was going to be very, very displeased. Zaid would have to rely on the usual, most effective weapon. "Then you will never see Khalaf again. Don't forget what I have done for you in the past. Who brought you the note from him?"

She pushed her hands deep into her pockets and turned away. A mist rose from the tracks where the train had rolled over them. Weeds pushed through the wooden ties. "Will you give Ahmed a message for me then?" She softened her tone and scuffed along the paint-flecked platform. A teenage boy leaned against the end of the building, a knapsack over one shoulder. He eyed them curiously.

"I don't know . . ."

"Ahmed thinks I'm dead, Zaid."

Zaid shook his head. "No. He said he left you . . . that you would be upset but . . ."

"I could have died, Zaid. That ought to tell you something." She touched his arm.

He shook her hand off. "These are extraordinary times, Zuleika. A war has started. We can't become involved in personal distractions."

She looked at his face. It was a face that would be forever boyish, grotesquely so, if he lived to an old age, with its pouting lips and upturned nose. How soon before he realized what he was doing? Not soon enough.

"You can tell Ahmed that I have something that belongs to him. A vial of toxin. Do you think that too much of a petty distraction?" She had his attention now. Rain was rolling down the back of his neck. He seemed oblivious to it. "Tell him that I will exchange the vial for one more visit with Khalaf."

"Why do you want to make such trouble, Zuleika?" Zaid pleaded. "You will have plenty of money. The freedom to live how you like. Just go back to Australia and lose yourself. You will forget all this one day. You can marry again. Live another life. Have another . . ."

She interrupted, "Tell Ahmed that I will expect a message to be left at the Paddington Hotel on Crown Street before noon tomorrow. If the message doesn't come the vial will be turned over to the authorities. The only price he has to pay is to allow me to see Khalaf once more. That's not asking very much considering the value of his little vial, is it Zaid?" The bluff meant everything. How well did her brother-in-law know her? Could he read her now?

Zaid bit his lip. Another train chugged in behind them, filling the station with fumes and noise.

At last he nodded.

Zuleika buttoned her coat with shaking hands. She had to continue the bluff. "And tell Ahmed that if anything should happen to me between now and then, the vial is in a place where it will automatically be turned over to the British. Along with a letter detailing all I know about his research, his family, and where he might be found."

She strode to the parking lot without looking back.

February 8
6:30 a.m.

August hit the ground running when the sedan pulled up outside the apartment building. It was one in a row in a treelined block just off the Heath. The call pinpointing Zaid Maher's new address had come through at 6:15 a.m. Zuleika had been gone for a little over twelve hours and the general alert had turned up nothing. She could be anywhere.

Zaid had bought the place after moving back to London in '89. All August could think about was that maybe, just maybe, Zuleika had come here. She'd given him the wrong address, maybe she'd known the right one. Had she planned this all along? Where the hell was she?

The night rain had washed the streets in a fresh jauntiness that London had lost long ago. A paperboy zigzagged his bicycle down the street, weighed down by the heavy bag over his shoulder. Seizing the wet railing August took the whitewashed stairs two at a time. A stained-glassed window of butterflies and robins greeted him.

"Riley!" Ward was coming from the bottom of the stairs, walking carefully up each as if entering church instead of stalking a felon. "Riley, please don't go barging in there too quickly. The backup is just getting into place. For God's sake, man! We don't want to alert anyone yet!"

August glanced up at the roof in time to see a uniform and semiautomatic duck behind the old chimney pieces that had once warmed these homes of the well-to-do. A young woman with swinging dark hair and darting eyes strode along the sidewalk. She was dressed in a tailored suit and carried a hefty briefcase. Her shoes were flat. He looked again after the paperboy. The boy was actually about thirty under his peaked cap. And that bag probably held more than the daily gossip which passed for news these days. He raised his brows at the Commander. Ward nodded, his usual prim expression suddenly transformed into one of deadly seriousness.

They startled the old boy dozing behind the reception desk. The lobby area was small but exquisite, with original oils and fresh flowers in porcelain vases. The desk was heavy and old and the caretaker was outfitted in a snappy dark blazer and crisp white shirt. His rheumy eyes jumped to attention when he saw them. It was 6:30 a.m.

"Mr. Maher?" The caretaker took his time examining a roster of neat entries. "He's been away for over a week now." His finger followed a line across the page. "Due back next week." He snapped the book shut. "I water his plants. Keep his mail. Things like that. Young Mr. Maher likes his holidays, he does." The man smiled almost fondly as if in indulgence of some youngster. August reflected that the old guy would probably have to work three lifetimes to earn what Maher squandered in a month.

The caretaker was reluctant to take them upstairs but acquiesced when Ward very patiently unfolded his identification and hinted at the "seriousness" of the inquiry. After being assured, a little to the old fellow's disappointment, August guessed, that his name wouldn't be involved, he showed them to the flat.

It was antiseptically clean and the kind of neat that only someone who was away all the time or had two cleaning ladies could maintain. All chrome and silver lines. Large abstracts covered most of the walls. A diamond-encrusted roach clip sat openly on a table beside the bed.

The crumpled, damp letter from Ra'ad's widow lay flat on a glass-topped desk in Zaid's living room. August's understanding of written Arabic was minimal, but he knew enough to sift a desperate plea from the words. And to wonder what a

playboy Jordanian was doing in receipt of a letter from a notorious refugee camp.

Ward ordered a forensics team to go over the place fibre by
fibre.

August didn't notice the package until they were on their
way out, the caretaker fussing ahead of them. The crimson
wrapping paper looked more pricey per square foot than most
of the actual gifts Riley had ever bought. The discreet signature of an exclusive jeweller swirled across one corner of the
box. A card was tucked below the velvet ribbon.

"What's this?" August picked up the package.

"That was delivered for Mr. Maher yesterday." The old man
winked. "The ladies like to keep him happy."

August prised open the card: "Darling, I can't wait to see
you. Just a little welcome home present. Love, Margaret."

August showed it to the caretaker who was thrilled to be
included. "Do you know this Margaret?"

"Think that's his latest. Only seen her once. But I'll wager
she'll be around again. Older woman," he said slightly disapprovingly. "But you'd never know it unless you looked close.
Great legs," he grinned.

"Do you know where she lives?"

"Haven't a clue, mate."

"Let's go," August said. "We have to find that jeweller."

He didn't wait for Ward this time.

7:00 a.m.

"I don't like it," Emma said, stalking the floor. Her hair was
wrapped in a towel and she had pulled around her a robe of
slippery silk and embroidered flowers she'd found in the bedroom. "You don't know this woman well enough. It's taking
too big a chance."

"You should be grateful I'd given you this address for us to
meet. If you'd gone to my place you might have been picked
up by the police." Zaid closed the curtains and pulled his shirt

from his pants, unbuttoning it. "Here we can get some rest. Ahmed and Khalaf are with a cousin in St. John's Woods until it's safe to leave. No one besides Ahmed knows we're here. Margaret's sulking on the Riviera. Getting all tanned for our reunion. Besides, we won't have to hang around for long. In a few hours I'll be on a flight across the Channel and you'll be — well, wherever you want to be."

Since his escape from August Riley and return to familiar territory, Zaid felt a new confidence guiding him. He'd barely slept. The pervasive fear had been replaced by exhilaration. Emma rubbed violently at her hair. Her scalp felt itchy and she could feel handfuls erupting at the roots. "Why does Ahmed insist on pulling the boy from school? Why didn't he wait? I don't think the message from his wife went over very well."

Zaid poured himself a scotch from Margaret's well-stocked liquor cabinet. It might be his last chance for awhile. "Ahmed can handle Zuleika. He always could. You can't blame him for wanting to make certain that Khalaf is somewhere secure. They're making it hard on Arabs now. The British are xeno- phobic enough — a war gets them wound right up." He picked up the innocuous-looking can of shaving cream he had placed on top of the cabinet when they came in.

"You mean Ahmed won't be very pleased about our joint venture?" she said slyly. Fool, fool, fool, she thought. You'll never get out alive. And Dr. Ahmed Maher will not get out of the country. One discreet phone call before the mission would take care of that. They'd arrest him before he had time to turn around.

He dropped onto the leather couch and pushed off his shoes, his shirt falling open. "Ahmed has always underestimated me. He likes to think of himself as the dedicated one and me as the dilettante. Nothing will change his mind until I do something. Besides," he tossed the canister in the air and caught it with a flourish, "as a couple we are far less conspicuous than we would be alone. And since our goals coincide — well, then, why not a little teamwork?"

"Don't be so casual with that," Emma said, taking the can from him and walking into the hallway where she placed it on a shelf above the coat rack, tucked securely amongst several mohair scarves.

He laughed. "I know exactly how to treat that little gem."

Emma came back into the room and sat down on the arm-rest of the couch. "But it's just for effect at first. Don't you forget that. We hold it until they agree to debate the '56 tests."

"And the Palestinians," he interjected.

She nodded. "Nobody leaves or enters the Chamber, or we threaten to release the contents of the vial. Right?"

He sipped at his drink and rubbed his chest. "We might not get out. Have you thought of that?"

"It'll be chaos. We'll leave separately. They can't possibly know which of us has the live vial." A certain satisfaction smoothed her features.

He lifted his glass in a mock toast. "To the House of Commons."

Margaret stood on the sidewalk in the midst of her designer luggage. A light gleamed from behind the drawn curtains of the flat. She really would have to remind Mrs. Wyjinsky to be more careful about leaving the electricity on. The woman was going to have to be let go anyway. Too many long-distance calls on the phone and too much watering down of the whiskey.

Margaret had gone straight from the offices of Abercrombie and Fraser to an antique jewellery auction in New York. She'd satiated herself on the excess of it and flown back wanting something real, something warm. Wanting Zaid. Sighing, she pulled out her keys and anticipated the hot bath she'd draw as soon as she got in.

Mr. Grutman was irritable and sleepy. He slid the heavy cage of bars back from the front door of his jewellery store, and August and Ward followed him into a tight vestibule. Flicking off the alarm just inside the door, he motioned them into the dimly lit interior. His hands flicked over the gleaming cases he'd tended for forty years. Their fragile appearance belied the fact that a sledge hammer wouldn't be able to break that glass. The fluorescent night lights illuminated the wallpaper in the same crimson as the wrapping paper on the gift at Zaid's flat. It shone like blood against the walls.

Most of the inventory had been locked away for the night except for a few pieces. Here and there the heads of distant-looking mannequins with thick false lashes and elaborate wigs peered out of the gloom, a few choked by heavy necklaces. August touched a tendril of one soft curl lying against a molded shoulder and thought of Emma: her pale, angry face; the power behind that white anger; the ruthless determination she carried with her. She was probably somewhere in this city right now.

He leaned against the counter where the cash register sat. His eye was caught by the display under his elbow. A tiny pendant in the shape of a hawk lay in a patch of velvet the deep blue of an Alaskan autumn sky. He leaned closer, trying to identify the bird. But the artist had successfully caught the sweep of a wing, the power of a talon, without specifying species. A tiny emerald chip formed the eye. August tried to remember the falcon he'd seen that day at Burnt Paw Lake. But all he could bring to mind in this exquisite shop on Bond Street was the rabbit, scurrying for its life — and losing.

Grutman came from the back, blinking his sleep-encrusted lids, his hair wisping from behind his ears, the collar of a candy-striped pyjama top askew beneath his overcoat. His thin lips were pulled down in disapproval. He'd made it clear that he didn't like being visited at the crack of dawn by any kind of police force. And August didn't blame him. But they needed to find the woman who had ordered the crimson package delivered to Mr. Zaid Maher, which turned out to contain a twenty-two-karat identification bracelet nestled in cream silk.

The proprietor pulled his glasses from a pocket and polished them with exquisitely slow movements before placing them precisely on the edge of his nose. "Yes. Mrs. Haden-Brown." He examined the two intruders over the edge of his glasses as if having second thoughts. "She's been a good customer of mine over the years. I wouldn't want to cause the lady any trouble."

Ward cleared his throat and tapped the edge of the counter with his well-manicured fingers.

August caught the edge of irritation in Grutman's eyes. This man had been pushed around by authorities before. He wanted them to justify themselves, to give him a good reason to cooperate with a clear conscience.

"Mr. Grutman," August said patiently, "we realize that this is very inconvenient for you. But a serious crime has been committed. Mrs. Haden-Brown may be able to help us. If you don't give us her address now we'll just have to go to headquarters and get the information from her driver's licence. All right?" August was counting on his respectful tone and Grutman's desire to get rid of them and back into bed with his plump, worried wife who had stood at the door of their flat, hand to her mouth, as Grutman had climbed into the car with them.

The older man gave him one long look and then glanced back at Ward. August prayed the Commander wouldn't offer one of his condescending prompts.

"Number Twenty-Four Stratley Gardens," Mr. Grutman said, snapping the book shut, the hard set of his mouth signalling that that was all they were going to get out of him.

Margaret's eyes swung from Zaid to Emma as if she were hypnotized by some invisible chain linking them. She tried to say something. Zaid wasn't sure if it was his name. He couldn't get used to her dark hair, her clothes, the outlandish makeup. At first he'd thought it was some stranger standing there in the doorway. A mistake. A terrible mistake.

He started to stand up, buttoning his shirt, knocking his drink to the floor. "Margaret. It's not . . ."

She stared at his bare chest. The dark liquor seeping into her white carpet. The thin woman poised on the arm of the couch. Dressed in Margaret's robe. "That's mine," she said idiotically. "Take it off."

Emma stood up slowly, turning her mind around the frenzy in this woman's eyes.

Zaid thrust one hand towards her. "Please, Margaret."

Damn! Damn! Damn! he thought. Get rid of her . . . Get rid of her . . . "Margaret, what are you doing here?" the question jumped from him.

"I live here, remember?" Her voice was surprisingly calm but the blood was pounding in her ears, making it hard for her to hear him. He seemed to be saying something else. She looked at the woman again. She could see her breasts rising and falling against the silk of the robe.

Emma didn't want to blink. The air was thick with threat.

And then suddenly Margaret crumbled in on herself. A puppet abandoned by the puppeteer. Her face collapsed like melted wax. Her shoulders were brittle and her knees suddenly pathetic in the little girl skirt. Neither Emma nor Zaid noticed her fists clenched to a bloodless white at her sides. Sobs punished her.

"Margaret. Please." Zaid was at her side, his arms around her.

"Don't touch me," she moaned, leaning into him, scrambling for some pride.

"Listen to me. It's not . . . it's not what you think." He was stroking her hair, pressing her to him.

She caught the woman's eyes. Measuring her. Measuring the years. Measuring Zaid's affection.

Margaret found her strength and pushed Zaid from her. "Just get out of here. Get out of my home." She could feel the mascara pooling in great dark globs on her cheeks. "And take your whore with you. Get out of my sight!" She ran into the bedroom, the door swinging closed behind her.

"I don't need to be told twice," Emma said, pushing past him.

Margaret leaned over her dressing table, choking on dry heaves of humiliation. The broken pieces of her delicate ornament, carried here in a futile sentimental moment to be repaired, were lined up in front of her like a mute accusation.

Zaid seized Emma's arm. "Not so fast. We have to think this out," he hissed. "I might be able to calm her down long enough to give us time. Bring her round."

Emma looked at Zaid with contempt. "You're a fool! There's no charming your way out of this one. The woman's devastated. We'll have to find somewhere else to hide until tomorrow."

"Where? Under the Arches?" He lowered his voice. "We need this place. It's secure. We only need a few more hours. Nobody knows we're here."

Emma leaned close to him. "Your girlfriend in there does!"

Margaret raised her head and gazed at her reflection in the bureau mirror. Puffy black eyes, her hair wired like some demented clown around her face. Lipstick smeared. The blush, much too bright. The eyes, too lost to be found again. By any-one.

She closed her eyes. But she could still see the two of them there in her mind. Carefully, she removed her diamond ear-rings, placing them in the proper spot in her jewellery box. The emerald crescent pin that Peter had given her the day he left winked up at her.

Coming back out of the bedroom, Margaret saw the woman pushing against Zaid. Pressing her face to his. The robe gaping open. They didn't care. She didn't exist. They had dismissed her in her own house as if she were a robot.

But she did exist . . . she did . . .

The gun was still in the bottom left-hand drawer where she'd left it. Her vision was blurred as she groped for it. The pounding was rolling in her ears again.

The look of horror on Zaid's face was worth it. Total recog-nition of her existence now.

She dimly regretted the tearing of silk as the bullet reached Emma's back. She heard a small gasp, like air escaping a tire, and heard Zaid shout.

She saw only the delicate threads of one embroidered rose on the sleeve of the robe. Her robe. That woman had no right to be wearing it. She wanted it back.

Zaid groped for the door behind him. Margaret's eyes didn't leave Emma. His coat. The canister.

Quietly. So quietly.

He opened the door and walked quickly down the first flight. Silence from above.

Running down the second and third flights, he knocked over a potted plant that sat in a rickety stand on the narrow landing.

Two blocks and onto the clear flight of the Heath.

Running. Running.

A yapping terrier caught at his heels, its owner chattering impotently at it. Zaid kicked at the dog. It hung onto his ankle, its tiny teeth deep into him. He kicked again, flinging it from him. The owner shouted, waving her umbrella at him.

He clutched the back of a bench, leaning against it, catching his breath, while the woman berated him and clucked to the howling white ball of a dog. Zaid could feel his leg swell and sting as he hunched over the bench, but he didn't care. It was a test. All a great test of his courage. He didn't need Emma. He could do this alone. Some power had allowed him to escape. Some power wanted him to succeed. He wouldn't let Ahmed down. He wouldn't let his brother down.

The fussing woman scooped up her dog and backed away from him.

Later, she would tell how the criminal foreigner had attacked Muffy in the park while they were out for their constitutional. She and Muffy dined out on the event for weeks.

Emma lay facedown on the carpet, her life pumping from her back. A streak of light from a crack in the curtains crossed her cheek. She could feel the woman tearing the kimono from her. Her bare flesh was exposed. She could also see the glint of the gun barrel in the light.

The shells of a wind chime shivered.

Emma wanted to live. If it was only the six months the doctors had given her. She wanted it. She wanted it more than anything else she had ever known.

7:45 a.m.

The desk clerk inhaled lazily from the stub of his cigarette and let his gaze linger over Zuleika's body. She didn't look like any of the regular hookers. Stained raincoat, damp hair, soggy shoes marring his floor as she moved from foot to foot. The earrings could be worth a bob or two. Room paid for in advance — it was usually rented by the hour so he wasn't complaining. She snatched the envelope from his hand without so much as a "thank you" and turned into the lobby reading it greedily. The clerk twisted himself from his usual position on the vinyl couch to watch her for a moment before turning back to stare at the television welded high up onto the wall. He chewed on the nub of his cigarette and opened his paper to the racing results. She wasn't his type anyway.

The instructions were to go to an office on Harley Street. Ahmed had a distant cousin married to an opthamologist who practised there. Zuleika memorized the address and crumpled the note in her hand.

The scream of the sirens sliced through the walls and a building wind rocked the wind chimes against the window. Ward gently unclasped the gun from Margaret Haden-Brown's hand and led her from the room. August bent over Emma, pulling the torn robe around her nakedness. Her lips were blue. He'd stemmed the blood with the heel of his hand and pulled her against him, rolling with the great shudders that were convulsing her.

Her eyes widened in bleak amazement as she recognized him. A yearning for mercy gnawed at her while the strange chime sang from a distance. She hadn't killed him. She hadn't killed him. She could atone for David later.

August Riley was alive. Maybe it was a sign. She had a chance. She out of all her family had a chance, after all.

August cupped the damp towel around her head. Hold me in, she thought. Hold my soul in, she tried to whisper.

He bent closer. "Where is he, Emma? Tell us. Where is Zaid? Don't let him do it, Emma."

Her eyes cleared for a moment. She remembered her father and the strength and spirit that had been sucked from him for thirty years, and she thought of her brother's grave next to his where she'd never been able to grow anything, her mother's bewildered eyes and distorted memories. A bile of bitterness surged in the back of her throat. "They killed my father," she rasped.

August bit his lip and looked to the ceiling. The wind chimes clanged in a violent gust of wind. "Don't take it with you," he pleaded. "Don't take this with you, Emma. Leave us something. Anything!" He wanted to shake her but instead pulled her closer, rocking her like a baby. Her eyes had glazed again, the blood had ebbed. "Emma. Your father was a soldier. Can you hear me?"

She shook her head weakly. "He didn't know."

"No, he didn't. But Emma," he gripped her shoulders, hard this time, pulling her up straighter. The blood released in a warm rush against him. The towel fell from her head, leaving her skull exposed with its tiny blue veins and tufts of hair. "Emma. The weather. Think of the weather. If there's an accident! You don't know what Zaid will do with the vial! If the wind changes it will be anyone. Anyone, Emma! Think of it! Mothers like your own. Brothers like Davie. Anyone!"

Foam bubbled at her lips. He gently brushed it away.

"House of Commons," she whispered. "House of Commons."

The siren screamed outside as he lifted her and placed her on the couch, vaguely conscious of Ward ordering around the paramedics. "It doesn't matter," he said quietly. "She's finished." He touched her pale skull once and then pushed past a couple of bewildered bobbies who'd been patrolling their normally benign neighborhood.

"Riley!" he heard Ward call. "Riley. Come back here, man!"

But the only response to the Commander was the sound of splintering glass as the storm rose and the wind chimes shattered against the window.

16

HARLEY STREET
LONDON
Same morning

It took Zuleika longer than it should have to make her way to Harley Street. She had paced the adjacent blocks twice before gritting her nerve to push the bell beside the freshly painted bright blue door. London was huge, she kept reminding herself. Even in these times they couldn't have a watch on every Arab national in the city. She had to hope that Dr. Haq Al-Zaqiz had kept his nose clean.

She remembered him as soon as he opened the door. A small man with kind eyes, his dark beard now transformed to a wispy goatee. He greeted her respectfully as the wife of his cousin and showed her into the inner office as if for a routine examination. Slipping around his equipment, he motioned her into the torturous-looking examining chair, flipped a chart on the opposite wall, and was gone.

She listened for the sound of Khalaf's laugh or the chatter of his voice somewhere in the house. But there was nothing.

Just the hum of traffic and the faint rumble of a subway train.

It took her a moment to realize that there was something odd about the chart. She moved from the chair.

A map was pinned over the vision test. A map of Hyde Park and the streets adjacent to it. A point was marked with a black x, with a time and date in Ahmed's familiar writing printed across the bottom.

Zuleika stared at it. What was his game? Why had she thought she could ever win against him — whatever her advantage?

She pressed her forehead against the map. And then carefully unpinning it, she walked from the office into the storm.

Zaid wasn't likely to get a taxi after he'd bolted from the flat — not in this weather. And he hadn't taken a car. There was only one station within running distance that could take Zaid Maher where he was going: the Northern Line straight through to Embankment, walk or transfer to Westminster. It would take him less than twenty minutes.

London had given August three years in the early eighties. A deskbound punishment from Wendell under the pretence of trying to relight the fires of the special relationship with the Brits. The exercise had been like rubbing two damp sticks together, despite Mr. Reagan's cosiness with Mrs. Thatcher. But he'd escaped the proper atmosphere of the offices on Curzon Street and embraced the strange grey appeal of the city. Ancient grudges and lost glories steamed from every crack in every old brick. The plunder of an empire was tucked behind the doors of a dozen museums and galleries. He had spent the winter hours lost in the past and avoided the crowded streets in the summer so he wouldn't have to witness the city's faded dignity painted up like an old tart, selling herself to the gawking tourists.

During his lunchtime escapes, when he couldn't face another drunken pub lunch, he'd follow the underground tube lines as far as they'd take him in search of some uncertain place. The

Heath had been one of his favourite destinations. The closest he could get at short notice to the illusion of wilderness.

He ran through the park, trying to pace himself but a jagged rasp in his lower chest pursued him. A woman sat on a bench hugging a piece of fluff that was passing for a dog. She stared at August. His shirt, still splattered with Emma's blood, flying from his pants, hair jumping from his head, two days' growth of beard. A wild man with demonic purpose. She clutched the dog to her and it growled halfheartedly from somewhere under a pink bow.

Should have stuck to that jogging program, August berated himself. He'd only lasted two weeks last time he'd tried it. The sloping streets of Hampstead offered some relief as he followed them past toy-looking brick houses with their perfect gardens and burnished door knobs. The streets were slick. Rain jumped off him, sliding down his bare neck. Another block to the station.

A news agent was gathering soggy papers from the sidewalk into a wooden shelter, drawing back a little as he saw August. The headline screamed at him as he turned into the station. *Gulf Debate Today*. Shit! Zaid's perfect platform. But he was clumsy in his commitment. Lacked the precision, the perfectionism, of his brother. But Zaid had a point to make. And he might be getting less fussy about where he made it.

August pushed a coin into the ticket machine. A group had gathered around the doors as the elevator rumbled up the shaft. The ticket machine jammed, blinking stubbornly red at him. He fumbled in his pockets, then dashed to the bored woman behind the glass of a cubicle, snapping the ticket from her hand. The elevator shuddered open. The group surged forward. August saw blood dotted against the dirty tile as he bolted around the ticket machines, one of them still blinking red.

His head jerked up. The alien, automatic voice from the loudspeaker was issuing its orders to stand clear of the doors. Zaid was squeezed against the elevator's back wall, a light shining clearly on his wiry hair, illuminating the features so uncannily twinned to that yellowing photo held in Phyllis Emory's arthritic hand. Fear flashed across his features as he recognized August. And then the heavy metal doors eased closed.

August jammed his shoulder against the squeezing iron. "Open up! Goddamn it! Open up!"

"I say, old man!" the voice was suitably disconcerted, the blue eyes beneath the sandy brows disapproving of the rude American. "We have reached the limit in here, you know!" the man added self-righteously as he punched the down button. The doors bounced closed, treating August to a line of graffiti as pungent as anything he'd seen on the streets of New York.

The station was the deepest in the city. The staircase interminable. August plunged down it, propelling himself with the railing, leaping over the oily puddles where the constant drip of century-old plumbing had worn away the cement. In places, the filthy white tiles that lined the walls had given way to weeping raw clay. His slipping footsteps echoed back round and round the curlicued iron banister.

Just a minute's grace. That's all he needed. Maybe two. Whatever else might be said about these archaic tubes — they were usually on time. And only one at a time could come through here, no matter how they sliced it.

Thirty feet to go. Maybe forty. He could hear the rumble of the train shaking Hampstead's foundations.

There was a rush of warm dirty air as the train pressed into the station.

Twenty feet.

He heard the hydraulic hiss of the doors, the automatic voice, this time warning Mind the Gap between the platform and the train.

Ten feet. Another hydraulic hiss.

He slipped and skidded past the benches and annual crop of winter ads for some mythical Grecian beach.

This time he jammed his arm through the door to the last car, managing to pry it open. The train lurched forward and then stopped. August grabbed the rail that ran along the ceiling inside the car and pulled himself forward. Discreet glances over high newspapers watched his progress, hoping the rough-looking fellow would keep right on moving.

The next section was full. Many commuters were superstitious about travelling in the last car after a series of gruesome wrecks. Several dark-haired figures ahead. Young men.

And then Zaid turned and looked directly at him. August's eyes flew to the bulge in the other man's jacket. The vial!

The train lurched again. Zaid squeezed through the door he'd propped open and onto the platform, loping towards the stairs August had just descended.

The automatic doors slammed closed. August heaved himself against them.

The train gathered speed, and the tunnel sucked them forward. And only a black wall surrounded him.

At Belsize Park Station he actually found a pay phone that worked. He got through to Ward immediately. And to give the man credit, he performed a minor miracle and shut the place down by the time five more trains had rolled through.

Londoners, by now used to another IRA scare — an untended package on a platform bench, a plastic Marks & Spencer bag shoved underneath a seat — had moved quickly off the trains. No questions, perhaps walking a little faster than usual. Resigned to yet another delay beyond the control of London Transport.

August was alone in the rattling, dusty train churning towards Embankment. The cars, lighter now without their passengers, clanged against their couplings, jolting August against the seat. The lights below ground had been doused. He had the eerie feeling of travelling in another time zone as the anxious driver, after twenty years of monotony, sped through abandoned station after station. The platforms were dark. A derelict, missed as a bundle of rags curled at the end of Leicester Square Station, lifted his head from a curdled wine stupor. He saw a bloodied man, silhouetted in a brightly lit car, speed by, suspended in the strange silence. He groaned and fell back against the pavement, pulling his rags around him.

Westminster was eerily quiet, as if the city had suffered a nuclear blast and August had emerged from below, a survivor.

He pushed away the compulsion to stay safe in the earth's belly. Zaid Maher was out there somewhere.

Big Ben thrust into the sky above him and rolled its gears to churn out nine o'clock as he scrambled up the stairs, fighting a wind and the slanting rain. Plainclothes were crawling everywhere. He could feel them. But they hadn't evacuated the streets around Parliament. Ward had used his territorial imperative to insist on that, afraid that it might scare Zaid off and force a showdown. This way they had more chance of taking him quietly.

August hoped like hell the Commander was right.

Spatterings of tourists were huddled around Churchill's hunched statue and at the entrance to a few sad-looking shops catering to what was left of the tour trade since the Gulf War broke. August jogged across Bridge Street. The light turned, and a limousine screeched to a halt, skidding on the slick road, its windshield wipers pumping maniacally against the steady downpour. An erect figure in the back seat, a slight man with grey hair was thrown forward. The driver leaned on his horn, grimacing at August. He raised a hand and jumped aside to continue walking down Millbank, blinking the rain from his eyes and wiping it from his nose, expecting to hear an alarm scream out any moment.

What the hell would he do? Where would the invisible poison cloud appear? Maher could be pulling the tab at this moment in the public toilets. Or next to Rodin's marvellous statue. Perhaps in a vinyl-covered booth in one of the cafes just along the block.

He could spot only two bobbies, instead of the usual one, standing at the public entrance to the House of Commons. God! What was Ward thinking of? They had to have more force. He scanned the rooftops, maybe Undercover were moving into place. Zaid could toss that thing anywhere. He knew he was a hunted man.

August slid to a stop beside the high iron railing that cordoned off the Parliamentary Gardens. He turned and let his gaze follow the limo that had nearly hit him as it carried the grey-haired man past him. It disappeared into the rain haze around the corner, each set of lights slipping to green as it approached.

And then he understood.

Number Ten Downing Street was less than two blocks away. Zaid only had to get within sight to target the Prime Minister!

A cruiser passed him, slowing down. August couldn't stop. Couldn't use them. Zaid would spot them a mile away. The cops slid the car up onto the sidewalk and cut him off. August yanked his ID from his pocket and waved it in their faces, shouting Ward's name before jumping over the hood of the car and taking the rest of the block.

The limo had turned right onto Richmond instead of left into Downing Street. Good. The driver was taking a delayed route. Once or twice around the block. Waiting for reinforcements.

August turned up his run. His ankle protested by crimping beneath him.

He nearly missed Zaid.

The flower stall was a block from Downing Street. The vendor was arguing with a late customer clutching what must have been three dozen carnations. "Sorry, mate, closing. Business rotten today." A wooden shutter slammed down, splashing water over Zaid's pure wool jacket. "'Urry up, squire! Got to get out 'a this bleedin' rain!"

August forced himself to a slow trot, stalling behind a rubbish bin propped outside a renovation project. His sight was blurred through the rain but he could still see the crimson carnations and hear the protesting vendor.

Zaid leaned forward and the vendor plastered a phony smile over his wet mug. He ripped some cheap green paper from a roller and wrapped it roughly around the flowers. Zaid pressed some bills into his hand. The other man offered a genuine smile this time and tipped his cap. Zaid turned away, his hand sheltering the bouquet.

August drew in his breath and stepped from behind the rubbish bin, resisting the urge to run after Zaid.

Zaid stopped suddenly and stooped to tie a shoelace.

August ducked into a doorway and pressed himself against

the vestibule wall. His shoulder trigged a bell. It buzzed into the grey day. An irritated uppercrust voice demanded his business.

Zaid glanced over his shoulder towards August.

August drew in his gut, vowing once again to stick to his diet, and plastered himself to the entry door. "Flowers for Mrs. . . . ," he hissed, sounding like the Boston Strangler, no doubt, and glanced at the nameplate, "Mrs. Dunham."

A put-upon sigh through the intercom. "There's no Mrs. Dunham at this residence. Miss Dunham will take delivery."

The door buzzed open. August leaned into it and swung through the glass door into a freezing cold lobby. He squinted against the glass.

And froze.

Zaid was walking back towards him!

A whiny voice was calling from the floor above.

What could he have missed in the five seconds his back was turned?

Zaid picked up his step. A little closer to the building now.

"You there! Are you the man from the florist?" The voice was even higher-pitched in life. A woman, all pink chins and red nails, was descending on him down the staircase. "I say, you there! I'm talking to you! What are you doing? Where are my flowers?"

The flowers! The goddamned carnations!

August pushed the door open as Zaid was hitting stride in front of the building.

Zaid Maher was strong and had a heavy dose of desperation propelling him. But the headlock choked off his first protest, the punch in the kidney, his second. Zaid clawed at August, kicking wildly as he was dragged back along the wet sidewalk, his pants tearing as they scraped the cracked pavement. They fell into the basement stairwell of a townhouse, tipping a full garbage bin back down the stairs on top of them.

The woman with the red nails gasped from the entryway, outraged at the hooliganism that had seized the city.

The limo's sleek body turned into the narrow street. Downing Street was less than a block away.

Zaid lunged, the power of a stallion, August hanging on like an amateur rider. August slammed Zaid's face into the iron railings, crushing the flowers against his chest.

"Did you release it yet, you bastard? Did you release it?"

Zaid choked out some gibberish.

August pulled his head back by the hair and aimed it at the railings again. "I asked you a question!"

Zaid spit out a tooth and shook his head violently.

Was he telling the truth? Or was he a suicider? A good little martyr?

The limo had slowed to a halt beyond them. A slamming door.

August's mind raced. An overzealous secret service agent might blow it. Might blow it all.

He pushed Zaid down the stairs, his ankle throbbing in revolt. Something cracked as Zaid hit the bottom. His knee was in Zaid's back as he pushed his face towards the bin. "Give it to me! Give it to me, you little bastard!"

Zaid hesitated. Blood streaming from his mouth.

God! Please don't let him be aiming for martyrdom! Don't let him be ready to let the next passing cloud dump this stuff on the next couple of hundred joes wandering in Green Park! Not ready to take me with him! I'm not ready to die vomiting some deadly poison over a pile of soggy banana peels and used tea leaves.

Zaid turned his head slowly and let the carnations, tumbling soft red, fall to the ground. He still held the green paper crumpled between his fingers. "Let go of me or you're a dead man," he hissed. "You and anyone else who happens to breathe today."

August's muscles locked into place.

"Let go!" Zaid's voice was clear now, every syllable clearly enunciated.

They both heard the footsteps splashing across the wet pavement at the same time. The squeal of the bobby's whistle. The woman from the flat shouting about "thugs."

Zaid lunged forward. August kicked his leg out from under him, his own ankle screeching in protest. Zaid stumbled against the moss-eaten stairs, and the green paper slid down his body.

They both watched it fall, as if in slow motion, to the stairwell's cement floor.

The bobby shouted.

Zaid darted towards the ground and seized the wet paper, green shreds of it sticking to his fingers. August kicked him again. A look passed between them that seemed to last a lifetime.

Then Zaid hurdled the stairs and bolted down the sidewalk.

The bobby descended on August.

August stretched his hand towards the wet slivers of carnations, petals and green paper, the dye smearing the ground. A purple bruise was rising like dough across his knuckles.

A canister lay cushioned in a wrinkle of paper. A curlicue of letters was embroidered across its smoky surface. The cap was twisted on its stem.

4:30 p.m.

"Ward will never agree. He wants to throw you in the Tower and let you rot," August said. "And I can't say I blame him. You risked everything taking off like that. Especially now that Zaid is loose."

She'd shown no remorse. Offered no apologies. Just appeared at the safe house and identified herself to the astonished Duty Officer. When August and Commander Ward showed up, she'd ordered Ward out while she spoke to August alone. The Commander had refused at first, but then a look from August had forced him, stiff-limbed and flush-faced, from the room. "I'll be in the garden," he said. A bark on his way out at the Duty Officer had to satisfy his fury. For the moment.

She stood leaning against the cold fireplace, biting her nails and swallowing cup after cup of black tea. Still trying to dance this dance to her own tune, August thought. And he wasn't in the mood to accompany her. "You set me up for a sucker once. That doesn't bother me too much. You're not the first. Or the most expert. But what does bother me — quite a bit — is that your brother-in-law just tried to toss a biological weapon into the middle of this city. If Zaid had managed to release your husband's little toy it would have killed every living thing within a five-to-ten-mile radius. And your husband is running around with God knows how many more of those gems in his back pocket. And," he leaned towards her, "you conveniently disappeared while all this was going on."

He pushed a hand across his mouth and eyes. Every time he thought he'd found a way out of the maze that was Zuleika, he turned around and found she'd added another impossible path. "You know it would help if you told us where Ahmed might be." He must have a safe house. Zaid must have made his way there after he got away from me."

"I told you — and I've told Ward a hundred times! I don't know! Ahmed and I led separate lives. They could be at any one of a hundred homes sympathetic to the Cause!"

August shook his head.

Something dismissive in his gesture brought her temper to the surface. "All right," she slid her cup and saucer onto the coffee table and sat down in the chair opposite him. "I thought that I knew what I was doing. I didn't. I know now that Ahmed will never let me have Khalaf. But I also know that he wants the other vial and is willing to risk quite a bit to get it. He thinks I'm desperate enough to try anything." She watched August, not letting him detect the fear in her voice. "Which I am. Right now — I have to trust you more than I trust him. All I want is Khalaf. And if I can get him — as we said before — chances are you can get Ahmed at the same time — right? What have you got to lose?"

August heard the bravado in her voice and felt the frantic search in her eyes as they studied him. Why did he want to believe her so badly? He stared at the dust-heavy brass candlesticks on top of the mantel. Gobs of melted wax and stubs of old candles, greyish now, were stuck in them. He wondered who on earth would have been inclined to light them for a romantic mood in this so-called safe house which seemed anything but? The memory of that one long, soft kiss by the window passed through his mind. He straightened his arms against the mantel and stared into the cold grate. They really had no choice, as she had said. They were up against a brick wall and Maher was a clever spider who could crawl between the cracks while Riley and Ward Inc. tried to bulldoze their way through all obstacles, thin or thick.

"Ahmed has agreed to meet me," she said to his back, her voice tremulous. "I have a time and a place."

He knew what that had cost her. He straightened up.

She tried to read his spine. "Please," she whispered. "One more chance. I'll do anything."

He winced and turned on her. "Don't beg."

She drew back. "All right," he muttered.

Zuleika waited rigidly. What was the condition? There had to be one.

"Ward still has to agree. I'll see what I can do. But I can't go over his head on this one. It's probably our last chance to get your husband. And," he watched her closely, "I'll have to be there."

She secretly shouted with relief. But on the outside she only allowed the slightest nod. Her appreciation was in her eyes.

"No! Absolutely not!" Ward leaned into the wind as if demonstrating his objection to the idea, pulling his collar up high around his neck. His hair was swept upward by a sudden gust. It was the most dishevelled August had seen him. "It's far too risky." He raised his sketchy brows. "You've already lost Zaid, for God's sake. We were just bloody lucky that safety seal hadn't snapped." He repressed a shudder. "One thing that we can say for Maher. He's damned thorough. Thank God."

"Granted." August didn't want to dwell on what might have happened in that garbage-tossed stairwell. "But look, Ward, for the moment we can assume that Maher and Zaid are still in the country. It's our last chance to stop them getting out with the toxin. We know he's got at least one more vial. If we can lure him to a rendezvous with Zuleika we've got a chance. If he gets a private jet — or even on the ferry to Calais — he's out of our range. We lose the chance to get him before he reaches his real destination. And if we incapacitate him, it increases our chances of nabbing his brother."

"His wife is in our custody. And we've got a vial. That's not a bad day's work," Ward said.

"Yes. But Ahmed's the real prize. Get him. Get the ultimate plan and whatever other cronies he might have floating around London." August tried to keep his voice calm. He could see by Ward's stiffening jaw and the twitch at the edge of his eye that the Commander was weakening — and fighting it.

"Look," August shoved his hands deep in his pockets and tried to ignore the way his soaked cuffs were sloping around his ankles. His eyes were gritty with exhaustion. The old flower beds in the narrow, brick-walled garden behind the house were drowning in mud. "I know you don't like me. But don't let that stand in the way of getting this bastard. I've gotta believe that you like Maher even less than me?" He tried a halfhearted laugh.

Ward punched his umbrella open and closed violently. "Don't flatter yourself, Riley. I'm only thinking of the operation." He dissected August with a look. "Your way, we risk losing both of them. Maher and his wife. My way, we at least keep the woman. A lot of information might be mined there. With a little patience." He snapped the umbrella again. "Why must you Americans always be in such a hurry?"

The rain was forming small rivulets in August's cheeks. "There's a war on, Commander. Remember? The Coalition has been screwing itself into contortions waiting for Hussein to dump this poison down our gullets. Some people are starting to say maybe we shouldn't worry quite so much. We Americans are natural optimists, you know," he grimaced wryly. "We'd like to think Saddam is just a lot of hot air and doesn't really know a chemical or biological bomb from his ass. Well, just think about it, Ward. One of the top biological weapon scientists on the planet is on his way — and I think we can presume jolly old England is just a detour to the Gulf — with at least one vial of a deadly toxin our scientists have never seen before, let alone produced an antidote. Unless he's decided to take Zuleika's offer, he's probably out of our hands anyway."

"Exactly. He might be out of the country already. They both might be."

August grit his teeth and squished the water from one runner, feeling it pump between his toes. "And he might not be. They could be coordinating another attack on London right now. But getting that other vial from Zuleika has to be important to him. Maher doesn't want us to get the formula. And he can't mix up another batch in a hurry. Every drop counts. You have the chance to pick him up tomorrow. Think about it."

Ward plucked at a dark leaf on a dying vine which was struggling on the chipped brick wall. "If we lose the woman as well we've gambled away not just the main prize but a pretty decent runner-up as well."

August hunched his shoulders and stared at the full-figured marble statue in the middle of an empty goldfish pond. "How about we have some of your clever boys bug the thing? It's detoxed now anyway." His voice rose an octave. "We let Zuleika keep her date with Maher at Hyde Park. She doesn't have to know the vial's bugged. That way, even if she wanted to she couldn't tip him off. And, if by some fluke, he gets the jump on your people — and me — we have a tab on him!"

Ward ripped the leaf from the vine and crumbled it slowly in his hand.

August squished the water from his other runner.

"Might be worth a try," Ward rationed the words like the last of his coin in a slot machine.

August punched him in the shoulder. "We'll get the bastard! We'll get him!"

Ward jerked his shoulder back. "For heaven's sake, Riley!" He was frowning but August could see the gleam of the hunt in his pale eyes.

17

Sunday, February 10

*L*aid had nothing against London. In fact, he'd grown to
rather like its eccentric grey ways. But this would be his
last day here. And he was ready to leave. To move on to the
real life that waited for him. His apprenticeship had lingered
too long as it was. He looked around the tube. He rarely rode
the stuffy underground and so it was appropriate on this last day
to travel the bowels of the city he was leaving behind. Sunday
shoppers and hungover Saturday night lovers lounged in the
corners of the cars, oblivious to him. The canister had been a
terrible loss. He had been cursing his clumsiness ever since his
encounter with August. But Ahmed had the right idea that
they should move on. They still had their true purpose to fulfill.
Emma Cowen was a detour. She was out of their way now.
There was nothing to stop them.

He enjoyed his inadvertent costume. The liberty of disguise.
Especially since it was an outfit he would never have imagined
adopting. The headscarf, the earring, the scruffy beard, and
scruffier coat. He looked as if he probably smelled and that was

enough to keep their eyes away. Ah, the meticulous hypocrisy of the British. It amused him for the last time. The train rolled into a station. He swung himself to his feet, resisting the temptation to whistle. Last stop for this gypsy. Hyde Park Station.

SPEAKERS' CORNER
HYDE PARK

The sky had cleared to allow thin slats of sun through the toss of clouds, enough to guarantee a respectable crowd. Ward had positioned his best Watcher, a blonde in jeans and denim jacket, near the Underground exit that crossed Oxford Street. She didn't look old enough for the job. But August had no choice. He comforted himself with the fact that no one, besides himself, wanted this bust to go down more than the Commander. Another tall woman with blunt cut hair was watching one of the fanatics who was unfolding a small stepladder, leaflets clutched nobly to his chest. There were at least ten other Agents working the crowd. And his own eyes were wide open.

He spotted Zuleika as she jumped from a double-decker bus and darted across the strip of grass between Park Lane and Speakers' Corner. There was always that brief moment of pleasurable surprise when he saw her. He was struck by the way her dark skin and eyes gave a glimpse of warmth in the February morning. And the way her clothes fell around her in an afterthought.

She threaded her way through the gathering fans and foes, tourists and regulars. Maher had picked his time well. The speakers usually launched their campaigns around 11:00. The spectators were starting to cohere into the safety of numbers, ready to shed their inhibitions in the anonymity of the crowd.

He moved closer to the concession stand. Bored faces resigned to the tedium of the lineup. Kids tugging at the adults' hands, swinging around their legs and tossing popcorn at each other.

His eyes scanned the thickening crowd. It would be hard to pick out Maher in this. An older version of Zaid. That was one face he knew well.

★ ★ ★

Qasim Daweesh was surprised when a stranger dressed in an expensive raincoat with a boy in a tidy school uniform approached him. But he graciously agreed to watch the young-ster while the man returned briefly to his car. He was proud that a fellow Arab would trust him in the heart of London to mind his son for a few moments. The boy seemed unconcerned when the father strolled away. Crouching down on pudgy knees, he watched between the adult's legs as two black dogs wrestled on the playing field behind them. Qasim shrugged, carefully removed the wrapping from another cigar and was glad his own four children were grown.

The blonde Watcher wasn't nervous. She'd thought she would be. Commander Ward had impressed upon her the importance of this assignment. It was her first big job since recruitment. Concentration was everything. Ignore the noise, the babble of languages. Concentrate on watching for the man in the photo. Lots of Arabs here. But this bloke shouldn't be too hard. Handsome. Particular glint to the eyes she'd caught even in the photo.

Thirty seconds later she saw him. The beard had been added. The hair less grey than in the photo. But it was him.

Dr. Ahmed Maher was walking right towards her.

August heard the strange thump as he leaned against the con-cession stand, an uneaten cone dripping down his shirt. A solid thump, thump. Iron beating against a velvet-covered anvil. He turned and saw the Queen's Guard cantering across the perime-ter of the playing field behind Speakers' Corner. Their peaked helmets glinted in the sudden flush of sun. And then they were galloping, the horses' thin, powerful legs flying across the ground.

Zuleika turned at the sound of hooves. The soldiers' crimson capes lifted and fell against the animals' backs. There was a murmur of appreciation from a group of tourists who swung their cameras to capture the sight.

And then she saw the boy, crawling between the tourists' legs. The blue and gold school uniform. The black tousled hair and white socks. He was hauling himself towards the playground of wet grass and huge toy soldiers.

He was inches away from the sharp, pounding hooves of two dozen horses.

Ahmed Maher brushed past his wife. He felt her hand clasping the brown paper bag. She was watching the horses beyond the crowd. Tugging it, he sensed an initial resistance. She turned her face towards him in a round, astonished *oh*. Their eyes met and her hand fell from the vial.

And then she had turned away again. Calling their son's name. Shouting August Riley's name.

August saw Zuleika's agonized face, her scream. He heard her call him. And then she was running. He saw the small black shoes, the fat knees propelling the boy forward. And the sharp hooves churning the wet grass into mud.

August's belly scraped the ground as he scrambled after the kid, pushing through the field of legs. A woman screamed, almost impaling his hand with a spiked heel. He grabbed the boy's ankle. The kid yelled and kicked at him. August yanked him back and swung him into the air. They were both covered in mud.

Horses galloped along the rattled line of spectators. August swung the boy towards Zuleika, who was pushing her way through the crowd like a bull at Pamplona.

The novice Watcher heard the shouts, the sudden alarmed shift of the crowd. Something was wrong. She strained at the microphone in her ear. Only indecipherable static. She'd been told to keep her eyes glued to Ahmed Maher. She did.

She saw the paper bag in his hand.

And she saw another man with a threadbare coat and a red spotted bandanna at his throat, gold hoop earring against rough beard. He was scooping the paper bag from Maher and putting it into a plastic carrier bag. He dodged across Park Road. Ahmed Maher disappeared into the Underground in the opposite direction.

She watched, memorizing the shape of his back and the

way he walked. She'd been told not to "give chase under any circumstances."

Ahmed ripped the false beard from his face and pulled the headdress over his hair. He threw the beard into the washroom garbage and folded his hands into the wide cuffs of the familiar flowing robe covering his body.

They were safe. Zaid was on his way. At last, the journey home had begun.

Qasim Daweesh offered prayers to Allah as the tall cold man and silent woman swept down on him. Handcuffs and brusque warnings. He knew he shouldn't have stayed in this country after the War began. He'd lived in London for twenty years and his shop had been vandalized for the first time last night. And now they had come for him. He tried to ask about the boy who had been entrusted to him but they wouldn't listen. Never in his life had Qasim had anything to do with the police. And now they were shoving him into the back of a cruiser in front of all these staring people.

Zuleika's fist was in her mouth, a storm of tears distorting her face. August held the boy, jostling him clumsily against his hip. But at the sight of Zuleika's tears, the youngster had started to cry as well, his face crumbling into fear as if he'd suddenly recognized the danger that had pressed him.

August stretched out his free hand and pressed her shoulder, urging the boy towards her. "It's all right," he said. "It's all over now." The boy cried louder and tucked his head into August's shoulder.

Zuleika looked from the child to August. "No," she whispered, shaking her head. "No . . ."

August wiped the boy's nose.

A man in a sleek grey raincoat scooped the boy from August's arms, muttering incomprehensibly.

"He's not Khalaf," Zuleika said. "That isn't my son."

PARIS
FRANCE
February 11

The Seine was murky grey and a stubborn sludge of snow had begun to fall over the embankment as the two men leaned over the rail and stared into the water. Ahmed pulled his collar close around his neck and tucked the scarf he wore tighter against it. But Zaid seemed oblivious to the cold.

"I've made contact with the Iraqis, Zaid. Things will only get more difficult. Can you carry on?" Ahmed asked.

The other man spit into the tumbling river. A rotting plank jumped through the grimy surf, rusty nails scraping the surface. Not far behind it the limb of some unidentifiable animal bobbed obscenely. "I can carry on for as long as you need me. Longer!" Determination churned his voice like the river. "I have only one thing in mind. And my mind will remain only on that until we have accomplished our task."

Ahmed studied his brother's face, measuring his expression. How much to tell him? "Your next assignment will require a certain patience — it will not be so exciting. It will require a larger appetite for the longer view."

"Amman?" Zaid's voice held a hint of anxiety.

"Yes. And once there you must wait. You must wait to be approached. Do not take action yourself."

He watched Zaid, trying to catch any sifting of commitment, any reluctance to surrender the centre of the stage. But he saw only curiosity. "Of course." Wet snow was falling on his face, melting into his dark hair and sliding off his chin.

Ahmed turned back to the water. He needn't worry, he could see that. Zaid would fly as far as Maher needed him to. "You almost have to admire their determination," he said. "They've bugged the vial. But we will use it to our advantage." In a small park behind them, centred with a roundabout and seesaw, a child screeched in delight as he swung high on a swing, his legs flailing in the air. "You must move around the city," Ahmed continued. "Go where you like. But keep the vial on you at all times. Change residences every night. Explore wherever you like. But move regularly. The longer you can distract them the more time I have. Remember, you are my decoy."

"And then?" Zaid asked.

Ahmed glanced towards the playground. He gripped Zaid's shoulders. "You know I trust you more than any man." Zaid held his breath. It was a great compliment, he knew. "And now I must rely on you entirely. However, there are some things, during these times, that I can't confide even to you, Zaid."

Zaid nodded, his mission stoking the flame that had been lit inside his belly twenty-three years ago.

Ahmed stared at Zaid as if to transfuse his own zeal to him. But it wasn't necessary. He touched both his cheeks to Zaid's and pressed his arms again. "We have work to do." He turned and waved to the child. The boy with the round, chestnut face and the golden eyes of his mother jumped to the ground, his pudgy legs stumbling as he ran to his father's open arms.

BAGHDAD
IRAQ

Zeinab Yalman stepped around the rubble that had been piled along the tight corridor outside Saddam Hussein's steel door and knocked. His hand, and the sheet of paper in it, was trembling. He had to restrain himself from barging into the leader's quarters.

Someone barked an abrupt order to enter and Zeinab opened the door to the inner bunker. Buried deep beneath the ground, reinforced with concrete, the walls still shook with each thud of the bombs. Zeinab had been trapped in this underground command post for ten days. Perhaps he could escape soon, if the news he carried was anything to go by.

Colonel Ojjeh, the leader's most recent second-in-command, was sitting on a corduroy-covered couch, his face sagging as badly as its overloaded springs. Saddam was stripped to the waist, standing at a small sink patting his face with water and spreading a thick layer of shaving cream over his chin. Zeinab's eyes swept from one to the other, trying to gauge the mood of the room. He hadn't lasted for three years as Saddam Hussein's liaison officer by not being able to hold a finger to the wind. Saddam picked up a razor that lay on a narrow counter next to the sink.

The air smelled of close detonation. A huge stain was spreading across the far wall where the concrete had finally split as a result of days of relentless bombing. The television set, placed prominently on a high sideboard, flickered with the serious face of the American commentator detailing Iraqi losses. Saddam drew the razor slowly and deliberately around his face in a careful ritual.

"What do you want?" Ojjeh was jumpy today. It was rumoured that one of his brothers-in-law had been amongst the pilots who'd fled with their jets to Iran last night.

Zeinab ignored him and spoke to his leader's bare back. He noticed the black tufts of hair sprouting beneath the shoulder blades. "The Professor has come through!" Zeinab announced, not bothering to disguise his excitement. "Dr. Maher has managed to get through. A message from Yemen. I brought it immediately."

Saddam Hussein put down his razor and patted his face with a towel. He shrugged into his khaki shirt, the knife crease of its sleeves standing rigid.

Ojjeh stood up. Dark circles were punched under his eyes. "Oh yes. Our precious Dr. Maher. He of the brilliant warning of a massive amphibious landing!" he sneered. The generals who had talked Saddam Hussein into responding to the amphibious landing had been buried by their families two days ago.

"He has the weapon," Saddam said confidently. "Ahmed Maher has the weapon which will bring us certain victory. The one weapon that the Imperialists fear the most." Saddam picked up a pair of small scissors and began to trim his moustache. "We will supply Dr. Maher with everything he needs to continue the production of his life's work. In exchange he is delivering a canister." He winced as a hair caught in the scissors. Ojjeh involuntarily winced as well. "A canister that will deliver us to victory." Only the dull thud, thud of the shells and explosives from above penetrated the bunker.

"What do you think, Zeinab?" Saddam asked finally, stepping back to study his reflection in the mirror.

Zeinab knew it was his chance. Ojjeh was watching him like a ferret over a rabbit hole. But the second-in-command was on his way out. And there was no immediate replacement in line. "I think that Dr. Maher is right. We should supply the weapons he recommends. Just a few biologically armed Scuds could end it. The Americans won't dare step into Kuwait."

Hussein replaced the scissors with a small comb. "Oh yes, twenty-six biologically armed Scuds could end it, all right." He touched the comb to his moustache, carefully separating the hairs. "But I don't think their destiny shall be Riyadh." He yanked a hair from his upper lip, wincing and puckering his mouth towards the mirror. "I think that perhaps it is the Israelis who would benefit most from such a lesson." Ojjeh and Zeinab glanced at each other. "It will bring them salivating into the war. No diplomatic dance will be able to stop them. Not after an attack like that. Even if just one of the twenty-six penetrates their defences, the situation will turn immediately. They will never be able to resist the public demand for vengeance. When have they ever?" Bitterness singed Hussein's tone.

"And to have them launched from what is technically Jordanian territory is the final cinch in the noose. They will never trust any Arab again or the Americans for that matter. Our Brothers won't stand by this time and let them overrun our land. Syria will gladly join us. And our enemy's enemies will become our allies. Just as I have always predicted."

Hussein was quiet for a long time, buttoning his shirt, watching Ojjeh's sullen face. Finally he nodded. "I think it's about time that I had some positive advice," he said, "instead of the snivelling whiners I'm surrounded with now."

Ojjeh shrank back into the couch.

"He says that he will personally deliver the vial to our Base," Zeinab said, proud that he held the precious information.

"Of course," Hussein fastened a button at his cuff. "It's his sacred duty. He is right to trust no one but himself to do the job." He turned to Colonel Ojjeh. "He's as clever as the reputation that precedes him. A man must always guard against being surrounded by fools."

Ojjeh cleared his throat again and wished fervently that he'd taken his brother-in-law's offer of a flight to Iran the night before.

LONDON
BRITISH MUSEUM

"Your Watcher — the young girl — she really pulled it off, Ward." August rubbed the nose of one of the red granite lions commanding the entrance to the ancient Egypt display area. "Never took her eyes off Maher."

"Virtually illiterate when she came to us, you know," Ward said proudly. "But a photographic memory. The girl had learned to notice everything — a survival mechanism." He shook his head. "There were those who argued that we shouldn't teach Treena to read in case she lost her edge." He shook his head again. "I can tell you, Riley, nothing people say or do surprises me anymore."

"And the contact?" August said impatiently. "The one she saw Maher pass the package to? Was it Zaid?"

"Yes. She described him practically down to the fillings in his teeth. Positively identified him from the photos sent up from Pine Gap. We think he took the tube straight out to Heathrow. But the blasted signal couldn't be traced underground. Then we lost it altogether until it was picked up again at Paris and then in Amman. At least that's what Cheltenham says." He looked grim.

"And where's Maher now?"

"Could be anywhere. Flights to Paris leave every half hour. From there he could go straight to anywhere in the Gulf."

August folded his arms and leaned against one of the lions.

It was winter in London, a war had been declared, and the museum was echoing and empty. "We'll just have to let the vial go. He must be planning to take it somewhere. And that somewhere will be critical. All we can do is follow it. And hope the bombing campaign doesn't interfere with the signal."

"But what about Maher's vial?" Ward didn't hide his irritation. "It's loaded with the real thing."

"I know. And we've got to find him. It'll be all over if he releases that poison before we get to him. Terror value alone could knock morale out for months."

"But how do we get to him? We've got virtually no inside contacts in the region now. And the few we do have are tied up pretty tight."

August leaned against the transplanted lion condemned to stare stiffly at tourists and school kids long after the fall of the British Empire. A woman, suffering from too many tranquillizers or too much reality, wandered past them and offered a lopsided smile before stroking the lion's cold nose. "Zuleika, that's how," he said.

Ward rolled his eyes. "We've tried that, remember? And that's the reason Maher is floating around the Gulf somewhere right now with a pocketful of biological weapons." He leaned closer and August could see the fatty deposits that had begun to collect on his eyelids. "It didn't work, Riley. It didn't work."

"Has anyone ever told you that you're beautiful when you're angry?"

The Commander sputtered. And then found himself, very much against his will, letting a caw of laughter escape him. He didn't remember the last time he'd laughed out loud. The sound spilled into the high-ceilinged room. The wandering woman, who was now gazing at an enshrouded mummy, laughed as well.

August held up a hand, knowing he could afford to surrender Ward's point. "Okay. We blew it. But remember this. Zuleika's still desperate to get her boy back. She's convinced that Maher might have taken him into the war zone. And she could be right. The man betrayed her totally. He got what he wanted and she got nothing. Just a big dose of fear and anger. Don't you see that we could use that? She knows Maher's family. Nothing that's happened changes the fact that Zuleika knows more about that man than any of the rest of us or a dozen analysts in DC or London could ever find out in years."

He drew a deep breath. "Ward. I'll go to the top if it's the chain of command you're worried about. I'll go to Riyadh — and take Zuleika with me. I won't let her off the plane if necessary. I'll accept total responsibility for this thing. But let me take her out there. She knows the country. She must have some idea where Maher could have gone. When we get on the ground we might find a trace of him. No matter how great our satellites are — they're never going to pick out an individual. It's human agents who still do that the best. And no agent can do it better than one with a motive. The whole communication system from out there is breaking down. It's getting impossible. We'll never be able to get any of this stuff through ordinary channels." He waited a beat and then added, "What have you got to lose?"

The Commander ignored the plea, rubbing his thumb back and forth across a tiny chip in the lion's ear. "Maher. And his wife. That's what we've got to lose. What makes you think this effort would be any more successful in nabbing him than the Hyde Park fiasco?"

"Nobody says Maher isn't clever. But London was just a sideline. Great if it worked — it would have punched a great big hole in the Coalition's morale. But if it failed he still had his other vial and the Hail Mary Plan. When Maher's wife got her hands on some of his supply of toxin it was worth the risk to try and get it back. Especially since he had the boy as a bargaining chip. Now he's got everything he needs. The vial. And the boy. He won't be putting himself in that position again."

"The chances of picking up both brothers are virtually nonexistent. If we alert one, we alert the other. You will step on all sorts of toes if you get caught over there."

August pressed one palm hard against the red flank of the lion. "Damn it, Ward," he gritted his teeth. "We know all that. Sounds very good in a report in triplicate. But now what? Just what's your alternative? Let him go — knowing what he's carrying?"

"Riley, I can't stop you from doing what you like. I can't really even retain Zuleika Maher much longer. Not if you get your people in Washington to pressure Whitehall. And once you set foot outside this country it's MI6's jurisdiction. But that doesn't mean I have to condone it." The Commander studied August. "Can I ask one favour of you?"

"What is it?"

"Don't tell the woman about the bugged vial. As you just said, she's desperate. She might use anything to get her way."

"Done."

18

RIYADH
GENERAL SCHWARZKOPF'S
COMMAND CENTER
February 13

Jamie's nervousness was confined to a slight twitch in his right knee. But he was glad he'd worn a tie and the good sports coat Nellie had nagged him into buying, even though the heat had almost overwhelmed him when he'd stepped off the plane. He'd hardly had time to sweat before the two giants in marine uniform hustled him into a luxury car that had the reinforced insides of a very wide, very comfortable tank.

There'd been no small talk when he'd entered the close room with the high slits in the wall. The General had a strong handshake, curt welcome. The guys with the sub-machine guns — it amazed him how much they looked like the heavy, plastic toys Jamie's sister bought her kid — kept distracting him. But soon the close questioning took all his attention.

There was no invitation to sit down. Jamie wanted to ask about August Riley, but Schwarzkopf's tight lips and narrowed eyes as he read the two sheets of typed paper Jamie had turned over indicated that the General would be doing all the asking. An air-conditioner whined in the background. Swinging from its slats was one of those tangy cardboard air fresheners in the shape of a pine tree like his dad used to hang from the Dodge's rearview mirror. Jamie had never smelt a real pine but he had his doubts as to any resemblance. The walls were plastered with some kind of nubby material, painted a sickly pink that the army must have ordered by mistake. The General's meaty hands were clasped in front of him and Jamie had to fight not to stare at the two watches ticking over on each wrist.

"Where the hell is he?" the General growled suddenly towards one of the two men who stood rigidly next to the door. The taller guy (compared to the shorter, who was maybe 6´4"), started to respond when he was interrupted by the sound of bolts and chains dragging along the wall like the introduction to some mediaeval dungeon. A door at the other end of the room swung open.

August stepped into the room, cautiously confident. He'd bought a new shirt at the PX in an unflattering green and yellow plaid and exchanged his jeans for a pair of hastily chosen cotton pants only to discover after pulling them from the package that they closed with a drawstring. It was too late to exchange them and so he'd pulled on the usual denim jacket, forced the bottom two metal tags closed and avoided the mirror as he left the claustrophobic room the Army had assigned him. He didn't stop to say good-bye to Zuleika, whose room was three doors down. Her silence and the guard's unblinking eyes kept him away.

Jamie was amused to see that August had also worn a tie, albeit already askew at his windpipe, his neck chafing red beneath it. Unexpectedly, he winked at Jamie but Jamie sensed it as a piece of bravado designed to put him at his ease. It had the opposite effect as the General loomed across him and stretched his hand to the newcomer, clasping him on the shoulder. "Appreciate your coming, Riley."

He held out both hands in a sort of folksy benediction and motioned them into the two hard seats on the other side of the table. He remained standing, one boot up on a wooden chair. Splinters were already falling to the heavily waxed tiles beneath it. "Now then. We have us a real problem. A problem that you two fellas can help us with." He raised one pale brow and eyeballed them.

A quick rush of nerves suddenly cramped Jamie's bladder. He'd probably start to babble any minute. Instead he found himself saying in a confident voice he hardly recognized as his own. "The bugged vial is in Amman, Jordan, sir." He flipped through the two sheets the General had left lying on the table. "Signal left London on February 10 on a flight to Paris. From there Pine Gap picked it up again in Ankara. Colorado got her in Aqaba. And I personally followed it through from there. Movement was steady, sir. And it's been sitting in Amman for twenty-four hours now."

"At least we know where the damned thing is. For the moment. What about the other vial? The one that's armed. The one that got away, so to speak." Schwarzkopf pinned August with his gaze.

"I believe Maher is carrying it personally." August had decided that direct and unequivocal was the best approach by far with this man. No dance of class conflict like the one he was forced to waltz with Ward all the time. No trying to dampen Ward's unconscious attempt to pin him and his status. Where did his father go to school? Where did he graduate from? What was the accent anyway? Where did it fit in the hierarchy? Sometimes he could almost touch Ward's irritation with the Yanks' tendency not to fit in! And what was worse, not even know they were supposed to! But with this man it was straightforward. He wanted information. And August was supposed to provide it. And if August wanted anything out of it he could just ask directly. He'd either get it or he wouldn't.

"The active vial isn't bugged. I want to follow Maher. It's a chance." August leaned forward. "It's our only chance."

Jamie's mouth dropped open and he turned his eyes slowly back to Schwarzkopf, who was leaning forward on his bent knee now, rubbing a scuff mark from the toe of his boot. Jamie noticed the high polish of the stars on his lapels gleaming against the drab khaki. "Why should you risk it, Mr. Riley?" the General asked quietly.

"We can't let the man loose in Kuwait or Saudi Arabia with a vial of biological weapon for which there is no known antidote, General. We have to try to track him. We have to at least try. I think he's probably going to consolidate his available supplies in Amman and strike out from there. We can't know in which direction. He could drop it here on the Base. A suicide mission by one Iraqi pilot is all it would take. One armed Scud." The shorter guard's eyes slid towards them. "Or he could drop it on our forward troops," he continued, "or on the Kuwaitis — just to show what they're capable of."

"Or on Israel," Jamie said quietly.

Schwarzkopf frowned and stared at him as if the idea were Jamie's own perversion.

"Shit, yes," August whispered.

"If he arms his Scuds near Iraq's western border, those weapons could send the biological stuff deep into Israel with barely any warning," Jamie said, his voice rising now.

August nodded, speaking quickly, "Even if an alarm were raised — once the germs were dispersed, thousands would die. Saddam would get one last chance to win one of his ultimate objectives. Involving Israel."

Schwarzkopf lowered his boot to the floor and folded his hands in front of him, pulling his sloping shoulders back. "There'd be no stopping the Israelis in sending everything into the war after that. As long as they think we're doing as well or better than they are they'll let us call the ball game. But something like this . . ." He shook his head.

"And nuclear will be the name of the game," August said. "We already agreed to the Israelis' request to shortcut the satellite's Pine Gap circuits, skipping Colorado and Washington, sending them straight through to Riyadh and onto Tel Aviv to increase their warning time of a Scud attack by two minutes. I believe you asked for that yourself, General?"

"Yep. The Israelis are watching our tail closer'n we are. They shot a missile into the Mediterranean two days ago just to illustrate that they're serious about fighting their own battle if we don't keep proving we're on top of this. And if push comes to shove . . ." He clamped the words off as if applying a tourniquet to the terrible possibilities. He looked from August to Jamie, and Jamie had the uncomfortable feeling he was being used to adjust Schwarzkopf's focus. The General walked to the door and stuck his head outside, mumbling to whoever was on duty.

August leaned forward and cleared his throat, tossing a nervous look to Jamie.

"Nothing can substitute for a motivated ground agent," August said to Schwarzkopf. He tried his favourite line. "What have we got to lose, sir?"

"You, for one thing. Even the most motivated ground agents get killed."

A rap at the door and a private entered and saluted. Schwarzkopf took the small, black box he offered and dismissed the messenger.

"If you're going to go in there as some kinda knight we might as well give you some damned armour." He rubbed the dull metal of the box. "Doesn't shine much though." Pulling a thin aerial from its side he handed it to August. "Satellite-Communicator. One-way connection straight back here," he raised his brows, "if the conditions are right."

August handled the cold metal.

Schwarzkopf continued, "Signal bounces straight up to the Big Birds, cutting out the tracking stations and then straight down to us again. Designed to help Commanders in the field. Guess you qualify as in the field, Riley."

"Thank you, sir."

"Don't thank me — it's not over yet."

19

AMMAN
JORDAN
February 15

The coolness of the garden and the heavy smell of honeysuckle was smothered by the scent of heavy perfume, which met Zuleika as she entered the harem, the women's quarters. The familiar musk drifted around her like a gentle noose. She almost turned and ran from the servant who was guiding her deep into the far reaches of the house. The old claustrophobia was creeping up on her, the sense that she was trapped inside a time warp that would never change. She blinked back the panic. She couldn't reveal her fear to Hoda. The woman had a reservoir of affection for her. But the reservoir was almost sucked dry.

Ahmed's sister had taken much convincing to agree to see her. Only the tantalization of tales of foreign experience, the bribe of fresh gossip, had won over her natural reluctance to risk her brother's anger. And Zuleika had been a favourite of Hoda's. They had played together as girls and learned domestic duties side by side after Zuleika's father, lost in grief over her mother's death, had sent her from the desert to the city.

Sheik Rifai had been buffeted by the changes in his land and this final blow of the loss of his wife had prompted him to send his precious daughter, first born and only child by his beloved Mahira, to Hoda's father, his second cousin who had made a successful place for himself in the city. He'd given Zuleika her mother's ring before he'd sent her off with her clothes tucked inside the best linen tablecloth.

Hoda had taken a different route than Zuleika. And was not unhappy for it. She had mothered eight sons and was held in high esteem and affection by her husband. He hadn't taken another wife and as such was greatly respected by the other women of the harem. But Zuleika knew her cousin's life to be a circle of indulged monotony, its colour and texture woven from whatever thin fabric Hoda could find within the walls of her admittedly magnificent home.

Zuleika clutched the two videos August had pilfered from the Embassy recreation room for her: a Disney cartoon and an adventure film about wild animals. She'd tucked them beneath the long dress she'd worn. Hoda would welcome the gift as a break in her boredom.

When she saw Zuleika at the entrance to the room, Hoda pulled herself from the brocaded couch where she lay, tossing an embroidered pillow to the floor. She moved in the old languid, sensual way that Zuleika remembered so well. Any evidence of the rigours of bearing eight children was hidden beneath the folds of pink satin laced with silvery threads that covered her from chin to toes. It was Hoda who had taught Zuleika to dance. Hoda who had giggled the surprising details of sex in her ear and Hoda who had comforted her during those early lonely months of separation from her father. And it was Hoda who had sent her the last letter from her son.

She took Zuleika in her arms and kissed her on both cheeks, grinning widely, a tiny diamond glittering in her front tooth. "It has been too long, my cousin. Far too long." The formal greeting over, she pushed her arm through Zuleika's and pulled her towards the couch. "Tell me where you've been! What have you been up to?" Her voice was eager with the starvation of a woman who lived her life as a voyeur of the world.

"I brought you a token," Zuleika smiled, suddenly a little ashamed of her offering. But Hoda accepted the tapes eagerly, jumping up to press the Disney one into the video recorder that sat on a carved stand beneath a huge television screen. She waited for the opening credits to flicker on as if suspicious of the film's existence and then clapped her hands with delight as the cartoon rabbit's exaggerated ears filled the screen before she turned the machine off and concentrated on Zuleika.

A servant entered and placed a silver tray before them. It held a coffee pot of creamy bone china and two tiny cups with silver spoons tucked inside them. Hoda poured for them both, the smell of spices wafting into the air with the coffee. She passed a cup to Zuleika along with a silver bowl overflowing with chocolates wrapped in mauve foil.

Zuleika forced herself to sip the coffee and select a chocolate. She amused Hoda with stories of Australia: the animals, the men, the outrageousness of the women. She spiced her life just enough to make it an entertaining story for Hoda but not enough to outrage her into doubting her fitness as a mother. She let Khalaf's name drift in and out of the conversation many times but Hoda didn't respond. Her cousin lay back amongst the thick cushions, nibbling chocolates and listening intently to Zuleika.

The servant returned with a carved incense burner and offered it to Hoda. She took the teakwood dish and tilted it under her nose, reverently inhaling the sweet smell.

Hoda reached over and swept Zuleika's hair from her neck. She lifted the incense to it, letting the pungent odour penetrate its mass in an old shared ritual. Zuleika held her head still, squinting the smoke from her eyes. The protected days she'd spent in the soft spell of this room drifted around her. How easy it would be . . . how easy to close those heavy curtains against the outside world. How easy to return to this security . . . this certainty. Worry would never disturb her again. Eventually, eventually, she would get Khalaf back. See him grow from a distance. But nevertheless, see him grow. Would it be so very bad?

"And what about our handsome Zaid, then?" Zuleika felt her neck grow rigid as Hoda twisted her hair, letting the smoke permeate it. She should have expected this. Zaid had always been a favourite of the women. He knew how to play his boyishness to advantage, to let them think they still held him in their sway as they had when he was a toddler.

"Fine," she answered quickly. Not too quickly, she hoped. Hoda knew her well.

Her cousin picked up a pearl-encrusted brush that lay on the floor and tugged it through Zuleika's hair. "My, my . . .," she clucked, "so many tangles. You've adopted slovenly Western ways. Hair such as yours must be groomed every day." She pulled the brush heavily through the thick waves. "Ahmed says that Zaid will be coming from London. To stay. And not a moment too soon." A note of censure crept into her normally buoyant voice. "The family will be together at last. I was sorry when Ahmed said you would be staying in Australia. I told him you would come home one day. But you know how he is. Tolerates no argument, that man!" she said fondly.

Zuleika was alert. It was what she'd been waiting for. "When did you see Ahmed?" She gently pulled her hair from Hoda's fingers, taking the brush from her hand to slide down her own scalp. "Did he have Khalaf with him?"

Hoda played with her bracelets. "He took the boy with him, of course."

"Where?" Zuleika touched her hand.

Hoda pulled away. "You know your husband wouldn't discuss his affairs with me." A sudden compassion traced her features and she pressed Zuleika's arm. "He's in school, no doubt. Ahmed was not pleased with the British schools." She sighed heavily. "You were always the impatient one. You'll know in time. Ahmed will tell you when he is ready."

"Is Khalaf with the family?" Zuleika insisted. "If I just know he's with the family I will be able to rest my head at night. You can tell me that. Surely, Hoda, for the sake of our old friendship, you can tell me that much?"

Hoda picked up the brush and pulled a strand of hair from the bristles. She twirled it around her fingers. "I'm the one who must live here, Zuleika. You have run away before. You might again. And I must live with the consequences. Ahmed wouldn't be pleased if I repeat conversations that I overheard between him and my husband."

"I would never say it was you, Hoda. Please. I promise you that. I would never say!"

Hoda slowly rose from the cushions and walked towards the video player. Two golden bracelets shimmered at her ankle as she walked.

"Please," Zuleika whispered to her back.

Hoda punched at the play button on the recorder with her toe. Her nails were painted lavender. "Ahmed is taking the boy to learn the Bedouin ways. He's gone to spend a month in the desert. We tried to dissuade him because of the troubled times. But he insisted that they would be safe. And you know Ahmed, he's always been a man to go his own way. Does what he wants. Just like you."

Zuleika jumped up and hugged the other woman, tears in her eyes. "Thank you, Hoda. Thank you so much. I'm in your debt."

Hoda turned back to the video.

Zuleika ran from the room, tripping over the tray and china pot. Dark coffee spilled over the carpet.

The last thing she heard as the cool marble door swung closed on the smoky room was Roger Rabbit's insane cackle of laughter.

KING FAISAL STREET
DOWNTOWN AMMAN

Zuleika stepped carefully along the hot street, keeping her face turned to the shop windows as if she were on an errand. She avoided her reflection. The cowled hair, the long shapeless dress, so anonymous, so comfortable, so undemanding. She'd forgotten the soothing protection offered by the tradition clothing. No fear of harsh interruption, a coarse male voice accosting her, ignorant shouts from groups of boys lingering at a corner. No self-consciousness rounding her shoulders over her breasts. No. She was safe within this soft armour. And she had to admit its appeal. Her emotions, her most private thoughts, tucked close to her, not exposed as in the West, with the concurrent need for a false mask of amiability to keep others from penetrating too deeply.

A young man brushed past her, automatically swinging his body away from her, even though the pavement was crowded. She remembered the humiliation of the sour-breathed man in an elevator in Alice who had clucked into her face and pressed against her backside, grinning lewdly as she'd turned a dozen shades of pink.

A woman stood in her path, dressed in a Western-style dress of bright cotton, her hair puffed and sprayed and pinned with bright barrettes. She held a small boy by the wrist, shaking a red-painted nail at him as he wailed after some forbidden treat. Perhaps it was possible to readjust. To loosen the reins just enough to allow some stride in her journey. In Jordan there was the taste of an alternative; fundamentalism didn't drench every part of life. The woman stroked the boy's cheek and murmured something reassuring as Zuleika hurried past them. Perhaps it was possible . . .

She had always prided herself on her pragmatism. Her rejection of the superstitious or religious had carried her stubbornly through the early years of her transformation. But her common sense seemed to be deteriorating lately, as if the training of her girlhood had been dripping against her will all the time. Silently, methodically, eroding her determination.

She was always aware that her father's agreement so many years before to let her explore the world physically and intellectually had been forged from raw love. He had protected her all his life as was his duty and had then released her to be educated in the West. Proud and radical in his own way, this had been his statement of a certain independence. But it had backfired when she had stayed away too long. Things would never be the same between them. But she could make it up to him during the years he had left. He had no wife and she could be a faithful companion. Loyalty had been almost a fault with her. This way she could put it to good use. And her father would find Khalaf. She knew he would get his grandson back. He would utilize every friendship he'd nurtured over sixty years. Yes, it would be worth it. To find Khalaf.

She moved a little faster, feeling already the urge to melt into the crowd, to match her gait with theirs. The comfort of familiarity closed around her like a soft fog. It was a pleasure hearing her own language, melodic and seductive to her ear. She'd missed it. The struggle to always communicate in another tongue took its toll on her energies. The uncertainty of never knowing how well you were expressing yourself. The polite confusion or outright irritation in a stranger's eyes as you missed a word or tripped back into an ethnic phrase. She'd gladly surrender that awkwardness.

But she needed August Riley as well. And his connections to the West. He had his own reasons for helping her, most of which she knew he was holding back. But he could call on resources that her father might not even imagine. The resources of the most powerful military machine in the world. As long as August's route was heading in the same direction as Maher she could help to guide it. She knew that the American wasn't actually lying to her — just omitting certain truths. Exactly as he'd accused her of doing. August had helped her before. He would again. He would help her find Khalaf if he thought he could snare Ahmed while he was at it.

She spotted the crudely lettered sign over the tired building that housed the Embassy flats and turned into the entrance, carved and round and low like the mouth of a dark cave.

August pushed open the wooden shutter of the tiny room. The sun screamed crimson against the horizon. He searched for a breeze but the day was still squeezing heat over the flat roofs. At least the floor tiles were cool on his bare feet and the trickle of a shower had offered some relief, lukewarm and rusty as the water had been. He stood, barechested, at the open window and tapped a cigarette from the package Jamie had tucked into his shirt pocket before they'd said good-bye in Riyadh. A plump pigeon cooed reassuringly on the roof opposite and pecked at the concrete. Somewhere a tin plate clanged against a hearth and cindery smoke curled into the purple blue air as the sun was sucked into the earth.

Where was she? She'd promised to meet him before dusk. His desire to see her was like the lull between thunder and lightning: dreaded, anticipated, inevitable collision. He realized he'd been scanning the heads of the people threading the alley below, looking for that odd, straight way that she walked as if expecting a challenge at any moment and ready, reluctantly, to meet it. So unfeminine. So compelling. He reminded himself that there was no reason for her not to come. She still thought she needed him to find the boy. He crumpled the piece of paper from Headquarters. Khalaf Maher had not shown up for his second day of classes at the exclusive school in the Amman suburbs.

He picked up a lighter and the message scrawled on the paper he'd placed on the paint-flecked window ledge. The communications from Jamie had been spotty and erratic. The lines were breaking down regularly. He read the latest signal again. Words were missing as the machine looped the loop somewhere between Riyadh and the Embassy's fax. But the coded message was still intact. He flicked the lighter's flame open and held it first to his cigarette and then to the crumpled message, before dropping it into the stained sink.

The exhaustion that had dogged him since Washington had been slaked, transformed by his fear of the repercussions of every move he made, into a single-minded fixation. The world had shifted into a clarity he hadn't noticed in years and never anywhere but in Alaska. And with it went a determination he hadn't experienced for a decade. He'd do this job. Take control of his life. Toss the drifting that had stalked him since Katy's accident.

He sat down on the bed and ran a hand over his chest, glancing at the cheap alarm clock for the tenth time in fifteen minutes. A second skin of sweat already covered him. He stretched to flick on the windmill of a fan tilting over the head-board. It ticked ominously and then fell to one side before suddenly righting itself and swinging into a lazy whirl. The thin stream of cool air wisped sporadically around the bed. A neon pink radio sat on the side table next to a glass of dusty plastic flowers. He switched it on but was offered only a gritty seam of high-pitched monotonous music. He left it on in hopes of a news broadcast.

August lifted his foot and massaged his ankle. It had stopped its constant throbbing at least. He smiled to himself. Damned Sam and their hunt for falcon chicks thirty years ago. The bug-ger had a lot to answer for this time. The sound of stalls being closed for the night reverberated from the alley. Men called blessings to each other and gathered their carpets and leathers and copper off the pavement. The tight little room was creep-ing quickly towards the night shadows. A sudden coolness prickled the sweat on August's neck.

He let his foot drop to the floor again. His manipulations had made it feel worse. Where the hell was she? He took a long unsatisfactory drag of the cigarette. She wouldn't try and search Maher out alone, would she? The man had left her for dead once. At the thought of it, fear pierced him and he stood up.

He was acting the fool. It was the heat. The tension. The solitude. She'd never wanted him here in the first place. Only agreed because she had no choice. And now she was as close to Maher and the boy as she was ever going to get — unless he helped her. He'd felt the warmth of her gratitude when she thought he'd pulled Khalaf from the horse's hooves. But it had been quickly dissipated by the atmosphere of Ward, of MI5, MI6, urgent calls from Washington, and the endless probing, skeptical faces that encircled her.

A shrill cry jolted through the window and a mother mur-mured to an infant somewhere in one of these cramped, hot rooms that thousands called home. The door of a stall slammed to the pavement, its elderly proprietor rasping to his son to help him steady it.

August shuddered and pulled his shirt on, stubbing the cigarette out in the metal ashtray on the dresser. The clarity of purpose he'd felt earlier had dissolved. Where the hell was she? He caught his reflection in the spotted mirror. A crack ran down it through the right side of his face, creating the illusion of a scar. He studied himself. Physical vanity had never been one of his faults, but lately his body had been demanding attention one way or another.

His looks were neither outstanding nor repulsive. Women were either drawn to him or not. He'd never had dozens of admirers but never had any trouble either. And the ones he'd gotten close to had usually wanted to stick around. His hair was slicked back across the receding hairline. Hell, maybe he'd just shave it all off. Not in this hellish climate, though. When he got home, where they still entertained the idea of a tree. He rubbed a hand over his chin. He was letting the beard grow in. It was preferable in this country — some tiny edge if Maher did spot him. But it was itchy and made him look ten years older. The shadow of a double chin lurked beneath his hand and expressed the general run of the rest of him. It was a good thing he had wide shoulders, they carried the extra weight for him. The raccoon rings that had encircled his eyes since this mess had started had finally faded. They seemed to have emerged from the murky haze that had enveloped them for weeks.

He didn't hear her touch on the latch and was startled to see her reflection suddenly appear behind him. He whirled quickly, embarrassed that she had caught his self-perusal. But she seemed unconcerned. "It's very difficult for a man to read his own soul," she said, with a half-smile that erased any sting of sarcasm.

"I was reading the lines of middle age," he joked awkwardly.

She pulled the shawl from her head. Her hair was pulled back from her face and it was a small surprise to see her face so plainly exposed. Her features, nude and unencumbered by cosmetics, shifted quickly from a glimpse of disappointment to confusion. "I spoke to my sister-in-law. She thinks that Ahmed has sent Khalaf to the Bedouin to learn their ways. It's been a tradition in his family." She pulled out the hair caught beneath

the collar of her long dress. "He might have taken Khalaf himself. They could be hundreds of miles away."

Her shoulders fell in anticipation of defeat. "Ahmed always
gets what he wants. Always."

August took her arm. A small muscle jumped beneath the
rough material of the dress. "What's wrong with you? You're
going to give up finding your boy without even trying?"

She turned, anger ready like a shield.

He dropped her arm and held up his hand to signal his
benign intent. "Please," he pleaded softly, "we can do it. Help
me and I'll go after him." He wondered what clumsy errors he
was weaving, but plunged on, "Let me speak with your father,
Zuleika. With your introduction he might help me. That way
I have more of a chance. And so do you."

"I don't know." She shook her head, the hair falling loose from
the pins that held it. "I know that you would have saved Khalaf
once. But that was different. Here — well, here . . . it isn't Hyde
Park. Not a green, soft place where things come easy . . ." Her
voice trailed off. A line of sweat dotted her upper lip.

He was conscious of not touching her. But wanting to. Pink
and gold shadow from the window crossed her face. She let her
head fall back. "It's so warm," she said. "I'd forgotten . . ." The
regret in her voice was for more than the temperature. She
loosened the ties at the neck of the dress and they fluttered
against the small bones at her throat. She put a hand to her
face, cooling her cheek. "I'm so tired."

"Of course," he said politely. The tinny Arabic music had
incongruously given way to Kenny Rogers moaning about his
latest lost love. "I didn't mean to rush you. It's just that . . ." He
gestured around the darkening room. "I've been waiting . . . the
day seemed long . . ." He wanted another cigarette, something
to do besides look at her.

Suddenly she had lifted his hands between her own as if
scooping his energy towards her. "I wish we weren't here," she
whispered. "I wish we were anywhere else but here."

He cupped her hand and kissed the palm. Her hand shivered
in his. He tasted salt on her fingers. She touched his shoulder.

"I like you," she said in a voice devoid of coquetry. "I didn't think I would. I didn't want to." She slipped her hands under his shirt and leaned towards him. His kiss was a question. He took her hands and wrapped them around his neck. Her look fought a memory of shyness as he slipped the loose dress from her shoulders. Beneath it she was covered with a light, muslin smock. He bent and kissed her breast through the thin material. She was an oasis of crystal snow, soft and cool and renewing. Pulling his blood from its sluggish route. Pulling him from the hard road he was building brick by red hot brick.

A moment's tentativeness as he lifted the shift and ran his hands along the smooth curved line of her back, bending his head to her neck. Somewhere she stiffened. Something in her pulled back. The fan whirred the air into hot gasps. He looked into her eyes. There was no hesitation in her gaze. And then it was as if she slipped some bridle and flew to him pressing her cool wide mouth against his throat.

August awoke to the crackle of a newscast. The room was chilled by darkness and the mirror reflected a cold moon slanting across the bed. The fan had died somewhere in the night and lay toppled on the floor. August rolled over and kissed Zuleika's ear through the wave of her dark hair. Then he lay rigid, holding himself slightly away from her as he listened to the announcer's excitable heavily accented English delineating the progress of the war. He closed his eyes and tried to pull the moment back to him, pressing himself against her. But he could feel it slip, hurtling faster and faster towards the hard future.

20

AMMAN
February 16

*Z*aid felt the joy of commitment threading his bones. He could smell his destination now. He was here. True, he had failed in London. But this success would be all the sweeter for it — and all the more necessary. He would play a critical part in his brother's triumph. And for now he would tease his audience a little longer. One last act and the curtain calls would be his. The vial sat snugly in the pouched belt hugging his body.

He ducked between the clogged cars that swelled King Faisal Street, pumping gritty exhaust into the air. A taxi honked and he jumped quickly to the sidewalk. The driver puffed a red face through the open window, shaking a fat fist. Zaid smiled grimly as he jogged up the street.

And now the old colours and smells and sounds of Amman embraced him, comforting him like a familiar face. The aroma of rose water and boiling syrup followed him through the alleys where the market stalls had been squeezed into every available foot. A moneychanger haggled with three tourists brave, or stupid enough to risk this part of the world these days. Retired teachers in drab dresses and hot, open-toed sandals.

Several women, raven-shrouded in traditional dress, hovered outside a goldsmith's booth. Their brown fingers darted and swept like small birds diving into the displays, and their wrists gleamed as they lifted them from side to side, modelling the bracelets. A Jordanian woman lingered next to them. She was dressed in a green suit, her tightly pinned hair threatening to escape to her shoulders. She peered through glasses shaped in an old-fashioned rhinestone design and held a dazzling brooch to the light. The sun fell in a pink slant across her smooth skin. Zaid admired the sharp tilt of her nose and full mouth. Perhaps he'd marry this year. It was late, but not too late, as his father would most certainly have agreed. He moved on as the woman turned to catch his look.

Wanting an indulgence, he tossed a stall keeper several dinars and helped himself to a thick *borma*, rolling the sugared pistachios slowly around his mouth. He lingered over a stall lodged deep into a thin alley between two blocks. Rich tapestried carpets waved in the slight wind and a tarnished flute lay carefully displayed in a bed of raw wool. He fingered the flute and tossed the last of the borma down his throat, chewing with vigour. He hadn't been so hungry in a long time. Paris and the French and their so-called haute cuisine! Muck for the most part. Indecipherable food drowning in thick unspeakable sauces. The French! Preoccupied with food and clothes and sex! Still not really aware that they were an Empire long lost, that they had discarded leadership and rule in the entrails of the nineteenth century. Full of airs about their culture and history — they were just as bad as the British, staring so long at their navels that they would never see the Sword of Islam raised over their thick, bent necks.

Zaid brushed the sugar from his hands and licked his fingers. He was still hungry. He looked at his watch: 4:50. A few hours at the cafe would end the day well.

As the afternoon died, Zaid held the water pipe towards the waiter and let him manipulate the long, clumsy set of iron tweezers, placing small chunks of charcoal into the pipe's bowl. Zaid sighed and breathed in deeply the aroma of fresh coffee as the boy poured from a large pot into his ceramic cup. This had always been one of his favourite stops. At the table next to him, two men argued amiably over a lazy game of backgammon. The comfortable murmur of male voices rose and fell on the cooling air just as it had when he was a boy — the last comforting sound at the end of the day.

The sun slanted across the faded tiles that covered the floor of the cafe and a worker bent lazily over a mop. Zaid sipped his coffee and sucked contentedly on the pipe. It was good to be here. Good to wait. And he would wait until he had fulfilled the last part of his destiny. One more call to make before he could complete his mission. One more call for Ra'ad's sake. His pilgrimage this far had been incredibly difficult — even frightening, if he was to admit it in the most private part of his soul. But when the victory was won he would have many wonderful tales to tell his brothers and sisters. Oh, that reward might not be immediate. But he could wait awhile longer. Patience, after all, had been a forced Palestinian virtue for forty-two years. A virtue that had worn away Ra'ad's life.

The smell, the heat, rode August like a bad conscience down King Faisal Street. He ducked through a maze of copper pots suspended from metal bars, sending them into a wild, toneless collision. A mane of scarves in aggressive fluorescent greens and purples brushed at his neck. Slabs of pastel prints — puppies with long ears, kittens playing with wool — were tilted against storefronts. Hisses and steamings from whistling kettles, the singe of burnt coffee pots never off the stove, tanged the air. A thick, choking-sweet smell married with the odour of caged chickens and old vegetables trailed him as he tried to separate the din of the crowded market from the signal at his ear.

The Ambassador had been suitably disapproving about handing over the tracking equipment, and the CIA's Station Chief had been grim and condescending about August's interference. But after the brief phone call from Riyadh they'd both zipped their lips and even skipped some of the paperwork.

There were still a few Westerners evident in the street, but nevertheless August felt conspicuous as he mounted the narrow steps worn to a dip in the middle by thousands of feet over a century, leading to what was evidently a cafe. The radio beep was reaching a crescendo now and he stopped as he reached the entrance to cup his ear and turn away from the curious old man shoving a grey mop across the faded floor.

He glanced around as he pretended to look for a handkerchief. The wide terrace was crowded. A group of men were gathered intently around a backgammon game and others lounged in their chairs, leisurely gossiping. There were two loners. One had a grizzled beard and was holding his creviced complexion to the sun; he was smoking a long pipe and wearing pants that rode too high at the ankle, as if they'd been bought for a shorter man. The other one was much younger. His face was partially obscured by a large, drooping plant in a corroded pot and he was turned away from August, pointing out something on the menu to the waiter. Lazy smoke from a few water pipes drifted into the air and the sole waiter moved from table to table now, the plastic-covered menu closed under his arm, adding coal to pipes, filling tiny coffee cups from a long-handled silver pot.

The beep was starting to drive a tight pain into August's ear. Mr. Smug at the Embassy had assured him that it was impossible for anyone else to zero in on the maddening sound. But as two old men followed him with slow eyes, one murmuring to the other from the side of his mouth, an edge of paranoia framed August. What if human beings still cradled a residual sixth sense, like a dog's, that might pick up such a grating intrusion, even subliminally?

He folded himself into a chair behind the most isolated table and reached into his jacket to flick off the receive button. His hand grazed the gun tucked next to his rib cage. The Station Chief had been grim and adamant in insisting that he wear it.

August gestured acquiescence to the waiter who had moved to his table and was holding the silver pot towards him, managing to suggest an element of distaste in August's presence.

The younger guy was moving, digging money from the pockets of his pants. He pushed his hand through his hair, laying several coins on the table before getting up.

August recognized Zaid immediately. He ducked away, keeping his hands steady, swirling the green coffee around and around in the cup, watching from under his lids. He flipped the receiver back on as Zaid passed his table. It nearly broke his eardrum. Zaid slipped down the curling staircase.

August doused the volume of the tracker and, flinging payment onto the table, rushed past the surprised backgammon players, down the staircase, and into the throng below.

He just caught the edge of Zaid jumping between the closing doors of a lumbering bus as it threaded its way up King Faisal Street. August had his doubts about the Ford the Embassy had reluctantly handed over to him with speeches about insurance and the "peculiarities" of Jordanian traffic. He had to gamble that it could keep up with the diesel-spewing relic lurching ahead. Shooing two boys who were playing with the windshield wipers, August jumped into the car and jerked it into gear.

The bus chugged out of the city, winding its way past the crawling blocks of sandy brown flats that looked as if they'd been designed for insects but actually provided a roof, and little else, for thousands of Jordan's Palestinian refugees and foreign workers.

The receiver was getting a tinny reception now. Mr. Station Chief had told August, explaining the workings as if to a six-year-old, that it was "state-of-the-art." The five-mile reception estimate seemed to be off about four miles. He wondered what the starched twerp would have to say about that . . .

He jerked along the road leading north, damping his rising nervousness with doses of reassurance about how busy the road was, how unnoticeable he really was amongst the gleaming rigs bursting with everything from antibiotics to spare tank parts and rusting pickups with braying animals swaying in the back, all making a buck from the embargo against Iraq. But the bus took a sudden tight turn and leaned into a narrow road that looked fit to lead nowhere, and might as well have, from the look of the squalid spread of tin-roofed shanties on a small rise of a hill.

Reaching into the glove compartment, August pulled out a flask. He drank half the contents straight and then pushed the lid back on. He was an American sitting in a 1985 Ford Wagon at the entrance to what he was pretty sure he remembered from the map was a Palestinian refugee camp! His nerves rose in a protesting lump at the back of his throat. Thank God the Embassy had had the sense not to put their plates on this crate.

He pulled off the side of the road into a small enclave where the hulk of a windowless Volvo lay tilted to one side, a dry bird's nest listing against the back window. A single skeletal tree, its roots atrophied claws in the thin soil, cast a bare shade over the spot.

The bus moved on a little and then groaned and spilled out a dozen people, including Zaid Maher and a group of weary-looking women accompanied by several bad-tempered children who scuffed along the dirt, heads down, whining. Zaid walked briskly, gripping a carryall and moving more quickly as he neared the first group of shanties.

The two whining boys looked back and stopped sulking long enough to scowl at August. One said something to the other and they picked up a stone and hurled it at the car with the expertise of a Nolan Ryan. Yeah, the league they were practising for was the majors, all right, August thought grimly. But not for three million bucks a year and fame and glory — more like the privilege of being blown to Kingdom Come at the altar of a suicide bomb or an Israeli sniper's bullet.

The windshield sprouted a hairline fracture. One of the women admonished the boys and they followed her, casting frowns over their shoulder at the dusty car.

August drew a deep breath, touched the gun at his side, and jumped from the car. Licking his lips, he muttered a few Arabic phrases. His voice sounded stiff and unnatural. The inflection was all wrong, the grammar awkward. His language coach had told him he was as good as he'd ever be. And August had settled for that. He wished he hadn't.

He'd have to think of something. A good reason to be here. A very good reason. An advisor? Yeah . . . that's what he was. A UN advisor come to check the camps. Must happen all the time. Reluctantly, he pulled his ID from his pocket and shoved it under the floor mat of the back seat.

The beeper was steady now. August watched Zaid duck his head through the low window of a hut a half dozen down and call out to someone. He kept a grip on his gun. People wandered desultorily down the narrow alleys that divided the grim streets. He held his hand lightly over his nose to block the stench of the open sewer that ran a few feet away. It didn't do any good.

Stiff ridges of baked mud challenged the children's bare feet and the worn tires of the bicycle ridden by a boy who was snaking through the houses, ducking beneath the laundry hung on drooping lines. The war had brought more refugees to try to carve out a niche in this inhospitable place and so August was, to some extent, just another body crowding into the precious space. A few suspicious eyes, mostly old men, scanned his face and examined his clothes. But most plodded apathetically past him, preoccupied with their own struggles. The young men were gone, either scraping what living they could in the city or gathering in the hills, having decided that dying in the Cause was better than barely living.

A girl of about eleven burst from the hut and into Zaid's arms. Her face crinkled into a wide grin that transformed her plain face. She hopped around him, touching his chest and neck, her faded dress too small for her gangly body. Zaid ruffled her hair and she ducked away like a shy animal. He put his carryall on the ground and unzipped it. The child peered over his bent shoulder. The scanner bumped up a tone in August's ear. Zaid pulled out a tiny doll and a small purse knitted in rainbow colours. The girl jumped up and down with excitement. Zaid laughed and handed the doll to her. Placing the purse tenderly over her shoulder, he kissed her on the forehead then zipped the carrier up before disappearing inside the hut.

The girl skipped down the dusty street cooing to the doll. A thin white dog, teats dragging near the ground, hauled herself from the shade. Something jangled. The girl cocked her head, dirty dark hair falling over her eyes as she pawed inside the purse. Beaming, she withdrew a shiny piece of metal and pushed the bracelet up her arm where it coiled above her elbow like a small snake. She stroked and patted it as if it were alive, and then humming softly, set off again, kicking her bare feet through the dust. August looked down as if studying the mud bricks piled along the side of the street.

The girl stopped to admire and adjust the bracelet. The doll fell from her hand and the dog moved to sniff it. She shouted, a quick panicky shout, towards the animal.

August swept the doll up. To his surprise it had the blank features, blue eyes and stiff yellow hair of the ubiquitous Barbie dolls, but it had been carefully dressed in a piece of muslim stitched in a design of tiny flowers.

"Pretty," August dared, handing it back to her.

She grabbed it from him, her serious, smudged face examining him suspiciously as she cradled it. "You talk funny," she said accusingly, screwing up her face disapprovingly.

August tried on a smile. God! Just what the hell was he doing anyway? Interrogating a child now. She was about Katy's age. "Is your bracelet gold?"

She couldn't resist a nod and a tiny hint of pleasure around her lips. "Zaid gave it to me," she said defiantly, as if he might challenge her.

"You're a very lucky girl."

"He always brings me things." She shrugged the purse up her narrow shoulder.

"Does he see you very often?" Jesus! Who would have thought the two week refresher course at Langley, "Principles and Pitfalls of Interrogation," would come to this?

Not one of his prouder moments.

She shook her head vigorously, tossing the flies from around her face. "No. He's far too busy to come all the time," she said a little pompously. "But I'm going to marry him!" she announced with a sudden, shrill confidence. And then quickly overcome by modesty, she ran up the street, clutching the doll, the bag slipping from her shoulder. The dog loped lazily after her.

August watched her for a long moment and then stared at the low entrance to the hut. Well, they knew Zaid's lair now. But this wasn't really the time or place to close in. He couldn't risk it alone. Ahmed Maher wouldn't be found here. Zaid had been a decoy in every sense of the word.

It was only then, as he turned to make his way back to the car, that he noticed the cluster of older boys gathered against one of the other huts. They lounged in a deliberate posture of threat, arms crossed, chests jutting forward. The biggest one was slowly punching his fist into the palm of his other hand. His eyes were black. Another tossed a large rock from hand to hand. A few more drifted from side to side. There was going to be no sliding past them.

August stepped to the side. Right into the open sewer. The rock presser guffawed like any arrogant teenager on any street corner in Chicago or Seattle.

Jumping to the other side, August scrambled up the shallow slope. At his abrupt movement they straightened up almost as a unit, a pack on the alert as the scent of the prey shifted. From a shanty on his right a tinny radio played a Beatles tune and something sizzled as a meal was prepared. August leaped through the open door of the hut, knocking over a spindly-legged table and the plastic plates that were waiting to be filled. The boys were shouting behind him now. A tiny grey-haired woman screamed. Men bursting through her home were not unknown, but every time another chunk of peace was torn from her. She clutched at her chest and fell back against the ancient stove, burning her arm. Another scar she'd carry for the rest of her life.

August tumbled through a grubby curtain, over a pile of bedding, and kicked through a plastic-covered square that served as a window. He fell hard on his ankle into a small patch of stunted vegetables. The pain shot up his leg like a drill. He pushed himself to his feet, the gritty earth cutting into his palms, and limped across a ditch filled with garbage, then lost his footing on some slime that was festering into a stagnant pool. He scrambled to get up again. But they were around him now. The old-young faces loomed over him, the younger ones with a fascinated curiosity, the older ones with naked hate.

One kicked him. Hard. It wrenched his shoulder and sent him reeling backwards. They moved six inches closer, closing off the sun.

No choices left.

The gun slipped easily from inside his jacket. Maybe Mr. Smug had been right after all to push for the holster. The weapon could have so easily slipped from his pocket. His palm was greasy, his grip tenuous.

He moved the weapon slowly back and forth across them. But they'd stepped back already. These kids knew what they were looking at. This was no Saturday matinee. Special effects and Super Humans catapulting across the screen in a spray of fireworks and hot pink laser beams. Most of them had seen the blood, the twisted tissue, and the sightless eyes a dozen times before the age of ten. They'd been weaned on death. They'd seen brothers, fathers, friends, die around the real pain of a real bullet. Their hands closed tighter around the rocks but no one moved.

August flipped the safety catch and made sure they knew it.

And then he saw the girl with the snake bracelet clutching her Barbie doll, its brilliant blue eyes staring back at him. The white dog was hunched at her side. A foreign regret yoked his heart as his eyes caught the child's and he saw the stark fear quivering there.

He swung his head back as someone shuffled and another cleared his throat. Another one spit. They were regrouping.

He backed around them. Swinging the gun steadily between them.

God help him if he had to kill one of them. Please . . . don't let it happen. . . . His feet touched the blazing pavement and he stepped slowly backwards. He remembered the potholes and prayed he wouldn't twist down into one of them. He forced himself to put all his weight on the sore ankle.

Don't let them smell the weakness.

Don't let it buckle on me . . . don't let it buckle . . . for Christ's sake . . . don't buckle.

He could reach the car in a few minutes at this pace. Hold them off. They might chase him. But they only had their hands, their young legs, and their fury. He had the gun and the car. Fair contest under the circumstances.

They followed him along the road. A few dropped back, but the more defiant ones still hurled hatred with their eyes, kneading the rocks.

The car was just behind him now. He could feel the shade of the solitary tree tapping him on the back. He'd be able to feel his way along to the door, unlock it by touch, keeping the gun on them. He patted his pockets with his left hand looking for the keys. Where were they? Where are you, you little suckers? Deep, dipping panic. And then he touched the knob of the rabbit's foot keyring provided by Mr. Embassy.

There was a swerve from the back of the group. The tallest boy tossed a Molotov cocktail into the air. Its narrow tailwind sighed on August's neck as it sailed past him to smash the car's windscreen.

A flash of flame instantly devoured the skeletal tree.

And then they were running.

August put his feet in motion but it was like treading water. The ankle refused and crumpled beneath him.

Something in the gas tank rippled with fury before it burst. Flames ripped through the car and August was hurled, the lining of his brain whistling like the fourth of July, across the road.

ALONG THE JORDAN–IRAQ BORDER

The jet stream ploughed the sky above Ahmed like a deadly comet guiding him to his destination. He was hugging the Jordanian border. The Americans would avoid dumping bombs here; for the time being at least they would have to indulge King Hussein's so-called neutrality. It wouldn't do to push the

King, however reluctantly, into a full embrace of Iraq. But the fence that the monarch was perched on was getting shakier and shakier. Any moment he might find it right up his backside.

The road was a theory, consisting only of whatever the tough Land Rover could punch out of rock and gravel, and the vehicle bounced and jolted over the scattered spewings of an ancient volcano. He'd avoided the main road from Amman. The convoys into Iraq were under tight scrutiny and anything might happen amongst that crowded, frightened line of nervous drivers and dilapidated trucks. He didn't want to be caught when the Americans decided to crack down or the van a mile ahead was rear-ended.

Ahmed pulled the headdress close over his face. It distorted his peripheral vision but the shade was critical. The vial, wrapped and rewrapped, sat on the back seat inside an orange cooler packed with ice which even now was pooling in the bottom. Ahmed could hear it swishing with every jolt of the jeep's springs. He would have liked to have the other vial as well. But it was certainly contaminated by the British. It was a useful decoy if nothing else. By now they might have tracked it. But by now Zaid would have carried out his mission.

By now Zaid might be dead.

Ahmed pushed the stab of pain aside. He must learn to duck and weave around these emotional obstacles for the moment. He could grieve later.

It had been difficult to leave Khalaf at the school in Amman. The boy had cried at the gate. Further evidence of the lethal softening of his character that his mother had encouraged. But at least he would be safe until his father's job was done. This was not the time for Khalaf to learn the ways of the Bedouin. That day would have to wait.

The jeep's temperature gauge was swinging towards the high mark but he had plenty of fuel and only a few more hours of travel. Somewhere in the outer sphere a jet whined and the eastern sky towards the south was streaked with black. On the left, a smudge on the horizon, he'd seen a small caravan. Bedouin perhaps. It was unusual for them to be travelling in the heat of the day but everything was unusual now, he thought, as the jet stream wound down towards Riyadh.

The steering wheel was sticky in his hands and the seat hot through his cotton pants. But soon it would be over. He had never wanted it to come to this. His life's work to be unleashed as an epilogue to the nuclear bomb. But better it be this way, in the midst of a Just War. There were always battle casualties. But no one was counting the dissident Iraqis, trapped inside their borders with Saddam Hussein running the show, no one was counting the dead in that hot, mad country. Ahmed grimaced at the thought of Hussein. He didn't have any illusions about the man, but he had to admit Hussein had two great virtues. The first, a desire to unite the Arab world, to bring them together in the great Brotherhood they were meant to be. The second, he would give the Palestinians a home. End this warring with the Israelis. End the Israelis. And return the Palestinians to the land they'd been driven from like a herd of sheep sent to the desert without an oasis.

Ahmed believed that history unfolded as the work of man. It wasn't accidental, nor was it evolution. He knew that this war was the turn in fate that could bring the Arabs together again. It would also return him from his exile, an exile that had only hardened the certainty of the road he had to take. He was totally convinced of the innate corruption of the West. The Koran condoned the waging of Holy War to spread the faith. It was time. The chance might not come again for another century. And by then all the oil revenue in the world would not have united the Arab Brotherhood.

Certainly his own personal chance to hurl the javelin at his enemies would never come again. He must succeed at this. Or fail utterly. Ahmed was exhilarated by the black and white of it. All his life Ahmed had spent carefully measuring, judging, holding back. Skepticism and caution had ruled his career as a scientist and his life as a man. And now the moment had come when he would be able to use every power — mental and physical — that he possessed, towards the ultimate goal. His hands tingled and his being ached for action.

The jeep bounced over a boulder and slid deep into a gouge in the earth. A rear wheel snagged the rim of the hole and sucked the vehicle backwards.

Ahmed stepped on the accelerator. The wheels spun. The back end was escaping him. The cooler jumped, the melting ice sloshing loudly. He reached back and gripped it with one hand. Damn! He'd have to get out and push. In this heat!

Twisting the steering wheel, he pressured the accelerator again. That awful wearing, rubbing sound, wheels against dry dirt, accosted him.

He didn't hear the burbling, the popping bubbles, until he flung the door open and swung himself out. Reaching back inside the car he popped the lever under the dashboard and pulled a rag from the glove compartment. He walked to the front of the jeep and lifted the hood. Wrapping the rag around his hand he tentatively twisted the radiator cap.

There was an angry hiss, and then a geyser of boiling steam hit the air, spinning Ahmed away from the jeep, his hands covering his face.

The flood was over as suddenly as it had erupted, the stream gurgling back into itself. He was left with only a blanket of heat folding around the shoulders of the horizon. Even the rocks beneath his feet were soldering irons. There was no chance now of cooling the engine long enough to refill it with water. And he was expected. He was expected somewhere for an appointment he'd been waiting a lifetime to keep.

He climbed up on the front seat and leaned out over the hood. Stretching, just stretching a little more, he could see the band of animals and people still plodding a thin line across a far dune. At least a dozen, maybe two. Certainly natives. Not army. A jeep, incapacitated or not, his cooking stove, the sleeping bag, air mattress, tent — all he carried — would be of interest to them.

Ahmed pulled the cooler from the seat and shoved it into a narrow band of shade next to the open door. That precious patch might last another half hour. If he was lucky. Pulling his headdress further over his face he leaned across the wheel and pressed on the horn. Eventually, slowly, as if at the lifting of some bad dream the smudge of camels and people on the horizon turned towards him.

As the Land Rover approached, Ahmed lifted his hand to shield his eyes from the sandstorm created by its speed. The markings of the vehicle were clear: Desert Police. Its driver's red-and-white headdress bounced around his shoulders as he bumped down the incline of the dune towards Ahmed. The police vehicle had emerged from behind the caravan of Bedouin that Ahmed had spied on the horizon, perhaps taking the opportunity to visit a relative. The Desert Police were all recruited from the tribe since they'd first been convened a half century before. But he hadn't expected to run into a patrol this far out. They must have stepped up the reconnaissance around this area because of the war. Their ostensible purpose was to help stranded travellers, but Ahmed knew that they gathered in hundreds of thousands in contraband every year. Smugglers unable to resist the harsh, but open, border. And the bounty was no doubt very profitable these days.

Ahmed raised his hand in the traditional greeting. "Praise be to Allah!"

The squat man behind the wheel ground down the gears and slowly got out of the cab, returning the greeting. A two-way radio crackled from the dashboard. "I see you have trouble, my friend," he gestured towards the open hood.

"Yes. Very fortuitous that you have come."

The man drew closer, his eyes swung from Ahmed to the jeep. "Well, we can soon fix you up." He was a full foot shorter than Maher and out of shape. Jogging around in a 1990 Land Rover all day wasn't exactly the hardy lifestyle of his Bedouin relatives. But Ahmed knew that he couldn't be underestimated. The competition for these jobs was fierce.

The Captain put his hands on his hips and swaggered closer to the incapacitated jeep. Steam still hissed lightly from the open cap. "Should have made sure the radiator was full, my friend," he said condescendingly. "You are not a tourist. You should know better."

"Yes. I should. However, I believe that the radiator may be defective."

"Hmmph . . ." The other man made it clear what he thought of such stupidity and leaned into the back seat. "You carry extra water in any case, I presume?" The voice presumed no such thing, as if Ahmed were capable of any stupidity. He noticed the cooler and pushed it with his foot. A slosh from inside. "Plenty of water here. You should have used this," he lectured, bending down to lift the lid.

Ahmed stepped behind him, lifting the gun. He'd hoped to escape the necessity of this. But all could be lost.

It must be.

Ahmed muttered a prayer of regret.

The Desert Patrol Captain, puzzled at what he saw in the cooler, glanced back at Ahmed.

He died with that expression of curiosity on his face.

The bullet passed cleanly through his neck, leaving little blood, to Ahmed's relief. He didn't allow himself to look at the face fallen to one side. Ahmed had disposed of many bodies in his time. Many dead animals buried for the Cause. This was only a variation of that. Most had died with less mercy. The sound of the shot was the worst part. Its echo travelled smoothly over the dunes, bouncing back at him for miles.

He dragged the body into the back seat of the Land Rover. Transferring his supplies and carefully lifting the cooler into the other vehicle, he steered the jeep north. He could dump the body a few miles from here. With any luck even a minor sand-storm would soon cover it, making it virtually impossible to find. And the Rover was well equipped to carry him the rest of the way.

He wrenched the wires from the radio and stepped on the accelerator. The Bedouin caravan had disappeared from view, swallowed by a sword-shaped dune. He was alone with the desert wind.

21

TWENTY MILES FROM AMMAN
February 17

"Father?" Zuleika was shocked at how ruthlessly age had marked his face beneath the dark eyes and scrap of beard. He sat at the far end of a wide carpet spread beneath a sway-backed canvas. The rough material had been stretched across the front of the modest house Sheik Rifai had bought when the desert had started to tire him. Arthritis was eating his knees but he could still retreat to this airy cocoon and cradle the illusion that at a moment's notice he could pack everything he owned and push away from civilization.

She lifted the canvas to allow a small goat to scuttle outside and stepped across the rich embroidered carpet of crimson and gold, stitched by her three aunts twenty years before.

Her father stood up. She didn't let him see that she recognized the effort behind his movements. He looked smaller, almost lost within the bleached material of his loose robes. He opened his arms. She embraced him and felt the old strength in his grip as if he'd never let her escape again. "You've come home, my girl," he whispered. "Praise be to Allah." He held her away from him with one arm and smiled. "Beautiful as ever. You are cheating time, my girl." He smiled again, wider this time as if accepting what luck had brought him.

"It's wonderful to see you, Father." She kissed the thin, brown hand.

He sank back into the cushions that covered the floor and gestured her to sit beside him, watching her carefully as she adjusted the shawl around her head and twisted the material at her wrists. He lifted her chin towards him. "What troubles you?"

"It's Khalaf, Father. Ahmed has taken him."

He took a water pipe from a low table and poked at the hot coals smoldering in the bowl. "It's a father's duty to see to the education of his sons." He frowned. And then looked at her again. "I saw to the education of my daughter and look what happened." He sucked deeply on the pipe.

Zuleika folded her hands in front of her and bowed her head. She would have to spend the rest of her life redeeming herself. But she had no time to make it up to him now. "A boy must also have his mother," she said, her voice low.

"Your husband can hardly be blamed for thinking you unfit. Ahmed Maher is a good man. An excellent match you made. But you disgraced my name after your marriage. You should be happy that you were allowed to return to my tent."

She heard the gruff pain that laced his words and kept her head bowed. "I can only beg your forgiveness, Father. I know that I'm in your debt for a lifetime. But if you could," she raised her head, "if you could just grant me one more request."

"And what of my request to you?"

"Father?"

"My request that you come home permanently. Back to your own country where you belong. You have experimented and gone your way. Another father would have disowned you. But it's not too late. I'm willing to welcome you back to the fold to take your proper place in this family. Who knows, you may even marry again."

Zuleika's throat filled with words she couldn't say. Words

she'd learned to throw so easily into the air without judging where they would land. But language was now a minefield to be picked through with exquisite care. A wrong step would end her hope of finding Khalaf.

She nodded. "I've made a great mistake. It is over." To her surprise, she felt tears rush down her face. And to her greater surprise and anguish, recognized that the words weren't entirely a lie.

He placed a hand on either side of her head and kissed both cheeks. "Welcome home, my child. Allah be with you."

She covered his hands with hers and repeated the blessing. "You will help me find Khalaf?"

"Don't you think I must see my first grandson? However," he said, "you must leave this with me." A protest jumped to her lips but he silenced it with a finger to his lips. "You cannot travel alone. And you would be an impediment to those who might go with you. Trust this to me. I will find Khalaf."

"But you'll need help, father. You aren't as young as you were. Ahmed is travelling with Khalaf to meet the Bedouin. He disapproves of the schooling Khalaf received in London. He wants him to spend time learning the old ways."

"That is understandable. But it's not right that he should take the boy without telling you. And the desert is very troubled now."

She seized his hand. "There's someone who can help us. He wants to find Khalaf . . . and he wants to find Ahmed even more than we do."

August felt the guarded curiosity from the other man as soon as he pushed aside the multi-coloured curtain to enter the makeshift tent. His ankle throbbed and his back still ached from the roasting the exploding Ford had given him. But he'd managed to scramble to his feet and run, his legs churning like an Indy 500 engine, to the main road. A group of puzzled Scandinavian tourists had picked him up and dumped him more than willingly outside the Embassy.

Zuleika emerged from the tent, a pale shawl covering her hair and half of her face, and gestured for him to enter. He sensed her lurking outside as he stepped onto the faded carpet towards the Sheik, who was sitting cross-legged amongst a pile of soft cushions. His eyes were drawn to the old man's, the same golden brown as Zuleika's, the same wary, but warmly amused expression, as if expecting a magician in disguise rather than a challenge.

There was a small movement in one corner. "Ah," August exclaimed. "A peregrine. Quite a bird!" The old man's eyes turned slowly to the falcon, reluctant to take them from August. But not before August caught the light of pride escaping them. "May I approach her?"

Zuleika's father gestured agreement, cocking his head to watch and making a small sound at the bird.

August picked up the glove that lay on a thick cushion and pulled it to his elbow. Fine hand-crafted leather. He offered his arm to the bird and gave his own call. It ruffled once and hopped onto the glove. August cooed and slowly lifted his other hand to trace a finger along its soft feathers.

The Sheik started to object and then drew back when he saw the bird acquiesce. He shook his head. "Damon rarely allows such intimacy upon first acquaintance. She's a very particular female. You are honoured." The voice was rich, a deeper version of Zuleika's, his English fluent.

"I know," August said, clucking once more to the falcon before replacing her on the intricately carved perch. "But I have respect. They sense it."

"Respect is a rare thing these days." Sheik Rifai gestured to the cushions. "I can't rise. My knees are rather brittle. Forgive me." He lifted a silver decanter and held it over two small cups. "Coffee?"

August indicated agreement and sank to the floor, folding his legs under him. The steam rose into the air and August realized that a chill was falling with the night. Sheik Rifai lifted a steaming cup and basket piled with dates and fruit. August took the coffee and helped himself to several dates.

They let the silence form a comfortable cushion between them, enjoying the refreshments. August knew it wasn't up to him to speak first.

"I understand that you wish to help my daughter find her son?" The tone was freshly skeptical.

"Yes. And in doing so, help myself."

Rifai's hand stopped with his cup halfway to his mouth. "Such honesty was not expected, Mr. Riley. However, I don't expect any American to do something that will not help himself. Especially in this part of the world."

August nodded. "Guilty. But I can guarantee that I'll do my best to find your grandson. Our intelligence services have narrowed down the possible sites where your son-in-law might be headed. But I'll need a guide. Someone who has an ear to the desert. It would be impossible for me to tackle that land alone. I would not have the arrogance to presume it."

"Ah . . . again . . . you surprise me — such modesty."

"I'm a realist, Sheik Rifai. You have no doubt heard the Western expression, 'You scratch my back, I'll scratch yours.'"

The Sheik smiled and August was treated to the end result of years of work by a top German orthodontist. "No, I haven't heard it before. But no translation is necessary. And what is your purpose for this undertaking, Mr. Riley?" The older man's gaze was direct.

August drew in his breath. He offered Zuleika's father an equally direct look. "My government believes that Ahmed Maher may be on his way to carry out a terrorist attack."

"In the desert?" The Sheik's tone had lost none of its skepticism.

"With respect, sir. That is all I can tell you. Except that if he succeeds, this war will take the blood of even more innocents. And if your grandson is anywhere near he will die also."

"Why would my son-in-law risk such a thing?"

August lowered his voice. "I tell you in confidence something that you mustn't reveal, even to your daughter . . ."

The Sheik chose another date and studied it for a long time before placing it in his mouth and nodding.

"The body of a member of the Desert Patrol was recovered yesterday by some Bedouin. We believe that an abandoned vehicle found nearby belongs to Maher. My government is convinced that he is a dangerous man. If he arrives at his destination, the President will most likely order saturation bombing of everything in the area. Every living thing will be decimated. We believe Maher has your grandson with him. He's been blinded by his mission. He believes he's safe now that he's back in the desert. He used his own brother as a human decoy to throw us off the course."

The old man pulled at his beard and August could almost see him push the image of Khalaf from his mind. "I have an idea where Ahmed may have gone. He borrowed a vehicle from his sister two days ago. He has been spotted since. My cousin is the best guide amongst our tribe. He will take you."

August contained the whistle of relief that pushed against his teeth and stood up, offering his hand.

The Sheik kept his contained in his lap. "We have a contract, Mr. Riley. Mine is fulfilled by its enactment. Yours is fulfilled with the return of the prize. If you do not bring my grandson back safely I will exact compensation."

"I understand."

August walked to the opening in the canvas. A hot wind lifted the rough cut door and he glimpsed the sky and dirt beyond. Zuleika was gone.

"Mr. Riley?"

August turned back, one hand supporting the canvas flap.

The Sheik was stroking the chest of the dark-eyed falcon. "I may tolerate self-indulgence and arrogance. The desert will not."

August pushed aside the canvas and stepped into the embrace of the suffocating sky.

Zuleika was waiting at the edge of the oasis that protected her father's home. Deep shade and the shawl hid her features from him. He cupped her face in his hands, the soft material of the shawl caressing his fingers. "It's arranged."

"I knew he would help us." She leaned her cheek into his palm.

"I have a guide. I'll leave before dawn tomorrow."

She raised her head slowly and he felt the coolness of her look dividing him from her like a new oar through autumn water. "Where shall I meet you?" she asked, knowing the question was hypothetical, forcing him to explanation.

He let his hand drop from her face. "You can't come, Zuleika. It won't work. I need to be alone. It's too . . .," he stopped before "dangerous" could leave his lips and remembered her bleeding fingers and torn nails as she lay amongst the dead animals in that obscenity of experiment. He had no right to talk of danger to her.

"I know more than you ever will about the desert, about Khalaf, about Ahmed. Do you just dismiss all that? Leave me to moan and wail on the homefront like every other woman in every other war? Even though it is my child somewhere out there? You know nothing. Nothing."

"What good will it do Khalaf if we're both killed out there? Besides, your father will never agree." He felt weak. Second-hand reasons had never appealed to him.

"Isn't the risk for me to decide? Or are you the authority on that, as well? Is this all for my own good, of course?"

He could only stand there under the pathetic shade with the heat already jabbing through quick gaps in the wide palm leaves and the desert at his back as he watched her move away from him towards the cool heart of the oasis.

AMMAN
One Hour Later

Zuleika lifted the crumpled paper and studied its singed edges as if the bare lightbulb over the sink would reveal more than the terse, officially typed words. An evening breeze lifted the heat as she walked into the cramped bedroom, the burnt paper clutched in her hand. She lay the remains of the message on the bed and smoothed the creases from it as if that might ease the nausea of shock jogging through her.

He already knew where Khalaf was. He already knew! And he was refusing to take her with him. Why? So he could do what he liked when he got there. No witnesses. Especially no witnesses like her. With so much to gain. So much to lose.

Crouching on the bed, her knees sinking into the sagging mattress, she encircled her pounding head with her arms. The defective fan ticked frantically against the headboard. She stayed that way, rocking back and forth, for a long time. And then very slowly, wiping the tears from her face, she got up and walked to the dresser.

August's matches still lay beside the tin ashtray. She struck one and held it to the edge of the paper, holding it between her fingers until it flared. She watched August's burning betrayal fall to the dresser, adding one more scar to its ugly surface.

ONE HUNDRED MILES EAST OF AMMAN
February 20

August was pulled into consciousness a heartbeat too late to reach for his gun under the mat and stop the man entering the tent. The intruder was standing over him, feet astride, black robe draped around him as naturally as a raven's wing. A rifle hung loosely from his hands and a full bandolier of cartridges hugged the unsheathed dagger that gleamed at his waist. Only his coal eyes were visible above the mask sweeping his lower face.

Sweat clung to August like a wet sheet. He struggled to wrench his mind, drugged by heat and exhaustion, back to the afternoon and the terrible moment that swam in the haze before him.

The ride had been hard, the grinding uniformity of the land broken only by mild undulations in the blackened stone. A suspicion stalked him, as the sun consumed hour after hour, that somewhere beneath the charred rock a volcano still seethed.

The tread of the camel's pancake feet had been chosen over a mechanized convoy that would guarantee the attention of Maher or his lookouts. One man alone along the border was a red flag to either side. And August didn't intend to offer himself as target practice for some novice sniper. The Satellite-

Communicator, awkward in this environment where survival on sparsity was the highest virtue, bounced against the sweep of the camel's neck.

His beast hated him, August was certain of it. The wide nostrils snorted and rode the nose ring, pulling far more than any of the other camels that formed their small caravan. Occasionally the round-domed, haughty face would swing towards him, thick, stubby lashes blinking widely. And then the thin lips would purse and spit violently into the ground, as if to express its true opinion of August's inexperience perched high on the winged saddle.

The animal's antipathy seemed only marginally less than that of the straggling family who had agreed to guide him as far as their spring camp. From there he was on his own. The weapon tucked securely across his belly seemed little protection from the dark, contemptuous glances whenever he ventured a question in his faltering Arabic. His loose traditional robe and headdress were barely camouflage against the desert's barren backdrop, offering no disguise of his ruddy face and his thick body compared to the lean, brown men with whom he travelled. The rocky sand had pared these people to their essence.

He was listened to courteously. Questions, though discouraged, answered quickly. His waterskin filled first from the well. His camel unhobbled before the others each morning. He was tolerated.

And he, in his turn, had to trust these hard men, their veiled women spread along the perimeter, searching out the occasional succulent weed to purge a thirst. They were guides and anticipators, aware of every dune and wadi for a thousand miles. Contemptuous of borders and acutely open to the next opportunity, to any brush of change along the horizon, any slight dent in the sky that might signal rain . . . or raid.

August was the interloper by whose fey ignorance they might profit, as they had skimmed the fat for hundreds of years from Western travellers. Although he did carry the blessing of Zuleika's father and so was folded into the tribe with a stiff nod to honour. Sheik Rifai's goodwill and the handsome price the foreigner had paid were worth three days and nights of toleration.

His compass had broiled the second morning out. Bouncing against the saddle, the heat had reduced it to a melted glob of indecipherable metal. Mahoud Taweel, the eldest brother of the band, had smacked his lips in disapproval and pulled his headdress closer, pointing towards the sheet of hardened lava that formed the desert floor, muttering that they would reach the next well in eight hours.

He had taken the rebuff as intended. A polite reminder that in this crucible no sane man relied totally on a piece of glass and metal pressed together by a machine in Tokyo. It was as foolish as betting a thermometer's measure against the frost crawling up your tent flaps on an October day in Alaska.

They were travelling fast. Sheik Rifai had personally ensured that their provisions were plenty. But this was not one of the clan's richer families and the desert dictated that even the most wealthy minimized the goods transported from one thin pasture to the next. Bedouin pride demanded a harsh self-sufficiency that, to the Western eye, was streaked with masochism.

Their band consisted of only twenty people: two brothers, their wives, and children. At first their mute acceptance had suited him as they sat astride the flat-footed camels, each wide hoof sending a puff of sand into the dry air.

August had never been one to seek out a human voice if he could avoid it and the nomads' stoic solitude was amenable to his mood. But out here a sense of isolation as tough as the unrelenting sky had crept over him. A desolation as hard and unyielding as the rock beneath their feet.

He was lost in this void. A thick dome had been lowered over the earth, closing out the sounds of life, suffocating his finer senses and reducing everything to an animal pitch for the search for water. The inadequacy of his vision was pummelled into him every day as each slight rise in a dune or a pale drift promised a well or camp . . . anything to punch a hole in the choking monotony and creeping thirst.

Here there was none of the Australian Aborigines' poetic

Songline, their graceful myth and texture stitched into the earth to guide you. Only baking black rock interspersed with a curl of sand or yellow weed here and there forming a mesmerizing pattern.

His semiautomatic was no comfort as he studied the desert's weapons: monotony, ruthlessness, sparsity, and the most parsimonious climate and vegetation he'd ever laid eyes on. Even the sight of a hawk sailing a thin wind high above the dunes didn't lift his spirit. The bird's cry was dry and thin as it coiled down to greet him from the hurting blue sky. He hadn't heard or seen another creature since he'd been out here. The raw earth ruled this place like nowhere else.

They'd finally made camp near a well that supported a scrub of bony grass. The unhobbled camels threw themselves on it like newborns on their dam's teat. A pitiful skewer of grey bark that had once resembled a tree threw a sliver of shade over the beasts' misshapen, life-sustaining humps.

The well was deep. August licked his lips as Mahoud tied the rope methodically, slowly, around the bucket's handle. He wondered if its rusty hooks would hold the weight of the water. Mahoud's brother moved off to gather whatever twigs he could and the women shifted around them, faces averted from August, calling to the children, readying the meal. The metal bucket swung deep into the earth, banging against the narrow sides of the deep pit.

Heat shimmered through the tent's camel-hair tarp suspended above him. It was late afternoon but the sun's hammer still pounded the land beyond their shelter's tethers. Somewhere a goat bleated and camels' feet shuffled restlessly in the dirt. A brass chime shifted listlessly in a shallow gust of wind.

There was that other chime in a pain-soaked flat in London. A wet and cool day when Emma Emory Cowen had died.

When at last the bucket had been pulled, hand over hand, to the surface, the water was brackish and sour. But August's thirst dictated his choices and once boiled in hot coffee, sprinkled with cardamom, he found himself reaching for a second and third cup.

After all proprieties had been observed, the meal suitably

yawned and burped over, they would arrange the bedding, submit to the intolerable heat. A sense that it would never pass, that he would never escape the inferno, gripped August as he crawled into the tent like a bear to a cave. The sour smell of his own body, saturated by the dust and sweat of the day's ride, clung to him. Perspiration dripped down the back of his neck as he tossed on the thin mattress, begging sleep to come. Water pouring in rivulets from his chest, soaking his bones.

He could feel the muzzle of his gun under the pillow. But something about the long, sinewy arms and sharp cheekbones of the looming tribesman told August that a dagger would be at his throat before he could blink, let alone reach for his own weapon.

August groaned and started to ease himself onto his elbows. The intruder mumbled something indecipherable. His fingers brushed the rifle.

Zuleika's father had warned August, his voice scandalized, about the tribesmen for whom raiding was still the preferred means of survival. And tradition was not always respected. Sometimes not an animal or tent or any provisions were left with their victims, as had been the custom for centuries. To offer the bandits hospitality was to invite danger to share your hearth.

The intruder grunted and pushed his black-sandalled foot against August's leg. A thick, distorted shadow was thrown against the length of the tent. Another raider? Or an animal seeking shade?

He could understand the thick words from behind the mask now.

"Get up," the raider was ordering. "Get up!" He kicked at August's limbs, pressing the cartilage on his bruised ankle.

August lifted his head slowly, sweat rolling into his eyes.

He turned on the mat, enforcing a deliberate sluggishness of his racing nerves as he edged his hand back up along the pillow.

The kick was sharp and to the target, the promise of a sore wrist delivered with it. The intruder was pointing the rifle now, the gesture unmistakable.

August pulled himself to his feet. A strange rumble had

started up outside, like some giant beast heaving its way across the earth. The tent suddenly heaved in a huge wind and the tethers shifted against their mooring. Somewhere pots and pans clanged together. August's robe clung to him, anticipating heat rash or fever.

He stumbled out ahead of the tribesman. August could feel the rifle butt nudging his spine. Mahoud and the rest of the family were gathered, bleary-eyed and hunched near the camels. The youngest child crawled in the sharp grass, pulling it and gurgling to herself. One woman leaned across the well, carefully disentangling her long, black robe from the dangling pulley. Wind was puffing the sand across the ground, twirling it into tiny circles. The sun had disappeared inside a black fist of sky.

August lifted a hand to Mahoud. He looked away and the women bowed their heads. August tried to think. There didn't appear to be any other tribesmen about. Was he being taken hostage? Robbed because he was believed to be a rich foreigner? Was it to be a bullet in the back? Left to rot under a desert sun because of a random robbery?

The tribesman pushed the rifle deeper into his back, urging him away from the family. August tried to remember the taste of courage but fear had sucked all his vital juices dry. The woman at the well pulled her black robe free of the pulley and jerked the bucket over the edge, spilling half of it, the cowl of her dress falling from her face, releasing her hair.

Zuleika.

She walked towards him, the familiar, long stride entwining her legs in the voluminous folds of the robe. A wind was wheezing beyond the camp and the camels had begun to bleat and snort in their tight space, jerking at their ropes. The single skeletal tree seemed darker, more bent than ever. But his pleasure at the sight of her pulled him from the suffocation of the day. As he watched her walk towards him, the shreds of his past seemed to knot together and offer a glimpse of a future even as he stood in this empty place with grit between his teeth and fear over the next ridge.

He raised his hand towards her and then, remembering the

audience huddled behind them, let it fall.

She muttered a few words in Arabic, some harsher dialect, and passed the man with the rifle some money. The tribesman convened the blessings of Allah on her. August watched him tuck the money into a leather pouch at his waist before lifting his eyes to the clouds with the skepticism of a teacher marking the exam of a known cheat. "Sandstorm," he muttered.

August followed his look. Beyond the next rise, the dunes were churning against low cloud whipped into orange foam by the hidden sun. The low rumbling he'd heard in the tent had changed to a thin hiss. The camels were shifting slowly and methodically, their skinny tails flicking nervously, moving their backs into the wind. Behind them, Mahoud was scurrying towards the tents. The women and children had scattered like pigeons, sweeping up, only to descend a distance away and set themselves to covering the food, securing the animals' tethers, and gathering the packs and waterskins around the tent.

"Why didn't you tell me they suspect Ahmed has killed a man? That he's heading towards the Military Zone? That he might have Khalaf with him?" Her eyes were watering, not from tears but the cindery ash that had settled in the air about them.

August blinked back the sting behind his own lids.

"How did you find out?" he asked.

"You should be more careful where you leave your little notes from home."

Mahoud shouted a warning across the slash of hot wind.

"Your father?" August asked, dreading the answer. "Did you tell him?"

"I'm desperate, not stupid. I lied to him. He believes you've found Khalaf and are returning to Amman with him. But he's very worried. I convinced him to let me ride with his old trading friend," she nodded in the direction of the disappearing tribesman, "to meet you. Suleiman Toukan has been ordered to bring Khalaf and me home safely. It's a reflection of my father's prestige that Suleiman agreed to take a woman alone into the desert. But he isn't pleased about it. And he doesn't trust you."

The intruder glared at August from near the wall. The

imprint of the gun's muzzle was still cold against August's neck. "I gathered that."

She pulled her hand away and jerked the hood of her robe up over her hair, tightening it against the rising wind. "You demanded that I trust you," the anger in her voice was kneaded by sadness. "And yet you kept all this from me." When he didn't answer she pushed a hand against his shoulder as if she might shove the words from him. "You used me to get my father's help. To get yourself a reliable guide." Her lips were dry and brown, chapped from her journey.

August sighed. A mistake. A deep frown pressed between her brows and darkened her eyes. But his sigh had been of regret, not irritation. "Because I knew you would do exactly what you have done. Follow me. And in this job I have to move fast. Without any restrictions."

"A job to help your war. Not a job to help me find my son."

"Both," he said honestly. The wind was spinning their robes, swirling in a black and white dance.

"Well, now I'm here to help myself," she said, the slight trace of Australian accent which had curled around her vowels over the years, tripping her words. "You take me with you. Or Suleiman takes both of us back to Amman." There was no defiance in her tone. Just factual insistence. She swept past him, head bowed to the spraying sand.

He grabbed her elbow, turning her towards him. Fighting the tent enclosing him, looking for a tear in the fabric of her determination through which he might escape, he shouted against the wind, "It's going to be dangerous. We might not be able to get to Khalaf."

"This way I'll know for myself, won't I? Not have to rely on whatever you may tell me after the fact."

The wind hit them. A stinging nettle of sand and harsh intent flaying their exposed skin and pummelling her into his arms. He cradled her head against his chest and, dipping against the wind, swung her away from it. They ran, tripping across the rolling dirt. A tin mug bounced across their path. August yanked at the tent flap. It fought and slid from his hands as the wind wrenched it back. Stumbling under the lowered camel skin, he pulled Zuleika into its shelter after him.

They huddled together on a straw mat, his arms around her, while the storm heaved itself against the tent walls as if to devour them.

22

Sam Whitman closed the book he'd been reading, a text about the Aymara, a Peruvian tribe who'd miraculously developed a language compatible with computers, and rubbed his eyes. There was so much to do and find out about. His life had been narrow and obsessive, rigid but filled with drama. Somewhere he'd left the love and curiosity wanting.

The light bending over the chair was cold yellow. The night was pulling in its lines, sweeping all the thoughts that had driven him from sleep into its dark net.

The house was silent. The silence of emptiness, not peace. The cuckoo clock Christa had salvaged from their tour in Germany whirred and the ugly little bird popped out and squawked four beats. He'd always hated that thing. Guess he could get rid of it now.

He picked up the mug of coffee and took a swig. It was stone cold. He flipped idly through the discarded book, trying to concentrate on the coloured photos of people intently weaving a coat and tilling the hopeless soil. Solid, exhausting tasks with a solid, clear end in sight. But the book had failed to provide its usual balm. Restlessness had eaten at him all night. He had an awful feeling it might chew on his vitals for a long time yet.

Christa's texts and a spiral-bound notebook were still piled on the coffee table. He got up and walked over to them. She must have been in a real hurry to get out of here if she'd left her books behind. As she had said, her voice strained between sadness and anger, she could come by any time to pick up the rest of her things because chances were, nine times out of ten, he wouldn't be there.

He let his fingers trail over the books: *Freudian Psychology and Its Relevance to the Late Twentieth Century*; *Jung: Symbol and Myth*; and a new one, *The Myth of the Warrior*.

He looked out the window . . . he hadn't bothered to draw the drapes . . . and stared at the driveway he'd strolled up less than twelve hours ago, adrenalin still pumping after the Gulf briefing session. Looked like his unit would be going in soon. The guys from B Company had been over there for a week already. The call would come any day. He'd retire after this one. He'd done a good duty. Seen more action than most. It was time to be with the family now, enjoy the baby. The Army'd find him a good job. Training new recruits would be satisfying. He'd actually been whistling as he strolled up the drive, deliberately irritating nosy old Macy Walker who lived next door.

Christa's mother had passed him in the driveway, the baby clutched to her chest as if he might snatch it. His wife was standing just inside the door, a sloppy pink bag of diapers and bottles and some soft, formless toy clutched in her hand. Her cheeks were chapped with old tears. He'd found her rings later, lined up on the desk in his study. She'd broken the lock on the door and left them on top of a stack of combat manuals.

She stood at the door with trembling lips, her belly strangely flat once again, and told him in that alien voice that it was over. She listed an accurate litany of his offences, in that new, cold, quiet tone, each word pushing him further and further from the barbed-wire boundaries of her life.

He'd left her when he knew the baby was coming any day. Someone else could have gone to get August Riley in the back of beyond. Someone else could have done the dirty work. After six years of sweat she'd earned her B.A. and gone to the stage to receive her degree with only her mother to congratulate her. The neighbour had held her hand in the delivery room. And her best friend had brought her home from the hospital. She wasn't spending another hour alone. And certainly not the next thirty years.

He wandered through the house. It smelled different. Talc and scalded milk and something more pungent. He'd been glad the baby was a girl. Boys were always in competition with the father. Either despising the old man in the end or drunk on failure because they could never live up to him. Girls always adored Dad. You had to be a real loser to blow it with them.

Looked like he'd blown it before he'd started.

The huge card covered with red roses and a white dove that he'd sent for their anniversary flopped from a cupboard door in the kitchen. The tape that held it was losing its grip.

He crumpled the card in his hand and leaned over the kitchen sink. Turning on the faucet he threw handfuls of cold water against his face, then straightened and stretched. The view from the kitchen window faced a row of militarily manicured patches of lawn saluting a brigade of identical row houses, the only attempt at individuality being the lemon yellow or robin's egg blue paint jobs. Each house had its allotted quivering aspen planted exactly five feet from the edge of the driveway. No wonder Christa had rebelled at the thought of staring at this for the rest of her life.

The phone rang and he recognized the brief dip and start of his heart rate. Welcome relief. He'd think about her after this assignment. Just one last assignment. And then he'd transfer out. Make her see he meant to stay around from now on.

He grabbed the phone on the second ring, lifting the receiver from the kitchen's wall unit. An army ant had crawled in through the open window starting a patrol along the hem of Christa's yellow gingham curtains. He flicked it back outside.

"Sam Whitman here."

It was the boss. Colonel Jake Brown, Commander of Delta Force. "It's August Riley. Again. We're on standby. Riley's in the middle of nowhere. We gotta cover his ass, Sam."

For the first time in his life Sam forgot to lock the door behind him on the way out.

NEAR THE IRAQI–JORDANIAN BORDER
February 23

Suleiman Toukan had taken the last of August's money and two camels in exchange for returning to Amman without them. He'd agreed to turn over the jeep belonging to Zuleika's father only after Zuleika cajoled and shouted and August made loud but vague threats.

"Jesus Christ!" August hissed, propping his elbows more securely against the sand to support his weight. He stared through the binoculars. "Jesus!"

Zuleika pushed herself up from where they lay crouched on the lip of a curving s-shaped dune tucked like a giant piece of pale driftwood amongst the beach of rock. "What is it?"

August seized the edge of her robe and yanked her back to the ground. "Get down! If they see you we're dead!"

"But it's deserted. There's no one there."

August inched up again until he could see into the shallow valley folded between the gravel dunes. He swept the binoculars across the area, wiping the sweat coagulating along his brow. "It might not be Times Square on New Year's Eve . . . but this joint isn't deserted," he muttered. "Not by a long shot."

He could just make out the two long, low mounds like massive graves in the centre of a partially buried complex. A high fence of scalpel wire slashed menace into the sky and a needle-thin minaret punctured the northern horizon. Concrete bunker roofs girdled by a catwalk were nosed into the earth. A wide, circular space, resembling a grotesque bull's eye, the complex being the dartboard, lay between the bunkers. As August watched, a bulldozer trundled out of the complex.

He rolled onto his back, crooking his arm over his eyes, shielding them from the sun. The sky was a grey shield, waves of heat beating at it from some furnace behind. "It's quite the setup Mr. Maher has down there. Probably a fully equipped lab. He just has to scurry underground with his formulas," disgust pushed the words, "and manufacture a few barrels of toxin."

"But if Khalaf . . .?" Her voice trailed off and she stared at the sand in her palm as if the answer to her unspoken question might be found there.

He stroked her arm beneath the sleeve of her robe. Smudged streaks of sand riven by dried tears marked her cheeks and bruised sleeplessness held her eyes hostage. His own face and forearms were swollen and sore, broiled by the sun.

He kissed her. He had no words to wrap around her. Or for her son buried alive somewhere inside this place. He had no inkling anymore of what might drive Ahmed Maher. He had no idea of tomorrow. Only the insane heat and the iron band around his head. And her cool face and blistered lips against his own.

She touched his neck. "Can we get him out?"

August picked up the binoculars again and searched the landscape. "God only knows how much more they've got underground. The bastard has made sure it's not only technically inside the Jordanian border which makes taking it out dicey for the Coalition, but he's got it reinforced like a goddamn nuclear launch site."

"But . . ." Confusion crisscrossed Zuleika's face. "I just don't believe," she hesitated, "I don't believe," she repeated, more certain now, "that Ahmed would take Khalaf to such a place . . ."

August studied her from under the hot shade of his arm. Grains of sand flickered along her thick lashes and her robe was stained with remnants of hurried meals. She sat cross-legged, her face wrinkled in concentration, like a girl scout at a campfire, the dark robe billowing out around her knees. He wondered what he was leading her to. But she had made it clear that she lived her life by choices. And this was one of them.

They were totally alone. The beat of their blood, the net of their skin, and whatever primitive intelligence scented survival was all that stood between them and the morning light.

Mahoud had watched them grimly, and August felt his disapproval of their journey with every turn of the man's head. But then on the morning they separated, Mahoud had seized August by the shoulders in a surprising display of emotion and kissed him on both cheeks before leaving them and turning his thin caravan into the sun, towards the closest transients' camp.

An engine started up somewhere inside the complex. August adjusted the binocular lenses and edged up closer to the lip of the dune. Four trucks were rumbling up the scratchy road, the bulldozer lumbering ahead of them. The cabs pulled extra long beds, their cargo covered by flapping tarpaulins. One had come loose and the red fin of a weapon jagged from beneath it.

August pinned his sight on the last truck. It jolted over a hole in the sand and then jumped again. After the vehicles had been waved past the guardhouse and inside the fence, the driver hopped from his cab and flipped the tarpaulin up, pulling and adjusting it.

August rolled over onto his side, his fingers white around the binoculars.

The goddamn trucks were loaded with Scud launchers!

The frightening realization sucked at him like quicksand. As he fought against acknowledging what his eyes and brain were telling him, he was pulled deeper into the quagmire, his own intellect working against him. "Maybe Ahmed doesn't know it's a launch site," he said hoarsely. "Maybe he doesn't know that's where he's taken Khalaf."

He looked at Zuleika. Her expression of despair mirrored his understanding. She started to babble in her native tongue, her hands pummelling the sand. August pulled her down the dune. They slid against the waving sand, missing steps and tumbling over their own feet, towards the jeep sizzling unshaded where they'd left it before tackling the climb. He reached into the back seat and pulled out the pack he'd set there, grunting under its weight.

The Satellite-Communicator was ugly and squat, forged from a dull black material. A mute but powerful animal. The minaret on the north of the complex was no doubt some kind of communication tower in disguise but the Sat-Com should beam directly to Riyadh. Just one bounce to a Big Bird, cutting out all the middlemen in Pine Gap and Colorado Springs and then straight down to Command Center.

The static was unbearable. He forced himself to speak slowly, turning the dials with meticulous care. Zuleika, careful to stand away from him, not crowd him, passed him the waterskin. The desert started to ease out from under its suffocating heat and slide into the coolness of night. The dune's shadow caught them like insects in a giant's dark web.

A harsh burst of static. Finally.

"This is the Traveller." August felt like he was on the dark side of the moon. "Repeat. This is the Traveller."

"Total eclipse." The code for cover. "Emergency. Repeat. Total Eclipse."

A high squeal from somewhere. Had the minaret tower tracked them after all? Was a laser narrowing its deadly pupil on them at this very moment? He watched the sky as it was slowly coloured by a deep purple dye seeping from the bony ridges of the horizon.

August had to guess their coordinates. "They're bringing in Scuds. At least four from what I can see. Probably arming them right now." He drew in his breath, conscious of Zuleika, rigid at his elbow. "Biological weapons. Note. Biological weapons. Possibly on their way to Israel. Tonight."

Silence. Only the sizzling and ticking of the line as August's blood catapulted through his veins.

He felt like screaming for a voice. A contact.

Only scratching static. And a satellite tumbling somewhere through space trailing his burst of words across the sky.

Zuleika pressed his arm.

He spit out the code again. "Total eclipse. Possible civilian inside target area. Repeat. Civilian inside target area!"

Silence. Air rushing from a balloon. Zuleika's breath escaping her like a stiletto had been plunged into her belly.

Static pushed August from the Sat-Com. He repeated the coordinates and squeezed the black box between his hands.

He watched Zuleika. There were no words of comfort.

They didn't see the truck with two soldiers inside it push over the seam of the dune and turn towards them.

The Apache pilot pulled on the tinted face mask, adjusted his night vision goggles, and honed in on the controls on his headset. A thumbs-up to his Navigator, his right arm with a brain, tucked into the seat above and behind him. Night was a purple promise on the horizon. They'd be flying under its cape within thirty minutes. He synchronized watches with the tower and touched the gears of the AH-64 helicopter.

The machine was smooth in his hands. Yep, after five years of training, he'd finally run smack dab into the real thing. Not a dummy run, played out a hundred, two hundred times. Not even a video simulation where no matter how tight your concentration or vivid your imagination, you always knew that the storm churning on your screen or the turbulence threatening your control could be unhitched with the flick of a finger.

This was it.

He set his coordinates and gripped the cyclic control. The huge blades began their slow, inevitable rotation and he touched his gloved hand to the side of his head in a lazy salute to the four Apache choppers rumbling on his flank. To Sam Whitman and the dozen men of Delta Force crouched inside.

Through the tinted glass dome of the closest machine Sam tossed a high sign back to the pilot. The same keen wave galloped across his gut as he'd felt the first time he'd clambered into a dilapidated biplane behind August Riley and chugged towards Burnt Paw Lake.

Two minutes later the Apache and its buzzing entourage hovered briefly over the secret airstrip three hundred miles from Riyadh and then lifted straight up into the air. Millions of dollars' worth of hardware suspended on a gamble over some of the most uncompromising land on earth.

★ ★ ★

Ahmed Maher watched the great guns swing into place. He was exhausted. He'd been working for five days to ensure the timing devices were accurate, the containers secure. He watched as Colonel Ojjeh, Saddam Hussein's second-in-command, faced the armed missiles like a wrestler before his opponent.

But this was not what Ahmed had been led to believe. The guns weren't facing west; they weren't facing the lines of battle. He started to protest.

"Please, Dr. Maher. I don't want you to think that we don't appreciate your work and effort. But remember, you are a scientist, not a military man. We promised you a laboratory. And you have one. Not up to your Australian standards perhaps, but," he smiled condescendingly, "in this country we have been fighting wars for many years. We learn how to pare a little here and there. We must all be ready to make sacrifices," he lectured.

"It's not the quality of the equipment I object to, Colonel Ojjeh. It is the use of my development. The virus."

"Well, what did you expect?" Ojjeh leaned tentatively over the reinforced block containing the toxin that sat beside the launcher, ready to be loaded. "This isn't a cure for cancer that you've found." He didn't hide a sneer this time as he waved towards the soldiers preparing the missiles.

"I was told that the virus would be placed on weapons aimed at the battleground. To kill soldiers. Not civilians."

Ojjeh leaned his granite face towards Maher. "Have you any idea how many of our civilians the Americans have slaughtered since January 15?" With an obvious effort, he lowered his voice. "Please forgive me, Doctor," he said sarcastically, "but your years in the West have distorted your perspective. Separated you from reality." He glanced around as if afraid that even here, nearly six hundred miles from Baghdad, someone might hear. "Do you have any idea what is happening out there? We are losing this war. Do you understand that? And we are losing catastrophically! They have bombed us out of the twentieth century while our Arab brothers sit on their thumbs and we once again sacrifice Iraqi blood to the Cause. Our last chance to make them see the truth is to force Israel into this fight. The Jews may tolerate a few casualties since most of our Scuds have been lost before reaching their targets. But they can't shoot down the weapon that this missile carries, thanks to you, Doctor. The virus will spread over and through the population before anything can be done. And the Israelis will never restrain themselves. It goes against everything they believe. And then, finally our brothers will stand up and be counted."

"I refuse." Ahmed pushed past the Colonel, disgust distorting his features. "I cannot be a part of this."

An arm stopped his progress as surely as a steel bar. "Oh, I think you better take your time over this decision, Dr. Maher. Assuming that you want to see your child again."

Ahmed hesitated. A cruel bluff. Surely? "Don't be so primitive, Colonel. My son is at school in Amman. I left him there myself."

The Colonel unbuttoned a shirt pocket. He retrieved something from its depths and opened his hand like a conjurer about to reveal a trick. The ring that Zaid had carried to Khalaf from Zuleika. The ring Khalaf had insisted on wearing on his first day at school.

"Where is he?" Ahmed whispered.

"Safe below. In his own private room. We even have a few toys for him."

"And afterwards? What about afterwards?"

The Colonel shrugged. "You will stay here as our guest, until the war is won, of course. And then no doubt, you will be feted and medalled as is your due. You will always be valuable to our country. You will perhaps gain honourable Iraqi citizenship."

Dr. Ahmed Maher watched as the soldier loaded the end result of his life's work onto the Scud.

The weapon's muzzle turned slowly against the bruised sky.

Towards Israel.

"Let me talk to them!" Zuleika hissed, pulling the veil across her face, receding into anonymity. "Get in the car! Quickly!"

She pulled the gun from August's hands and gestured violently towards the jeep.

August jumped over the low door and slid into the passenger seat, pushing the Sat-Com under the edge of the floor mat. He hunched down, pressing his chin against his chest. Jesus! His pale skin was sunburnt and blistered, his hands dangled from the ill-fitting robe, and his green eyes were bloodshot. Christ! He couldn't pass as even fourth cousin to an Arab. His robe gleamed white and conspicuous in the quickly gathering twilight.

He gripped the revolver beneath his thigh.

Zuleika drew in her breath and tried to think over the pounding blood in her ears. She kept the veil high to her face so that it covered her mouth and nose. The hand that held the gun in the folds of her robe was trembling. She looked to the ground as the soldiers jammed on the brakes and jumped from the truck. They tried to veer past her, towards August, towards the man. "Peace be upon you," the older of the two said automatically.

"And upon you be peace," she said offering the traditional reply. "Please. My brother is ill. Please. Don't go near. He is frightened. He . . ." She ducked her head again. "He has the mind of a child. We are returning from the city to my parents' home. I had taken him to the new hospital in Amman. To the doctor there."

"Alone?" the older soldier barked.

The other glanced at him, surprised by such a harsh tone to a woman.

"My father has been travelling with us. But he suffered from the heat and was taken in by a passing tribe. My mother is expecting us so I volunteered to drive my brother to her."

"You drive?" the older soldier demanded disapprovingly, peering over her shoulder, examining the jeep.

Zuleika's mind raced. "Some of us did learn. It is necessary. My parents are old now and this is my only brother," she gestured helplessly towards August.

The man snorted and put the butt of his gun against her shoulder, easing her aside.

The younger man was scandalized. "Mohammed Heikal!"

he protested, "do not speak to the woman in such a manner." Abdel Ibish had been relieved of guard duty this shift . . . the arrival of the so-called great scientist had made only that much difference to him so far. But he'd welcomed the relief of this reconnaissance jaunt with Mohammed even though the man was a notorious grouch. And to come across a woman was enough of an event to help him plough through another week.

"What are they doing out here then, so far from the main road?" Mohammed growled. "So near . . ." he gestured back over his shoulder towards the plant.

The cold was cutting across the desert with an icy knife. Zuleika shuddered and raised her eyes helplessly to the younger man. Real tears starting in them. Desperation halting her breath. "I was hoping to teach my brother to drive. As you say, it is not right that a woman should have to do so. But he wandered too far from the road and we had been trying to get back when," she added quickly, inspired, "when we heard your truck and hoped that someone might help us."

"Of course," the younger one murmured.

But Mohammed was moving past them towards August now. The last rays of the sun were slanting against the jeep's bumper.

"Mohammed," Abdel urged, following him, "we can guide them back to the road. They can . . ."

August heard the heavy boots scraping through the sand. He could smell the soldier from here. He should have moved earlier. He might still be able to take one of them with him. Zuleika would be left alive.

He clutched the gun.

The Sat-Com cackled some indecipherable communication.

August's eyes swung up to meet the soldier's.

Zuleika jerked the gun out from under her robe. She'd had one lesson from August before they'd left the tribe. And she had every reason to remember it.

The bullets made a strange, pinging sound as they hit the men's flesh. A sound that would wrench her from sleep many times until well past the age that her hair had turned white.

Tiny spots of blood spattered over her, immediately absorbed by the dark material of her robe.

The older man managed to release one shot that careened across the desert, screaming their presence. But the younger had simply turned towards her with a look of terrible surprise before slumping into the sand, a rill of his blood mixing with the black sand.

August stood up, swaying his gun back and forth over the bodies as he climbed from the jeep. He ran to her. She was standing absolutely still, holding the gun rigidly away from her body. Her voice was a stiff whisper. "I had to . . . I had to . . ."

He pressed her shoulder. "They would have killed us, Zuleika. The older man would have pulled the trigger without hesitation."

She nodded mutely, her eyes seeking the blank eyes of the young man.

August seized her chin and twisted her face towards him, his eyes hard. "You had to do it! Understand? They would have killed us! You would never get near Khalaf! Do you understand me?" He was shouting now.

"Yes," she said. "I do understand." And then she was pulling the hood from her head and pulling the robe from her body. Beneath it she was dressed in a cotton shirt and loose pants. She moved towards the dead men. "You take his uniform," she pointed towards the older, heavier man, "the younger's will fit me."

"Zuleika . . ." He didn't like the edge to her tone. It had the high pitch of a novice ready to dive into an icy canyon before judging its depth.

"What?" She turned towards him, hands on hips, legs astride, her face a hazy mask in the evaporating light.

The vestige of optimism he'd clung to when he'd held her while the sandstorm raged around them was disappearing with the day. "Nothing," he said.

She pulled the boy's shirt roughly from one thin shoulder. "We have the truck. We have uniforms." She cast a glance back at him. "That means we have entry."

★ ★ ★

They waited in the cold truck cab sharing cigarettes. Zuleika removed a tattered Koran from the dashboard and placed it in the glove compartment. Two pairs of faded gloves and a clumsily knitted scarf, sent by a mother or a wife, lay on the floor between them.

They hovered in a time of sick dread enfolded by exhaustion. Alternately dozing and sitting silent. August could smell the dead man on the clothes he wore. He ached to see his daughter. He ached for ice and water and sweet, clean air. For another chance.

It seemed the soldiers must have been sent on a lengthy patrol since no one had ventured after them. Or else they're just too busy, August thought. With darkness the subterranean world below had come alive as if someone had thrown a phosphorescent light over an insect colony to reveal all the activity going on beneath the surface. The dull hum of an electrical generator throbbed through the night and a repressed glow covered the area in a watery glaze.

It was somewhere in the dead hour of the night, while Zuleika was slumped against him in a fitful doze, when August heard them.

Helicopters. Low. Very low.

The thread of his excitement reached Zuleika and she jerked awake, automatically reaching for the weapon, her eyes blurry.

"This is it," August said. "Sam and the boys are coming. They're coming in."

She seized the steering wheel. They'd agreed she should deal with any questioning. His Arabic was too clumsy.

August put his hand over hers. It was ice cold. "We could wait. The Force could do it. They'll watch for Khalaf. They'll pull him out if they can."

She shook her head. "You don't have to come. I would never blame you for wanting to stay here." She was looking straight ahead.

"I owe you one. Remember?"

She stepped on the gas as the first Apache rose over the far crest, its monstrous face distorted in the desert's flat visage.

★ ★ ★

An alarm screeched, sending the ant figures spewing from the bowels of the earth. The sentry's face was distorted as he was ripped from his midnight dream by the sudden realization of the nightmare he inhabited. August tossed the dead soldier's ID towards the terrified guard, the dead man's blood leaking through the shirt, staining him as he gripped the edge of the dashboard. Zuleika crashed through the gate, leaving the sentry waving his semiautomatic in the air. A narrow line of paving, just wide enough to hold one vehicle, snaked into the heart of the complex down amongst the tunnels. It was deserted. Spotlights waved erratically over the walls and the siren's wail bounced against the truck.

The copters hovered in a tentative dance then landed around the complex. One by one they spilt open, spilling men and machinery across the sand. An elaborate dune buggy, with three men crouched black and tight over their weapons, zipped towards the guardhouse and the paralyzed sentry. Commandos slithered down the concrete battlements, tossing tear gas. They hit the ground at full speed.

A volley of bullets sliced the side of the truck, sending it careening into a concrete barricade. The car lurched to the side, wheels spinning in the air. August hit the floor, pulling Zuleika with him. This was it. They were going to die in a stupid car accident. As if they'd been tooling out on the freeway beyond DC. As if in a second's carelessness, a drunk had hit them in a blind spot. No chance to fight it. His stomach and nerve ends scattered somewhere in the spiralling reality of the coffin of the truck. Zuleika was a graze of warm skin and harsh breath.

Beyond them the Scud launchers gleamed in a bizarre circus ring lit with blazing light, surreal sculptures thrusting at the black sky.

Zuleika was crawling through the shattered front window. Sharded glass was slicing her, blood bubbling along her arms. He scrambled after her, calling. Beating back panic.

She couldn't hear him.

He leapt after her, pressing her against the wall as another explosion lifted the ground at their feet. Her heart was ricocheting against his chest.

Rumbling spewed from somewhere deep below them like a prehistoric mammal rising from sleep. They must be close to the main bunker now.

Somewhere radio traffic was cackling wildly. And then silence. The lights wavered and died, leaving them with the erratic pop of gunfire and the stench of explosives. Darkness. The boys must have hit the transmitter. Sam had bought them some time.

A flicker and then the emergency generator kicked in, illuminating the Scuds all over again in a garish cobalt light.

Zuleika escaped him and ran to the door ahead. She crouched and then jumped forward, her gun steady, like a big city cop at a drug bust. Screaming for Khalaf.

Her voice was drowned by another volley of shots and the thud of a fresh explosion. She ran from the room, pushing August aside with stunning strength.

He kicked open the next door. A shower of gunfire pinned him against the wall, the sharp gravelly concrete pressing a design into his face.

He swung forward and hit the room, emptying a cartridge. Silence.

He kicked the door farther. It swung back, clinging to the wall this time. Two men lay inside, one sprawled across a cluttered desk, the other's hand still clutched at the controls of a radio.

August reloaded and aimed. The radio went up in a sizzle of hot wires and bulging, popping bulbs. Its dials spun crazily and the screens zigzagged a last, final message.

He straightened up, trying to pull his reason back into step with his instinct, suddenly aware of the dead man's clothes clinging to him as if with hundreds of tiny, sharp claws. Shaking his head, perspiration flew into his eyes. His neck and head were steaming, the gun slippery in his wet palms. He'd never felt colder in his life.

He ducked back out the door.

Zuleika was ahead of him. Frozen to the spot where the half-submerged tunnels widened out towards the launch area.

Ahmed Maher stood in the centre of the launch pad, a yellow pallor covering his face. Behind him was a man dressed in the colonel's uniform of Saddam Hussein's army. Preparing to give the final order to launch.

August felt his blood congeal.

He could see Sam now, carrot red hair escaping his black helmet. He was moving along the far wall, swaying like a spider on its thread. Delta Force had to go easy around the Scuds and their toxic cargo. A change in wind and all of them and every living thing within a hundred miles would be dead in a week.

A strange whine had erupted from Zuleika.

August seized her shoulder; she was shuddering like a wild animal in pain.

The Colonel was issuing orders to two soldiers grappling with the long missile, juggling it into its container. Terrified, they twitched in minor seizures each time another explosion lit the sky in phosphorescence, revealing the ant figures in all their human clumsiness screaming and running across the bulging backs of the concrete bunkers.

Maher was trying to speak.

Zuleika saw the sharpshooter, his curled figure suddenly outlined by a tumbling flare, at the same time as August did. Her face was crimson in the reflection of the inferno devouring the door behind them. The sniper was locked in on the Colonel, his weapon lodged against his shoulder. Ready for the final order through his earphone.

One of the soldiers loading the missile cried aloud and fell to his knees in prayer. Maher stepped towards him, blocking the sniper's view of the Colonel.

And then Zuleika was running, running to her husband, her feet crunching through crushed glass, her figure in the blazing light next to the missiles. "Ahmed! Tell me where he is! For the love of God, Ahmed! Tell me!"

August was after her. Blind, running . . . running . . . a speed propelling him that had to take him beyond these few yards of horror.

The Colonel was turning on her, his face a study in cold

consideration, his gun levelled.

From somewhere August heard Sam's voice. A command to the sharpshooter. The sniper took out a spotlight next to the Colonel, shattering it at his feet.

And then August was on Zuleika, pulling her down, rolling along the hard hot ground beneath the launcher, its black form looming over them.

Turning to see the gun at his head. Sam dropping behind the Colonel. That hard grace he'd always had since he was a kid. One shot. And Ojjeh had fallen. And then a volley of sharp gunfire from the catwalk lifting Sam from the ground. Spilling across to Maher. The scientist tumbling. His white suit soaked in blood.

Sam lurched once, falling forward across his gun, seizing his throat. Another explosion. The last spotlight hissed violently before dying.

Screaming for the medic, August crawled on his elbows and knees towards Sam, edging towards him in the blackness lit only by the choppers' rotating blue and red lights. He pulled the other man to his lap. "Don't . . . Sam . . . don't . . . come on, now . . . just hold on . . . we'll get the medics . . . just hold on . . ."

Sam was murmuring. A half smile on his face. Dark blood seeping as if invisible through the black combat suit.

August leaned closer, his ear at Sam's mouth. "You've really got us in trouble this time, Riley . . . you've really got us in trouble . . ."

August turned his face to the sky. He felt Zuleika move behind him, begging him to come away. And then the fiery whine rode the rage of the last detonation as the launchers were hit and were tossed into the firelit sky like grotesque athletes.

A rioting hot wind before the searing pain pierced August's eyes and robbed his vision.

Flaming night.

It was over.

EPILOGUE

February 23, 1991

They found Khalaf Maher huddled under a set of bunks in a small room carved from the far end of a far tunnel. He clung to Zuleika as the Apache lifted into the air, throwing violet shadows over their faces. All he would remember of that night in the years to come was his mother's face, hot with tears, buried in his neck and his father's body in a crimson white suit growing smaller and smaller as the helicopter swirled away from the flames below.

Four hours later, Zaid Maher said good-bye to the smudge-faced girl in the faded cotton dress and walked out of the refugee camp north of Amman. She never saw him again.

LONDON
ENGLAND

Margaret Haden-Brown pointed towards the box of donations for the sullen-faced man from the charity. He looked like he expected a tip. But Margaret never gave anything to any man anymore.

The flat was nearly empty now. Always had been too big, too gaudy, for her tastes. The house in Devon would be fine. She might even take up gardening. The police and the judge had been rather reasonable about it all in the end. Too many questions, though. And the embarrassment of having to bring Peter into it all again. Rehashing the divorce. Terrible nosiness. That part was a bit too much. The pills had helped. And it had all worked out in the end. She had no trouble at all in believing that Zaid Maher was an internationally wanted terrorist. And the woman dressed in her silk robe, his accomplice. And from there it was easy to accept that Zaid had really murdered the woman. If she could accept that, it would be so much easier for INTERPOL to hunt him down. It had all been explained. Because he had murdered the woman in a way, hadn't he? Bringing her to Margaret's flat and drinking her liquor and wearing her clothes.

Yes, she might plant roses in the garden of the little house in Devon. She'd heard that they take a lot of time and patience. "Keep busy, Margaret." That was what the doctors had told her.

"Just a minute," she said, as the disgruntled charity man turned to leave. His face settled into lines of expectation.

She reached into the heavy stand next to the door and pulled out the bright pink umbrella. She tossed it on top of the box he was holding, weaving under its weight. "Take that," she ordered. "I don't ever want to see it again."

RIYADH
One Week Later

Her musky fragrance drifted through the antiseptic hospital room before Zuleika's lips touched his. They were still rough and chapped. The mark of the desert would take a long time to heal. He grasped her hand, surprised to feel the brush of the robe's long sleeve against his arm.

She lay her cheek against his. Her fingers lightly touched the bandages on his eyes as if to confirm they were really there. "How are you?"

God! He wanted to look into her eyes . . .

"Not bad for a guy who can't see or walk. Aside from that I'm just great."

She stroked his cheek. "August . . . I . . ."

He pushed his hand behind the nape of her neck and pulled her to him, pressing his mouth over hers. She clung to him as if he was a long-lost oasis. She caressed the bandages, his jaw and chin, resting her mouth in his hair, her cool palm at his throat. "I'm going home today."

He leapt for the fantasy, knowing there would be no net if he fell. "Alice Springs isn't really my idea of paradise. But I'll follow you anywhere . . .," he joked.

"No." Her fingers were at his lips. "I promised my father. And Khalaf is confused. Lost. He needs something solid. Unchanging."

His eyes stung. "Zuleika . . ."

She kissed him once more.

Her scent lingered long after she was gone.

BURNT PAW LAKE
ALASKA
July 1991

The rising sun slipped in a crimson sheen across the lake. August winced a little against its bright shimmer. But the second operation on his retina had been more successful. The only sound was the steady lap of small waves at the edge of the sand.

He clenched his fist inside the thick glove. The falcon, Zuleika's parting gift, unfurled her feathers and expanded her chest as if embracing the chill air. August loosened the leather jesses, tossing them over the side of the boat.

The bird moved her head once to watch him with wide

golden-brown eyes before turning her sharp profile back to keen over the rippling lake.

And then she rose from his hand. Just a few inches, clenching and unclenching her thick talons.

August stood up slowly, holding his arm close to his chest. The bird's feathers touched his face. He could feel the flutter of its heart. Then he pushed his arm into the air, all the lost years behind him propelled with it.

The gyrfalcon rose, her powerful wings pumping lazily, and then with one massive surge she hurled herself to freedom. Catching a high wind she soared over the trees. Beyond him.

August shouted once into the silent dawn.

It was good to be home.

ACKNOWLEDGEMENTS

This is a work of fiction. But at the heart of it is the very real suffering of the soldiers and civilians who were in the Australian outback when nuclear weapons were being tested. My first acknowledgement must be to them and their long struggle for recognition and compensation.

I thank my friends at Malaspina Library, who with good humour and grace continue to encourage me. To Francine and Dave Ritchie and Elizabeth and Robin Pack: my gratitude. Also many thanks to new friends who have been one of the joys of this writing life: Shawn Montgomery — we were in the right place at the right time to meet you; Ray Beaumont; Daniel Kolos; Paul Stevens; Ray Grasse, who was a silver lining on some dark days; Laura Lee, who combines "sense and sensibility"; Paul William Roberts for the long-distance laughs; and, of course, the team at Stoddart, especially Lynne Missen, for making another dream come true.